# THE OF
# OF K/

## BOOK TWO OF THE EMBERJAR

## VERONICA GARLAND

Imprint: Independently published
ISBN-13:9798711502142

# THE ORANGE

# OF

# KASHIQ

# THE ORANGE OF KASHIQ

## DEDICATION

For those I love, and for you.
May your roots spread far and deep,
and, when the flowers fade,
may their fruit nourish you
and grow anew.

## CONTENTS

# THE ORANGE OF KASHIQ

# THE ROOT

## CHAPTER 1

J ember!' Gladia was calling for him loudly now, her voice effortlessly penetrating the mud wall behind which he crouched, his shoulders juddering with stifled laughter. I eased up from the beehive I was tending in the garden nearby and made a suggestion.

'If you don't go soon, Gladia will catch you and then there will be no fresh oranges from Kashiq when Benakiell arrives back in Mellia! She will make you do chores, maybe even sort out all her threads for her, and we will all enjoy our treats in front of you!'

Jember rolled his eyes at me. He had impossibly long and curly eyelashes which framed his dark, almost black eyes, and a mobile, impertinent face. Like all seven-year-olds, he seemed part child and part adult, with glimpses of both the babe he once was and the man he might become making an appearance.

'Can't you tell her I am helping you with the bees, Aunty Talla, please? I don't want to do her silly old chores!' My mouth twitched at the corners, still amused at the way in which Jember addressed me as Aunty, even though I had no kinship with him or his mother Bellis. I certainly had no kinship with his unknown father, one of the OutRider soldiers who had used his mother as an Angel all those years before. We had all agreed not to speak to Jember of how he came to be, and he was instead told that his father had tragically died of a fever in a far-

3

off land before he was even born, and that Bellis did not like to discuss him as it hurt her too much. This last, at least, was true. So far, Jember showed little interest in his ancestry, and relied on Benakiell for manly advice, doing his best to outwit the redoubtable Gladia. She saw him as something between an imp and angel and could have rivalled Ashkana in her devotion to teaching Jember to work hard. We had all noticed how Gladia enjoyed having a small boy to boss around, and ever since Jember had passed into the Second Age some months before, she had been firmly resolved that he should not grow up to be a worthless layabout. This also afforded her the chance to sit on her veranda more.

'I cannot tell lies to Gladia, Jember,' I answered sternly. 'The bees might find out and then all the honey would be bitter, more bitter than the skin of one of those Kashiqi oranges you are waiting for – if you do all of Gladia's jobs!'

Sulkily, he stood up and yelled to Gladia, 'I'm coming, you old slave driver!' I gasped at his impudence, but he hopped over the wall and galloped off towards her before I could scold him. Tutting to myself, I pondered on what would have befallen me or his mother Bellis in the Temple had we dared to say such a thing to one of the Priestesses. There is no doubt we would have got a slap from the nearest Maid in their Third Age, and then a telling off and then a punishment, usually something awful like cleaning out the wastepits or scrubbing the Temple steps until they shone, and then doing them again and again until finally we were released, resolved not to transgress again.

The air was pleasantly fresh. We were edging slowly towards springtime, and the sharp, cool nights were losing their edge. Some trees were in bud, and the bees were becoming more active as they roused themselves from their winter slumber. It was the time to clean out the hives, remove any old beeswax and replace the new slats on which the honeycomb would be formed. The springtime honey would be light and delicious, just like the season, full of promise, and readily consumed by all, whereas the winter honey which I had just removed was a deep, dark brown in colour, strong and powerful, best used for physics and other medications. With the new season's flowers about to blossom, Achillea and I would be busy making physic and bottling honey back in Gabez when we returned there later in the month. These were Maren's bees now, of course, for she had taken over these beehives. They had only been under my care for a few months, after all. Before that, they had belonged to Achillea's mother before she died. I had offered to do some cleaning of the hives for Maren in exchange for some of the honey her bees produced. Her garden was rich in both lavender and Paradox blossoms and both the honey and beeswax were good to use in calming and soothing salves.

Returning to Mellia always reminded me of when I had first arrived there, a Maid, clad in the drab, walking mindlessly out of a life on the inside of the Temple to a vastly different life in the Outer, one which I could not have foreseen, even in a dream. And yet it was now a good few years since that first visit. While much remained the same, much else was now different, changing constantly, unlike life in the Temple which seemed to me to be a solid constancy, a place where the same things were said and done decade after decade; a place where the same aphorisms were taught, and the same mistruths declared. Thinking about it always made me feel angry, and I brought myself back to the garden in Mellia by telling myself sternly that the beehives would not clean themselves.

Looking down into the hive once more, I watched the bees crawling busily about, each intent on her journey and her work. I thought that perhaps the Goddess was similarly intrigued when she looked down upon the Temples of Oramia and watched the Priestesses and Maids busily going about their business. I could see the Queen of the hive; she was larger than the rest, with a longer body, and unlike the others, she was not busy. She had no job other than to lay eggs and so she tended to look rather lazy in comparison to the rest. The other bees also seemed to avoid her somewhat, crawling carefully around her, so that she looked like a small island amid all the activity. I wondered if our Queen, Lunaria, noticed the same thing happening to her when she met others. My mind drifted back to the events of almost eight years ago, when we had found Lunaria in the Temple and taken her to be acknowledged as the rightful heir of the old Queen. At one point, I had even considered the possibility that she was my sister, that I was her DoubleSoul, but that thought seemed absurd to me now, for we had even less in common than we had before. We certainly bore no resemblance to one another as many DoubleSouls did.

Ostensibly, I had no contact with the Queen, nor with her Vizier, Lord Ambar. I had been told, on my departure from the Court, on the day that Lunaria was made Queen, that there would be no returning there. However, small occurrences which took place once or twice a year led me to believe that the eyes of the court were still following my life. Occasionally an OutRider would come to my market pitch where I traded common physics and salves for coughs and stomach ailments, as well as honey, and would ask me questions in a way which seemed different to the way they treated others. There was at once more deference and a sort of keen focus on my activity. I tried to answer their questions quietly and calmly, for I dreaded being taken away from the life I now led.

I lived and worked now in Gabez, the town to which Achillea, Tarik and I had travelled after the death of Ashtun, the beloved of Achillea. Originally, we had thought to travel somewhat and then perhaps to make our way back to Mellia, but weeks had become months and then years, and we were happy in our own dwelling place, just outside Gabez. We had taken over a place which Tarik had found for us. We never asked how he had come by it, and he had repaired it and then built himself a smaller dwelling at the other end of the garden. Somehow, there was enough made by the three of us to trade for food and other essentials, and we began to make and trade new physics and salves using the plants we gathered from the garden and beyond. Tarik could also repair metalwork and made leather straps for carrying gourds and the like. He was unfettered by the expectations of the Outer that only one craft should be learned and was always eager to learn more. He was, like me, one who had not been raised in the Outer, and he picked and chose his own rules of living. I envied him that freedom, which I did not feel I had. As an OutRider he had travelled through the Outer, unlike me and had the sort of confidence that comes with experience. I also had a feeling that it was rather easier for men to go against the system than it was for we women, at least in Oramia.

Not long after we began living in Gabez, I awoke to a deep humming sound from outside. Looking out, I saw a large dark ball of activity, a swarm of bees who surrounded their queen, ready to die for her should I prove aggressive. I took this as a sign from the Goddess, a message that this was a good place, for the bees had found me and wanted to stay. I lashed some rope to an old hollow branch, eaten out by termites, and hoisted it into the tree where they were resting. Neither Achillea nor Tarik were surprised that the bees had once more become a part of our lives, and there was soon honey to add to our trading. I now had four hives hung from the Paradox and Kosso trees which stood in the middle of our garden. Shaking my head, I disturbed myself from the thoughts of my own hives, to finish attending to the work in hand.

I had been disappointed to find that Benakiell was not there on my arrival, as he had gone travelling and trading, away to Kashiq, the land which was close to Gabez, although he had not travelled there through Gabez, but through a more secretive route.

Kashiq lay just across the long, border river Gabish from Gabez, and there was much trade between the lands, with traders crossing the river regularly over the big wooden bridge to acquire goods which were not available in their own land. The OutRiders patrolled the riverbanks regularly, to try to ensure that no goods were smuggled over, for every trader had to pay a tax to the Queen on leaving and entering Oramia; a proportion of their goods was removed and sent to the Court of the Queen. Many were forbidden from making the journey because their offerings were deemed to be too common or too cheap to be worth the tax. Consequently, Gabez was full of traders who all tried to make a good trade for the wares which they had often carried for long distances in the hope of returning with a beneficial trade; unusual goods which they could then trade on for items of even higher value.

Benakiell had traded across with Kashiq in his younger days, and something in our journeying years before had made him want to revisit that activity which he had ceased at the behest of his beloved wife Velosia. She, however, was long dead, and for the past five years or so, he had been steadily trading, firstly in Oramia and, latterly, and more regularly across the border in Kashiq. I was not sure how he managed to cross the river, but I had my suspicions that he did not travel on the conventional routes, for he was circumspect about how much tax he had to give when I asked him. He would avert his eyes and stroke his beard and change the subject to something else, glossing over his travels even though he knew I wanted to hear more about them.

'Aunty Talla, Aunty Talla!' Jember came pelting down the hill, full of excitement. 'Benakiell is coming home! I saw him in the distance from the Kosso tree I climbed!' He stopped next to me, his skinny chest heaving up and down with the exertion of having climbed down from his tree and running to fetch me.

'And what were you doing in the Kosso tree, Jember?' I enquired, severely, yet unable to disguise a lightness in my tone, caused by the welcome news which he brought me, 'Gladia wanted you to do chores, not climb trees!'

Jember was unabashed. 'She asked me to go and pick beans, so I did go, but the tree was on the way and was more interesting, and I thought I saw a bird's nest, and then I was just looking out and I saw him coming down the path!'

'Did you tell Gladia?' I asked him, knowing that she would want to know before Benakiell arrived home from his travels.

'No, I came straight to you, Aunty Talla!' answered Jember, still breathless. I stopped what I was doing and gave him a shove.

'Run straight away to Gladia and tell her now, Jember! And don't tell her you told me first!'

Jember galloped off happily, as unconcerned as a butterfly, flying happily from one activity to the next, and I finished my task on the hive somewhat hurriedly so that

I too could go and await Benakiell. I envied Jember his unconcerned approach to life. Bellis, his mother, worried about him and what he was doing, simultaneously anxious that he would end up in terrible danger and trusting that the Goddess would care for him regardless. I also envied Bellis's continued faith in the Goddess if truth be told. She had been betrayed by the Priestesses in the Temple in the most soul-destroying manner, and yet she still held on to her belief in a benign, creator Goddess, who cared for the land and all living things in it equally and without prejudice. The things I had seen in the times before Jember's birth, and indeed in the years after it had made me cynical and distrustful of anything which came from the Temple or from the Court of the Queen or her OutRiders. It amazed me that Bellis, who had been abused and tortured with the knowledge of the Temple, never associated that pain with the Goddess who was the focus for the Temple.

I put the leaves and flowers I had picked from the garden into my basket along with the gourds of honey which I had taken from the hives and began walking up towards Gladia's dwelling. In the years since I had first been to Mellia, the village had firstly shrunk and then grown and there were now around twelve inhabited dwellings. It had been ransacked by the Outriders while they were searching for me, and the dwellings had all had to be restored by Benakiell on his return. Now, however, it was a thriving village, with fertile land to grow crops and new people had gradually moved in. I was getting to know some of them more when I visited Mellia and was relieved that there seemed to have developed an unspoken rule that neither my nor Bellis's upbringing in the temple would be referred to except amongst those os us who knew.

We had both become convenient distant relatives to Gladia and Benakiell and the village accepted us as such, since we had been there before them anyway. Gladia treated Bellis as her daughter and was by turns indulgent and critical of her, telling her off if she felt she was being lazy or not disciplining Jember enough, but also stitching her brightly coloured netelas and making her honeyed flatbreads. Bellis loved Gladia in the same way that she had loved the Goddess in the temple, simply and unaffectedly, and she had learnt to work hard as a stitcher, putting together the robes and tunics worn by both men and women. Gladia would then embellish them with embroidery and they would be traded in Sanguinea, or by Benakiell on his travels. A new family had moved into the village recently, and the man and his two sons were weavers, who made cloth. Gladia and Bellis were much excited by this development, since it meant they would no longer need to travel so far to trade for the cloth to sew the robes, and the weaver likewise was spared the travelling.

I arrived at Gladia's dwelling to a scene of frantic activity as she tried to persuade Jember to move his bits and pieces away from the outdoor mat under the Paradox tree, and simultaneously exhorted Bellis to making good strong coffee for Benakiell. On seeing me, she bustled up and announced importantly that Benakiell was almost home! I evinced surprise and delight convincingly, and Gladia beamed, happy to deliver the good news in person. Jember smirked at me from a distance, pulling silly faces of exaggerated joy to mirror my own. That boy had a talent for making me want to laugh out loud. I had grown much more able to laugh at silly little things in the years since I had left the Temple.

When I first emerged into the Outer world, I used to tell myself off for finding amusement in little things instead of dedicating myself more wholeheartedly to working for the good of the Goddess, but gradually, I come to enjoy the feeling it gave me; a feeling of community with the others around me and a light and happy atmosphere. Even Gladia had noticed my more relaxed approach and had declared, somewhat begrudgingly, that perhaps I had learnt something in Gabez after all. She was forever trying to persuade me to move back into the village of Mellia, along with Achillea, but we were happy in Gabez, and in some ways, leaving the security of my friends in Mellia behind had been a little like leaving the Temple; simultaneously exciting and terrifying. But I had learned so much by living away from them, and, strangely, now appreciated even more the time that I did spend with them when I returned. I could even forgive Gladia some of her sharp poking – both into my upper arm and into the progress of my social life, in which she showed far too much interest.

Bellis came to stand next to me, calm and placid in the face of the whirling excitement. She had grown into a well organised woman, under Gladia's tutelage, and had also developed her own way of dealing with Gladia's brisk interventions by being outwardly calm and placid. I wondered about her mind, sometimes, and whether it really was as calm as she portrayed. Knowing her history, it concerned me that sometimes she must be hiding her anxiety under this calm exterior, but it was the way in which she chose to live, and she seemed to cope best that way.

'Gladia is very happy,' she remarked, brushing away a fly which was buzzing around. 'She has been getting grumpy without Benakiell here!' We smiled at each other, both of us knowing how much Gladia enjoyed looking after Benakiell. He liked her too, in his way, but he enjoyed his wandering life and his frequent travels. Like me, he was endlessly curious about other lands and their peoples and I looked forward to asking him more about his trip to Kashiq.

Benakiell trudged up the path from the gardens, Jember already dancing alongside him, asking him questions, and breathlessly telling him all of his news from the birth of the goat kids in the village to the discovery of the birds' nest to Gladia boxing his ears for impudence. Benakiell grunted from time to time in response to something that Jember said, but otherwise continued walking steadily, his large heavy bundles making him stoop his back. He only stopped when he reached us, waiting as we were by the mat under the Paradox tree.

'Talla!' His eyes lit up with recognition and pleasure and I felt a warm glow inside to know that he was as happy to see me as I was to see him. We smiled at one another and he spoke to Bellis, asking her how she had been and noting that Jember had not yet learned the art of listening although his talking was very advanced. This said with a twinkle in his eye.

Later, after Benakiell had delivered the various goods ordered by the villagers and accepted their trades for them, we sat around the fire at Gladia's, relishing the oranges which he had brought back from Kashiq. There were those who tried to grow oranges in Oramia, but they were always bitter, pithy fruits, unappealing and infertile, the trees often dying after only a few years. The Kashiqi oranges were quite different; plump and round with fragrant skin and sweet juicy flesh which you simultaneously ate and drank.

'Tell us about the orange groves, Uncle Ben,' pleaded Jember, the sweet juice making sticky tracks down his chin. Bellis reached over with a scrap of cloth to wipe his face and he twisted away from her, embarrassed at her treating him like a little boy. Benakiell smiled at him indulgently, no doubt seeing the way in which Jember's eyes lit up when he listened to Benakiell's tales of distant lands. Gladia, on the other hand, was having none of it and seized the cloth from Bellis's hand and grabbed Jember, scrubbing his face vigorously. When she was done, she poked him and told him off for refusing his mother's attentions.

'You should have let Bellis clean your face, young man,' she told him. 'She would have been much gentler than me!' Jember scowled, and moved closer to Benakiell, ignoring both his mother and Gladia and pulling a dreadful face as he turned past me, and I struggled not to laugh. That was a very cheeky boy. Benakiell chuckled and stretched out his legs, his knees cracking and picked another orange out of his basket. This one still had its stalk on, and a dark green, dry leaf.

'This orange began its life in an orange grove in Kashiq,' he began. 'It is warmer in most places in Kashiq than it is here in Oramia. There is a lot of sun – look at this orange – it's just like the sun itself and that is what makes them so sweet. But a lot of Kashiq is too dry to grow oranges and it is only in the springs towns where the orange groves grow.'

'What's a spring and a grove?' interrupted Jember, who was intently following the description Benakiell gave.

'Most of the towns are built around wells or springs of water from deep in the earth. Kashiq doesn't have many rivers, aside from the River Gabish which makes the border, so where water is found, people settle, and then they use the water to grow plants like date palms and fig trees, oranges, and apricots. A grove is just a collection of fruit trees.'

'What's an apricot?' interrupted Jember again. Gladia gave an exaggerated sigh and rolled her eyes.

'It will be time for you to go to sleep soon, Jember,' said Bellis gently. 'If you ask too many questions, Benakiell will never get a chance to describe the orange groves to you.'

Benakiell patted Jember's shoulder. 'I'll tell you all about the apricots tomorrow, Jember. I will tell you about the orange groves tonight and then you and I must get to our sleeping; it's been a long and busy trip.' I admired the way in which Benakiell spoke to Jember. He always took him seriously, despite his young age, and always spoke to him just as he might speak to an adult. I usually felt awkward when I spoke to children, although I was accustomed to Jember, having been there on the day he was born. Children seemed simultaneously ignorant and wise. I paid my attention back to Benakiell as he described the orange groves. He told us of the orange trees, kept quite short so that the fruit could be easily picked by workers who carried large baskets on their backs. He described the sharpness of the scent of the leaves and squashed the leaf on the orange that he held so that Jember could smell it.

'In the springtime, the trees are covered in small starry flowers which have such a strong scent. You know that though, Jember, it is the smell of Aureus. I am sure that Bellis has made sure you know your colours and scents.' My mind drifted back, stirred by the mention of the scent of orange flowers. My time in the Temple was sometimes opaque, but the colours and the scents could transform that. It was as if they cleaned my mind so I could recall clearly the swaying embroidered orange cloths which adorned the Goddess and that deeply sweet and yet sharp scent of the orange blossom. 'When the orange trees are all in flower, the groves are full of the sound of bees, Talla, they love the orange blossom. The honey in Kashiq is very often from orange blossom. The orange growers keep the ground under the orange trees clear and just keep their beehives under there. I will talk to Talla about the hives tomorrow.'

Jember's eyes had drifted off, no doubt imagining the orange groves of Kashiq, and Benakiell tapped him on the shoulder. Bellis got up, coming round to fetch her son to take him back to their dwelling to sleep. It was late for him to be awake and I suspected he would soon be dreaming again. Bellis could have returned to us once he was sleeping, but she preferred not to, and instead would sit with him and then sleep herself. Perhaps she was concerned that he might run away and hide or perhaps that the OutRiders might come and steal him away. It would not be unheard of, after all.

Once he had left, I turned to Benakiell, interested to hear about the Kashiqi beehives, but he yawned widely and confessed that he was exhausted and ready for a rest himself. Promising to talk with me further the next morning he heaved himself up and wandered off to catch up on his sleep. This left Gladia and I still sitting by the fire, watching the sparks fizz and flare. I rather enjoyed the brief silence which followed, and the warmth of the fire, but Gladia was intent on finding out some information from me, so she settled herself down more comfortably, nibbling on another fresh fig which Benakiell had brought for her, knowing her weakness for them.

'How is Achillea and why did you not bring her with you on your trip?' Gladia always got straight to the point in her conversations. There was none of the elaborate dancing and weaving about that so many people indulged in; she just got straight to the point, like a kingfisher spearing a fish with a single dive.

I sighed and replied mildly, trying to keep my mind's emberjar from flaring up. 'Achillea is very well but she is very busy.' It was an evasive answer, and I knew that Gladia would see it for what it was; an attempt to not speak about why Achillea had not come to visit. The last time she had visited was months ago. She and Gladia had exchanged sharp words. It was unlike Achillea to hold a grudge for so long, but she could be very stubborn, and had resolved not to return to Mellia until she was sure that Gladia would not repeat the incident. Gladia huffed.

'I suppose she is still in a mood with me,' she said finally. Her round face looked sad. I had thought she might be more combative, sturdily standing up for her own viewpoint, but instead she looked regretful, possibly even remorseful. This expression did not last long, however. Just as I was building myself up to try to be comforting and sympathetic to her, her dark brown eyes flashed at me and she commented, 'If only she would accept that she is wrong, we could all be friends again!'

'Achillea says much the same thing,' I remarked, unable to bite my tongue and stifle my words. Gladia pursed her lips and looked disapprovingly at me. In the years since I had first met her, she had become even more self-assured – one might almost say bossy – and had blossomed in her new maternal role towards Bellis and Jember. This had made her even more convinced that she was always right. Achillea, too, had matured and become more self-confident. She no longer sought approval from everyone, happy as she was with her love for Tarik, the source of the argument.

'Why can you not be happy for Achillea and Tarik?' I asked finally.' You know how deeply grieved she was by the death of Ashtun, and how long it took for her smile to return, and yet now her smile is there every day, you disapprove of her.'

17

Gladia looked at me sharply and I wondered if I too might end up distanced from her by her stubborn refusal to see Tarik as a worthy man for Achillea. When Achillea had told Gladia and Benakiell of her happiness at discovering that her friendship with Tarik, whom she had known for so long as a steadfast friend, had now moved into being a loving relationship between he and her, both of us were surprised by Gladia's angry reaction. She had always trusted in Tarik; he had treated her wounds and looked after her and you might have thought she would have been glad that Achillea and Tarik were now so happy together, but she was not. She disapproved, she told Achillea, because Tarik was brought up as an OutRider. Even though he had left the OutRiders and quietly become part of the Outer, as I had myself, she did not think he should be entitled to be with a woman of the Outer. Achillea and Gladia were quite as stubborn as each other, and the more that each tried to express their point of view, the more fixed they became in their opposition.

'You know what the OutRiders did, and no doubt still do, to the Angels,' she reminded me. 'How can a man like that be trusted to look after a woman of the Outer? Why, for all we know, he could be Jember's father!'

I pondered on what she had said, for there was truth in it. But Tarik was different. He had made many personal sacrifices and had proven his loyalty and his patience many times over, and I knew that he deeply regretted his upbringing as an OutRider and their attitude towards those known as the Angels. Even though we had seen no evidence of Maids being cast out from the Temple and being picked up by OutRiders for some years, I knew in my heart that it must still be happening, somehow. Gladia was so deeply entwined in all these occurrences; her own baby daughter had been taken from her by her parents when she was young. The baby girl was left at the Temple, and I knew she felt great guilt about that. When Bellis had appeared, close to giving birth to the child of an unknown OutRider, Gladia had seen her as her own possible child. Her deep love for Bellis, who stood for the daughter she had never had the chance to rear, meant that her loathing of the OutRiders had intensified over time. She disapproved of Achillea's love for Tarik, and indeed of his love for her, and was mutinous in her opposition. Achillea had always been an easy-going person, ever since I had first met her, happy to see the good in others and willing to trust where some might be more circumspect. But she too, over the years had realised that it was important to stand up for closely cherished ideas and principles even if it might upset others.

When I had talked to Achillea and Tarik about a return to Mellia, Achillea had surprised me with the strength of her anger. It was usually me who had to dampen down the flames of my rage in the emberjar of my mind, but this time it was Achillea who exploded at the idea of having to repeat the same ill-tempered conversation with Gladia about Tarik. I had looked to Tarik, helplessly, hoping that he might guide Achillea to some form of compromise, but, in this instance, he remained silent, wrapping his fingers around Achillea's, entwined like a clinging plant.

'Neither of us wants conflict,' he said wearily. 'I have always liked and admired Gladia, and although I can understand her misgivings, I must also admit that it wounds me deeply that she might think of me like this. Until Achillea told her of our love for one another, she was happy to treat me as a good and trusted friend, and now she is suspicious and distrustful of me.' He looked at Achillea fondly. 'To me, our love is a rare and precious thing, just like Achillea herself. As bright and warm as one of her songs.' Achillea nestled her head on his shoulder, stroking the back of his neck where his hair stopped. I watched them, fascinated by their intimacy and their longing to be so close to one another. Since I had left the Temple, I had learnt a great deal about life on the Outer; how to chat about inconsequential things to set a person at ease, how to listen to a person who needed to speak, even, occasionally, how to put my arm around the shoulders of another who might be sad or grieving. In the years after Ashtun's death I had many chances to practice these skills as Achillea sought to recover herself from her loss. But I still had no understanding of the relationships between those who loved one another as Achillea and Tarik did. I understood the feeling of loyalty and trust, of enjoying the human company of another, working in partnership with another, but not this hungry desire to be with someone. Tarik spoke again.

'I do not want Achillea to be made sad by Gladia's disapproval,' he said. 'I agree with her decision to not go to Mellia until Gladia has reconsidered her attitude to our love.' Achillea beamed.

'You see, Talla, I am right, I knew I was! Tarik is so clever and if he supports me, I know I must be right,' she said triumphantly. I sighed under my breath, knowing that there would be no budging either of them while they stood so staunchly together.

'But will you not miss seeing Benakiell and Bellis and Maren and little Jember?' I enquired, trying to tempt them both into travelling with me. Achillea looked wistful for a moment at the thought of what she might miss but then confirmed that she would not be going back to Mellia. They had travelled with me as far as Sanguinea, along with some salves, gourds of honey and dried herbs. I had continued to Mellia along the main road, enjoying travelling on my own and relishing the silence as I walked. And now, here I was, embroiled in this seemingly intransigent argument between two people who I cared for, each wanting me to take their side. I tried to pick my words carefully.

'Tarik cared for you when you were wounded,' I reminded her. 'He has been a good friend not only to Achillea but also to me for the past few years now. I think if he had meant any of us harm, he might have acted by now.'

'Friends are one thing, lovers are another,' maintained Gladia. 'We should not dignify OutRiders by letting them become lovers of our womenfolk when they have abused them and wounded them so terribly. How can you forgive that, Talla, when it made you so angry when you first found about it? I have seen Bellis's pain with my own eyes. Even now, seven years on, she cries in the night in her sleep as she relives it in her dreams.'

'And what about me, Gladia,' I asked, curiously. 'What would you think if it were me and not Achillea who were the one who loved Tarik? Or what if I met a man of the Outer and he loved me?'

Gladia sat back, trying to marshal her thoughts, and form an answer.

'You're different, Talla,' she said, finally. 'You are a woman. You are from the Temple and you seem to know nothing of love nor know anything about it, for all your clever learning. You have not hurt men of the Outer in the same way that the OutRiders have hurt countless women.'

'But those women were of the Temple, not the Outer,' I answered, bewildered by her reasoning and a little stung by her blunt statement about me knowing nothing of love. 'The Angels who were wounded so grievously by the men of the OutRiders were women of the Temple not the Outer.'

Gladia paused for thought. 'But some of them came from the Outer,' she responded triumphantly. 'People of the Outer do still leave unwanted babies at the Temple for the Goddess, after all.'

'So, by the same token, Tarik could yet be a man of the Outer. He might have been left at the Temple himself when he was a baby by some woman of the Outer who could not care for him.' I countered, sensing a way to at least make Gladia pause for thought. She was silent for a few moments and then heaved herself up from her station by the fire.

'I feel quite weary,' she said as she rose. 'All this talk and the excitement of Benakiell returning have made me ready for sleep. I will see you in the morning.' I watched her wander off in the shadows, a stout, determined figure. It seemed unlikely that she would change her mind in the near future. I sat watching the fire as it gradually went from a fierce red flame to orange embers. There was an owl somewhere in the Paradox trees which called gently, whether to its mate or to its competitors, I could not tell.

# CHAPTER 2

T he next morning, the air was fresh. We were a long way from the stifling days of the hot season, and it was the time of year when wrapping a netela around your head and shoulders was for warmth rather than protection from the sun. I was grateful to feel a steady warmth building from the fire. I was staying with Maren while I visited Mellia. She had taken over the dwelling in which I used to live, along with the bees which worked in the garden. I had thought that Achillea would have had more of an attachment to this land and to her dwelling and that of her late mother, but I think that she associated the place with sadness, firstly the loss of her own mother and then the death of Ashtun, her first love. Once we had decided to settle near Gabez, she happily packed up her belongings and a few small plants from the garden in Mellia to grow in our new garden in Gabez, and then gave her dwelling to Bellis and Jember and the one which she had allowed me to use, the dwelling of her late mother, Cassia, she had given to Maren, on condition that we could stay with them when we returned to visit.

Maren was happy to live in Mellia, guarding the bees for the village. She was also trained as a BirthMother, and her knowledge of herbs and salves made her a useful member of the village. There had been only three births in the village since she had started living there, but the women who had been aided by her were grateful to her for her knowledge. Her long years of impaired vision had made her patient and adept at listening to others and, in fact, I had heard some in the village say that talking to

Maren was almost as good as visiting the Empath. I woke first I tiptoed out quietly to start the fire from the emberjar, leaving her snoring gently on her sleeping mat.

I had already been in Mellia for a few days, but I was not due to meet Achillea and Tarik for two more and, having done all the maintenance work I had aimed to do, there was not a great deal for me to do. A lack of work made me restless, and the Aphorisms of Ashkana still came into my mind when I felt like I had been idle for too long. I had not become accustomed to the Outer habit of sitting and doing nothing and valuing it. Being raised in the Temple meant that this kind of behaviour had never been encouraged. The Goddess had worked tirelessly in the creation of the world and it was our duty to continue that tireless work to her glorification. Or so they told us in the Temple. It was a good thing that Benakiell had returned from his travels because it meant I could talk to him about his discoveries and the people he had met on his trading trips, and indeed he had mentioned last night that he wanted to discuss something of interest with me.

Living near the town of Gabez, which was on the river border between Oramia and Kashiq, there were good trading opportunities, for there were trading markets situated between the two lands. These were patrolled by the OutRiders, and their equivalent armed soldiers in Kashiq, and had been constructed in order to try to regulate the trade between them. There was no quarrel between the two lands, and they were happy to work together on keeping hold of the taxes on traded goods, each for their own. Benakiell, however, was, and always had been, reluctant to give over any portion of his trades to the OutRiders in taxes and his attitude had not changed over time. He had some more circumspect route into Kashiq, but when asked about it, he would wave away my questions and gruffly comment that it was not important for me to know these things. He seemed to bring back much more than other merchants, while producing small quantities for the OutRiders who patrolled the markets demanding their tax. For them, he showed trades in oranges and figs and incense bark and silk threads, but there was much more that appeared once he got back to Mellia, metal objects, jewellery, pictures, spices and oils. He also delighted in bringing back small curiosities and scraps of parchments for me to read out to him. I had tried to teach Benakiell to read and to scribe, but he had lost interest, wishing instead that he might intuitively know how to do both. I had explained to him how long it had taken me to teach myself to scribe and read when I was in the Temple, but he brushed off my experience. He was fascinated by the processes, but he preferred to deal with people face to face, so he could see the truth in their eyes. Which was all very well when you could see their eyes, but when faced with a Priestess or an OutRider, whose eyes were hidden from view, the truth only went in one direction.

Benakiell often brought back scraps of parchment and scrolls from Kashiq. They made the parchment out of goat skins there as they did in Oramia, but they also made a kind of a parchment from the bark of certain trees and the inner part of a plant which grew along the riverside. This type of plant parchment fascinated me, and I had scrutinised the scraps brought back by Benakiell, hoping to divine how it was made. The language of Kashiq was scribed in the same way as the language of Oramia. Benakiell said that the people of Kashiq did sound a little different from Oramians when they spoke. You could not hear this in the scribing for it sounded in my head just as the voices of the people of Oramia might sound.

I drank my coffee and ate my flatbread before Maren awoke, and after exchanging a few words with her, I walked off in the cool morning to see if Benakiell was yet awake. I wrapped my netela around my shoulders as I went, running my fingers over the stitching. It was one which Gladia had made for me a couple of years ago, and I tried to always wear it when I came to visit, to show her how much I liked it. I had three netelas now in various colours, and I enjoyed being able to choose what colours and patterns to wear each day. Having spent the three ages of childhood wearing the drabcoat and then anticipating wearing a red Priestess robe in the colour of Flammeus, it had taken me some time to get accustomed to the Outer life of choosing any colour to wear. I was still drawn to the warmer colours of Flammeus and Aureus, but I also admired the deep purple of Lilavis. Benakiell, on the other hand, was a man of habit, and tended towards colours like green and blue. I had never seen him wear an item with red on it. I asked him once, and he told me that he liked colours that allowed him to blend into both crowds and natural landscapes. He preferred to be the observer than the observed, that was certain.

'You are awake bright and early,' said Benakiell, in greeting, as I arrived at his dwelling. It was still the most well-tended dwelling in Mellia. He weatherproofed it every year with Paradox oil in some secret method and trimmed and replaced the reeds and canes in his roof assiduously. I returned the compliment, noting that even though he was tired the night before, he was already awake and busy around his dwelling. He smiled and sat down on his stepped veranda, beckoning me to do the same.

'It's good to see you again, Talla,' he commented. 'It seems a long while since I last saw you, although it may only be a few months. It's a shame that Achillea and Tarik could not be with you, too.'

As I pondered on whether to discuss the disagreement between Achillea and Gladia with him, he reached for one of his bundles which were neatly stacked next to the dwelling wall and produced a new fruit, with a flourish. It was a small, light orange fruit with a smooth, golden, velvety skin. He encouraged me to taste it. I bit into it slightly dubiously, wondering whether it would be sweet or sour, or full of gritty seeds. I liked to taste new foods, and Benakiell delighted in producing exotic items for me to try. This fruit had a firm flesh which gave slightly under my teeth but was not slushy or too juicy. The flesh was as orange as the skin, and there was a hard stone in the middle which my teeth met as I bit into it. It had a pleasant taste, slightly sharp but sweet with an almost honey like flavour to it.

'Do you like it?' enquired Benakiell. 'It is one of my favourite fruits from Kashiq, aside from the oranges. It is an apricot. If the orange is the sun of all the fruits, the apricot must be the moon or the stars.'

'It is very good.' I acknowledged. 'They are only small fruits, but they are rich in flavour. I wonder what the honey tastes like from the bees which collect from their flowers.' I examined the stone at the centre of the now finished apricot. It looked like a small brown pebble, and I wondered if I might be able to grow it in Gabez, which was close to the border with Kashiq. I suggested this to Benakiell.

'It may grow.' He acknowledged. 'But in Kashiq the apricots are grown further inland where the days are warmer, and the nights are colder. They say the apricot wants the best of both worlds. We cannot always grow everything that we might want, after all. Every land has something interesting to show us and there would be no point in travelling around to trade as I do if we were all the same. Anyway, please keep the apricot stone; it may

27

grow for you back in Gabez after all. Now, let me tell you about the beehives there in Kashiq.

'To see the beehives, you have to travel some miles inland from the river between Oramia and Kashiq. If you take the time to travel a little further away, you can often find more interesting things to trade, and you see more of the people. The orange groves are there, too so you can get the best oranges. I did a lot of trade with my building reeds there and worked on some fencing for the groves too. The beehives are the same kind of shape of ours but instead of being made from hollow logs like ours are, in Kashiq, the beehives are made of clay. A hollow pipe is made of clay, and it is sealed at each end by a flat disc of clay, with a hole in it so the bees can get in and out. Some of the beehive covers are decorated so you can tell whose beehive it is. In Kashiq, both men and women can be Beeguards. They stack up the clay pipe beehives in rows between the orange trees and make life easy for the bees by giving them the flowers they want to make the honey. They get good oranges and good honey and also use some of the orange blossoms to make neroli oil!'

I was fascinated by this. I thought back to how little I had known when I left the Temple in the First Age. I knew how to clean and how to pray and chant and how to oil the statue of the Goddess. I knew how to do as I was told without question. I had taught myself to read and scribe, secretly. But since I had entered this world of Oramia, I had learned so much more. I had learned to talk to other people and to listen to them, I had learned to trade in the markets and to make salves, to guard bees and even to ride a horse, although I had not ridden one since Lunaria became Queen. The thought that in each land there was an equal number of new ideas to understand and new skills to learn and new foods to try filled me with excitement. Why, in seven years, I had not yet learned half of what there was to learn in Oramia. One could spend one's whole life learning new things.

Benakiell chuckled at the look on my face. 'Now perhaps you see why I love to travel so much. I had forgotten how much it meant to me. After I met Velosia, I was more interested in her than in my wandering, and somehow I lost my desire to find out more. Velosia was like a land unto herself.' He paused, then, lost in his memories. I wished I had been able to meet Velosia, for everything I knew about her had come from the memories of Benakiell, Gladia and Achillea. It seemed to me that Gladia might have wanted to replace Velosia in Benakiell's heart, but, whilst she was a dear old friend to him, he did not seem to show any interest in her as a wife or lover.

As Benakiell got to his feet, he told me that he had found something interesting for me to take a look at while he had been trading in Kashiq. He went over to the bundles and rifled through the contents of one of the smaller ones. I could hear some metallic clanking. Perhaps Benakiell had brought back some metal vessels I could store honey or salves in. There was not much metal in Oramia except at the Queen's Court and among the OutRiders, who used most of it to make their armour and the fittings for their horses, for their arrowheads and their swords and throwing knives. Those who sought to trade metal goods in Oramia were heavily taxed and the OutRiders were well known for taking much of the available metal, leaving only the knives used for food preparation and for cutting and stripping the reeds, and needles such as those used by Gladia in her stitchery.

When Benakiell returned, however, he was holding a small strip of parchment. It had been torn raggedly so it was incomplete. There was no illustration on it, merely tightly placed script in a faded dark brown ink with many curves and flourishes.

'It was wrapped around something given to me in trade for my help in rebuilding a dwelling. The woman there needed a lot of help to make her dwelling safe and warm again. I asked her if she wanted the parchment but she said no, that it was of no use to her, so I brought it back for you. I have been a bad learner when it comes to reading and scribing and I must admit I am curious about what it might say or be about. We might learn something interesting from it, don't you think?'

I reached out for the parchment and smoothed it out to flatten it. The scribing was small and cramped but was in orderly lines. I already knew that I would be frustrated by the fact that it had been torn in half. I wished Benakiell had thought to ask the woman if she had the other half of the parchment. I drifted my eyes over the script quickly to see if there were any familiar words on it before I began trying to decipher it. Close to the bottom, I saw a name I recognised, and my interest was sharpened immediately. It was a name which I recognised from the Temple, although it was not one that I often saw scribed.

The words of the prophet Ashkana, child of the Goddess were the words by which we Maids had governed our lives. The Aphorisms of Ashkana offered on how to fill your time working for the Goddess, and each Temple possessed a scroll with the Aphorisms scribed on it. The Reader came to our Scholar classes to read to us from the scroll. Each day we would be read one of the Aphorisms and would then chant it over and over until we had learned it off by heart. Since we Maids did not read, this was the only way that we could learn from the wisdom of Ashkana. I still carried all the aphorisms with me in the emberjar of my mind, even though it had been some years since I had devoted much time or effort to them. I had taught myself to read in the final years of the last age of Childhood and had read the name of Ashkana from the scroll, following with my eyes as the reader read from the scroll. So, I knew it well. But what was her name doing on a parchment found in Kashiq? Ashkana's name was sacred in Oramia. No Maid nor woman of the Outer could be given her name, for it had been given to her by the Goddess herself, so it seemed unlikely that it could refer to anyone else of the same name. But perhaps things were different in the land of Kashiq. I knew nothing of the land beyond what Benakiell had told me, and he had never mentioned anything about what standing Ashkana might have in that land. I began to read the parchment, starting with the lines above the name. Benakiell hovered near me, waiting impatiently for me to tell him what the parchment was about. And now, for some reason, I wanted to read this parchment on my own, without him peering over my shoulder.

'It is a difficult script to read,' I murmured, shifting away from him as I rolled up the parchment. 'It will take me some time. It seems to be an account scribed by someone from some ages ago, but I cannot yet tell what it is about. May I take it back to Maren's dwelling where I can spend some time on it? Maren is planning to see Gladia and Bellis and Jember today, helping them to harvest the chillies so I can try to work it out more quickly, since I know you are eager to hear what it says.'

Benakiell's face fell slightly. He had clearly been anticipating me reading out the parchment straight away and he really wanted to know what it said. I felt a slight pang in my heart as I considered his disappointment but balanced it against my need to find out what had been scribed about Ashkana first. I had never been able to rid myself of my desire for secrecy, for keeping information

31

close to myself. I felt that if I shared too much with others, that somehow, I lost something of myself.

'Will you come and tell me when you have read it?' Benakiell pressed me and I promised I would come and find him again soon, after I had read as much as I could of the strange parchment. I was eager to get back to it now and, thanking Benakiell again for the apricot and for bringing me the parchment, I headed back towards Maren's dwelling.

# CHAPTER 3

I ran my hand over the torn parchment. I could tell it was old. It was thin and soft and had been made smooth with a sandrock. The ink was dark brown, faded to a lighter, redder colour in some places. I briefly wondered how much of the scroll was missing and then laid it out so that it was flat and weighted down the corners with smooth flat pebbles and began to read, tracing the scribing with my finger, and then painstakingly copying it out for myself so that I made no mistake, leaving out all the ornamentation with which the scribe had seen fit to decorate the scroll.

'...was only ever seen in its entirety by the Blessed Ashkana and by the Lord Rao. The Orange of Kashiq was made by Lord Rao as a token of devotion for Ashkana during the time of their great love. Ashkana it was who broke the honeygold orange when Rao's passion for her was no more, and she swore there would be no knowledge of love until the orange could be made whole again. She kept the key and returned the pieces of the orange showing that the Orange which had once been one united by love was now broken asunder. The pieces of the orange were sent by Ashkana to...'

I turned the parchment over, looking desperately for the continuation of the sentence, my mind feeling both full and strangely empty. In this short parchment, most of what I knew or had been told about Ashkana had been recomposed. Perhaps it wasn't true. Perhaps it was a fanciful story. But I knew this was recorded by one who believed what they wrote. Ashkana. The prophet who instructed us all on the power and the reason for work. She who inspired us to work harder and harder on behalf of the Goddess. There was no mention of the word love in any of the Aphorisms of Ashkana. My early childhood ages had been spent memorising the Aphorisms of Ashkana in preparation for my work as a Temple Maid in the Third Age of childhood. Those seven years of hard work were taken by the Temple and we were exhorted every day to work harder by the words of Ashkana. We had been told that Ashkana had devoted her entire life to work, that she knew that this would please the Goddess who made us all, and that her devotion to the Goddess was never swayed by human relationships. That she was the one who began the building of the Temples as centres for the work of the Goddess, carried out by us, the Temple Maids. I shook my head, trying to make the jumbled threads inside it fall into neat, tightly woven lines, but it remained a tangled mess. I read the parchment again just to make sure that it definitely said Ashkana. There was no doubt it was her; they even titled her Blessed. I carefully rolled up the parchment with the scribing on the inside, to preserve it from fading further, and tied it up with a piece of embroidery thread I had picked up on the path from Gladia's dwelling last night. No doubt Jember had been given some left over threads – or perhaps had taken them – to use in his play. I placed the scroll and its copy in my light wooden carrybox and closed the lid, as if that might make my thinking go away.

I had acquired the carrybox in Gabez. I had never seen one in Sanguinea before, nor even in the Temple, although there were, of course, boxes aplenty there, as there were at the Court of the Queen. But all those boxes stood on their own, sharp cornered and difficult to carry for any distance. They protected precious items much better than a carrying gourd, because they were more secure and an easier shape to get into. Many boxes that I had seen before were made of strong, heavy woods, constructed to stay in one place: heavy chests or ornamental boxes for jewellery or other treasures. Achillea had one such box in which she kept her necklaces and other pieces of adornment. I did not wear jewellery. I had once owned a bee pendant, briefly, and had given it up to the Queen, Lunaria. If I could find a necklace like that again, I might use such a box. This carrybox was made of a light wood, though. It did not open like many boxes did from the biggest surface, but rather from the smaller one. Because of this it was not wide and flat, but rather tall and narrow. It was held in a woven net of bands and could be easily carried flat on one's back as one walked along. One strap went over the shoulder and the other under the opposite arm and they could be tied fast. Benakiell also had one though he mostly still bundled his goods together in squares of cloth or in baskets or gourds. I had noticed that as he grew older, he carried fewer large objects and did more trading for smaller things, valuable spices like cinnamon, metal objects, embroidery silks, coffee pots and the like. Still, I marvelled at the strength of his back.

I knew that I would have to talk to Benakiell. It occurred to me that I could tell him that it was about something else, that I could lie to him about its content and that he would never know, since he did not read. Benakiell had an uncanny knack for knowing when I was being evasive, however, and would often continue questioning until he received the right answer. Besides, without Achillea and Tarik there, who were usually the ones to whom I spoke, he was the next best person to confide in. I felt dubious about involving Gladia and Bellis, however. Bellis, like me, had been raised in the Temple, and, unlike me, was still devoted to the Goddess.

She had even visited a Temple with Gladia recently to give thanks for Jember's First Age of childhood. I tried to steer clear of them, myself. Normally, Gladia would stay away too, but for Bellis, nothing was too much effort, and Gladia accompanied her to the Temple near to Sanguinea. If the new information about Ashkana were correct, I knew it would have a profound effect on Bellis. On the other hand, Benakiell sometimes confided in Gladia, who, in turn, would doubtless talk to Bellis. Bellis had developed a close friendship with Maren and Maren would then undoubtedly find out. I sighed. The links between people were like a complicated spidersilk with each line affecting another one.

I walked down to the gardens where Jember had found me the previous day. The coolness of the morning had drifted away, and the sun was shining, not with her full strength, but with a pale determination, and the sensation of the sun on my back warmed me and brightened my heart. I resolved to go and talk to Benakiell after I had joined Maren at the hives.

She looked up as I arrived and smiled in greeting. Her eyes, now fully cleared of the effects of poisonous smoke, were a deep, warm brown. Her eyelashes were sparse, perhaps from years of rubbing at her sore eyes, and her eyes had deep lines fanning out from the corners which contrived to make her look older than she was. For years she had kept her hair shortly cut since she could not see to tend it in any way. Her close companion, Anglossia, had tended to her hair while she was alive, but when Anglossia died, Maren had cut her hair very short and so it had stayed. I noticed that it was longer now than at my last visit, and the ends of it were curling up. I commented on her hair as I sat down beside her, reaching for some bark strips to plait into a holding rope for the hive she was finishing off. She smiled shyly at me.

'Bellis persuaded me that wearing it longer suited me,' she said, smiling slightly and pulling her fingers through the curls a little self-consciously. I pondered this, at first surprised that anyone might change their hair based on what a friend might say and then recognising that I too had sometimes moderated my appearance or what I wore based on what Achillea advised. I was more surprised that Bellis would take an interest in the hair of another woman. She had been raised in the Temple and we were not accustomed to making comment on the appearance of others. 'Keep your eyes on your work not on those who work with you.' And 'The Goddess has no care for what you look like, only what your work looks like'. And here I was, repeating the words of Ashkana to myself even though I now knew that she had not always been so single minded in her approach to work. I continued to plait the strips of bark absently, drawing in new lengths as old ones ended while I thought.

I heard a lot about love in my time in the Outer. The love of Achillea for Ashtun, now dead. The love of Achillea for Tarik and his love for her. The love of Bellis for the Goddess and for Jember. The love of Benakiell for Velosia. I had heard tell of the great love between Princess Paradox and her OutCommander, father of Queen Lunaria. I had listened to songs of love and squabbles between lovers in the marketplace. But I had never felt it. I had not felt the love for a parent, nor yet the love of a parent for a child. I had not loved another as a partner. I cared for my friends deeply, but I was not sure if this was the same love. I wondered how Ashkana knew and resolved to discuss it with Maren in a general kind of way, without mentioning the parchment.

'What do you know of love?' I asked. Maren seemed surprised at my question, and then looked away briefly before she addressed herself to my query.

'I can only tell you of the love that I have felt, sister Talla,' she acknowledged. 'It may not be the same for all. I guess that you do not mean the love of a parent for a child or for family, but rather the sort of love between such as Achillea and Tarik? It seems they have a strength of love between them since they do not bow to Gladia's concerns.' I shifted uncomfortably, reminded of my discussion with Gladia the previous night and my desire to try to resolve the conflict between them. I hoped Benakiell might have some good ideas for me in that regard. But really, I did not want to talk about other people's love but to hear about it from one who knew for herself. Slowly, I realised I might have asked the wrong person, for Maren had never married. I suddenly became concerned that I might have upset her with my questioning. Although I was curious about love, I had no ambition for myself in this regard, but I knew that for the people of the Outer it was something that preoccupied them. I turned towards her, ready to offer my apologies for having spoken too hastily, but she was smiling at me, about to speak.

'So many people tell of how some feature about the appearance of the one they love is the thing which drew them together, but I did not, of course, remember anything of how Anglossia looked – and in any case, she was so badly burnt in the fire that she told me she looked quite different from her former self. So, I never fell in love with her beauty or only that which I could touch with my hand. It was something in her manner of being with me which caused me to love her. It felt like she was the other half of me. All the things I seemed to lack, she seemed to possess. Her love for me made me strong. She made me feel encouraged and worthy of love.'

My face must have told Maren some tale in its expression, for she smiled a little self-consciously and continued. 'There are those who would tell you that only the love between a man and a woman can be truly crowned as the jewel of love, for only they can create a child, but there are many in this world who have a love not founded on making a child but on a love for one another. I have never felt any of the same kind of love for a man that I have felt for a woman. It is the way the Goddess made me, in her wisdom, and she made others too who feel like me and who, in turn can love me in the same way.'

It seemed that there was much more to this thing called love that I needed to understand. I knew that Maren had lived with Anglossia for many years but had always thought of them as friends or companions, not lovers. Every time I thought I had learned and understood this world of the Outer, something new occurred. I had thought that one of the reasons that the Goddess had separated her world into the women of the Temple and the men of the OutFort was so that they did not meet one another and become lovers or have children, but if one could love one's own kind as well as another, it made me wonder why it had not occurred in the Temple between the Maids or the Priestesses. It was all becoming more and not less complicated and talking to Maren had not helped in the slightest.

I thanked Maren for telling me of her love and she asked me curiously why I had wanted to know. She suggested that perhaps I had met somebody that I loved too. I looked at her, horrified at the conclusion she had drawn from my question, and assured her that it certainly was not so. She laughed again. She seemed so light-hearted, quite different from the quiet, sad person she used to be, even the last time I was in Mellia, which was only a few months ago. I wove the last piece of the bark strip I was using into the rope and gave it a tug to make sure it was strong enough to hold up the hive. I helped Maren to strap the hive up and then we raised it up into the canopy of the tree where it hung like a floating branch, aloud with the noise of disturbed bees.

# CHAPTER 4

My journey to Sanguinea began in the early morning. The air was fresh and sharp and there was the smell of heavy dew on the dusty path. I shifted my carrybox so it hung more comfortably and tied my gourds to my waist. Maren had filled them with dark, syrupy honey. I would trade some of them and use some of the honey in our salves and physics. Maren had told me a few things which she would like me to find in Gabez and bring back with me on my next trip, including a necklace in the form of a flower. I was surprised at this request, but reasoned that Maren was entitled to trade her honey for whatever she wished and recalled how happy the little bee pendant had made me all those years before.

Gladia had refused to talk to me further about Achillea, contriving to look both mournful and stubborn at the same time. She reminded me of Jember when he was being told to do something he had no intention of doing. Benakiell had nothing useful to advise me regarding this mutinous battle between Achillea and Gladia and only counselled me to let them resolve it in their own way – currently by ignoring one another. I found this a deeply frustrating attitude and told him so; the spark of rage in my mind's emberjar rekindling, infuriated by their steadfast refusal to talk to each other. Benakiell had chuckled and told me that I could be just as stubborn about other issues, and that when Achillea and Gladia were ready, they would talk to one another.

'You cannot always have things happen according to your desire,' he warned me, mildly. 'That, after all, is what leads those in power to make choices and decisions which are only of benefit to themselves. It might be that some time away from each other is what they most need.' I subsided, knowing that he was right, and resolved to try, once again, to learn more patience in my dealings with other people.

I had talked to Benakiell about the parchment and told him what it said. He was as shocked as I was, and at a loss to explain what it might mean. He had never heard this story before, although as he reminded me, he had not known to ask about it while he was in Kashiq.

'There is something about those involved in the Goddess and her messengers which makes ordinary people secretive and defensive. The only way you could really find out more would be by asking the people of Kashiq more about what they know of this. Rao is one who is honoured in Kashiq, just like Ashkana is here in Oramia.'

I gaped at him. Although he had not heard of this particular story regarding Ashkana and Rao, he had heard of this Rao, described in the scrap of parchment as Lord Rao. If Rao was a real person, then it made it much more likely that this parchment was based on truth. I asked Benakiell for more information, but he was vague, and told me that while he traded over the river from Gabez in Kashiq, he tried to remain quiet and unobtrusive so that he could do his trades without drawing attention to himself. He said he knew a few people in Kashiq, but only those who he traded with, and that they did not discuss much aside from their trading, and a little about how the fruit was grown and how the wooden boxes were made and so on. He had heard people invoking the name of Rao, especially when faced with a problem which they could not solve, and said they often used the phrase 'Rao, share your great wisdom', seemingly as an entreaty to this Rao to solve their difficulties. He gave me the parchment to take back with me to Gabez, saying that he had no need for it now that he knew what the words said.

I realised I had missed having some complicated puzzle to untangle in my mind, and that my mind had grown quiet and tepid over the past few years I wondered if I might be able to ask some of the Kashiqi traders who came into Gabez with their wares about this Rao. I might even talk to Tarik about it. Since he used to be an OutRider, he was more widely travelled than either Achillea or me, and he may have heard of this Rao as he travelled through Oramia. I felt impatient to get back home now, and although I would miss my friends here in Mellia, I knew I would be back soon, and hoped that I would have both more information for Benakiell and a flower necklace for Maren. I had seen Kashiqi jewellery for trade before and planned to do both tasks at the same time by asking a Kashiqi jewellery trader about Rao.

Jember hopped around like a dizzy cricket, suffused with excitement, even though it was only me departing, something he had seen many times before. He seemed to feed off the energy of others in the way that I took my energy from coffee and honey.

'When are you coming back, Aunty Talla? Will you bring me something from Gabez? Will you bring Aunty Achillea and Uncle Tarik?' The questions were endless, and I admired his capacity not to be daunted by the lack of answers, for he just kept on asking the questions. Bellis smiled at him indulgently, and Maren smiled at Bellis. Gladia thrust a cloth wrapped bundle into my hands as I prepared to walk off and told me that had made me some cinnamon spiced flatbreads for my trip. I was touched that she had thought kindly of me before I left, but she brushed away my thanks and went to stand next to Bellis and Jember. I turned down the path and then turned once more and waved again before resolutely setting my face towards the path and walking briskly on.

I had arranged to meet Achillea and Tarik at the market in Sanguinea. It was a place I now knew well, having visited it many times over the past seven years. My mind drifted back to the first time I had visited there, a time when I had never been to a market on the Outer, never been surrounded by so many people, so much noise and colour and so many different items for trade. I did not know then how to interact with people, how to exchange light pleasantries with potential customers, or how to balance my trades. Nowadays, Achillea and I tended to take our goods to market once a month and we had got to know some of our regular customers. Some of the perfume traders traded for our salves and for my beeswax. I had thought that I might try to make the perfumed creams myself if I could acquire some of the scented oils. Achillea made the salves usually, singing away as she stirred together the beeswax, paradox oil and honey before pouring them into the tiny gourds we grew in the garden, along with the herbs and flowers we grew for my bees.

Tarik worked more on the physic. He had learnt how to make the tisanes and poultices and infusions while he was an Outrider. He was also a skilled metalworker, but rarely had the opportunity to practice his skills any more since the OutRiders were the only ones who had access to the stocks of metals. We on the Outer could only buy certain metal objects; small knives, saw blades and hoe blades, needles, and the like. Tarik did not like to be pressed on his life as an OutRider and although he had spoken of it openly when we first met, since he had quietly left, he had not spoken much of it and was taciturn when asked questions. Achillea seemed untroubled by this and insisted she had no interest in reliving the past. But perhaps they spoke of these things when they were alone.

My journey to Sanguinea was uneventful. It remained cool even when the sun shone brightly. People I met along the way hurried along; more to keep warm than anything else. Some of them wore double thickness shawls wrapped around their shoulders and heads. I wondered if I might be able to trade for one at Sanguinea when I got there. I preferred the warmth of the sun as we left the cold season and moved into the hot season. I could almost hear Gladia in my head muttering about how some people were never satisfied. She was right. I never did seem to be satisfied. There was always so much more to learn and to understand and to improve at that I felt I needed to spend my life trying to fulfil as much as possible. And yet when I sat out in the garden plaiting a rope or cleaning a beehive or pulling up the creeping weeds from my herbs and flowers, I felt more fulfilled. There was something about it which quieted my mind and stopped it from chasing itself around in circles. I had found the same freedom in the Temple, strangely enough. As I worked at my cleaning, which, although physically taxing was not mentally demanding, my mind wandered along teasing out the answers to questions and problems. I needed that quiet. Achillea on the other hand loved to talk to people and managed to do so all the time. She chattered to anyone about anything and I admired her ability to coax a smile from even the most recalcitrant face. Tarik was a quiet person like me, although he could talk for a long time on certain subjects. He loved to listen to Achillea, and he listened well, often recalling things she had told him about this person or the other.

Achillea chatted away without pausing to take a breath when I caught up with them both in Sanguinea. They were preparing to pack the goods away and she told me some of what had happened while I had been in Mellia for the past few days.

'We have traded all the honey, of course; we even had some people waiting for us to unpack it, they were so eager. There seems to be less honey around now and that meant we got some excellent trading deals; I'll show you those later. Tarik has also traded all the physic; there has been some sort of sickness travelling through Sanguinea and many people wanted to trade for the ginger tonic and the Achillea physic.' She preened herself slightly as she told me this. Tarik had taught us a great deal about wildflowers and herbs, and Achillea had been thrilled to find out that there was a flower from which she took her name. It was a useful herb and Tarik made wound salves and tonics out of it. The wound salves stopped the bleeding of wounds and the tonics helped to stop stomach ailments. She showed me some of the things which she had traded for; flour for flatbreads, figs and dates, coffee, some plain thread for mending and some needles, and the small gourds which we used for so many of the salves. She had done well, and then she showed me two extra things triumphantly.

Achillea had acquired two bags made in a cunning new design. I say it was a new design, but really it was like a large underpocket. We all had underpockets in which to keep our precious small items as we journeyed or even if we had items which we just wanted to keep safe, like small pieces of jewellery. They were made from a circle of fabric which had a sequence of small holes cut around the edge. A plaited string was then threaded through them and gathered up and could then be attached to an underbelt. These new bags were much larger, and I saw immediately how useful they might be to us. We could use them to gather herbs and flowers or to carry quantities of small gourds in and it would be much easier. I praised Achillea for her choice and she looked pleased, her large dark eyes softening at the edges as she smiled.

'And look Talla,' she continued, 'they have been beautifully stitched on the outside! I chose this orange one for you, with the little green leaves, and I thought I could have the blue one with the white flowers. But I don't mind,' she added, hastily. 'If you prefer the blue one, you can have that one either.' I assured her that she had made the right choice and that she had chosen well for me. Although I was born under the day of Flammeus (or so the Priestesses told me), the colour of red and the scent of cinnamon, I had become more attracted to other colours and orange seemed a milder version of red. It suited me better now, and I was happy to have the bag, and happy to be with my friends again. I wanted to tell Achillea the news from Mellia, but I felt that it was better kept until we got back home to Gabez. Instead, I was content to listen to her going through the gossip from the market traders in Sanguinea. Along with the illness travelling through Sanguinea and the shortage of honey, it had been reported that the OutRiders had been visiting Sanguinea with more frequency searching for items made of metals. Achillea told me that this news had worried Tarik and that he was glad that we would be going back to Gabez soon.

As she told me this, Tarik turned and waved, finishing his conversation, and hoisting his bundles onto his back. As usual, we were planning to sleep one night on the way back to Gabez, and we needed to start walking now if we were to make it there before dark. Not for the first time, I thought longingly of the horses we had ridden seven years ago and imagined how much faster and easier it would be if we had a couple of horses. Of course, we couldn't own horses, for they were the sole preserve of the OutRiders and of the Queen. I felt a familiar twinge of anger as I contemplated the unfair system which we lived under, but from which there seemed no escape unless I were to move and live in some other unknown land.

That evening we sat close to the fire after we had eaten, drinking hot coffee, and trying to keep warm while I told Achillea and Tarik of my visit to Mellia. I did not talk of my conversation with Gladia but concentrated instead on the funny things which Jember had said and done and on how the garden and the bees were doing under Maren's care. I also talked to them about Benakiell and how he had returned from Kashiq with oranges and apricots. Tarik was immediately interested in all the information that Benakiell had brought back with him from Kashiq. He asked me so many questions about what Benakiell had said that I began to wish that he had come along to Mellia so that he could ask Benakiell all his questions himself.

After a silence, Achillea enquired in a casual tone, 'And how is Gladia? Does she still disapprove of me and Tarik? Are we welcome in Mellia yet?' She laughed, but it was a brittle laugh, betraying her anxiety. Tarik patted her hand affectionately and assured her that she would always be welcome wherever he might be. She leaned her head on his shoulder, and inched closer to him. I could feel the pain in her question. It was important to her and yet she was trying awfully hard to make it appear trivial. I pondered my words before I spoke.

'Gladia is concerned about your relationship still. Benakiell says we should let it alone for some time and she may change her mind.'

Achillea sighed, looking downcast. A single tear rolled down the side of her sharp nose and dropped into the fire with a small hiss and a grey puff of fine ash. Tarik wiped her cheek tenderly with his thumb. I myself never really thought any more about his past life as an OutRider. Years had gone by and I knew him far better now. I reflected on what Gladia had said about him, and about the possibility that he could have been Jember's father, although even Gladia had acknowledged that it was unlikely. Even so, ever since Gladia had raised it the day before, I had been thinking more about his background. How could we be sure that somebody raised as an OutRider would respect Achillea and cherish her? How did we know that he would not see her as the OutRiders saw the Angels, as empty vessels for the using? The conversation I had with Gladia was clearly lodged in my mind and I gave myself an internal shake. I knew Tarik well and I, of all people, should know what it was like to be judged based on where you came from. I still remembered the looks of some of those I met when I had first left the Temple, wearing my drabcoat. I had resolved to always be kind to any Temple Maid I might come across in my life in the Outer, but I had never yet met one who had been sent out by the Temple since I had left. I wondered if the Temple had changed their arrangements for the removal of the Maids who did not pass muster.

In order to give Achillea something else to think about aside from her fractured relationship with Gladia, I told them both about the mysterious parchment scrap which Benakiell had brought back from Kashiq. This had the desired effect, and Achillea was immediately fascinated.

'I wonder what happened between them for her to do that. Did this Rao not really love her? Did he find another? I would love to see what the Orange looked like; it must have been beautiful to have been made for

Ashkana herself! I wonder if the Goddess made Rao not love Ashkana so that she could do work for the Goddess instead! What do you think Ashkana looked like, Talla?' This last question was an unexpected one for me. I had never even imagined Ashkana as a real person before, someone like me or Achillea. Ashkana as a person who combed her hair or cooked a meal or washed a dish seemed unlikely. And yet this small section of parchment which stated that Ashkana had felt love for another and that the same person had felt love for her made her more real to me. As a Maid in the Temple, I had only ever thought of her as the one whom the Goddess had chosen to scribe down instructions for us on our duties in the world, especially regarding work and how to glorify the Goddess with our efforts. I had never thought of her as a person. I thought now of her sitting in a room somewhere, perhaps in a Temple, with a parchment and a reed pen, scribing out her Aphorisms that we might all know them. Every Temple had a copy of the Aphorisms of Ashkana, from which the Reader would read to us when we were young, that we might learn it all off by heart. There was no need for us to read it there, for we recited the Aphorisms so many times that I could scribe a copy myself. But was this all? Perhaps the Priestesses only read to us the parts which they thought were most useful to them. Perhaps Ashkana wrote many pieces of wisdom and only the Aphorisms were shared with us, to exhort us to work even more.

Tarik pushed another stick onto the fire; tiny orange sparks flew off it briefly into the dark, purpled night sky. He was, it seemed, more interested in the Orange itself and how it was made and what it may have looked like.

'We used to use Kashiqi metals in our metalworking sometimes, in the OutFort,' he said. I was surprised because he rarely spoke of those times now. 'We used them to make our armour mostly, the little discs for the horse's armour and the meshes for the helmets. They do have a tradition there of making silver goods too, but we did not usually get a lot of the silver because it tarnishes too easily. We used more of the honeygold. I remember seeing some very ornate daggers and sheaths once. Perhaps this Rao was a master metalsmith. I wonder if it looked like a real orange or was a flat shape or a picture of an orange engraved on honeygold. I would like to make you such a token of love, Achillea,' he said, turning to look at her fully.

'What would you make for her?' I asked, with interest. I too enjoyed making things. There was real satisfaction even in making a well-fitting cover for a salve gourd.

Achillea's eyes lit up and I felt pleased that she was feeling happier, and was not dwelling on Gladia, at least for now. She looked at Tarik, with her eyes dancing, waiting for his answer. As usual, when it came to Tarik, he had been thinking carefully.

'I would make you a golden bird, my love,' he replied fondly. 'You sing so beautifully. I could listen to you all day. And I would make it of honeygold, if I could but find some, and then I would make another bird for myself, and the honeygold would always be a force between them. They would belong together, you see, just like we do.' Achillea sighed happily and nestled closer to him while I rolled my eyes in the dark. I was happy that Achillea and Tarik loved one another but sometimes it got a little over fanciful. There again, what would I know; I had never loved someone, nor indeed, as far as I knew, been loved by someone in this way. I made my excuses and crept off to sleep, leaving Tarik explaining his idea to Achillea in gentle murmurs.

# CHAPTER 5

We were halfway back to Gabez when our journey became rather more eventful than we had anticipated. It was a long walk, but the path was quite flat, and because it was the cold season, it was pleasant enough to make our way along it. We did not have to rest in the shade at the hottest time of the day and we made good time. It was as we approached the crossroads that we became aware of a person standing at the stone which marked the splitting of the paths. There was a familiarity about the figure, an intangible presence. I glanced at Achillea, but she was evidently oblivious to my feeling. Tarik, however narrowed his eyes slightly, and shifted his hand. I knew that he still had his throwing knife from his days as an OutRider. It was small enough that he could keep it discreetly hidden. I had never seen him use it since he had used it to kill the OutRider who had murdered Ashtun, but I knew that he would if he had to, to defend Achillea. Ahead of the waiting person was a small knot of travellers standing around, apparently casually, a little way up the road. There was something aware about them. They held themselves upright, and they had too few bundles to be genuine travellers. I had heard in Gabez of there being small groups of men who robbed travellers of their goods and then used them to trade for themselves. This was contrary to the teachings of the Goddess, but it didn't seem to stop them. The figure began to lazily stride towards us, raising his hand in greeting and calling his greetings to us. I caught my breath. It was Ambar. Vizier Ambar, Lord Ambar, companion of the Queen.

He looked much the same as he had done when I had last seen him seven years ago. His beard was still closely trimmed and his eyes still a golden brown like rich honey. He was not as lean as he had been back then; there was a softening of his silhouette, much as there had been with Tarik. He wore a standard robe of the Outer, but I doubted this was his normal garb as the Vizier of Oramia. As the Queen's consort, he would no doubt now be accustomed to wearing richly embroidered fabrics. He gestured behind him to the small knot of onlookers, who turned away, presumably following orders. Tarik suddenly began using the sign language used by the OutRiders. I suppose, like any other language that a person might be fluent in, it could not be easily forgotten. I had tried to persuade Tarik to teach me the silent language many times since then, but he refused, implacable that it was not something he needed nor wanted to use any more, now that he lived a new life in the Outer. And yet, here he was, using the very same language to address Ambar, whose eyes narrowed as they followed Tarik's gestures and whose clenched jaw muscle throbbed. He turned away from Tarik and faced me.

'My greetings, Talla Velosiana,' remarked Ambar, his honeyed tones mild but instantly familiar to me. I was shocked that he knew what my chosen family name was, here in the Outer. Those of us born in the Temple only had one given name, for we had no family except for the Temple. In the Outer, a woman would take her mother's given name with -na on the end of it. Benakiell and his wife Velosia had never had a child and I had asked him if he would mind if I used Velosia's name for my own family name. Blinking a little, he had kindly agreed and ever since then I had happily settled into my new name. All

53

this, however, had taken place after we had left the Court of the Queen. I was not sure how Ambar had found it out, but it did confirm my suspicions that those of us who had helped to install Queen Lunaria were still being observed.

'I greet you,' I responded shortly. Vizier or no Vizier, Ambar had treated us all shoddily after Lunaria had become Queen. Having been a good companion to us all with his charming manner and his ability to make one feel interesting, once he had found out who the real Queen was, he had thrown everything behind her and left us all without looking back. Despite this, I had missed his company sometimes.

Achillea's mouth had dropped open rather comically so that she looked like a baby bird with its mouth open for more food. She gaped at Ambar, and then, as she recovered from her surprise, travelled her eyes over his clothes critically. Achillea would have expected the Lord Vizier to be wearing clothes which were elevated beyond the means of we ordinary people of the Outer, and she was disappointed by what she saw.

'Do you not have any nicer clothes than that?' she asked finally. Like me, it was clear that she would not be standing on ceremony for Ambar. His lips twitched at her apparent impertinence. Perhaps he missed being spoken to like an ordinary person rather than being spoken to by ingratiating courtiers and earnest OutCommanders. His eyes flicked back to Tarik, whose hand still rested near his concealed throwing knife. He had been Ambar's closest companion for some time, but like us, he had not seen him since we had left the Court.

'Come,' he said mildly. 'My men have made us a shelter and a fire with coffee brewing. Let us sit a while together as we used to do, that I might tell you why I have sought you out.' He pointed over to one side of the path, near a large, dark grey boulder and there was indeed a cloth shelter or tent open on one side which had been set up with a fire. One of the OutRiders was tending to a coffee pot while the others stood by their horses, alert for any danger to their Lord Vizier.

'But how did you know we would be here?' asked Achillea, finally, bemused by his seeming prescience. Tarik turned to her.

'His spies will have told him. How else would he know of Talla's family name? He has been keeping track of us for years now.' He turned to Ambar, and, while he spoke in his usual calm manner, there was no mistaking the warning behind his words. 'He must be wary of such behaviour. It may be an easy part of Court life, but there are those of us who know more than the courtiers do about the story of the Queen, and he would do well to remember that.'

Ambar raised his arms in mock surrender, smiling. 'Come, come, brother Tarik,' he said. 'I mean you no harm, and I only try to keep up with you all. You were my companions, and it is natural to wish to know how you are all getting on, surely? Sit down with me and take some coffee.' He moved his hands quickly and the OutRiders who attended him melted away to stand by the trees, out of earshot but not out of sight. We followed him over to the fire, glancing at one another. We sat down on the cloths that had been laid out on the floor, the three of us on one mat and Ambar sitting on his own on another one. He poured the coffee into a set of plain clay beakers and handed them to us. We all remained silent, almost as if we had agreed on this beforehand; perhaps we were all unsure of what to say. It made me uncomfortable to think of the detail of our lives being reported back to Ambar and Lunaria up there in the Court of the Queen which rose high above the plains of Oramia. And here was Ambar, apparently still travelling the world, his true status unknown by those he met. I wondered whether he did this often, or if there was a special reason why he had left the Court and whether he meant us harm. It was so hard to tell. As if aware of the anger sparking in my mind, he turned to me with a placatory smile.

'Well, I see I will have to try to convince you of my sincerity,' he began. 'The Queen and I have often thought of you, our companions, and indeed the reason we met for the first time. As brother Tarik has pointed out to you, we have occasionally followed your progress, and that of Benakiell and Gladia, and Maren and Bellis. We heard of the birth of Bellis's son, too. In other lands, perhaps we could have remained friends more easily.'

This all seemed too simple to me. He and Lunaria had turned away from us without even expressing regret. And poor Achillea had lost her love Ashtun. When I thought of how much pain she had endured, and how hard we had all worked to rebuild our lives, it made me angry to think of Lunaria and Ambar looking down on our lives much like the Queen's Court itself looked down on the plains of the Outer. I was about to say this to him in forthright terms, when Achillea spoke.

'It must be so hard for Lunaria...I mean the Queen...not to have friends who have known her since before she was the Queen. There must be so many around you both who only want all the rich furnishings and food and who will tell you anything you want to hear.' She blinked and reached for Tarik's hand. 'But if you can travel as you have done today, without fuss, why have you not been to visit us before? You obviously know where we are and what we do.' She paused, and then continued, rather more indignantly. 'Poor Tarik has worried for years that someone will come from the OutRiders to take him away! In all of that time you could have got a message to him to reassure him! Unless, of course, that is what you have come for now!'

Ambar looked away, evidently somewhat ashamed by the scolding which Achillea had just given him. I felt a smile beginning and struggled to keep my mouth closed. Her admonishment would have had far more impact on Ambar than mine would have done; he would have expected hot headed rage from me but not from her. His fingers twitched, as if he wanted to speak privately to Tarik, but then Tarik spoke too.

'I no longer use that language of the hands, Ambar,' he said. 'I was caught off guard earlier, but I have not used it in years. I am a man of the Outer now, and prouder and happier for it than I ever was as an OutRider of the Queen. If you have something to say to me, you may say it in front of Achillea and Talla too, for we do not hide such things from each other.'

Ambar was taken aback again, and, despite myself, I began to feel sorry for him. It would have taken a lot of organising to arrange this meeting here with no others around, and some patience to find out our travels and to plan for it. I looked more closely at him. Although he was only an age older than me, there were lines of worry on his brow and a weariness around his eyes. It would surely do no harm to listen to what he had to say, and to his reasons for engineering this meeting after all these years. What could possibly have made him seek us out? I sipped my coffee, relishing its richness and purity. There was at least the advantage in drinking high quality coffee while we listened.

'Let us hear what he has to say,' I suggested. 'We all know Ambar, and he knows us, so there must be some reason why he has sought us out. We have nothing to hide, after all.' Immediately after I had said this, I realised that, in fact, we all had something to lose and plenty to hide, at least from the Outers. I could tell from Tarik's face that he had also thought the same thing, but thankfully his nature was to be cautious in his responses and he merely inclined his head slightly to indicate his assent. Achillea, seeing this, also nodded and asked Ambar to tell us why he had sought us out. He settled down more comfortably and began to tell us his story.

# CHAPTER 6

I come to you for assistance,' began Ambar. 'I am not sure who I can trust at the Queen's Court. Although I am the Lord Vizier to the Queen, there are still those who wish to use the Queen for their own ends. It has taken long years for me to show the Queen the extent of my devotion to her and for her to place her trust in me.'

I thought back to when Ambar first met Lunaria and how he had seamlessly transferred his apparent interest in me (who he initially thought to be the Queen) to Lunaria when her real identity was revealed. I had been stung at the time; there had been sharp pain and then a dull and plaguing ache and the lingering belief that I had lost something which I did not even know I had. I had not found any special relationship with another person above friendship. Perhaps it was my Temple upbringing, but I did not feel able to be comfortable with men who were interested in me as something different to a companion. I realised that Bellis too had not found such a relationship although it was scarcely surprising, considering her treatment at the hands of the OutRiders. Hearing that Lunaria had taken so long to commit herself to Ambar made me feel somewhat comforted.

Ambar explained that he and Lunaria had become close and that he now wished to become her official consort, to marry her and to give her children, to carry on the royal line.

'Lunaria is determined that she should not make the mistakes of her Grandmother, the old Queen,' continued Ambar. 'She wants our children to be raised under the love and care of the Goddess and to learn justice and fairness from an early age.' I almost snorted aloud at this statement, delivered quite earnestly by Ambar. He, who was now the Vizier and had, when he was seeking the Queen, stood up against the old systems run by the land of Oramia, and spoke against the use of the Angels, those who had been discarded by the Temple. Since Lunaria had become Queen, there had been no outward sign of any system having been dismantled at all. It still incensed me, and what made me even angrier was that I had no opportunity to do anything about it myself, for I never encountered any of the Temple Maids who had been ejected from the Temple to become Angels. I felt impotent against this hidden system which was neither just nor fair.

'How can we help you, Lord Ambar?' asked Tarik, being careful to accord Ambar his honorary title, to maintain his distance.

'There is one at the Court who Lunaria places much faith in,' answered Ambar slowly. 'She is the one whom they call the Reader of Dreams. Not only does she do all the reading for the Queen, for Lunaria does not read, believing it, as you know, to be the gift of the Goddess, but she also is believed to have the gift of interpreting the dreams of the Queen. The Queen relies upon her interpretations, and although in many matters she takes my counsel, in these things she will only listen to Silene, the DreamReader. It is she who has interpreted Lunaria's dreams with the help of old scrolls and told her that until she acquires a particular item, she will not be able to have children with me or any other man, nor be permitted by the Goddess to marry. If it is found, then it will be a sign from the Goddess that she blesses Lunaria's choice of partner.' Ambar sighed and looked dejected. I knew how implacable Lunaria could be once she had set her mind to something, and I didn't envy Ambar in trying to change her views. If this Silene had convinced her that the Goddess was sending her messages in her dreams, Lunaria would believe her. The longer it had been since I had seen her, the more unlikely I thought it that I really was her DoubleSoul sister. I think I trusted in my own interpretations of my dreams far more than I would the words of one such as this Silene.

'What is this object?' asked Achillea, suddenly. 'Is it a piece of jewellery, like the bee necklace or the brooch that Talla had? Can you not have one made by the Court Jeweller? Oh, but then,' her face fell as she realised the flaw to her plan, 'Lunaria is the Queen, and she would find out! Do you want us to try and find you a good jeweller here in the Outer?'

Ambar smiled at Achillea, with a hint of his old warmth and charm.

'It is no piece of jewellery, but a kind of ornamental fruit or some such thing,' he sighed. 'It was apparently owned by Ashkana herself according to Silene, but I suspect that is just a tale she has dreamed up herself to stop Lunaria from marrying me for she does not trust me with the Queen.'

Tarik and I looked at each other, the same thought having occurred to us both. Could this be the very same item which I had read about on the parchment scrap which Benakiell had found in Kashiq? Ambar might be tired and somewhat careworn, but he had lost none of his acuity and the swift glance between me and his old comrade had not escaped him.

'Do you know something of this? Before I even tell it? How can this be?' he asked, surprised and suspicious.

Achillea spun round, suddenly realising that we might all be talking about the same object.

'Of course! It must be the Orange! If it is about love, then of course Queen Lunaria will want to have it returned to her!'

Ambar looked surprised at the mention of the orange and then his eyes took on that focused look which I had observed many times before, the look of one who is planning several moves ahead. Again, his hands twitched and again Tarik looked away from them, refusing to engage in any communication that was secret from Achillea.

'I do not understand how this can be,' exploded Ambar in frustration. 'How can you know of what I tell you when the only ones that know it are in the Queen's Court? Is there some kind of spy there reporting back to you?'

I laughed, genuinely amused that Ambar could immediately make such an accusation when he had just admitted to spying on us. Achillea, too, burst into peals of laughter. Her laughter always sounded so melodious whereas mine sounded more like a jackal barking to me. Tarik's mouth twitched as he tried to maintain his normal serious face, but he was unable to resist joining in with the laughter and soon the three of us were chuckling at Ambar's high-handed accusation. He looked exasperated at first, but the crosser he looked, the more we laughed until eventually he began to laugh too.

'A spy,' chortled Achillea. 'Why yes, Lord Ambar, we have our very own network of spies who we often send to the Queen's Court to spy on her and listen to her conversations!!' This sounded even more ridiculous and we laughed again. Eventually Ambar spoke again.

'Forgive me, I know you cannot have a spy there; I just cannot imagine how you could know that I speak of an orange when I have told nobody of this and, unless Silene herself has spoken to another, as far as I know, it is only her and the Queen and myself who know of the supposed existence of this orange. I had dismissed it as a fanciful story made up by one who seeks power over the Queen, but now I do not know what to think. How did you hear of this?'

Before Achillea or I had time to respond to Ambar's questions, Tarik spoke.

'We will answer that question after you have told us why you sought us out. For why would you search for us to help you with some issue of a dream, even one dreamed by our Queen? There must be something which troubles you or a reason why you came to seek us out rather than speaking to the wealth of people who are available to you in the Court. You were the one who sought us out so you must be the one to speak first.'

And so, at last, Ambar began to explain the story of why he had found us and what he wanted from us. Silene, the DreamReader whose opinion Queen Lunaria trusted so implicitly, had, one day, come to the Queen to read her dreams. In the same way that a Reader interpreted the symbols scribed on a parchment, so this woman purported to read the symbols seen in the dreams of the Queen. She had been a member of the old Queen's Court, and while many of those who supported the old Queen were removed from the Court, (Where did they go, I wondered), Lunaria had shown interest in the talents of this person. She began by only interpreting occasional dreams, but later she read messages from the Goddess in the dreams which Lunaria had. She had become a kind of confidante for Lunaria and when Ambar had spoken to Lunaria about his love for her and his wish to marry her and become her consort, she had asked Silene to interpret her dreams in the following days. Silene had introduced doubtful messages in her reading of Lunaria's dreams and had then told her that the Goddess had sent a message to Silene herself in a dream to say that the

Queen could only marry if she found and restored the famed Orange of Kashiq. Silene had shown the Queen a scroll of parchment and read to her from it, saying that the Goddess could only bless the marriage of a Queen with children if that Queen possessed the complete Orange of Kashiq. Silene explained that the Orange had been lost and that ever since all the families of the Queen had been cursed. If Lunaria did not want to be cursed as her own mother, the Lady Paradox, had been, she would have to find the lost treasure.

'I do not trust what this woman says,' said Ambar ruefully. 'She is the Reader for the Court and I do not read, as you know. Even if I am the Vizier, I cannot find a reader whose first allegiance is not the Court. I feel ashamed that I do not trust the Reader of the Court, but you know what the Court was like when Lunaria became the Queen. I came to find you because I know that Talla can read and I want somebody who is not of the court to tell me if Silene has told the truth about this orange.'

He stood up and went towards his pack. I wondered briefly how he had managed to get the scroll and bring it with him without Silene or Lunaria becoming suspicious. But Ambar was adept at getting his own way. His lazy charm and twinkling eyes oiled his movement, and he was skilful in misdirection. So far, his story rang true. Lunaria was a very self-contained person, but her greatest influence remained the Goddess. She had begun her training as a Priestess and her sudden and unexpected move to the Queen's Court had not changed her devotion to the Goddess. Silene sounded as if she had much influence over Lunaria, using the word of the Goddess as her weapon. I was doubtful myself about the Goddess sending messages to people in their dreams, but I did remember some strange dreams which I had myself experienced and dreams were mysterious events, whereby the mind could travel and reason and understand things over which one had no control. Perhaps they were indeed sent as messages from the Goddess. There were those who thought that the bees were the bearers of dreams, that they carried dreams from the Goddess and dropped them like the dust from the flowers. It was a fanciful thought, but one which pleased me. Ambar thrust a scroll of parchment towards me and broke my musings. I took it from him, curious.

The scroll was made of fine parchment, sanded, and pounced to a smooth, creamy brown surface. It had been scribed in a dark, berry purple ink which was faded in some places and was curiously thick for a fine parchment. It was a different hand to the scrap of parchment which Benakiell had found. I wondered again why Ambar did not just learn to read himself. It seemed so easy to me and would have certainly made his life easier. But it seemed that long held traditions lodged themselves in the minds of people, like large ungainly coals in an emberjar and blocked the way. There were still many who believed that reading and scribing were sent as gifts of the Goddess and could not be learned. It seemed that many incomprehensible things like dreaming and reading were ascribed to the Goddess which meant they could not be explained by mere people.

I began to read from it slowly.

'Until the pieces of the Orange of Kashiq are found and made whole again, it is said that the Queen of Oramia will not be happy in love, and her children will turn against her. Ashkana, the Blessed One, it was who said that love was broken when the Orange was broken.'

Ambar looked crestfallen. The scroll echoed what Silene had told Lunaria. But there was no mention of the Goddess in the scroll in the manner of her blessing anyone, nor was there any mention of cursing anyone

65

and I brought this to Ambar's attention. He brightened momentarily but then pointed out the mention of Ashkana, the prophet of the Goddess and the phrase about love being broken. He asked me to read it again twice more, then sat in sad silence.

'I do not know what to do now,' acknowledged Ambar. 'Lunaria will not marry me without the orange, Silene has made sure of that. But I do not know where to find this orange nor how to mend it. Silene is probably counting on that. She would prefer that the Queen stay under her power. But I know that I can take care of Lunaria and give her all she needs, and she must have children so that the line of the Queen continues...' His voice trailed off as he tried to find his way through the complicated maze that Silene had laid for him. If, as Ambar had told us, Silene was indeed more interested in her own power than in the happiness of her Queen, he had few options. Lunaria was calmly obdurate, she did not often change her mind and if Ambar tried to set her against Silene, she would likely go the other way. The Queen held all the absolute power and if Silene's influence were made stronger, even the Vizier might not be safe.

'You will just have to find the Orange,' declared Achillea decisively. We all looked at her, wordless. She looked back at us levelly. 'Ambar needs to find the Orange so that he and Lunaria can get married. We know that the Orange is in Kashiq somewhere, and Benakiell might even know more if he can remember where that other scroll came from!'

Ambar immediately seized on this and demanded to know what Benakiell had to do with this orange of which we had heard so much. Reluctantly, I told him about the scroll fragment that Benakiell had brought back with him.

'You see!' Achillea was triumphant. 'The Orange must be in Kashiq and it even says in the parchment that Ashkana sent the pieces somewhere. We know that this Rao came from Kashiq, and I am sure that Ashkana must have sent them back to him when her love for him died.'

It seemed to me a large leap to assume that Ashkana would have sent the broken pieces of the orange to Rao, but Achillea definitely knew more than the rest of us about the nature of love. And it was true that Benakiell had returned from Kashiq with the parchment which told us about the Orange of Kashiq. This was confirmed by the scroll Ambar had brought with him from the Court of the Queen. If only Benakiell were with us now. Not for the first time, I wished for him and his quiet wisdom to be here with us to advise us on what we should do. Tarik poured more coffee, looking thoughtful. His earlier antagonism towards Ambar seemed to have cooled. Perhaps he was feeling some empathy for his old comrade who seemed to be stuck in a gap in a rock, unable to go forward nor yet go back. He rubbed his chin thoughtfully, making a rasping sound.

'I cannot go to Kashiq to search for this orange,' said Ambar. 'It would not be looked upon well if the Vizier of Oramia were to travel to the land of Kashiq and try to take away some treasure, however broken it may be. It could even cause a war. Neither could I send OutRiders for the same reason.... However,' His honey-coloured eyes stopped on me, lighting up. 'You could go to Kashiq for me! You could go with Benakiell and find out more about the orange and the pieces and where we could find it! I am sure you could!'

We looked at him wordlessly. Why would we want to do such a thing? Benakiell had only just returned from Kashiq and would surely not wish to return for some time. The three of us were well settled in Gabez and had our dwellings and our gardens to care for, and, in any case, why should we leap at Ambar's bidding? There was a silent balance of power between us, for what we had endured together in order to have Lunaria made Queen held us together. None of us wanted to push the other too far for fear of what might be revealed in a hot-headed moment.

'Why would we do such a thing, brother?' Tarik asked finally. 'This mission is fraught with difficulty and likely to fail. There is too much that is unknown and too much that is at stake. We would be in another land, far from the security of your OutRider forces if there were difficulty. From my view, you have everything to gain and little to lose, whereas we three have much to lose and little to gain.' He smiled and used his hands to indicate a shifting balance, and then waited for Ambar's response.

Ambar looked crestfallen. It seemed that he had not considered that we might not have the appetite for this venture. Against the more sensible urging of my mind, however, interest was rising inside me. It sounded exciting and different from the lives we now led. When I had left Mellia with Achillea seven years ago, I left because I did not want to be tied down to one place. We had moved on to Gabez first, planning to move on again, and then, somehow, we had settled there. Originally it was just for a few months, so we could trade there, but the months had turned into years and there we still lived. At first, I had enjoyed making a new routine and learning new skills. I honed my skills with the bees and learned more about making physic, and about life in the Outer. We made regular trips to Mellia and Sanguinea, but this would be a good opportunity for us to travel somewhere new. Or at least it would for me; Achillea and Tarik seemed content to stay in Gabez. Once again, I ran my hands over the parchment which Silene had read to

Ambar. As I did so, I felt a slight ridge in the parchment and turned it over to examine it more closely.

On the other side of the parchment, I could see why the parchment had felt thick, especially at the bottom. It had been cunningly folded backwards from the front, where I had read the original words which Silene had read to Ambar and Lunaria. I ran my finger over it again. The other three had lapsed into contemplative silence as they pondered Ambar's plan. I walked towards the light to look at the parchment more closely and stopped at a flat rock. I laid it out and could then see where the parchment had been sealed against itself. I wondered if I could prise up the parchment where it had been sealed. A shadow fell on me as Ambar leaned over my shoulder, trying to see what I was doing. He had not been so close to me since before we had found Lunaria. We had ridden together on his horse and had been close up against each other then. I had felt the channel of empathy between us and had felt his feelings almost as plainly as I had felt my own. His presence made me feel stirred up; he simultaneously soothed me and excited me. Despite my distrust of him, there was something about him which drew me to him, even knowing that he was in love with Lunaria.

'What have you found?' His breath felt warm on my shoulder. My netela had slipped off to one side and I reached for it, wanting to put a barrier between us. I pointed with my middle finger along the line of the sealing of the paper.

'The parchment has been sealed here,' I explained. 'I wonder why.'

'Well let us see,' Ambar replied, with interest. He reached across me to pick up a small stick. Again, there was a warmth as our bodies brushed past each other. He began to scratch at the place where the parchment was sealed, but it was held fast with some sort of tree gum. Tarik and Achillea had noticed our absorption and got up to take a look themselves.

'Won't you just make a hole in it if you use a stick?' enquired Achillea bluntly. 'There must be a better way to see why it has been stuck down. Tarik, do you know a kind of physic that melts gum?' Tarik pondered.

'Sometimes you can use oil to take away sticky gum, but if you put oil on this parchment, it would soak into the ink and the parchment and ruin it,' he answered ruefully. Ambar continued to scratch away thoughtlessly at the parchment with the stick until I moved the parchment away to stop him. Then I recalled that warmth sometimes softened glues and gums, and we heated up some of the solid plant gums to make them more pliable if we were using them in the repair of the beehives. Perhaps if we warmed the parchment, the gum might soften, and we might be able to prise it apart. I looked over at the fire which Ambar's OutRiders had made for him to brew the coffee on. It was still crackling and hot, and I worried that it might cause the parchment to catch fire if I held it too close. They had used wood still redolent with a spicy scent which mixed pleasingly with the smell of the coffee still in the ornate coffee pot. It was as my eyes followed the curls of steam drifting upwards that I had the idea of holding the glued parchment in the steam so that the heat of it might soften the glue but not cause the parchment to catch fire. I took it over to the coffee pot and held the gummed edge in the steam. The others gathered round.

It took some time of holding the parchment in the steam before I could feel the edge starting to slide over itself when I pushed it with the tip of my finger. I held it in the steam for a little while longer and then took it out of the heat and used the small stick that Ambar had been

70

using to slowly prise up the folded edge of the parchment. The gum stretched out as I pulled the edge up and I had to push it apart with the stick. Achillea helped me by holding one side of the parchment as I pulled the other one apart from it until, eventually, we had separated out the parchment where it had been folded and glued. It had been folded twice before it was stuck, so I couldn't see why it had been folded until I pulled it out fully. There was another section of scribing, perhaps added on later because the ink used was darker. But perhaps that was just because it had been folded over and preserved without sunlight.

'Read it, Talla!' squealed Achillea in excitement. 'What does it say? What does it say?' Ambar and Tarik looked at me expectantly. I hoped that the added script was not scribed in some other tongue, or that it did not consist of idle scribbling of unimportant words which had been folded over just because they were irrelevant. However, the gum had been strong and well applied to make the parchment appear smaller than it was, so I hoped it might say something of interest. I began to read aloud.

'The Blessed Ashkana sent the pieces of the Orange of Kashiq back to the place it was made, to the Tower of the Wise in the city of Arbhoun, returning it to the Lord Rao.'

'Ha!' exclaimed Ambar triumphantly. 'I knew Silene was hiding something from me. She was clever, to read me the top of the scroll so I could not say she did not read it right. But I was cleverer!'

Achillea laughed. 'Listen to you, Ambar! It was not you who knew the parchment was folded back and glued to fool you, but Talla! She is the clever one!' Tarik smiled at her words. Achillea could always be relied upon to say the things that others were thinking. She reached across to me and patted my arm. 'I don't know how you do it, Talla. Your mind seems to delight in untangling the puzzles made by others. Well done!' I felt a warmth at her words. Ashkana would have said that 'Work is its own reward and pleases the Goddess most' but being acknowledged by those whose judgement I trusted gave me more reward than the work I did. Ambar took the parchment from me and traced over the words with his finger thoughtfully and then turned to Tarik, who was also looking thoughtful.

'What say you, brother?' Ambar asked in a deceptively casual tone. 'Does this alter the odds? We know now where to go to find the pieces of this blasted orange, and it will only be if I can find the entire orange that Lunaria will acknowledge marriage to me and have our children, which is all that I desire.'

Achillea cleared her throat loudly and deliberately, causing the two men to look up. Ambar looked baffled, but Tarik looked a little abashed.

'I do not think it is only Tarik who has a choice to make on this, do you, Lord Ambar?' said Achillea boldly. We often talked, her and me, as we worked, about all manner of things. We had spoken before about the assumption made by men of both the Outer and the OutRider that they were the ones who should make the decisions. No doubt it was this which she was thinking of when she interrupted the two men and their discussion. I thought back to my days in the Temple where work was completed in silence except for essential communication. There was certainly no chatting. 'Talking does not serve the Goddess,' we were told crisply by the Priestesses. Back then, I did much of my thinking in those times when I was cleaning. It was still the best way of resolving puzzles, to my mind. Occupying my body with some sort of repetitive task and allowing my mind to unravel its problems worked well for me, but I had also realised that sometimes talking things over with a companion while I worked could bring rewards and answers.

Tarik smiled warmly at Achillea and reached up his hand to hers from where he sat. 'Of course, it is not,' he confirmed. 'Why, we would never succeed without you and Talla, and besides, I would not want to go anywhere without you.' Achillea, mollified, took hold of his hand and looked at me expectantly. Why were they all looking at me?

I pondered what we were being asked to do by Ambar. He made it sound quite easy, but I knew him of old and he was adept at making difficult tasks appear simple. I did feel stirred and excited at the idea of travelling again though, perhaps visiting Kashiq and finding out about this Tower of the Wise in Arbhoun. But it would not be easy, and I did not want Ambar to think that he could command us at his every whim. A bargain of sorts should be made; a payment for work done. I would have preferred to have had some time to mull over this proposal. To sit with the bees and watch them working the flowers always helped me to make decisions. There was something about their single-minded dedication to their work which led me to the right conclusions. They would meet one another and make movements, the same sort of sign language, I often thought, as the OutRiders. Following their communication, they would continue with their business, the one returning to the hive and the other flying out to the flowers to collect the honey dust. Perhaps this was like when Achillea and I talked while we made our salves or went about our other work.

'If Tarik and Achillea would like to travel with me to Kashiq and we can travel on to Arbhoun, then I would be willing to go and see if we can find out more about this orange for you. But we must be back in Gabez by the month of Aureus at the latest, for we will need to harvest the honey by then, and we cannot stay in Kashiq on your quest forever.' I addressed Ambar, looking at him directly in the eyes. He was not accustomed to my new ways. The last time he saw me, I had been not long out of the Temple and was still used to looking at the floor every time I was addressed or every time I spoke to another person. Now I believed it was important if both people were unveiled, for it made both equal. I looked levelly into Ambar's eyes and he looked back into mine. His eyes were still the same honey-coloured eyes, sweet and warm and melting any further resistance I might have had towards his idea.

'I know that you will be the best people to take on this challenge. I trust that you will do your best for me and for your Queen Lunaria,' replied Ambar. I was more inspired by the thought of the travelling and learning that I might do than by serving Lunaria or Ambar, but he was very persuasive, and in the end it did not matter whether I was motivated by my own longing for knowledge or by his longing for the love of Lunaria. Achillea was inspired by the thought that she might be bringing love to the lives of Lunaria and Ambar and was quite swept away by it. Tarik was, perhaps a mixture of the two of us, and, with his OutRider training, I knew he would be alert for any signs of trouble while we travelled.

Ambar went to the OutRiders who still waited, watchful from a distance. Unsurprisingly, any travellers along the path were making detours to avoid them, and we were still on our own here under the weak sun. He returned after a short while with a quantity of flatbreads and a large, silk pouch. I wondered how he had managed to have the OutRiders accompany him without telling them that his mission was not sanctioned by the Queen to whom they all owed their undying loyalty. I could see how he would be the type of man whom soldiers would fight for. He had an easy way of talking to people, to put them at their ease. He smiled readily and inspired confidence. He had also been an OutRider like them. I wondered how this had been explained to the OutRiders - that their Vizier had been an OutRider and had forgone his vows to the old Queen in order to find the new Queen. Probably they did not even know. He would, in any case, wriggle out of any difficulty, I felt sure.

'We will need the help of Benakiell to help us to get into Kashiq discreetly,' said Tarik. 'Talla, do you think he would accompany us until we reach Arbhoun?'

Benakiell had only just returned from Kashiq and I thought it unlikely that he would wish to go back so hastily. I suggested that we should bide our time until Benakiell came to Gabez next month and talk to him then. Ambar was impatient, itching for us to depart upon our mission. He had never been a very patient person, but this time he would have to wait his turn. Achillea and I would need to prepare and organise some trading supplies to take with us to Kashiq and to ask our neighbour Kazima to look after our dwellings and gardens while we were gone. Kazima was very partial to the white honey I had recently started producing from my hives and I knew that she would be happy to take care of our property in return for a gourd or two of the honey. Reluctantly, Ambar agreed to the wait. Tarik reminded him that it might take up to three months for us to find out about the Orange of Kashiq once we got to Arbhoun and that even if we did find anything out, we might not be able to return with the mended orange.

'Always looking for how the task might not succeed,' grumbled Ambar. 'I would rather think of how much Silene's power over the Queen will be reduced when I show her the famed Orange of Kashiq!'

A thought suddenly occurred to me. Silene would no doubt be checking her parchments and scrolls and would know that the scroll's secret had been revealed if Ambar replaced the scroll as it now was, unglued and unfolded. Luckily, the gum was still on the parchment, so I warmed it up again and we carefully refolded the parchment and glued it back how it was. Ambar replaced it in the pouch he had brought and withdrew several small drawstring bags which contained cinnamon, frankincense and other costly spices and another with a variety of small, gold necklaces and earrings. He gave them to Tarik to use for trading once we were in Kashiq, where spices were much in demand, to help us on our mission.

As we rose to take our leave of Lord Ambar, he came up to me and put his hand gently on my shoulder, making me turn around to him. 'Please do this for me, Talla,' he said quietly, so the others could not hear. 'You are dear to me and I trust in you. If events had been different...' His voice trailed off and he looked into my eyes as if searching for some sort of truth. The way he looked at me made me feel warm and a little flustered and I looked away, lost for words. Achillea bustled over and the moment dissolved into the air like the steam from the coffee pot.

We collected up our belongings and prepared to leave. Tarik spoke to Ambar, trying to work out how we might let Ambar know if we had been successful. We could not just approach the Queen's Court since Queen Lunaria and Silene would then know that Ambar had been in contact with us and so we needed to find a way to get a message to Ambar. We could not send him a scribed message since he could not read himself and we could not be sure that the message would not first be read by Silene and altered in the telling. Eventually, Ambar had an idea and reached into his pouch once more, withdrawing a small, finely made wooden box which had previously contained frankincense. He scratched a small star inside the box so that he would know it was the same box. They agreed that if we had been successful, we would send him the box full of cinnamon sticks, and if we could not find the pieces of the Orange of Kashiq, we would send it full of dried chillies. It was an ingenious plan which I wished I had thought of myself, and Tarik explained that as OutRiders they often used these kinds of messages to ensure that no other could interpret them, and that the message went to the right person. As I had learned in the case of Silene, even scribing and reading were open to deceit, and it seemed that the only way to be certain of a message was to agree in advance what each message might look like. I wondered what would happen if chillies or cinnamon were not available to send the message, or if the sender filled the box instead with salt or lemon leaves, but could think of no better method, and kept my doubts to myself. Once Ambar received the box, he would find a way to meet us again.

We walked back down the path to Gabez after we had taken our leave of the Vizier. He had insisted that we leave first, explaining that he had told his OutRider force that we had brought him a trade intended as a surprise for the Queen, and showed us a beautiful necklace hanging on a fine silver chain which he had acquired earlier, somehow. It was made of a shining substance which glimmered and gleamed like the sheen on a ripe berry. It was a milky white and as hard as stone. The back of it was coated in polished silver and at the centre were two small milky white stones so that it resembled a sort of seed pod. Tarik looked at it critically and then, having examined the clasp and the links in the chain declared it to be fine work. Ambar told us that it came from a far-off land, near a huge expanse of water, and that the substance came from the shells of animals which lived in the water, as did the milky white stones. As I gazed at it, I felt such a pang of longing for this necklace. It was not just because it was beautiful, but also because Ambar had chosen something so beautiful to give to his beloved Lunaria. I remembered the little bee necklace which he had given me and which I had then had to give to Lunaria when she was declared Queen, and the sparks of rage in my mind sparked and flashed.

# CHAPTER 7

The bees hummed around the hives. I was checking over them before leaving them to look after themselves while we ventured to Kashiq. For all Kazima's interest in my honey, she had no desire to have anything to do with the bees while we were gone. She was happy to pick and store any fruits and vegetables which could be stored for us while we were away. The rest she would trade for us, taking some of them for herself in payment for her caring for the dwellings and the garden. She was fearful of the bees, having been stung by them several times. I had never been stung by my bees. I didn't really think about it anymore. The bees would fly away or, sometimes, remain in the hive and crawl over my hands as I worked to remove the honeycomb from the hive. We had an understanding, the bees and I; I provided for them and they provided for me, and we lived this way in balance. I did not harm them, and they did not harm me.

Kazima was respectful but fearful of the bees, and if one appeared near her, or came to investigate a plant near where she was working, she would shriek and wave her netela vigorously at the bee, flapping her hands in an attempt to drive it away. This only served to aggravate the bee and make it more likely to sting her. I had explained this to Kazima, somewhat impatiently, but she was resolute that, while she found their honey tasty, she did not find them easy companions. I sometimes thought that the bees deliberately sought her out and even, perhaps, saved their strongest stings for her. I had seen her hand once when she had been stung; it had swollen up in an angry looking lump and you could still see the thin black line of the bee sting like a miniature arrow. I scraped it out with edge of my fingernail and looked at it in wonder while Achillea bustled off to get Kazima some Calendula tonic to bathe it with, and a honeysalve to soothe it. The bees would be fine without her care, I thought to myself with a smile. They might even appreciate a small rest in their honey making labours while we are gone.

There was a loud humming from the Kosso tree which grew in the corner of the garden, its large, pendulous red blossoms were just emerging after the cooler weather and they were popular with the bees, but this was a louder sound than normal, so I went to investigate.

There was a big group of bees flying around the flowers but not collecting the honeydust. They were anticipating something, and I knew what they were waiting for. I had seven hives now hanging on the trees in the garden, each with its own queen. Over the past years, I had spent a long time with the hives open, studying them as they went about their business. The queen was somewhat larger than the other bees and spent almost all her days laying eggs into the honeycomb cells. They lived a lot longer than the ordinary bees which were constantly being replaced. Perhaps it was because they worked ceaselessly and never rested. When the old queen bee died, a new queen came into being and before she confined herself to the hive forever, she would fly out to these groups of anticipatory bees where she would mate frequently before her return to the hive. I had observed it before, but I was still intrigued, and put down my basket of bark rope and sat on a rock to see if a new queen might be arriving soon.

It was warmer in Gabez than it had been in Mellia and it was pleasant to sit with the sun warming my back for a few minutes. Just as I was preparing to get back to my work, a bee arrived at the cloud of buzzing suitors and the level of noise instantly rose, along with the activity of the frantic bees as they attempted to be one of those whose offspring the queen would produce. They were completely absorbed in their activity and everywhere that the queen flew, she was followed by a dark knot of male bees. It was a frenetic spinning cloud and once the queen had been mated, her admirer fell out of the sky, embracing death as his fate. They seemed to be impelled by a strange force stronger even than the fear of death, or perhaps they did not ever know they were to die.

When I turned and left the new queen, I headed back to the dwelling with my basket. Achillea and Tarik were at their dwelling, arranging our goods for trade into bundles, and Benakiell was sitting with his back against the wall in the sun, taking some moments to rest after organising his own bundles.

'Talla,' he called out as I got nearer. 'Come and tell me again about Ambar's parchment. Was it the city of Arbhoun that it said?'

I confirmed that the parchment had stated that the Orange of Kashiq had been returned to Arbhoun to the intriguingly named Tower of The Wise, and asked Benakiell if he had been there before. He confessed he had not, as it was further than he normally ventured into Kashiq. He preferred to do his trading in the settlements which were within a day or two's walk of the border and Arbhoun was around five days walking from the border. But some of the people with whom Benakiell traded came from Arbhoun so he had heard some stories about this large city in the centre of Kashiq. He was excited about our journey to Kashiq, I could tell. There was a sparkle in his usually serious eyes, and an eagerness in his questioning which reminded me of the days when we were searching for Lunaria. I wondered aloud how Gladia would take the news that he would be away for some time, and he told me, somewhat guiltily, that he had not thought of sending her any kind of message to say that he might be longer than his usual three weeks.

'She will only worry,' he grumbled mildly. 'Besides, I do not need to tell her where I am all of the time.'

I looked at him as sternly as I could, just as Achillea and Tarik came around the corner, she with her arm casually linked through his, he with his arm around her shoulders.

'What on earth has poor Benakiell done, Talla?' exclaimed Achillea, laughing. 'It must be something very bad!'

'She is trying to make me send word back to Gladia to tell her how long I am going away for,' muttered Benakiell. Achillea's eyes widened in shock.

'Oh, Benakiell, of course you must send word to Gladia that you will be away for a long time! Think how worried she will be when you do not arrive back after the normal amount of time! We must send word with one of the traders who is heading towards Mellia to let her know!'

'I didn't think you would care so much about Gladia or how she feels,' retorted Benakiell, stung by the rebuke delivered to him by a young woman more than half his age. 'You and Gladia never seem to agree with one another these days anyway. If you tell me to do something, she will think I should have done the opposite!'

Achillea looked wounded by his scolding, but continued, nonetheless. 'No, really, Benakiell, I beg you to let her know. I know that she worries about you when you are not there. Whatever her quarrel is with me, she would agree with me on this one thing.'

Benakiell cast his eyes towards the sky but eventually conceded defeat and we worked out a message for Gladia which was reassuring but still slightly vague, to please all parties. Tarik knew that Shanif who traded in coffee pots and other cooking vessels would be going towards Mellia in the next few days, and so a short message was given to him to pass on to Gladia, along with a small gourd of my white honey for her and a similar one for himself. I hoped he would remember the message accurately and wished again that all could scribe and read so that messages could be sent back and forth with ease. I wondered what Gladia's reaction would be to the message Benakiell was sending her and was pleased that I was not going to be there to have to explain it. It did feel a little sad for Jember, since I knew how much he looked forward to Benakiell's returns from his travels.

'How will we get into Kashiq without the knowledge of the OutRider Guards?' asked Tarik, later that evening. Mostly, those who wished to trade across the border had to cross over the river which made the border between the land of Oramia and the land of Kashiq over the gated bridge east of Gabez. The two lands remained separate from one another, and trade was only permitted between the two towns of Gabez in Oramia and Pirhan in Kashiq which lay at the other side of the river.

Benakiell looked evasive.

'There are a few different ways to avoid the notice of the guards', he replied, shifting slightly. It was only now that he was realising that he would have to share his secrets with us in order to get us into Kashiq without the OutRiders noticing us. 'It will be better if I do not tell you my plans beforehand, just in case we get separated or caught by the OutRiders.' It sounded rather suspicious to me, and I pondered on how Benakiell appeared to have somewhat shifting ideas of what was right and wrong.

'Will we leave from Gabez?' enquired Tarik, casually. I could see he was trying to find out a little more than Benakiell was willing to share. 'We will need to know because if we have to travel far, we will need to take with us more food and water for the trip.'

Benakiell considered the question and reluctantly informed us that we would not be leaving from Gabez, over the bridge, but would instead be taking an alternative route which would begin some half a day's travel north of Gabez. He stroked his chin absentmindedly and then told us that it would be better if we waited until midday to set off.

'But that will make it night-time by the time we get there,' interrupted Achillea. 'If we left in the morning, it would give us all afternoon to get to Kashiq and find a place to rest overnight.' She looked at Tarik, her brow wrinkled in bewilderment and her big eyes looking up at his, searching for an answer. Tarik stroked her arm.

'I think Benakiell has in mind the sort of travel which is best done in the dark,' he smiled. 'Am I right, Benakiell?' Benakiell acknowledged that he was. I thought that Achillea might shy away from the challenge of trying to get into another land under cover of darkness, but instead she was excited and declared herself even more committed to our quest, saying that she thought it sounded exciting. This brought a chuckle from Benakiell who told her that he had missed her brightness and her optimism. It was unlikely that anyone would ever have the same thing to say about me, I thought to myself ruefully. It was interesting however to find out more about Benakiell's trips, about which he had been consistently elusive in the past. Benakiell had been the first person of the Outer who had supported me. He had been loyal to me almost all the time I had known him; the exception being when he felt that I did not do enough to save Gladia from pain. I did not blame him for that though. I still felt now that I had not done enough, even though Gladia had long since forgiven me. It was a shame that she could not be so forgiving towards Achillea and Tarik, but I had hopes that Benakiell might be instrumental in persuading her to change her views – especially if he were to spend more time with us all and see how much they loved each other and how good Tarik was for Achillea – and she for him.

I was a little less enchanted with the idea of crossing over the border into Kashiq at night-time. The river Gabish was a long river which wove its way along the border between the lands of Oramia and Kashiq and so we would have to find some way of crossing it. All the bridges over it were manned by OutRiders so there must be some other way which Benakiell knew about. All these times he had been to Kashiq and he had been doing it secretly. Of course, those crossing the bridges were subject to the OutRiders taxes. Benakiell was no supporter of the OutRiders, so it did not surprise me that he did not wish to give them any of his own hard-earned trades.

# THE STEM

## CHAPTER 8

T he silence spread around us like the water we travelled over, silky, and all-encompassing. Benakiell had warned us to make no sound as the boat moved across the river between Oramia and Kashiq, and Achillea and I huddled under the cloth, masquerading as bundles while Benakiell and Tarik pushed the boat through the water with long poles taken from Benakiell's bundles of roofing materials. We were on our way into Kashiq, using one of the routes which Benakiell had devised in order to cross the border without having to pay a tax to the Oramian border guards. I assumed there might also be guards on the Kashiqi side, but Benakiell had not mentioned them, only saying, with his customary quiet firmness, that he had no intention of paying a share of his trading goods to the OutRiders of our land.

After some time, there was a fine grating of shingle and we felt the bottom of the boat scraping on the ground beneath us. Neither Achillea nor I moved even though we could sense Benakiell and Tarik rocking the boat as they moved off it and then heard them quietly splashing through the water to tie up the boat. We continued to wait. It was steamy and warm under the covering cloth, and I longed to throw it off and breathe in the cooler night air but made myself wait. Footsteps approached the boat. I hoped it was Tarik or Benakiell, but I could not be sure, and, until I was, I lay still, next to Achillea, clasping her hand tightly as we waited.

The cloth was thrown off and Benakiell's gruff voice told us to get up and get our things out of the boat before he and Tarik hid it. We hastened to do as he asked, remaining silent even though Benakiell and Tarik conversed quietly between themselves as they unloaded the building supplies and the numerous bundles and then dragged the boat beneath the trees and covered it with old branches and leaves. I wondered idly what might happen if someone else found the boat. What, I wondered, would Benakiell do? He was a quiet man, but bull-headed in his way, and, like Gladia, not one to suffer fools gladly. He always walked with a sturdy staff which he could use as a cudgel, should the need arise, and he was wiry and strong despite his age. He and Tarik, having hidden the boat to their satisfaction, began to hoist their bundles up on to their backs and hang them off their shoulders. Achillea and I were already weighed down with the smaller pieces and as we trudged off, I thought we must look like a group of tortoises walking slowly along with a large amount on our backs.

Dawn began to tinge the sky and warm the air and after walking some way from the river, we stopped to drink water and eat a flatbread with some figs. I looked around me curiously, my first view of a new land, the land of Kashiq which lay across the river from Oramia, the land of my birth. It seemed very flat here, with only undulating shallow hills, and none of the mountains which we saw in Oramia. The ground was stony and dusty and the soil was lighter than the red earth across the river, mixed with sand. Straggly thorn bushes grew here and there, and there was a sporadic palm but, in general, it seemed quite bleak once we had left the cool green vegetation which thrived along the riverbank.

'We need to go as quickly as we can while it is still cool,' urged Benakiell, as Achillea and I dawdled, looking around us, trying to take it all in. 'The sun here is unforgiving when you are in these waterless plains. The travellers' path is not far from here now, and once we are on that, it will take us perhaps three more hours to get to Rishkar where we can trade some of our goods and where we can find out more about the journey to Arbhoun.' We sped up dutifully, and I walked alongside Benakiell in companionable silence while Achillea chatted away to Tarik, who did not say very much himself, but was content to listen and occasionally respond. They walked behind us, and I reflected on how the years had brought about this new relationship.

It had unfolded quietly over the course of three years or so, after we had moved to Gabez, in part to get away from Achillea's memories of Ashtun, the man whom she had loved and who had died in the defence of the Queen. In those years, I had concentrated on keeping Achillea busy and, although she still had a tendency towards idleness, she worked much harder now, perhaps because she had discovered that she enjoyed working with the physic, making the creams and unguents, the tinctures and cordials that we traded at the markets. She sang as she mixed them up and, in a fanciful moment, I imagined that something pure and soulful from her singing was dropped into each physic she made, and that was what made them so successful. Tarik had travelled with us to Gabez, and although we expected that he might then leave us, perhaps to return to the life of an OutRider now that the Queen was securely on her throne, he never did.

Somehow, there was enough traded by the three of us in the beginning to trade for the food and other essentials that we needed, and we began to make and trade new physics and salves using the plants we gathered. Tarik could repair metalwork (though he made sure to keep his fixings simple) and made leather straps for carrying gourds and the like. He was always eager to learn more and do more. He was, like me, one who had not been raised in the Outer, but he h ad learned more varied skills in the OutFort, where he had been trained not only to fight and defend himself but also to make and use physic and to use and make things from metal for a variety of usages.

I had noticed his regard for Achillea early on; the way in which he watched her as she spoke or sang, and the way in which he would try, in his understated and grave way, to make her giggle. He brought her small offerings – flowers and herbs he had found or sets of small gourds into which she could pack the salves. I liked Tarik. In comparison to his more charming and cunning comrade, Ambar, I did not feel that he had too many hidden layers. He did not try to sway with the words he spoke but rather listened carefully and responded in a measured way. When he told Achillea that he loved her, her face had lit up and she confessed that she felt the same way about him but had not wanted to compromise their friendship. I had pondered on this many times, musing on how they knew that they loved one another. It was not something I had ever felt, in truth, this kind of love. I had not looked for it either, truth be told. I preferred to keep to myself. And somewhere inside my mind was still the feeling that, having been brought up in the Temple for the service of the Goddess, I could not and should not feel this kind of love. I was happy that Achillea and Tarik were together, and there was plenty of space for us all to live companionably together. I liked my own space anyway and was happy to spend time on my own. Eventually, Tarik and I swapped places and he and Achillea lived together in the larger dwelling, and I lived happily in the smaller one which he had built for himself when we first got to Gabez.

'Have you still got my scrap of parchment, Talla?' asked Benakiell, breaking into my ruminations. The torn parchment was one of the reasons that we had set off on this journey to Kashiq in the first place and perhaps he, like me, was speculating on what the rest of it might say, were we to find it.

'Why, do you think we might find the rest of it? Was it in Pirhan that you acquired it?' I asked curiously.

'No, no,' he answered. 'But I was thinking that perhaps we could visit the place where I did get it – Rishkar – on the way to Arbhoun. It was a welcoming place, and I am sure that the woman who traded with me and gave me the parchment would search to see if she had the other part.' He smiled, slightly smugly. I could imagine that he would be popular with the widows in the villages who needed building work done. He had a strong, calm presence and was good at his job, as well as being easy to talk to. It had not occurred to me before that he might enjoy the company of other women than Gladia and I felt a little disconcerted. However, I did not want to have an argument about it, especially at the beginning of our journey, so I made no specific comment, and we walked on in silence, taking in the scenery around us.

We had left the banks of the River Gabish behind us now and the land here was much different to that near the river. Along the side of the river grew many river plants which Benakiell told me were the ones which the Kashiqis used to make a sort of plant parchment by weaving strips of them together. There were many of them growing, tall with fluffy heads and firm, dark green stems. We saw some groups of men working on the reeds who turned, curious, to watch us as we walked past. They were standing up to their knees in the water of the river which flowed past sluggishly, wielding curved blades on sticks and clearing the reeds out on to the riverbank as they worked. Benakiell raised his hand in greeting as went past and they raised their own hands in response and then returned to their labours. It had not taken long before we moved away from the river and its overabundance of green life and now we were walking along a stony path which looked much like many of the paths in Oramia. There were certainly no large trees like the Paradox tree and the Kosso tree here, and the landscape was unremittingly plain and uninspiring. We were walking east, into the morning sun, and, without any shade, it was very bright against the eyes. I imagined that wearing a veil such as was worn by the Priestesses in Oramia would, on this occasion, be a welcome relief, with protection for the head from the sun and for the eyes with the woven shaded section. Both Achillea and I pulled our netelas up over our heads to help to shade our heads. Benakiell told me something of what the differences were between life in Kashiq and life in Oramia as we walked.

'In a lot of ways, life here in Kashiq seems much the same as it does in Oramia, in any of the towns. People trade their goods for things they have gathered or made or grown and just as in Oramia, there are many who travel around making trades, like me. But there are many things which are made here which we cannot trade for in Oramia, and many things which we grow or use which they do not, so you can make good deals once you have learned which goods command the best trades. Craftspeople here compete with one another and are always trying to get better at their craft. Each tries to find something unique which only they can make; a silversmith may only make jewellery in the form of flowers, another may make ornamental boxes for spices, yet another will make fine tools for others to use. There are items which they will not trade with us from Oramia, however. You cannot trade a weapon of any sort, nor any bladed tool such as those scythes which they use for cutting the parchment plant. Their guards will take away all the things you trade if they catch you or the Kashiqis trading such items. I wish I could trade for some of their metal tools – think how many more bundles of grass or reeds I could cut in the right season if I had one of those big reed knives...'

'Many people work for a Craftmaster,' continued Benakiell, enjoying the fact that he was educating me about something of which I was ignorant. I had noticed that although he liked to learn, he did not himself like to show his own ignorance. I myself had no qualms in that direction and loved to find out about new things. I asked him to tell me more about the Craftmasters, looking back to where Tarik and Achillea were walking along behind us, hand in hand, talking to one another.

'The Craftmasters are people of great learning. They find out all they can from scrolls and parchments about their craft. They learn about the best materials and draw out the best designs. They get examples of good craftsmanship and sometimes even take them apart to learn how they have been made. They recruit people who have shown they have skill, perhaps in carving wood or in making plant parchment or in silverwork and then they learn how to get better and better. Of course, this means they get better and better trades for their craftwork. There is even a Craftmaster for stitching, though I can't imagine Gladia taking any kind of orders from anyone, Craftmaster or not!' He chuckled, imagining, as I was, how Gladia might react to having her embroidery taken apart to learn from.

'Where do they find all these scrolls and parchments which they learn from?' I asked, intrigued at the thought that so many more people here in Kashiq appeared to be able to scribe and read, or at least preserve pictures and diagrams on parchments.

'Every town has a small hall where some scrolls are kept by the Craftmasters, but they do say that vast quantities of them are kept at the Tower of the Wise in Arbhoun. People go to Arbhoun from all over Kashiq, and even from other lands, they say. It is said that all the wisdom of the land can be found in the Tower of the Wise. It is a good thing that they have found how to make parchment from those river reeds, to make all the new scrolls they need to make. Otherwise, there would not be enough goats in the country to make the parchment out of!'

I had many more questions, but I knew that Benakiell would not know the answers to most of them. I hoped to find out more when we reached Arbhoun. Benakiell had never been as far as Arbhoun in his trade visits so it would be new to us all. I reminded myself that we were here with a task to fulfil for Lunaria and for Ambar and not to answer all my questions, but I couldn't help but hope that some of them would be answered in the course of our search. I could see, now I had found out more about Kashiq, that my reading and scribing would be invaluable here. Kashiq seemed to be the kind of land that would suit someone like me who wanted to find out so much.

Achillea called out to us and gestured towards a large sandstone pillar over to the side of the path. It was casting a shadow and certainly looked very inviting. In Oramia it had been cool, but here in Kashiq, the sun was hot and there was not a lot of shade, so we headed over to it gratefully and took off our packs and sat down.

After we had eaten and drunk some water, Benakiell suggested that we should rest for some time and carry on with the journey a little later when the sun was not so high in the sky. He rearranged his bundles into a mound, rested his head against them, closed his eyes and rapidly went to sleep. The rest of us were not so weary and remained in the shade of the large rock talking and, in Tarik's case, wandering around, looking closely at the rocks that littered the ground. Every now and again he would pick one up and scrutinise it carefully and then either toss it down again or put it in his carrying pack. Achillea and I watched him curiously for a while and then Achillea went to fetch a small gourd of salve from our bundles. Now we were away from the relative humidity of the river area, the air was very dry around us and we could both feel its effects on our skin. Achillea was much interested in maintaining her fresh, velvety skin, and insisted on applying salves to it at every opportunity. I was not so concerned with how my skin might look but I did acknowledge that the salves made my skin feel less tight and more soothed. We had found that adding a small amount of honey to the salve (which we made with Paradox oil, beeswax and perfumed oils) made it softer and easier to rub into your skin. Tarik grew and dried the small gourds which we stored the salves in. They fit neatly into the curved palm of my hand, like a tiny pumpkin, and Tarik had also devised a way to keep their lids attached to them by boring a hole in both the base and the lid while they were still green and then tying them together with bark string. Tarik was particularly good at inventing new ways to do things and would often take what he had learned in one craft and apply it to another.

Achillea rubbed the salve into her face and arms with a sigh of pleasure.

'Do you think we will find this Orange of Kashiq, Talla?' she asked, evidently pondering on our quest. 'It will be such a gift for Ambar to give to Lunaria...he must love her very much to go to all this effort.' It seemed to me that it was we who were making the effort, not Ambar himself, but I held my tongue and nodded agreement, whilst trying to answer Achillea's question as honestly as I could.

'I really do not know. We know nothing about this Rao who is mentioned in the parchments, and I have never heard of him before, even throughout all the times we were read the Aphorisms of Ashkana in the Temple. I cannot help wondering if this is just some tale that has been told over the years and become something it is not. And even if it is true, the pieces of the Orange may have been lost or stolen over the years, or even traded with others from other lands. It seems to me a very unlikely quest to succeed in.' I replied, trying to be realistic in the face of Achillea's shining hope. She looked crestfallen, but quickly brightened.

'Well, it will be an adventure, anyway. We are sure to find new things to trade for and to take back with us which will let us do even more when we are back home in Gabez. Tarik and I would like to build a bigger dwelling in time. How do you think we will find out where the pieces of the orange might be hidden? It must be hidden somehow, for surely, otherwise, someone else might have already found the Orange and taken it for themselves.'

Achillea's face fell as we contemplated the fact that someone might have already remade the Orange for themselves. It might be being kept in a special case in Arbhoun somewhere. Just because there was an old manuscript which told about it did not mean that it was still there. It seemed a high and difficult mountain that we were expected to climb up and it reminded me of our trip up to the Queen's Court, situated as it was on top of a stony massif. Each step was hard, and we could have fallen at any moment. But, I told myself, we had indeed arrived at the top of that stone mountain by taking our trip one step at a time and not looking too far ahead. Our first step was to reach the city of Arbhoun and, once we got there, we could work out our next steps.

Tarik walked over to us with a handful of the strange rocks he had been picking up from around the sandstone pillar. He uncurled his hand to show us what he had found. The rocks were a sort of bluish green colour, for the most part, intermingled with a light sandy rock.

Tarik smiled at our looks of incomprehension and told us that he believed it was a stone which had a metal mixed within it. He had seen similar stones before in the metal working workshops when he was an OutRider. He explained to us that the stones had to be crushed up and then heated until they were so hot that the metal within them began to melt. I had never thought about how metal items might be made – or rather how the metal itself was made – and this was interesting. I had never seen such stones in Oramia and asked Tarik if he had ever seen them on the ground on his travels in Oramia either. He shook his head. 'The riches of Oramia are not found in the stones, Talla,' he said, slightly ruefully, and I thought of how much he had sacrificed to stay with Achillea. He was made happy by her presence, and so the interests of his previous, single, OutRider life were put in the shade by the brightness she brought to him, but I wondered if he missed his old life sometimes; the metal working especially, for there was no provision for any man of the Outer to do metalwork in Oramia, save for softening and remoulding small items and sharpening of knives and arrowheads. Tarik asked Benakiell if he knew anything of the metal melting that must occur in Kashiq. We were all looking to Benakiell as the one who knew everything about Kashiq, and yet it was becoming apparent that his knowledge was more limited than we might have wished, for he told us that he had never seen the melting of the stones.

'I do not know a lot of people to ask these questions of,' he reminded us, mildly. 'The Kashiqis are always happy to trade, but they guard their secrets as carefully as we do in Oramia. They would no more tell me about the melting of the stones than I would describe how to build a dwelling, especially to a woman. Normally I just like to keep myself to myself and concentrate on the trading.'

'Do they have OutRiders here?' asked Achillea, curiously. Tarik shifted uneasily, I thought. Benakiell shot him a look, having noted his discomfort.

'They have their own force here. They are not called OutRiders, though,' replied Benakiell. 'But they do the same job in the same kind of way. After all you could colour a bee purple, but it would still sting you. They wear different armour and carry different weapons, but they still control ordinary people by force. What do you know about them, Tarik?' He turned to Tarik.

Tarik sighed and sat down again. He wiped his forehead absentmindedly with the edge of his tunic, making a clean dry streak through the sweat which had gathered there.

'I do not know a great deal about them, although we learned a little about the forces of other lands from some of the OutCommanders. I never went to the border areas of Oramia while I was an OutRider. They are called the Defenders, but I do not know who they swear allegiance to. They are well trained and efficient, I know that. I saw some of their weapons; they have many sharp weapons, because of their knowledge of metalworking; different kinds of knives and clubs with sharp metal spikes pushed into them, and long spears which they can also throw as well as arrows, of course. Their armour is lighter, made of thin metals linked together.'

Achillea listened attentively, but I knew it was only because it was Tarik who was speaking. Achillea had no interest in how land was governed nor who ruled it. She had explained to me that it had no impact on her life, and besides, it was something that Tarik wanted to leave behind him. I, on the other hand, was becoming more and more interested in how lands were governed, and how their rulers made choices which we, the ordinary people had to live by. I had been on the cusp of becoming part of that governance when I had been offered the supposed choice between being a Priestess and leaving the Temple. Of course, even that had not been a choice made by me – or wasn't meant to be. My mind warmed with my interest in this new land, and I knew that even if we failed to find the Orange of Kashiq, I would certainly find something, even if I did not yet know what I was looking for.

When we set off again, Tarik asked Benakiell where we might rest that night. Benakiell told us that he thought that the settlement of Rishkar would be a suitable place to stay. He told us that it was as far to the east as he had travelled and that we might perhaps find out more about the journey to Arbhoun while we rested there. He sounded a little gruff as he suggested this, and I shot a look at him.

'Might this Rishkar be the same settlement of which you told me earlier?' I asked, trying to catch his eyes with mine. Even though I had been in the Outer for seven full years, it still did not come easily to me. I did know however that it was one of the easiest ways to see the direction a mind might be taking but he looked down and fiddled with the bark cords of his bundles, avoiding my gaze.

'Aye, it is,' he replied. 'I thought it would be a good idea to stay somewhere that I know, and where I know we will be welcomed. It's also a good place for me to trade and just possibly, Shira may have the other part of the parchment which started this whole thing off in the first place.'

'And who is Shira?' asked Achillea swiftly, seizing upon this name. 'Is she the one you traded with who used the parchment as wrapping? Do you learn all the names of those you trade with in Kashiq, Benakiell?' And she turned to him innocently, with wide eyes trained on his flustered face. I looked down to hide my smile. Benakiell had never been any match for Achillea, who had a way of eliciting information from even the most recalcitrant of sources. She had an ability to make people want to answer her apparently naïve questions.

Benakiell stopped walking for a minute and rubbed his hand through his beard rather self-consciously before he answered her.

'Shira is a woman of Rishkar. She is a … good friend to me when I am here,' he said. He must have known that the questioning after that would be merciless, but perhaps he thought that it was best to get it over with before we reached Rishkar and the awkward questions presented themselves at an even more inappropriate moment. I was amused whilst also concerned for the feelings of my friend Gladia. I had never forgotten the day when I had first visited the Empath Erayo and had taken on the burden of the feelings of others and had seen Gladia's yearning for love. Gladia and Benakiell had always been together in my mind and it seemed strange to try to pull them apart from one another. Like plants, they had grown close to one another and disentangling their roots was difficult. I couldn't imagine how Benakiell had managed to keep it hidden from one such as Gladia with her knowing looks and her probing questions. Perhaps this was what lay behind her recent intransigence regarding Achillea and Tarik, and her insistence that people should stick to their own kind to make relationships with.

Tarik chuckled suddenly, surprising us. He was often a quiet man, a listener rather than a talker, and preferred to keep in the background of discussions, listening and observing but rarely drawing attention to himself. He was obviously deeply amused by Benakiell's confession. After a short pause, Achillea joined in and somehow the laughter spread amongst us until we were all laughing, even Benakiell himself.

'I wondered why there had been so many trading trips to Kashiq in recent months,' grinned Tarik. 'But I never imagined that this was the reason. I look forward to meeting this paragon of womanhood when I arrive in Rishkar. Is she very beautiful?'

Achillea and I looked at one another, both feeling a pang for Gladia, who had never been described thus. Gladia was a formidable character; honest, determined, funny and able to withstand much pain by implacably continuing with her own path, but she was no conventional beauty. Her hair was flecked with grey and she was short and stout. Her dark brown eyes were splashed with surprising flashes of green above a rather squat nose and a mouth that was almost always busy talking. She had never married, although she had had a child when she was young, who had been left at the Temple. Benakiell, on the other hand, had been married before, to his dear Velosia, although they had never had any children, and she had died quite some time ago now. Neither Achillea nor I felt able to ask Benakiell about whether Gladia knew about this Shira. We waited to hear what he would tell us about her.

'She is...pleasing to the eye,' he admitted finally, with an embarrassed smile. We waited for more details but there were none.

'Tell us more,' urged Achillea, desperately curious. But Benakiell shook his head and told us we must make our own observations when we arrived at Rishkar and that we should do more walking and less talking if we wished to reach Rishkar at all, so we walked on, talking little, each of us exploring our thoughts about the news which Benakiell had told us.

# CHAPTER 9

Rishkar bustled, especially in the evening. It was evening when we arrived. Benakiell had told us that the markets there only opened when the sun was starting to slip and the heat that shone off the orange sand had eased. During the hot time of the day, the Kashiqis stayed inside and slept and then stayed awake for longer after dark. We from Oramia were used to living with the light of the Goddess. Each morning she shone upon us, waking us up for the new dawn. The light showed us that it was time to wake and to work. When the Goddess brought the day's end, the work could stop, but we were often tired from the day's labours, and after eating and a little talking, sleep came, gifted by the Goddess. She also sent us our dreams where we could do all manner of things and never be tired, even if we dreamt of running all day or lifting a huge boulder. So, a day in which the work was carried out after dark would indeed be a new experience.

It was a dusty place, and the dwellings were made of moulded clay bricks. They reminded me of the dwellings of the Outer in their shape; they had either a flat or domed roof which in the Outer was made of reeds and thatch, but which here was made with clay bricks They seemed curiously blank and I realised that they seemed not to have many openings for light and air, beyond the entrance which was made of wood and a vent in the roof. It made sense that, as there were not as many trees here as in Oramia, there would be less use of them in the dwellings. Some of them had been covered over with a lighter orange clay which perhaps served the same purpose as the Paradox oil and mud covering used in Oramia, which Benakiell was an expert in. These dwellings, however, were situated on the outer edge of Rishkar, surrounding a large central courtyard. In the middle of the courtyard was a well under an ornate woven canopy which offered welcome shade to those who were drawing water from it. There was a line of people waiting to fill their large earthenware pots which were held in nets made from plaited date palm leaves. The full pot was then placed upright in the net and carried hanging on the shoulders.

The traders were situated around the well, in the courtyard. It was much more orderly than the markets of Oramia, and the courtyard was laid out in a series of alternately coloured large squares. Each trader fitted themselves and their goods into one square. I wondered idly what happened if there were more traders than squares, but I could see quite a few places which remained empty, so I followed Benakiell to an area where there were two squares close to each other and he began to set out his items on one of the squares, whilst we set out ours on the other.

I noticed how well Benakiell knew what would make good trades here in Kashiq. He brought with him things which might be common in Oramia, but which were rarer in Kashiq; small pieces of dark wood from the Osho Mountains, cinnamon bark, flexible reeds, gourds of Paradox oil and carved peg and loop sets which could be attached to a door to hold it shut. Around us everybody was chatting and making bargains just as they did in Oramia, and while they spoke the same language, their voices lilted more musically than ours in Oramia, rising and falling like a birdsong.

'Will they want to trade with us at all, do you think?' asked Achillea anxiously looking around her. 'There are a lot of fine items here, as well as the food we might need. Of course, in Arbhoun it might be different again, so it's hard to know what we need. Why don't you take the first turn in looking round and Tarik and I will look after the trades for us all, and then you can look after them while we go.' I agreed readily. We were so accustomed to our weekly trading at the market in Gabez that by now it felt like second nature to me to be in a market. I thought back to the first market I ever went to in Sanguinea and smiled wryly at how naïve I had been in the ways of the trader. I was much firmer now, more able to pretend a lack of interest to drive a better bargain. We had only laid out a few things here in Rishkar as we were hoping for more valuable trades in Arbhoun for our salves and physics.

It was not yet evening, and the day still wore about it a dusty, rosy quality. The dropping sun burnished everyone. The Kashiqis already had skin the colour of dark honey and the sun made them glow even more. I felt a little self-conscious walking around as there seemed to be nobody else wearing clothes like mine. Their clothes were looser and made with more fabric, but the fabric itself was thinner, some of it almost as thin as the silks we used to use in the Temple to glorify the Goddess. The men wore a loose longer tunic over baggy trousers and the women also wore a tunic or robe over trousers. Even though it was much hotter here than in Oramia, they wore more clothing, to protect themselves from the sun. Achillea and I would need to trade for some of the trousers, as would Tarik, though our robes might suffice. I was curious to see how they were stitched, and I was sure that Gladia would be interested in this too. There was a trader who had rolls of the plant parchment and metal nibbed pens and small metal canisters of powdered ink. I lingered, thinking wistfully of how much I might like to acquire from him before moving on and making note of the foodstuffs which were readily available here.

I had learned that you could make the best trades with those who only brought with them the common stuffs. I saw large baskets full of dates and oranges and lemons. There were figs and pomegranates and some small squashes. There were mounds of flour, so there must be areas where water was plentiful enough to grow the wheat and barley and there were also people trading cooked food. This last enterprise was a surprising one to me, but it seemed that the people of Kashiq were fond of trading not just for the basic items from which one could make one's own food, but here one could trade for a sturdy flatbread smothered in spicy stew or a small doughy ball soaked in honey. My mouth watered. I had never learned how to cook at the Temple, and although my companions had done their best to teach me, I did not seem to have the patience or the skill to make very tasty meals. Even Tarik could cook better than I, and he had been raised in the OutFort. It would be good to live here, I thought. I could trade for some ready-made food and not have to cook my own. I passed a man trading honey and paused to chat with him. It felt strange to be discussing bees and honey and beehives with a man when in Oramia only women could be Beeguards, but I asked him some simple questions about what type of flowers the bees drank from and he told me that his honey came from the orange groves. In Oramia we used a peeled stick to offer tastes of the honey, but he had a set of tiny bone spoons which he kept in a jar of water. This was another idea I thought we could return to Gabez with. I tasted the honey critically.

It was deeply scented with orange blossom and was of a pleasing orange hue. It was light and flavoursome and very tasty. We did not grow oranges in Oramia, so I had never tasted honey made from their blossoms before, although of course I was familiar with the heady scent of orange blossom since it was the scent for the day of Aureus. I wondered if one could cause the bees to make a honey for each of the days of the week. I imagined a cinnamon infused honey would be a delightful thing. It was good honey, but of course I did not need more honey. I looked around at the rest of his trades; there were some oranges and dates, some small clay jars and some flat clay bowls filled with beeswax, with a short string poking out of the top. The trader told me they were lamps which everyone needed in Kashiq, living as they did in dwellings without openings for light. This was more interesting to me, not only because we might need such a source of light, but also because in Oramia we did not use beeswax for this purpose; it was almost all used for salves. In Oramia we used Paradox oil for our lamps. The advantage of the beeswax lamp was that it would not spill as an oil lamp would (and often did). I moved on, telling the man that I would return later.

Out of the corner of my eye I noticed a tall, slender woman lingering by Benakiell, chatting to him. Achillea was busy trading and had not noticed, or else thought that this was just another person who wanted to trade. I, on the other hand, could see the ease with which they conversed and wondered if this might be the woman whom Benakiell was so close to here in Rishkar. As I casually made my way back towards Benakiell, he glanced up and saw me and said something to the woman, who melted away into the crowd. I felt the spark of anger flare at Benakiell who evidently wished to be in control of every aspect of our meeting Shira. Instead of stopping to talk to him, I carried on past him and returned to take my place in the trading. Achillea told me that the salves had been most popular, and that she had traded for enough food for the three of us for the next few days. A lot of people had also stopped to see what we had to offer and were interested in our coughing tonics, and in my white honey. Tarik had gone off too, to see what items he might be interested in trading for, and had taken some of the physic with him, and some of the small carrying gourds.

'Did you see that woman who was talking to Benakiell?' I whispered to Achillea. 'I think she is Shira.'

Achillea shook her head, disappointed not to have had a look at this mysterious woman and asked me what she looked like.

'She was tall, taller than me. Slender. I could not see her age because she has her hair hidden under her headdress. She looks nothing like Gladia.' I replied, still feeling angry that Benakiell seemed to have betrayed his friendship with Gladia. Achillea looked thoughtful.

'She might be very nice, Talla. Just because Benakiell has a friendship with another woman does not mean that he does not care for Gladia. But love does not take account of convenience, unfortunately, although it might be easier to just choose the right person, but love shows itself in funny ways. I never thought I would meet someone after Ash died, and more than that, I never thought I might fall in love with someone who was once an OutRider – but I did, and I couldn't be happier.' She turned to fully face me and then, impulsively, put her arms around me and squeezed me briefly. 'I hope that one day you will feel that way about somebody too, Talla.'

It made me feel warm and comforted to hear this, that my friend wanted me to feel happy. There again, I did not feel that I was missing anything in my current life. I was working hard and learning new things. I had my bees. I lived simply but did not lack for anything. I had friends and a dwelling and now I was travelling and visiting a new land. I had never felt for any person this thing called love which seemed to drive people and change them, and I didn't think I wanted to either.

We stayed at the marketplace until it grew dark and then Tarik suggested we should find a place to sleep, and asked Benakiell if he knew of any good places to stay the night. Benakiell frowned. I think he was tiring of our teasing but, perhaps with a view to pleasing someone who was none of us, he answered that Shira had offered to let us stay in a spare dwelling which she usually used for storage. Achillea wrinkled her nose dubiously at the thought but we were all curious to meet Shira and followed Benakiell towards the west of Rishkar. It was a short walk, which I was grateful for. We had walked all day and then worked in the market and I was ready to eat and to sleep. Truthfully, I had little appetite for social chatter with someone I did not know. But this woman was not only close to Benakiell, who was my first friend on the Outer, but also the one who had owned the torn piece of parchment which had first told me of Ashkana's hidden story. I hoped she might have the other piece of parchment which would tell us even more of the story.

The spare dwelling was small and dark, although Shira had thoughtfully placed a beeswax lamp on top of a light, wooden cupboard. They had cupboards in the Court of the Queen and in the Temples, but the people of the Outer usually hung things up on pegs in the wall, or just stacked up in piles, or in baskets. Tarik ran his hands over it enviously, taking careful notes of how the pieces of wood had been joined. The doors to the cupboard were carved with patterns made of straight edged shapes like triangles and squares.

Benakiell placed most of his bundles along with ours by the side of the dwelling but he did not drop his small bundle of personal belongings, and instead made some muttered remarks which I could scarcely hear. You couldn't really tell who they were addressed to, nor what he meant to say, but he sidled out of the dwelling and headed toward Shira's dwelling. After he had gone, we all turned to each other and laughed. None of us had ever seen Benakiell like this before. He had contrived to keep all mention of this Shira away from us on the last few times we had seen him, never mentioning her. Perhaps it was because we always seemed to see him in the presence of Gladia.

'Do you think Gladia knows about Shira?' Achillea asked me, pensively. Despite her recent disagreements with Gladia, Achillea remained tender hearted and loyal, so she was divided; on the one hand she wanted Benakiell to be happy and loved after so many years of grieving for Velosia, but on the other, she did not wish to think of Gladia being upset. I could not imagine that she knew and said so. She appeared to behave exactly towards Benakiell as she always had, indulging him with extra treats, sewing his tunics for him and generally looking after him and telling him off in equal measure. I was the only one who knew the real depth of Gladia's feelings for Benakiell, and that had only come about by accident when we had visited the Empath Erayo. Somehow, I had taken on all the feelings of those who had seen the Empath onto me, and I had taken on all Gladia's feelings, including her feelings for Benakiell. Tarik frowned slightly.

'Do not judge them, at least not yet,' he said mildly. 'Think what it must be like for Shira, if she sees you take against her for no reason of her own making. You do not know that Gladia does not already know of her. You can see Benakiell is suffering under your scrutiny – and Achillea, I know how much you like to tease!' We laughed again but promised to be well behaved. There was a clay pot with water in it standing by the dwelling wall, and we took it in turns to wash our hands and faces and prepare for the evening meal. I looked forward rather greedily to eating some hot food made by someone else for a change.

Benakiell returned not long afterwards and walked with us to the dwelling next door where Shira lived. I was interested in her home, since the dwelling we were staying in was merely a shelter for storage, whereas her dwelling was a much more personal place. It was dark outside, and even if it were not, it would still have been dark inside the dwelling as it had no light openings, save for a hole at the top of the steeply domed roof. There was a fire held in a metal basket under the hole and the smoke moved efficiently upwards and out of the dwelling. Over the fire was a shallow clay pot with a richly scented stew bubbling away. My mouth watered.

Shira smiled as we came in, her smile lighting up her face. She wore a dark red tunic with matching trousers and the headdress which all adult Kashiqis wore. It comprised a square piece of thin fabric covering the head and neck which was held in place by an embroidered headband. Shira had a yellow square, and her headband was red, with orange embroidery on it.

'Welcome to my dwelling, visitors,' she said, formally, but with a smile. 'It is good to meet friends of Benakiell.' Benakiell introduced us all individually by name to her and we spoke a little about the market and how we had traded some of our goods and which goods we noticed were different to those of Oramia.

'And what brings you all to Kashiq aside from the trading?' asked Shira, curiously. We exchanged glances but left it to Benakiell to answer. He knew her best, after all.

He answered her smoothly, barely pausing before he spoke. 'Talla here has an interest in the Tower of the Wise. She has a skill in reading and scribing and wants to learn more. Achillea and Tarik,' as he waved his hand vaguely towards them. 'They like to trade and to travel, just as I do. It seemed a good plan for us all to travel together. This stew is as delicious as usual, Shira, if not more delicious. What have you put in it?'

Shira glowed in response to his praise and seemed to forget her earlier question. Achillea quickly seized on the opening and asked further questions about how the stew was made and what her own method of making stew was. The moment passed and never returned, but we had all noted that while Benakiell might indeed be close to Shira, he did not share every detail of his life with her. Shira appeared to be an easy-going woman, full of droll stories about people and recent incidents, and she smiled readily. She had an easy grace as she moved, and often used her hands to help her to explain what she was talking about. She listened earnestly to whatever Benakiell had to say, focusing her large, dark brown eyes on his face when he spoke, and waiting respectfully for him to finish speaking before she replied. A little different to Gladia, for sure, although personally, I preferred Gladia's brisk and slightly bossy manner. Gladia had a knack for aiming straight for the point and was quick to spot inaccuracies and evasions in the stories of others. She was a little blinkered, especially regarding Achillea and Tarik, but I hoped that she might change her mind on that issue, given time. Gladia did hold strong opinions, but she had been known to change her mind completely. Benakiell had always been taciturn, keeping his own counsel, preferring to observe conversations rather than join in with them, but Shira seemed to inspire him to talk more, and to laugh more, and deferred more to his opinion. Perhaps, I mused, this was what he had been like when he had been married to Velosia, and the Benakiell I had got to know was, in fact a different version of him, and that this one that I saw now was more like his real self. I still felt like an outsider looking in on the world of the Outer, despite having now lived for a whole age of adulthood in it. I realised that Shira was speaking to me and I had not heard a single word of what she had said to me, being lost in my own thoughts.

'Benakiell has told me of your prowess with the bees,' she started again, after my apologies. 'But he also said that you are a scribe and a reader. Which of the Gods do you seek guidance from?'

We all looked at one another, bewildered and unsure what to say. Benakiell stepped in, again.

'Remember we are all from another land,' he said mildly. 'Why not tell my friends of how things work in Kashiq? We are all interested.' He looked at her fondly.

Shira moved casually to sit closer to Benakiell and then began to explain how life was lived in Kashiq. We listened in rapt attention, for it was considerably different from all that we had known and been brought up with, whether we were of the Temple or the OutFort or the Outer. Shira spoke with a low, calm voice.

'Well, here in Kashiq we are governed by the guidance of our Gods and Goddesses in all the aspects of our lives. Whatever way we live and work is under the guidance of one of the six. So those who produce honey, for instance, they come under the guidance of the Goddess Ashkana, because she is the Guide for those who work to bring forth harvest from the earth; those who grow crops or dig out rockmetal or cut parchment plants or harvest honey. If you were one skilled at reading and scribing and learning new things from that which others have recorded, then Rao would be your guide.'

We exchanged glances. The very two that we knew were connected had been mentioned in the first few sentences. Achillea's eyes widened even further, if that were possible, and she turned her full attention to Shira.

'But in Oramia, we do all sorts of different things. Our work is divided only by whether you are a man or a woman not by which God guides you. There is only one Goddess, who made us all, and Ashkana is her model for us here. Which God would guide me in the making of salves, for Tarik, Talla and I all make salves and tonics and other physics, and we do not harvest our salves from the ground, although we might use the things that have been harvested from the ground?'

'Soren is the Goddess of healing and caring, so she would be your Guide here in Kashiq,' replied Shira. She is the Guide for all those who seek to heal wounds and soothe harm and give comfort.'

Tarik was listening intently, absorbing all this new information, and no doubt storing it where he could access it later. 'So,' he asked curiously, 'how could I choose for instance, for I grow crops in the garden, and I make items to trade like pegs and clasps, and gourd containers, and I work with the physic. By your reckoning, I would be guided by Ashkana, Maliq and Soren. Can a Kashiqi be guided by more than one Guide?'

'No,' replied Shira. 'You would need to choose which Guide to give your allegiance to, and trade for the other items. So, if you chose to be guided by Soren, you would trade with others for the herbs and plants you needed for your tonics, and for the containers which had been crafted to keep them in.'

We all fell silent for a moment, thinking of how our lives in Oramia differed from the lives of the Kashiqis, and all of us, no doubt, were grateful that we were able to do so many different activities ourselves. Even though we were only allowed to do certain jobs by virtue of being either a woman or a man, there were many jobs which all could do, like growing and cooking and making simple items.

'I think you have mentioned four Guides,' prompted Benakiell, after a while. 'Who are the other two?

'They are the two whose life forces are constant for us all, for we are all given into life and we are all taken into death. The Goddess of life and creation is Asmara. She is the one who brought us all into existence, and those who take Asmara as their guide pledge allegiance to her. They care for the places of worship and they glorify the Gods and Goddesses and intercede on our behalf. The God of death and destruction is Yael. Those who take Yael as their guide are the soldiers and defenders of Kashiq, those who bury and honour the dead and care for the dying and those who butcher animals for meat.'

I was glad that I was leaning back against the wall of the dwelling, somewhat in the shadows that leapt behind the flickering beeswax lantern, so that Shira did not see the surprise on my face. In some sort of way, Kashiq and Oramia must be connected to one another. Those who were guided by Asmara, the Goddess, were like the Priestesses of the Temple in Oramia, although I did not know if they wielded the same power in Kashiq, or even if they had Temples. Likewise, those guided by Yael, the God of death and destruction, were similar to the OutRider force in Oramia. In Oramia all were united under the one Goddess who made us all, but here in Kashiq, they acknowledged her opposite force too and not only acknowledged him but gave him equal standing to her. There was much to think about here, and I was pleased that, with her customary happy acceptance of new information, Achillea moved on to asking Shira about what it was that she did, and under whose guidance she lived her life.

'I am under the guidance of Maliq,' answered Shira. 'I make date sweetmeats and cakes. I have a friend who is of Ashkana and has a grove of date palms and nut trees, and I use her fruits to make my goods. Date cakes, made of pounded dates mixed with ground nuts and honey and dried fruits are very popular here in Kashiq, and I trade well for them at the market. I also trade dates stuffed with chopped nuts and honey or orange syrup. Benakiell here has a fondness for those, don't you?' She patted his arm and he smiled back at her. As far as I knew, he had never brought back any of these delights to Mellia, more's the pity. My mouth was watering at the thought of them and, when Shira then offered us all a piece of one of her date cakes, I waited for my piece with anticipation. It was made of a layer of plump sweet dates mixed with powdered almonds and a little honey, followed by a layer of honeyed nuts of different types and then another layer of the dates. It was sweet and delicious, and only a small piece left me feeling full of sweetness. I licked my fingers and then stopped, aware of how greedy I might look. Shira laughed at my consternation.

'It shows I have made my date cake well if you like it so much, Talla,' she reassured me. 'Maliq guides me well in my craft.' Not long after we had eaten the date cake, Tarik yawned, rather ostentatiously, and a little unlike his usual unobtrusive self.

'I think we need to sleep now, since we have a long day of travelling to Arbhoun ahead of us tomorrow. We thank you for your hospitality, Shira, and for the tasty cake.' He rose to leave, offering Achillea his hand to help her up. I followed them, leaving Benakiell and Shira in her dwelling, already talking quietly to each other.

'Why did we leave so early?' complained Achillea. 'I was interested in what Shira was telling us!'

'I thought Benakiell and Shira might want some time on their own,' answered Tarik. 'You know how difficult it is to get time on our own!' They gazed into each other's eyes and I felt suddenly unnecessary and somewhat alone. In one dwelling were Benakiell and Shira, with eyes only for each other, and ahead of me were Tarik and Achillea who only wanted to have their own dwelling to be together too, and here I was, in the way of all of them.

'I think I might go for a walk,' I announced airily. 'I am not very tired, and I think a short walk will be just what I need, having eaten all that delicious food at Shira's.' And before Tarik and Achillea could stutter any protestations, I wandered off into the night.

I pulled my netela over my head for the night air carried a sharp edge. The dry wind stirred the leaves of the date palms which grew close to Shira's dwelling. I walked down the path towards them, relishing the silence against the chatter of the day. There was a low wall built near the trees, and I went to sit on it. The sky was a dark, endless black, dusted with stars like honeydust on a flower. I wondered what it might be like to want to spend time with another person just like Achillea and Tarik, or Lunaria and Ambar or even Benakiell and Shira. There had been nobody who wanted to spend that sort of time with me, no man who had lingered by my market stall with a twinkle in his eye, no man who had ever spoken to me in the way that Ambar once had. Even that, I believed now, was probably just a story in my mind. Ambar had made me feel warm with his talking and the way in which he watched me. He had made me laugh and want to embark on his quest. And now here I was, once more fulfilling one of his requests. And he was not even here! I shook myself. Thinking like this would not solve any puzzles. Ambar had, unsurprisingly, chosen Lunaria, the Queen, over me. Who was I, after all? An unknown Drab escaped from a Temple who did not even know where she had come from. I had thought, once, that I might have been the Queen myself, but now I knew that was not true. Even if I were Lunaria's DoubleSoul, born just after her, there was no proof. And, in any case, I did not really know what Ambar felt about me. For all his charming words and gestures, he had never really told me how he felt about me.

I tried to put these thoughts behind me and thought more deeply of the story Ambar had told us, and of the parchments which had told us of the relationship between Ashkana and Rao. Even Ashkana, I thought bitterly, Ashkana with all her aphorisms about the importance of work and her devotion to the Goddess, had been found by one who loved her – at least at first. And now we knew he was the God of Learning, of Scribing and Reading. I felt like I was a mixture between Ashkana and Rao in my own interests. The thought of going to visit Arbhoun with its high reputation for learning, made me suddenly eager to continue to travel, to go and sleep so that we could set off again early in the morning and find out more. My gloomy thoughts forgotten, I sprung off the wall and walked back to the dwelling.

# THE LEAF

## CHAPTER 10

I shifted my feet restlessly. I was standing in a long line again. When I first came here to the Tower of the Wise in Arbhoun, I was much more patient, but now, a scant three days later, I found the whole process of waiting to be given the whereabouts of the new scroll you had requested tedious. I cast my eyes towards the ceiling of the Tower, far above me. I had never been in such a tall building before I had entered the Tower of the Wise. Even the Great Hall in the Court of the Queen was not as high. This huge tower had six equal sides, like one of the sections of a honeycomb and all those walls were lined with shelves made of cedarwood and sandalwood, pinewood, and camphor. The scent from these woods mingled and swirled around us, and, incidentally, helped to protect the scrolls from the insects which liked to eat them. There was a narrow staircase which wound its way up through the different sections into which the scrolls had been sorted. I had never in my life seen so many scrolls. They were of all shapes and sizes; some were tattered and curling, turning brown and ragged at the edges, some were held in boxes of loose sheets, some were protected by ornate silver scroll holders. When I had first entered the Tower of the Wise, I stood in awe, gazing at all the reading and scribing in evidence around

118

me. I had longed to turn and exclaim about it to Achillea, but she was not with me.

Achillea and Tarik were not permitted inside the Tower of the Wise because neither of them could read or scribe. Any person from another land, or indeed any Kashiqi had to prove that they could both read and scribe before they were permitted to enter the Tower. Achillea and Tarik were turned away at the entrance. I told them I would meet them again at the end of the day by the wall of the Tower, and they left, rather crestfallen. Then, I moved into the entrance vestibule where there were several angled boards holding scrap pieces of plant parchment, each with a metal-nibbed pen. I stood in line here, too. The scholar who sat on a grand chair next to a box of scrolls looked at me superciliously. His eyebrows were exceptionally fine; they had perhaps been plucked that way, and his moustache was trimmed and oiled. His beard, too, was highly groomed and had been trimmed to a point. His fine eyebrows rose disbelievingly as his eyes travelled over my Oramian garb.

'Seems unusual to see one such as you here at the Tower of the Wise. I've seen a few of the veiled ones before, but never one like you.' He sighed. 'Well, I suppose I shall have to go through the motions, since you have declared yourself under the guardianship of Rao.' He thrust his hand into the box beside him and drew out a piece of script randomly and handed it to me.

'Read this,' he directed, with an air of continued disinterest, presumably expecting me to fail. My mind's emberjar, much more controlled these days, flared briefly at his tone. I looked down at the scribing on the parchment and began to read it out loud, although it made little sense to me.

'...herds of goats, flocks of birds and swarms of bees. It is full of delightful surprises around every ornately

119

carved corner...' I began, casting my eyes down toward the paper, avoiding the gaze of the scholar for fear that he might see the anger in my eyes. He listened to me read the rest of the parchment to the end and then made a small mark next to my name, which he had scribed on a list.

'Hmmm, well you read well enough.' His eyebrows moved downwards slightly. 'Let us see if you can scribe in a legible manner. Go and scribe me six lines on...' he cast his eyes upwards, as if searching for inspiration, '...food and drink.' I looked back at him, baffled. In Oramia, scribing was used as a functional device; it passed on instructions or laid out official ceremonies or sequences of events; it was used in the Choice ceremony, in scrolls of Permission and so on. We did not simply scribe on diverse subjects plucked out of the air, but apparently this was what I needed to do to progress further within the Tower of the Wise. I retreated to one of the wooden slopes and picked up the metal-nibbed pen tentatively. I chose to scribe the requested six lines about the apricot which Benakiell had given me to taste, checked them through and then returned to the scholar, who read it through, occasionally frowning in a critical manner. When he had finished, he tossed it into the box with the other parchments and gave me a small piece of plant parchment on which he had scribed my name. He then took a small scoop of warm beeswax from the lamp and put it on the paper and embossed it with an intricately carved seal which hung from a fine chain around his waist. He thrust it back at me and said in a disinterested tone. 'You may enter the Tower of Wisdom; may it bring answers to your questions and questions to your answers.' I took the parchment mutely and he waved me away, already focused on the next candidate.

Over the past three days I had made my way around the Tower, finding out how it worked and in what manner to behave. The lower hall, beyond the entrance vestibule, was full of standing easels for scribing and of benches on which one could sit for reading the scrolls and parchments. If you wanted to find a scroll, you had to approach one of the scholars, of which there were six, and explain what you were looking for. If you were a higher scholar, they would then direct you to the box, basket, or shelf where the scroll or parchment might be found. You would then go up the staircase and work your way through the scrolls until you found the one you wanted. For other scholars, such as me, you had to ask for the type of scroll you wanted, and they would fetch it or, more commonly, send someone to fetch it for you. It was very time consuming, because you had to read it and then scribe any notes and then return it before you could look for others. I spent much of my time reading and dismissing scroll after scroll before I started to find some small items of interest. And here I was, waiting, yet again, for another scroll. I was trying to find out more about the supposed relationship between Ashkana and Rao, in the hope that it might offer me clues about what had happened to the Orange of Kashiq. I was also searching for any piece which referred to the Orange of Kashiq at all. Sometimes it felt as if I were drowning in the cacophony of voices which I read from the scrolls.

I sighed rather loudly. I had not spoken to many of those who worked here, preferring as I did to work quietly on my own. In any case, the scholars frowned upon chatter and insisted that it should be saved for the times when one went for a break in the courtyard garden. In truth, I spent far too long out in the courtyard garden. It was so pleasingly made. There were channels of flowing water which fell into large metallic vessels and from thence into dark pools of water. There was a complicated system of returning the water to the channels which I was sure Benakiell would have been intrigued to see, although he, like Achillea and Tarik, was not permitted in the garden which was reserved for those who attended the Tower of the Wise. In any case, Benakiell was no longer travelling with us. After walking with us to Arbhoun and seeing us settled at trader dwellings, he had explained that he intended on returning to Rishtar and Shira, rather than staying with us. He promised that he would return to us soon, but that he wanted to see if he could find the other part of the parchment which he had got from Shira, and that he thought if he were alone, it might be easier. Tarik counselled him not to speak of the reasons why we sought the parchment to Shira, and he promised that he would not, and that, in fact was why he thought it better to do it on his own. It was, perhaps, just an excuse to spend some time with Shira away from us.

The man in front of me in the line turned and glanced at me as I sighed, a wry smile playing around the corners of his generous mouth. He wore the standard Kashiqi clothing, a long tunic and wide, flowing trousers and a headband over a piece of cloth. His tunic was a dark, blood red, and his trousers an indeterminate, grubby colour. His headband was green and was embroidered with red triangles over an orange head cloth. He caught my eye as I looked at him and smiled again. I found myself smiling back and then looked forward again to the movement of the line, but I could feel his eyes travelling over me. I suddenly felt rather self-conscious in my scruffy orange tunic. Achillea and Tarik and I had all traded for a simple pair of the wide trousers worn by all Kashiqis, but had decided to keep our own tunics, to save on trades. I had a pair of blue trousers. There was not, in all honesty, much choice unless we wanted to trade a great deal more, so we chose the older, scruffier pairs in the market. I now wished, for some reason, that I had traded some of my honey for the beautifully embroidered orange ones I had seen, which would match my tunic. My netela was draped lightly over my head so that, although it was clear I was not Kashiqi, I could pass in a crowd more easily. The line moved again, and it was the turn of the man in front of me to say which scrolls he sought.

'I am looking for the scroll scribed by Scholar Tafir about Lord Rao and his mechanical orange,' he said to the plump little scholar who sat on an equally plump cushion.

'But that's the one I want to read!' I burst out, infuriated. I had stood in the line for quite some time, pleased with myself at having finally found a reference to the orange and Rao, and here was this man asking for it before me! Who knew how long he might take to read it? He turned to look at me, surprised at my interjection.

'You can read it after I have finished with it,' he suggested amiably. I simmered. Surely, he could choose something else to read? The plump little scholar looked at us both, his shiny, black eyes twinkling with amusement.

'Might I suggest that in order to save time for all of us, Ravin, that when you finish you could bring the scroll to...' He scrutinised me intently and then looked at me, raising one eyebrow quizzically.

'Talla,' I replied shortly.

'Talla. Just so.' He sent a scholar who was working with him up the stairs to fetch the scroll for Ravin. I had no other scroll in mind to look for, so I chose to go out into the courtyard garden and wait a while, hoping that this Ravin might quickly discover that he did not need the scroll after all.

I wandered out, under the carved arched doorway. It was hot outside, but the garden courtyard had been planted with a variety of tall leafy trees and palms. It was laid out in a pleasing pattern of square flowerbeds and water channels, each surrounded by clay moulded benches, coloured white to keep them cool. In Oramia we planted plants which produced useful things, fruits and vegetables, oils and seeds, herbs and physics, wood and reeds. In this garden, the person who had planted it had thought of the colours and the scents of the flowers, and the shade qualities of the trees. I sat by one of the pools of water and thought of what I had learned so far in my study at the Tower of the Wise.

I had read several parchments which confirmed that Lord Rao and Ashkana had had a relationship of some sort. I had not found it easy to discover any scrolls which detailed the reasons why Ashkana had been in Kashiq in the first place, nor any yet which told of her departure from Kashiq to Oramia. I had also read several rather condescending parchments relating to the land of Oramia. Most of them dismissed it as a land full of ignorant people who had no interesting or redeeming qualities. One of them mentioned that Ashkana must have gone into exile in Oramia after she had left Rao, for there was no other reason to go there. When I read these, I felt angry. These scribes, no doubt, knew nothing of Oramia and had, in all likelihood, never been there. Even though I had a long list of my own complaints, these sneering remarks were making me reassess what I thought of the land of my birth, and I now felt very protective and defensive of it. Because I had not found out very much about Ashkana and Rao, I had turned my attention to trying to discover any further references to the Orange of Kashiq, which was, after all, the focus of our travel to Kashiq. I knew that the Orange was in fact made from honeygold, not silver as I had originally thought. Honeygold was a light golden colour and was close to a silvery tone. Ambar had told me that the little bee pendant which I used to wear was made of honeygold. I had learned that Rao had designed the orange himself, although he had used his most skilled craftsmen to make it. The scroll which the irritating Ravin had requested sounded as if it might give me lots of detailed information about what the orange looked like and how it could have been broken into pieces by Ashkana.

The wind rustled the drying leaves of the date palm trees above me. I glanced down at the flowerbed beneath it, which had been planted with lavenders and a sort of deep red flower which I had never seen in Oramia. There were bees tracing journeys through the air, back and forth to the flowers, their gentle humming adding a somnolent quality to the hot, still air. It seemed that there were bees in every land, busy working and making honey which we then used to make physic or eat or make delicious sweetmeats with. Of course, Benakiell had told me when we were still in Oramia that there were bees in Kashiq that feasted on the flowers of the oranges and apricots which grew in groves around the outskirts of the cities. They made me feel more comfortable and at home in this place which was so far away from my homeland. I moved to sit on one of the cool white benches and leaned against the trunk of the tree which grew behind it.

'Well, I have rushed through reading this scroll because you were so eager to read it yourself, but here you are, sleeping in the garden!' An amused voice woke me up with a jump. My netela had slipped off my head and hung loosely off my shoulder. I did not normally sleep during the day, especially as I was usually working hard, but I was finding that all the reading and scribing I was doing was making me feel very languid. The cool calm of the garden made me feel at ease and now here I was looking very disinterested in my study. I could feel my cheeks heating up – from the emberjar within, rather than the sun.

'I thought it would take you longer to read it,' I retorted. Ravin's eyes crinkled up at the corners, amused by my answer. I realised, too late, how impudent it might sound, and my cheeks flushed even further. 'I did not mean to insult you,' I stuttered. 'Only that it would take me longer to read a scroll like that.'

Ravin laughed. 'Have no worry, Talla, was it? I take no offence. I have read most of it, but I thought it best to allow you time to read it as soon as possible since you were so eager to read it too. Perhaps when you have finished with it, you will come and find me so I can peruse it again?' He looked at me quizzically as I struggled to think of something more seemly to say to this man who seemed very cordial and friendly despite my awkwardness.

'Why did you want to read the scroll?' I asked, hoping that he might be able to tell me something more about the scroll. Ravin looked at me curiously and then indicated the bench I was sitting on.

'May I sit down beside you while we talk? The sun is hot on my back and your bench looks much cooler and more pleasant. Besides,' Ravin stretched, 'I have been bent over my scribing board almost all day and I need a rest. Have you eaten?' Feeling flustered, I replied that I had not eaten and shuffled along the bench so that he could sit down on it. He had a piece of fabric which had been stitched together into a bag which could be drawn up by two cords and was slung over his shoulder He took it off his shoulder and placed it on the cool white surface of the bench and then eased the cords down so that it opened out flat. It was a charming thing; it carried his portions of food and a small metal vessel of water and so when it was opened out, it served as a mat for his food. I told Ravin how ingenious his little carrybag was and he smiled again and said, 'I like things that can be unwrapped.' He shared his meal with me. It was a thin, chewy sort of a flatbread which had been folded around some oiled and salted vegetables and a piece of a nut-filled sweetmeat. We ate in silence, and I thanked him for his generosity, savouring the flavours in his meal. I licked my fingers of the remnants of honey, and then wiped them again on my netela so that, when I got to work, I would not leave any traces on the scroll.

'Stay a while before you go back to the scrolls,' urged Ravin. 'You can tell me about what you are trying to find, and I can tell you about what I am looking for and you never know, maybe we are looking for the same thing!' He laughed again, seemingly amused at the idea that we could be looking for the same thing. Considering the content of the scroll, it seemed highly likely to me that we were, but I held my tongue, and suggested that he start. I had no intention of sharing the real purpose of my research with him, but I thought I could ask more about the relationship of Ashkana with Rao, which he must surely know more about me than me.

'Lord Rao had a very clever mind,' he began. 'He invented many different devices and ways to move things. I am interested in finding out as much as I can about all of them, so that I can learn from his mind and go on to make some of my own clever objects, using some of his ideas. Even a quite simple thing can change the way we behave and think. Look at my little carrybag. It allows for me to share my food politely with a beautiful woman in a beautiful garden and have a conversation with her. No doubt if I had wrapped all the food up in a big mess and then offered it to you, you would have declined my offer and swept off with the scroll and not even a backward look!' He chuckled again. I felt my cheeks grow hot again when he described me as beautiful. Me, Talla, the Drab from the Temple who did not even know how to braid hair some years ago, and who was always clad in a patchwork drabcoat. I had not, of course, ever seen for myself what I looked like, though I caught a glance in still water sometimes, or in the polished side of a coffee pot. I had observed Achillea the most, and she was certainly attractive with her big eyes fringed with long eyelashes, and her small, pointed nose. She had clear skin and a generous, smiling mouth which was usually either talking or singing. Achillea had told me before that I had lovely thick hair, which was good to braid, and when oiled with Paradox oil, it gleamed pleasingly. But I was not beautiful, for surely someone else would have said so by now if I were? Ravin continued, unaware of my pondering.

'The scroll which I have already looked at, and which you are about to look at is about a little device that Lord Rao is supposed to have made. It has been regularly scribed about, but nobody can say where it is now, nor even tell us exactly what it looked like or how it worked since it was a gift from Lord Rao to Ashkana, when he loved her. Scholar Tafir, who scribed it, was said to be one of those who worked on parts of the Orange of Kashiq. I wonder if it is just a story though, for there is precious little detail of how it worked, nor yet what became of it, save that the Lady Ashkana sent it back to Rao broken, as their love was broken.'

'I would have liked to see a diagram of the moving parts but Tafir just describes it which gives me little to go on. I want to understand how the Orange opened, for we are told in the scroll that it could be opened and closed using the stem and the leaf of the orange. But, enough of what I wanted to get from the scroll! You will have your own reasons for wanting to study it. Are you also interested in how things are made and dreamed up?' He turned to look at me. He had a burnished skin, glowing with the sheen of sweat. His eyes were warm and kind, a deep brown, almost black, with glints of mischief dancing in them. His moustache was oiled and tended to in the manner of the Kashiqi men and he had a short, neatly trimmed and shaped dark brown beard.

I looked away swiftly, lest he should think that I had been staring at him too hard, and then turned again to look at him as I answered his question.

'I am interested in this tale of the love between Rao and Ashkana,' I said. 'I am from Oramia, where nobody knows of this, and it was a surprise to me when I heard of it. So, since I am travelling with my friends now and staying here in Arbhoun, I thought I might spend some time finding out about it.'

Ravin rolled his eyes comically. 'I should have guessed! All the ladies like a tragic love story more than an ingeniously designed device! Even though Lord Rao spent so much time and effort in designing and making the Orange of Kashiq, you are still more interested in the fact that his love for Ashkana did not last – or perhaps it was her love for him that did not last. In any case, she ran away to Oramia and broke up the Orange. Imagine doing that to such a beautiful thing! You will not find a great deal about this famed love affair in this scroll, I am afraid, Talla. The scroll is much more of a description of what the Orange of Kashiq looked like, and what it was made of than its history. I would love to have seen it when it was whole … it must have been amazing …' His voice trailed off and there was a distant look in his eyes as if he were seeing it in his mind. After a few moments, he shook himself out of his dreaming and stood up.

'Come then, Talla,' he said. 'Let me hand over the scroll so that Scholar Faroon can see that I have done my job. He will be getting itchy already because I have left the scroll at my scribing board for so long!'

I leapt up, worried that I had kept him in the garden too long and that he might get into trouble on my behalf – or even that I might not be able to read the scroll when we returned inside the Tower of the Wise. Ravin chuckled again. He seemed to find much in life amusing, and although part of me was irritated by his almost constant good humour, I found it lightened my spirits and made me smile too. I might be able to find out a lot of information from him while I worked in the Tower, and he might even save me some time too.

After Ravin had handed me the scroll under the watchful eye of the Scholar, I thanked him and asked him if I might ask him some more questions about Rao's designs at some other time. His eyes lit up with interest and could see that I had asked the right question. He patted my hand, which was curled over the scroll, which inexplicably caused it to tingle. I started and he smiled at me again as I walked off to my scribing board.

Spreading out the parchment scroll on the board, I moved the ingenious leather straps which were held at the back of the board over the corners of the scroll, laying it flat against the board so that I could read it as well as possible. It had been scribed in a sparse, spidery script. I imagined that the scholar who wrote it must have been a very tedious person to listen to. His scribing was precise but rather too detailed for my interest. However, I did glean some points of information. As Ravin had pointed out, Tafir did describe the Orange of Kashiq in more detail which allowed me to imagine it better, and at least know what sort of thing we were looking for. I, for one, was happy that he did not go into the kind of detailed information which apparently Ravin craved.

It appeared, from what I read, that Tafir had been engaged by Lord Rao to do the engraving on the Orange of Kashiq. By the time I got to the end of the scroll, I also wished that there was a diagram of the Orange because the words I read did not paint a sufficiently detailed picture of it. But I did find out some useful things; the orange was the same size as a real orange and was definitely made of honeygold. Tafir described it as having an ingenious opening device comprising a leaf and central stem, and that there were six sections in the orange, each one made to look like the segment of a real orange. Each of the segments was a small opening box of sorts and was engraved with intricate flowers and leaves. Tafir described his work thus:

'The pieces of the Orange of Kashiq have been skilfully engraved by me. I was engaged by Lord Rao who had heard of my prowess with honeygold. The engraving was so fine that you could not see where the catch was that opened the segment. It is still my finest work...'

There was more in the same sort of vein. Tafir was, I think, intent that his contribution to the Orange of Kashiq should be recorded forever. I scribed some of the details down, along with the other notes I had made that day from the scrolls I had seen, and then rolled up my own scroll and tied it with a scrap of thread. All around me everyone was collecting up their possessions, as the scholars of the tower had just chimed the gong to warn everyone that it was time to go. I headed for the arched wooden doorway along with several others. I felt a hand at my elbow and turned to see Ravin again, just as I spotted Achillea waiting for me on the corner of the path.

'Will you be in study again tomorrow?' he asked diffidently. 'I can show you some more of the scrolls I have found about Lord Rao's orange, if you are interested in it. Perhaps we could share the study to make it more interesting?'

'Yes,' I stammered quickly, conscious of Achillea's eyes on me. 'That would be ... useful.' Ravin smiled again and raised his hand in brief farewell as he turned to walk around the corner of the path. My eyes followed his slight figure as he went, the evening breeze ruffling his head cloth.

'Who was that?' asked Achillea immediately, her eyes alight with curiosity. 'Who is your new friend? What have you been finding out today? When do you think you will discover something definite? I have been trading for some of the Kashiqi salves and oils at the market today so that we can copy them when we get back to Oramia. And I heard a beautiful song earlier today when some Songmakers came to the market; I think I have remembered nearly all of it. Just imagine, here in Kashiq you can sing all day and people will trade for the joy of listening to you! That would be a wonderful life, wouldn't it? I will try and sing it to you when we get back. Tarik has gone searching for places where they craft silver and metal boxes in case he can pick up any stories there, or so he says, but I think he just wants to do some more metalworking; I know he has missed his old life...' She drew breath finally and then looked at me expectantly to hear my answers to her many questions. I laughed, relieved that she had talked for so long that I had had the chance to order my thoughts.

We talked as we walked back to our dwelling, and I told her of what I had discovered about the Orange itself, which we agreed Tarik would find most useful since he was the one who knew about metalworking. We still had no further information about the whereabouts of the Orange – if it were well known, I was sure we would have heard about it by now, but my suspicion was that all the parts of the Orange had been cast away, perhaps in a fit of anger by the Lord Rao after Ashkana had returned the broken pieces to him. I was doubtful that we would find any of the actual pieces but more hopeful that someone somewhere might have scribed a little of their story after they had been sent back. It was strange to come to a land where everyone knew the story of the great love between Lord Rao and Ashkana and yet we who came from Oramia where Ashkana was honoured and respected as the daughter of the Goddess knew nothing of it. I had always thought of her in one kind of way, as a stern, joyless, determined, hardworking and pious figure and now I was having to reconsider what I thought I knew. I asked Achillea some questions about the salves and her day in the market and she had just finished telling me what she had discovered when we arrived back at the place we were staying. Tarik was not yet there, but we went inside, grateful of the dark shade inside, and lit the lanterns and the fire for our evening meal.

When Tarik returned home, he told us he had also had an interesting day. He had been to visit the metalworking area of Arbhoun. There were some strange allocations of work in Kashiq. Because each person was aligned to one of the six Gods through their profession, some of them were obvious; those who grew crops, for instance lived under the guidance of Ashkana, the Goddess of Working and those who read and scribed were, as we now knew, under the guidance of Rao. The metalworkers were all under the leadership of Yael, the God of death and destruction. Achillea shivered dramatically when Tarik had told her this and protested that she felt sure that they might be more likely to be under Maliq the God of crafting. However, Tarik suggested that, because metal was used by the soldiers of Kashiq for all their weapons and armour and that it might either cause death or protect from death, this could be the reason for their guide. In any case, it was not our job to allocate professions to the gods and goddesses of Kashiq. I wasn't sure what I thought of their enlarged group of gods and goddesses. Perhaps because I had grown up in the Temple, I struggled to imagine more than one Goddess. Here in Kashiq, Ashkana was considered a goddess like Asmara, she whom we knew as the Goddess, the Creator of all things. It did not feel right to me. As I often did, I drifted off into my own mind, which this evening seemed to feel cosy and warm, and was thinking about the events of the day again when Achillea poked me in a manner reminiscent of Gladia. I rubbed the spot on my arm vigorously and tried to pay more attention.

'You will have to tell Talla again, my dear,' said Achillea, giggling. 'She has a new friend who seems to be quite occupying her thoughts today!' Tarik raised his eyebrows, encouraging Achillea to say more, much to my discomfort. 'She has been very careful to avoid the subject since she came out of the Tower of the Wise, but I will tell you what I saw. I saw a very nicely turned out young gentleman of Kashiq who was deep in conversation with Talla when I saw them. He looked quite transfixed by her, in my opinion and his eyes never once left her face! I think she was almost as transfixed by him; I have never seen Talla so interested in a new person!' Tarik grinned.

'Do tell us more about your new friend, Talla,' he urged, in innocent tones. 'We shall have to meet him and judge if he is an appropriate admirer for you!'

I was pleased we were sitting by the fire and that the warm flush on my cheeks could not be seen. I felt very foolish, having such a reaction to my friends' good-natured teasing.

'He is not an admirer,' I insisted plaintively. 'He is just someone who is also studying the Orange of Kashiq and who might be a useful person for me to get to know. He may have clues about where we can find it!'

'Of course, of course,' soothed Achillea, mockingly. 'You must meet him again and endeavour to discover more.'

# CHAPTER 11

W hen do you think the Orange of Kashiq was made?' I asked Ravin as we sat and ate our midday meal in the garden. 'How many years do you think it has been missing and broken?' I looked up at his by now familiar features. We had fallen into the habit, over the past days, of meeting at this time and discussing what we had found out through our reading of the ancient scrolls regarding Rao, Ashkana and the Orange, the symbol of their love. Ravin had become more interested in the story of what had led up to the creation and subsequent destruction and it really did feel as if we were getting closer to finding out what might have happened to the broken pieces.

So far, we had mainly found scrolls scribed around the time of the creation of the Orange. Some of them were more complicated descriptions which Ravin took great interest in, and he spent long hours copying the fine diagrams of the structures in the Orange. He had in his possession a beautiful metal nibbed pen with a very fine nib. I thought back to when I had first used an ink pen and the carved reeds which Benakiell had made for me, and which I had used to scribe the Permission Scrolls. I liked to watch Ravin from my scribing board which was behind his and somewhat to the right of it. He would peer closely at the scroll he was reading and then dip his pen in the ink. Then, using curious instruments, he would draw circles and lines in a very light-coloured ink. Then he would use a darker ink to sketch out the lines of the Orange, as he thought it might look. I had watched it growing over the days and was impressed with the way in which he linked such disparate, tiny fragments of knowledge together to make a detailed drawing of the structure. I sometimes found myself just sitting back and watching how he moved as he scribed, or the way in which he would adjust his headdress while he was thinking, or the way in which he ran his hand over his beard as he pondered his next move.

Ravin looked back at me, instantly interested in my question.

'It is hard to tell. They do say that it was a hundred ages ago when they talk of the Lord Rao. But I am not so sure. I do not know if the parchments are the same ones that were scribed at the time for surely they would be by now so faded and fragile that they would have crumbled to dust in a hundred ages? But perhaps they are all copied, at the end of every age. I believe the Tower has the Scholars copying any important scrolls which show signs of wear.'

I reflected on this as I finished off my daily flatbread and licked the oily sauce off my fingers. Ravin's eyes followed my fingers to my mouth and watched me. My cheeks flushed warmly. I tried to think of another question. It was now time for us to go back inside and return to our scrolls but spending time here with Ravin had become almost more important to me than the work I had come here to do.

'Why do you think that Lord Rao chose to make an orange for Ashkana instead of something like a flower, or a ...' I cast my mind around...'a bee or something?' Ravin smiled at me again and adroitly produced, from within his little carrying bag, a whole orange.

'When I first heard about the Orange of Kashiq, I also did not know why it was that he chose it. It seemed such a complicated thing to choose to make. But then I began to realise that he had chosen an excellent example, for the whole thing was a sign of love.'

'Can you explain that to me a bit more?' I asked. Ravin looked back at me and placed the orange into my hand. His warm fingers brushed over mine as he did so and I felt their warmth travel through me, like the channel of empathy which Empath Erayo had opened in me all those years ago. I closed my hand around the orange, feeling its slightly rough yet polished feeling skin.

'Love is just like an orange. It grows naturally in the garden of our heart just like this orange grew in a nearby garden, fed by the goodness of the soil, the refreshment of the water and the warmth of the sun. But when you choose to pluck an orange, you do not yet know how it will taste. It looks ripe and juicy, satisfying, and sweet, and yet we do not know. To find out, we must go a little deeper.'

Ravin took the orange gently from my hand.

'It holds such sweet promise, this firm, round fruit. It is shielded by a thick skin which has a bitter spray, to warn you off if you do not have good intentions, to test your resolve to taste the fruit.' He dug his nail into the orange and began to peel it smoothly, until all the outer rind had been removed. 'And then, there is another barrier, this layer of soft fluffiness which has no substance.' He began to strip off the white inner pith fastidiously. I watched his fingers as they moved over the flesh of the orange. His nails were trimmed closely and completely clean even though he had been drawing with ink earlier. I leaned forward, fascinated to find out more in this impromptu lesson on love. He paused and looked at me. I did not instantly want to look away when he looked at me anymore; I liked to see his eyes as he spoke to me; the brief flashes of mischief and laughter and the darker flashes of impatience. It was he who moved his eyes away first. He split the orange up into segments and lay them out on his palm and then offered them to me.

'Choose one,' he urged, smiling. I hovered over them, trying to guess what part of his explanation my choice might play. Eventually I chose one and lifted it off his hand. 'Eat it,' he said. 'Enjoy it.'

I bit into the plump segment of orange that I had picked. It was sweet and juicy and filled my mouth with an almost scented flavour. Ravin took a segment too, and then placed the remaining segments down on to his cloth.

'Imagine I am Lord Rao,' he said grandly, puffing out his chest importantly. I laughed. 'And you,' he turned to me, serious suddenly, 'you are the Lady Ashkana whom the Lord Rao loves. How can he show her the meaning of love when she does not comprehend it yet and has never encountered it before? Perhaps, one day, I, Lord Rao, was eating an orange when I first came up with this idea.

'Love comes in different forms, each quality like the segment of an orange, and each part makes up the whole orange of love, held together by these connective threads. I offer you my love, one segment at a time and you take them, not knowing how they will taste. Some are larger than others, some have many seeds, some have none; some are sweet and juicy, others are bitter or sour.

'I offer you my love as I offer you the orange, segment by segment. Your lips close around the orange and take in the sweetness of my love. It is overflowing as you eat it and the juice spills out onto your fingers. You are greedy and lick up nearly all the drops. It is delicious now, but with time its sweet stickiness will irritate you and you will wash it away.

'But, one day, you take a segment of this, my orange of love, and you will expect sweetness and refreshment. Instead, your tongue will curl up with its sourness and you will want to spit it out and reject it. And even though it is but one small part of the whole orange, it will affect how you look upon the whole orange. If you were to blend all the segments together, you would not notice the bitterness so much. An orange must have some bitterness to make its flavour whole, and yet you think it should only ever be sweet and replenishing. And now, whenever I offer you my love, you wonder if it might be bitter, and soon you are too afraid to taste it again...'

Ravin gazed off into the distance, over the roof of the Tower of the Wise as he finished his little speech. I was amazed by what he had said to me, and how clearly he had explained the Orange of Kashiq and how Lord Rao had made it, and probably what had caused Ashkana to reject both the Orange and Lord Rao; some small, bitter kernel which was but a chance part of the orange of love he had offered her. Ravin turned back to me, his face serious again, and stripped of his pretence at being Lord Rao.

'What do you think, Talla? Do you see now why Rao chose an orange to make for Ashkana? He wanted her to understand that love had many aspects, but she only wanted the sweetness, and when she tasted the bitterness, she mistrusted herself and could not try again in case it happened again.'

'I do.' And I really did understand why Lord Rao had chosen the Orange as his symbol of love and how, in her way, Ashkana had made it a symbol of her own by breaking it up into its segments and returning her love, broken, to Lord Rao, because all she could taste was the bitterness. It made me feel sad for them both, that they could not try to repair their love, just as they could have tried to repair the Orange of Kashiq. And I also understood more about love. Like Ashkana, I had not been raised with any knowledge of love save that of the Goddess. None of the Priestesses spoke of love or indeed expressed it. I had seen those I cared about taken over by the forces of love and yet had failed to understand it as well as Ravin had explained it to me. He picked up the remaining orange segments and offered them to me.

'Would you like to try a segment of my orange?' I hesitated, wondering again which one to choose, remembering the story of the bitter segment. He laughed out loud at my indecision, startling a bird which was pecking in the flower garden close by. I quickly chose one and bit into it. The thin skin gave way and juice sprayed out over my lips and my chin. We both laughed again and then Ravin reached out his hand to my face. He wiped a droplet of juice away with his finger and then deliberately licked the juice off. He moved closer to me and raised his hand once more towards my face, drawing it closer to his own, and then very gently touched my lips with his own, like a butterfly stopping at a flower to drink the honeyjuice before it flew away. I closed my eyes, unwilling to halt the warm feeling which flowed through me. Ravin sighed and stroked my cheek again. I opened my eyes to see his eyes very close to mine, warm and kind, but questioning whether I welcomed his actions. I moved slightly closer to him to show him that I did, and once more he kissed me, this time for a little longer.

We sat next to one another, each of us unwilling to break the silence which seemed to wrap itself around us so comfortingly. At last, Ravin turned to look at me again and spoke.

'Ah, Talla. I have offered you just one of the segments of my orange, and you took it, even when I had told you about Lord Rao and the Lady Ashkana. You trusted me and you trusted yourself – I shall endeavour to show you that your trust was not misplaced. I have given you just one small taste of my love, but I would give you the whole orange, or, better yet, an orange tree which gave you hundreds of oranges or maybe even an entire grove of oranges... but for now, my heart sings that you have tasted just one of the pieces of my orange and I thank you for it.'

I stammered back, disconcerted by the sudden rush of feelings which flooded through me as he spoke to me, trying to make sure that I did not say the wrong thing.

'May I bring an orange for us to share tomorrow?'

# CHAPTER 12

The next days passed suffused in a haze of warmth and excitement. I only kept it a secret for one day before Achillea wheedled it out of me, having seen me walking closely to Ravin as we emerged from the Tower of the Wise. Concentrating on our studies had become difficult for both of us in the face of our mutual fascination, and only two days after Ravin had first kissed me, we arranged to move the positions of our scribing boards so that we stood next to each other. This was, if possible, even more distracting, but it did allow us to combine our study and not look at the same scroll twice. It reminded me of the attraction between the little bee pendant and the Queen's brooch, both now in the Court of the Queen. You only had to hold the little bee near the flower brooch for it to move, seemingly of its own volition, through some invisible force, so that it became firmly attached to the flower.

Achillea was unduly fascinated, I thought, and continued to try to make me talk more about my feelings and how it felt between Ravin and I. Even Tarik recognised that she wanted to know too much and patted her on the arm to remind her to stop asking me questions. I had, so far, managed to avoid them meeting and had even asked Ravin to leave before me or after me to make it less likely that Achillea would engineer such a meeting. But I knew it was only a matter of time. Besides, Ravin himself was curious about my companions and wanted to meet them too. He had not told me much about his own circumstances, preferring, he said, to hear about mine. I told him something of the length of time I had been friends with Achillea but had told him nothing of the quests which had united us all, nor of my childhood in the Temple. His care for me was so precious that I feared telling him the details of my life in case he should think that I was too strange or be otherwise disenchanted by me. And, despite having become accustomed to having my own possessions after a childhood of having none, having a person who was mine was a new feeling to me too. In truth, I did not want to share Ravin with anyone, even Tarik and Achillea who had been nothing but supportive and kind to me over the years. One evening, Achillea approached me directly.

'Talla, we want to meet Ravin. We know he is important to you, but do you not see that this means he must be important to us too? For you know both of us and we love one another, and we only want the best for you. We are worried that he is turning your head with flattery and might not be a suitable man for you. He is of another land and we know nothing about him, and we need to make sure you are safe.'

I laughed. The thought that Ravin would mean harm to me seemed unlikely. I tried to explain this to Achillea and Tarik, but I realised that the only thing that would satisfy them would be to meet Ravin for themselves so that they could judge him and understand that he only wanted good for me, as I did for him. Tarik looked at me kindly as I struggled for words to try to explain myself to them.

'More than anyone, I think I know how you feel, Talla. After all, I too was raised without mention of love. The only thing we were told of was the Angels, and we all know that there is nothing about love there. I had no one to tell me how it felt to truly love another person. I watched others – I saw Ambar, my comrade and how he seemed to feel – first for you and then for Lunaria, the Queen. I saw how much Achillea and Ashtun loved each other, and I saw how the loss of that love affected my dear Achillea. With time, I began to feel what I now know to be love for Achillea, but I had no idea whether she felt the same for me, and for some time, I was too frightened to ask her. But when I did, and found she felt the same way for me, it was such a lifted burden. It will not hurt you or Ravin to share your love with others who also care for you; we do not wish to take it away from you. Achillea and I have seen how much you smile these past days, and the way that your eyes light up at the thought of him. Let us meet, and then Achillea and I can see for ourselves. It is easy to be blinded by the bright light of love, and it is for us, your friends, to make sure that Ravin is not trying to take advantage of you.'

'Ravin does not seek to take advantage of me,' I retorted. 'What could he gain from me? He is much more learned than I am and knows much more. There is precious little that I can offer him except my company. I do not have riches to offer him, or wisdom, or beauty. I cannot make tasty sweetmeats for him, nor even sing to him as Achillea can sing to you. And yet, he wants to spend time with me, not for any of those things but for being with me, and I feel the same.' I stopped suddenly, feeling a little ashamed by my outburst, and feeling irritated that I could not express myself clearly enough that they could understand.

'Well then, it will do no harm for us to meet, if he is as unassuming and pleasant a person as you say,' said Achillea firmly, reminding me, in a small bright flash of memory, of Gladia with her uncompromising attitude. 'It is never easy to see outside a closed room, after all. Tarik and I will be your windows, so you can see both in and out.' Then she burst into laughter. 'Listen to me, with my wise words! I sound like Ashkana herself! I must be soaking up your knowledge and wisdom like a piece of cloth in a puddle. You'd better be careful, or Ravin will be kneeling at my feet in amazement at my wisdom!' She chuckled again. I was still unsure, but I could see no way out of it and so we agreed I would ask Ravin to wait with me for them after the next day at the Tower of the Wise so that they could meet, and that we would plan to meet again to eat together, perhaps on the next Day of Light.

It had taken us all some time to understand how the days were managed here in Kashiq. They had the same names for the days as we did in Oramia, but that seemed to be the only similarity. There was one Day of Light each week, and it always fell on the same day of Aureus. In Oramia, each day was linked to a colour and a scent, with which to glorify the Goddess, and each week a different day was chosen as a special day of worship, so that each might take their turn to be special. Here in Kashiq, one day was set aside for the praise of all the gods and goddesses. All stopped work on that day and made their way at a time of their choosing to the Place of Prayer, where they would approach the God under whose guidance they worked and offer prayer and praise and make offerings. These were received in turn by the Guided of Asmara, whose work it was to tend for the Places of Prayer, to keep them clean, to tidy them and to ensure a quiet reflective atmosphere. The rest of the day was left free to spend with family or friends, perhaps in one of the large walled gardens of Arbhoun, or in one of the six orchards which encircled Arbhoun or in doing things at home. Even the markets were not open on that day, which I had found very annoying when I first realised it was the case. It meant that one had to plan for one's food, and I had never been particularly good at that. Luckily, Tarik was a great planner, and after that first time, always went to the market on the day of Flammeus to select our food for the next day. Without our garden in Gabez, there was precious little to keep us going, save what we traded for, except for dates and oranges which grew in abundance on every street.

'Have you found out any more about where the Orange might be, Talla?' asked Tarik, breaking into my thoughts. 'We have been here some time now, and although we now know much more about what the orange looked like and how it was made, we still have no idea about where Lord Rao sent the pieces. You found that scroll which said that he had placed them in the safekeeping of those who would hurt any that tried to remove them, but has there been no further clue? It sounds as if they will be well guarded so they may be locked in a secret room surrounded by soldiers. If they are, we may as well give up now, and return to Ambar empty handed. We will not be risking our lives for him just so that he might turn the head of Lunaria towards him once again. I do not myself think that it can be a true love, if it needs a trinket to evoke it, but we did give Ambar our word that we would try, and so we shall. I just wish we knew more.'

I felt slightly guilty. In truth, I had not been paying as close attention to the scrolls as I should have been, knowing what we needed to find out. I had been swept along by Ravin's enthusiasm for finding out more about how the Orange of Kashiq was made and had let my own objectives fall behind. Tarik had reminded me that there was one other scroll which had been scribed at the same time as that one which he referred to, and by the same scholar. This scholar, Finzari, was fond of riddles and puzzles, and never quite putting things down plainly so that they could be properly understood. I think he thought he was cleverer than everyone else, and it pleased him to make little word jokes, and even to add in tiny drawings between his scribings to give little clues away. It had been in a scroll which Ravin was examining, but he soon cast it off because it had nothing in it which he could copy for his immaculate drawings and notes about the construction of the Orange. I had not closely examined the scroll as it had been near to the time that Ravin and I went into the garden to eat our meal, and so I had relied on him to tell me what was in it. I resolved to request the Finzari scroll the next day and see for myself. I could not decide whether I needed to tell Ravin more about our quest or less or what impact it might have on our relationship if he knew that I had not told him everything. Truly my mind turned in circles, this way and that, trying to see a clear path before me, but all was unknown. There was no scroll to tell me how to act in this circumstance.

# CHAPTER 13

I think I understand how the Orange worked,' whispered Ravin to me, excitedly, as I stood at my scribing board, trying to decipher the ornate curlicues of the calligraphy of Scholar Finzari. I looked up, tempted away from my work by his obvious excitement and the glow of satisfaction in his eyes. Ravin loved what he did. There was a simmering joy in him which almost reminded me of the simmering rage which still built up in the emberjar of my own mind. The more time I spent with him, the more my anger diminished and the calmer and lighter I felt. It was hard then, and remains hard now, for me to know what it was exactly that made us fit together so well. What is it about one person which suddenly illuminates our world? I only knew that he made me feel buoyant and free, like a flower floating on a flowing stream.

'Tell me about it when we go into the garden,' I suggested, quietly, aware of the sharp eyes of the daily scholar watching us. The scholars did not approve of discussion within the scribing room, and I could understand why. If everyone started talking at the same time, it would be a cacophony and trying to read or scribe a difficult passage needed quiet concentration. Ravin smiled, his lips parting over his teeth and his eyes wrinkling at the corners and slowly closed one eyelid. It was a trick which never failed to amuse me, and which I had tried many times before, but I could not make only one of my eyes close in such a way.

149

'Shall we go now?' he asked. Again, the scholar glared at us and, to prevent him calling us to his table to be admonished and possibly have our scrolls taken away for the day, I rose, leaving Finzari's scroll on my board. We left the Tower of the Wise through the eastern door and strolled across the courtyard to the area where the date palm trees grew. The cool white clay benches were there and there was a faint underscent of some kind of woody herb. There were less people in the Eastern garden than in the Western one where Ravin and I had shared our first kiss. I was uncomfortable with other people being near us or watching us when we spoke, and Ravin laughed at my propriety, telling me that there was nothing more natural than that he should be enjoying the time he spent with a lovely young woman like me. He charmed me with his sweet words, I will admit. It had also been something that Ambar was practiced at; the ability to give compliments, but whereas Ambar used his compliments and his honeyed tongue to get what he wanted from people, I had never seen Ravin say anything similar to anyone else. He did not allow the compliments to flood out, nor use them to get his own way, but simply expressed them as though they were a truth.

We sat on the bench, and he laid his arm along the back of the bench, encircling my shoulders and pulled me with a gentle pressure to sit closer to him, despite the warmth of the midday sun. I leaned against his shoulder and shut my eyes, breathing in his scent. He wore a perfumed oil on his beard as many Kashiqi men did. Even Tarik had asked Achillea if he should get some for himself, and she had mixed a few drops of scented oils together to make him a light scent of lemon and lavender. And now, in the same way that I used to associate a day with a scent in Oramia – and still did, for that matter – I associated Ravin's scent with him. There was the familiarity of cinnamon in there, but also a stronger, sharper scent perhaps frankincense, and then a sweet, musky smell like a ripe fig. His hand which rested on my shoulder moved upwards and suddenly tweaked my orange netela so that it fell off my shoulders. He grabbed it playfully from me and dangled in front of me.

'What will you give me for this fine netela?' he asked, his eyes twinkling. 'It is of exceedingly high quality and very stylish. All the fine ladies of Kashiq wish they had such a thing! Let me see.... I know the exact price for you, madam. It will cost you one perfect kiss to get it back!' And before I could respond in any way, he pulled the netela over both our heads so that we were enclosed by it, and the light shining through it was a suffused dark saffron. He kissed me, gently at first and then with increasing passion, and our lips both parted and we became as one, tasting each other, almost trying to step inside one another's minds and bodies. I wished that we could go somewhere where we could be alone together. Achillea and Tarik spent time together behind their curtain at night-time in our dwelling and where once it had not bothered me, now I tried to leave them alone more in the evenings, taking long walks as the sun set so that they could love each other without concern. Perhaps if they liked Ravin then he could come to our dwelling more, and perhaps they would take their own sunset walk one day and leave us alone together. When Ravin and I kissed it truly felt as if we were but one person with the same mind.

Later, after we had eaten and before we had to go back into the Tower, I told Ravin that Achillea and Tarik wished to meet him after we finished for the day. He looked at me, his dark eyes tinged with concern. 'Should I be worried? Are they angry with me that I cannot resist you? I have tried not to do anything ... untoward –

though it is increasingly difficult.' His eyes lightened as he smiled again at me. I explained to him that they merely wanted to meet the one who made me smile so much more. I did not want him to feel as if he were being assessed for his suitability, although it felt like that to me. Then I recalled the rest of my conversation with them and thought of what my original aim was in going to the Tower of the Wise in the first place, and asked Ravin if he had come across any clues as to the whereabouts of the pieces of the Orange of Kashiq while he was trying to work out how it was designed and made.

'No. But then, I haven't been looking for them,' he answered, reasonably. 'What I really want to do is to understand how Lord Rao made the Orange so that it could open and close, and how it could be split into pieces by the Lady Ashkana without being broken.'

I looked at him, a little puzzled. 'But how do you know it was not broken? I thought we just knew that it was in pieces, not that they were pieces that could be easily fixed back together.' My heart had begun to race a little, quite separately from how it always raced when Ravin was there. I realised that because I had always been purposely unclear with Ravin what my interest was, that there were things he may have read in the scrolls he had seen which could be significant to our search for the actual Orange itself, so that we might find it and take it to Ambar to present to the Queen, Lunaria.

'I read it in one of the scrolls I saw, I think before I met you, for I had been here some months already when you arrived like the bright sun in the dark Tower of the Wise. It was scribed by that one you are reading at the moment, Scholar Finzari, in another scroll which I found wrapped round one I was looking at which dealt with the metalworking which could have been used for the Orange. He was quite certain in his scribing that the pieces which had been returned to Lord Rao by Ashkana were returned whole and unbroken. Perhaps even in her grief she did not wish to completely break their love. But Finzari only mentions six pieces, all the same, and the other scrolls I have found from earlier, when Lord Rao designed and made the piece, talk about seven pieces. I think this seventh piece must be the piece which holds them all together, and there is precious little scribed about it.'

So now I knew that there were six whole pieces of the Orange of Kashiq which had been separated from the seventh and returned to Rao here in Arbhoun, and that he had hidden those pieces somewhere safe and well protected, according to Finzari's other scroll. I felt a rush of increased interest in our quest, such as I had not felt before. I could also see a way in which we could all help one another if we were able to trust in Ravin. I felt like I trusted him implicitly already, but the words of Tarik and Achillea had lodged in my mind, glowing like a hot coal. They needed to see and meet Ravin to know if he could be trusted with being told more, and I knew it was not simply my choice about what to tell him. There was much, after all, which I had not told him and there was much he had not told me. I resolved to try to find out more, not only about Finzari and the location of the six parts of the Orange but also about Ravin himself. He had not spoken much about his family, saying only that he came from a village in the far south of Kashiq and had travelled many months to reach Arbhoun some years before. I knew he lived in a dwelling on the south side of Arbhoun. He shared his dwelling with the man who owned it, a man in his Seventh Age who could not do the more physically demanding tasks anymore. In return for his room, Ravin would do those tasks for the man, whose name was Shafir: carrying wood and pots from the market, maintaining the dwelling, collecting, and moving the jars of water and so on. Shafir was a wood carver, a craftsman under Maliq, and he continued to carve the wooden boxes and screens for which he was well known in Arbhoun. He traded well for them and lived comfortably, trading with Ravin for occasional scribing and reading tasks. It seemed to suit them both.

'You seem to be deep in thought,' said Ravin, breaking into the path of my mind. 'Is it something I can help you with?'

I did not want to speak falsely to Ravin. I wanted him to know and understand me even more, but I worried about it, and so I answered him with a step to the truth; it was true but did not explain everything that we were here in Arbhoun for.

'I think I need to read more scrolls scribed by Scholar Finzari,' I replied firmly. 'I have become much interested in his accounts of the Orange of Kashiq, and I wonder if he may have scribed the exact place where the pieces of the Orange were hidden. But Finzari is clever in his scribing and dresses everything up in layers of words, so it will be difficult to tell if he scribes the truth or if he merely plays games. But just imagine,' I turned to Ravin, suddenly excited for him, rather than for myself, 'If we did find the pieces, you could understand how it really worked!'

Ravin looked at me curiously. 'Well, indeed I could, although I suspect that if anyone heard about it, it would be taken away from me very quickly. The Defenders of Yael may search for the Orange too. They already possess great power, since they decide and preside over matters of death, but they seek yet more and might think to preside over matters of love too. However, if Scholar Finzari interests you so much, I will be sure to give you anything I can find which is scribed by him or about him. On one condition...'

'What is that?' I asked, a little nervously, wary of making bargains I could not keep, even if it was with Ravin.

'That you look after me and protect me from these frightening friends of yours that I am to meet!' He laughed. 'Why, it worries me more than an encounter with the Defenders, to meet these fearsome guards! What will they ask me, or be watching me for? What shall I say to them to make them like me, so that I can spend more time with you?'

We laughed together. It was one of the things which I most enjoyed about being with Ravin; he laughed so freely, and we often laughed at the same time and for the same reason. Laughter was not evident in the Temple in Oramia where I grew up. Childish giggles and light heartedness ended with the First Age, and from then on, we were encouraged not to waste time in laughter but to work and to glorify the Goddess. We had all we needed to live in the Temple; food, water, clothing, our own dormit to sleep in. We could bathe every day and improve our working abilities but there was little joy, despite the Priestesses telling us that the Goddess brought joy. I felt closer to the Goddess when I laughed with Ravin or with Achillea and Tarik than I ever did in the Temple.

I decided to copy Finzari's scribing as far as I could, and, when we went back into the Tower, I began to scribe the scroll I had been working on. He had ornamented his scroll around the edges with plants and flowers whose elaborate, curling tendrils and leaves edged towards his scribing. To complete the scene, which I must admit was distracting me from the wording in the same cunning way that the Scrolls of Choice did back in the Temple, he had drawn tiny flying creatures. I peered at them more closely, struggling to make them out as the sun had moved away from the pierced wooden window near where I worked. But the light was going, and it was time to return the scrolls to the Scholars for safekeeping. If you wanted to re-examine a scroll on the next day, you had to tie on your name paper as you handed it back, and the scholar would place it ready in a basket for the following day. I rolled it up and tied on the name and accompanied Ravin back to the Scholar to return the day's scrolls.

'Finzari, eh?' Scholar Mazin looked up with alacrity. 'An interesting choice. Finzari was a true scholar of Kashiq, and a fascinating character. I studied his poems and tales myself. There is also a scroll which details his life, back in the days of Lord Rao, if you might be interested.' His small black eyes glinted beneath his bushy eyebrows, and I could see that he had a great interest in this subject.

'I would be most grateful, Scholar Mazin,' I replied, casting my eyes to the floor in respect. 'I am indeed finding his scribing interesting and would like to see these other scrolls.' Mazin made a note. The Scholars here had a sort of shortened way of scribing which reminded me of the silent language of the OutRiders. It was somewhat like ordinary scribing, but they omitted certain characters and changed others. Just like the silent language, it was something I longed to learn for myself. Ever since I had taught myself how to scribe and to read, I had had a fascination for these other ways in which people communicated other than by speaking. Ravin left his scrolls, all of which he had finished with, in the appropriate baskets for the Scholars to replace the next day, and we walked out of the Tower of the Wise together.

Achillea and Tarik were waiting for us, standing under a tree at the corner of the street. The orange sand skittered along the way, blown by the evening breeze. Achillea had clearly taken the trouble to wear her nicest robe and her face was gleaming. Tarik always said that this glowing exterior was Achillea's kind heart shining through. Although I agreed with him about Achillea having a kind heart, I knew it was somewhat more to do with the liberal amount of scented salve which she applied to her face twice a day. Tarik looked much the same as usual, his clothes neat but unremarkable. He had acquired a simple headdress and band to wear while we were in Kashiq, which made it easy for him to blend into the crowds here in Arbhoun. I recalled how easily he and Ambar had done the same thing in Oramia, changing their appearance in subtle ways so that they blended in and yet were unobtrusive. I led Ravin over to them, feeling unsettled.

Ravin touched his middle finger formally to his heart and then to his forehead in greeting, in the manner of all Kashiqis. In Oramia a formal greeting consisted of saying 'I greet you' but here in Kashiq there was this wordless acknowledgement of the presence of another before one spoke. Benakiell had explained it to us as we first walked into Kashiq from Oramia. He had no doubt learned about it from Shira. I wondered what he was doing and when he might eventually arrive in Arbhoun, for it had now been some weeks since he had returned to Rishkar. He had told us that the simple gesture referred to first the heart of the person and then to their mind, indicating a willingness for friendship. It was an easy enough movement to learn and it was certainly helpful in all the trading we had to do here in Arbhoun. Tarik returned the gesture but Achillea being Achillea forgot all about it and merely offered her beaming smile to Ravin, turning her large owlish eyes on him excitedly.

157

'At last, we can meet Ravin! We have heard so much about you from Talla here!' she exclaimed.

'Really?' Ravin looked at me, amused. 'I cannot quite see Talla telling long stories about me around the fireside; it does not sound like her.' In that moment, I felt how well Ravin knew that I would not spend long hours talking about him to others because it was not my nature. He had spotted Achillea's mischief making straight away and adroitly stepped aside from it. Tarik grinned and took hold of Achillea's hand lovingly.

'Achillea is perhaps exaggerating,' he murmured. 'Talla has told us very little in words about you, Ravin, for, as you obviously know, she is not given to idle chatter. However, we have noticed the things she has told us not in her words but in how she acts since she first met you. Talla has not always been given to smiling, and yet she has competed with Achillea in recent days.' He stroked Achillea's forearm affectionately. 'We look forward to finding out more about you, for Talla is very dear to us both. You are welcome to join us for some food at our dwelling. It will be good to talk.' And Tarik then repeated the gesture of greeting, but in reverse, touching first his head and then his heart, as if to reinforce the presumption of friendship. I was intrigued, for I had never seen this before, at least not in the Tower of the Wise, but Ravin acknowledged it by repeating the gesture, and we all turned to walk down to the dwelling.

Achillea was irrepressible and chattered happily all the way back to our dwelling. We had not lived there long enough to call it home and it was a basic place in which to live, but there was room for us all there, and in the small courtyard at the back of it were some palm mats to sit on and a low wooden table on which to put the food. My original worries began to ebb away, and I relaxed into the evening. When Achillea and Tarik rose to go and cook the flatbreads and serve the goat stew that Tarik had made, Ravin moved closer to me and stroked the back of my neck, under my netela.

'I like your friends,' he said. 'They are watching me and asking me careful questions to try to see if I am a good enough man for you.'

'Do you not find it annoying?' I asked, for I myself had got a little tired of all the carefully worded questions and veiled references that Achillea and Tarik had clearly discussed between themselves before we had met them.

'No. It is only a sign of how much they value you, as I do myself. For you are, after all, a woman of great worth. I only hope that they will judge me to be of adequate value to court you; I would be terrified of them both if they found me wanting!' He looked into my eyes, his own eyes now serious and without their customary teasing glint. 'Ah, Talla. I never felt the way I do about you for any other. When I see you, it is as if the stars singing in my heart. You make me feel strong and clever and somehow, almost invincible!' The warmth of his words melted into me and I turned to kiss him. Sometimes I could not put into words how Ravin made me feel and kissing him was one way in which I felt like he knew what I wanted to say. I, who prided herself on her careful use of words was fumblingly inarticulate when it came to expressing myself to him. But he did not mind.

There was a loud cough from Achillea as she walked back into the courtyard while we kissed, and we scrambled apart as she bent to sit down with the flatbreads. She poked me in a deliberate gesture as Gladia would have done had she been there and I could barely contain my laughter as she met my eyes, her own sparkling and happy. I realised at that moment how much she meant to me too. Not in the same way as Ravin did, but in a different way. She loved me and wanted to see me happy in the same way that she was happy with Tarik. It would be a good evening.

# CHAPTER 14

F inzari is the name of the Scholar, much beloved by Lord Rao. It is said that Lord Rao himself learned to read and scribe at the knee of Finzari and held him in great respect until the end of Finzari's life. It was to Finzari that Lord Rao turned when the great love between him and Lady Ashkana came to an end, and it was the scrolls of Finzari which comforted and gave wisdom to Lord Rao throughout his life. For it is truly said that those who know wisdom and scribe it can share of that wisdom even after death.'

The following morning, I continued to read the scroll which Scholar Mazin had found and given me triumphantly, along with an assortment of scrolls of poetry and short stories and other assorted texts relating to him. It had been hard to get away from Mazin, who was much enamoured of Finzari's scribing and life, and perhaps saw me as a new acolyte for Finzari. He urged me to read all the scrolls carefully, for, he said, there was distilled wisdom in almost every word Finzari scribed. This, I doubted. Finzari wrote in an overly complicated style with explanations of explanations until my head spun with it all. However, now that I knew that Finzari was such a key person in the life of Lord Rao and that he had been involved in the construction of the Orange (and therefore possibly in its safeguarding after its return by Ashkana), I was resolved to search out every clue.

Ravin was not at the Tower that day since he had to do some tasks for Shafir, the man he dwelt with. I missed him and wished he were there, but I also knew that I would work harder and with more concentration if he were not there and resolved to have some real information to report back to Achillea and Tarik. I turned back to the heavily ornamented scroll I had been reading the previous day to examine it again. I was weary of the scroll which detailed the life of Finzari and from which I had learned little of interest to me. I lifted the other scroll up towards the light, recalling that previously I had struggled to see what the tiny flying creatures were. On closer inspection, I discovered that they were bees. Finzari had drawn little swarms of bees throughout his scribing, with single bees appearing to land on certain words. I remembered that Finzari was celebrated as one who liked to scribe in puzzles and riddles and felt a pulse of excitement. It felt to me like a message, that there were bees on this scroll.

Here in Arbhoun, there were many less opportunities for me to observe the bees. My own bees were far away in Gabez and I missed my quiet times in the garden as I tended to the flowers, their source of life, and to the hives. I often found that when I had a problem or was angry or irritable that if I went to sit next to the hives and laid my hand on the wood of the hive, that the almost imperceptible humming carried through the wood into me and I felt at peace and ready once more for the vagaries of life. There were many beehives in Arbhoun, but they were all sited in the orange and lemon and apricot orchards which surrounded the city. It was traditional in Kashiq for the bees to be in hives in orchards of trees. It was much hotter and drier than Oramia away from the settlements which were all built around abundant springs and wells of water and so there were less flowers growing, except in the gardens such as the ones which surrounded the Tower of the Wise. Those we would call Beeguards in Oramia were like farmers here, efficiently harvesting their honey. But the honey was very light; there was not much variation in colour or consistency, and the treasured white honey which we used in our salves seemed not to be made by the bees here. Although I did not bear the mark of the bee as Lunaria did, I had always felt their importance in my life, and if ever I felt that the Goddess was guiding me, it was through the bees. I began to read the scroll again, making careful notes of the words or letters which the tiny drawn bees seemed to perch on. It was a long scroll, closely scribed. At first, I wrote down the words on which the bees were found, but soon realised that it was a list of no meaning, a jumble of random words. I sighed in exasperation and started again, this time noting the exact letter they seemed to touch on each line.

'them
ostprec
iouso
range
ofallisf
oundin
thekee
pingoft
hesegu
ardsalla
round
arbhoun...'

I looked up as I got to the end of the scroll and saw Scholar Mazin heading determinedly towards me, his body so round that it bumped the scribeboards as it passed them. I hastily placed my own scroll behind the one which I had been using the previous day to copy out the words of Finzari and rolled up the scroll I had just finished with.

'Ah, Talla, isn't it? I have come to see how you are enjoying the words of the great Finzari. Is he not a true and wonderful scholar? Have you learned much from him already?' His eyes drifted away, perhaps pondering the times when he discovered these scrolls for himself. I wanted to find out more, and I very much wanted to look at the letters I had scribed, but I also did not want his suspicions to be raised at all that I might be searching for something forbidden. I quickly asked him what he would recommend, in his capacity as an expert on Finzari. He preened himself as I described him as an expert using that slightly breathless tone which Achillea had been known to use to get her own way.

'Well, I am not an expert scholar like Finzari himself, but, yes, I do have some expertise,' he conceded smugly. 'For a beginner reader such as you, I would recommend his Poems of the Trees collection and perhaps his Tales of the Orchard to accompany it.' I kept my eyes to the floor until I had dulled the spark of anger I had felt at being considered a beginner reader, and then raised them gratefully up to him and simpered that I would indeed take great pleasure in learning not only from the great thoughts of Finzari, but from the recommendations of Scholar Mazin. He patted me gently on my hand as he left, promising to find me the scrolls he had mentioned. I was glad that Ravin had not been here to witness this even if it had achieved my aims.

I pondered what I knew so far. I knew that we were searching for seven separate pieces of the Orange of Kashiq, and that six of them had been returned intact to the Lord Rao by Ashkana. If we could find these pieces, we might be able to work out what piece was missing from the study that Ravin had done on how the Orange was made. We knew that the pieces of the Orange had been placed in safe, secret, guarded places by Rao, and I suspected that Scholar Finzari knew where the pieces had been hidden (and had possibly hidden them himself) and could not resist leaving clues as to their whereabouts. I believed I had found a secret message contained within his scribings, and possibly there might be more in his other works.

I was slowly getting used to the Kashiqi way of using scribing as a means not only of communicating facts, but also of communicating feelings, and of conveying messages through instructive and amusing stories and poems. I thought of the songs which Achillea loved to sing, and how it might be interesting to scribe them one day, so that others might learn them. But for that to happen, more would need to learn the art of scribing and reading in Oramia and that seemed unlikely when they were used to keep a firm hold on power as they were now. I glanced around the room and saw, with relief, that Scholar Mazin was now hoisting himself up from his cushioned perch and preparing to leave the Tower. The Scholars stayed in their position for half of the day and were then permitted to work in the workrooms upstairs where they could work in peace, away from the bustle of the main room. He was being replaced by Scholar Avenda.

Scholar Avenda was a tall, angular woman. She had an interest in counting and calculation, and in designing patterns of regular shapes, I had seen some of her drawings, where she had made identical shapes fit together in new and intriguing patterns, and then painted them in two or three different colours to give different effects. It reminded me a little of my pounced embroidery patterns which I used to make for Gladia. My way of doing it had involved making the pattern once and then tracing over it many times, whereas Avenda used a measuring stick to make her patterns. She was not a

Scholar who talked a great deal, unlike Mazin, and she sat at the Scholar's scribeboard and administered to the students efficiently and then returned to her patterning. It would be safe now to return to the letters I had copied out.

At first, the letters from the scroll did not make sense to me, and I wondered if I had been wrong about the deliberate way in which the bees had been posed on the scroll. Then I spotted that the final letters spelled Arbhoun. I wrote this word down at the bottom of the plant parchment piece I was using for my notes. I looked again at the letters but could only see the further words 'range', 'them' and 'round'. Exasperated, I counted how many letters were in each of the words off each line of the scribing, but they varied from five letters on one line to eight letters on another. So, I scribed all the letters out, one next to the other, in a long string. I turned the plant parchment around so that it lay longways on my scribeboard and began to patiently scribe the letters again. I could scribe much more quickly now that I had a metal nibbed pen, and a ready clay vessel of ink instead of the carved reed pens and berry inks I had used in Oramia, but even so, scribing in ink still required you to pause after each letter to allow the ink to dry; there were times when I still longed for a slender twig of charcoal to scribe with. Finally, I looked down at what I had scribed on the parchment.

'themostpreciousorangeofallisfoundinthekeepingofth eseguardsallaroundarbhoun'

Immediately I could see what Scholar Finzari had scribed:

'The most precious orange of all is found in the keeping of these guards all around Arbhoun.'

Disappointed, I leaned back. We already knew that the Orange was in the safekeeping of guards. This had not helped in the slightest and had been a waste of my time. Then I read it again and saw that the clue was there, in front of me. Finzari had used the word 'these' to describe the guards. That must mean some guards in particular, possibly mentioned in the scroll. But there had been no mention of any guards in the scroll. And then it came to me. Finzari was talking about the bees. When he said 'these guards' he meant the tiny drawings of the bees which swarmed over his scroll and had directed me to the hidden letters. He meant that they were both the guards of the secret on the scroll and their guards in real life. The bees guarded 'the most precious orange' from any who might seek to find them, and the bees were found in the six orchards which ringed the city of Arbhoun. It was to these that we needed to go to seek the pieces of the Orange of Kashiq.

My heart was thudding in my chest, and I looked around to ensure that my excitement was not obvious to any other. Luckily, there was nobody working right next to me since of course Ravin was away and the student behind me had just left to go and get another scroll. I folded the piece of plant parchment up into a small wad and then rolled up the scrolls on my scribeboard neatly, before picking up my wrapped food and exiting to the Eastern gardens. I stopped to use the wastepits on my way out, taking the chance to put the small wad of plant parchment into my underpocket. In Oramia this hung under my robe, and here in Kashiq, many wore something similar between their upper robe and their loose trousers. I, however, kept mine under my trousers which were loose enough not to show where it might hang. Once I had tied it in firmly, I washed my hands using the tall earthenware jug of water poured over my hands and into a larger clay pot. This water in turn was taken to the gardens to water the plants and flowers.

As I ate my meal abstractedly, I thought about what my next steps should be. I needed to discuss this information with Achillea and Tarik, and we needed to discuss what to do next. I also wanted to tell Ravin about what I had found out. It was hard to know whether to share this with Achillea and Tarik or just to go on my own feelings and tell him first. If my conclusion was correct, and it was in the orchards which surrounded Arbhoun that the six returned pieces of the Orange might be found, then I would need to find out more about the orchards and where the hives were kept. I could not think how it would be possible that the pieces of the Orange, however small they might be, to remain hidden for so long without being accidentally discovered. I decided to try to find out more at the Tower of the Wise first, and then to go to the evening markets and see what I could glean from the honey sellers there.

I returned some scrolls and requested two further scrolls from Scholar Avenda, who sighed with scarcely concealed irritation and got up to go and fetch them. While she was gone, I looked over to her scribeboard where she was working on a regular pattern, perhaps of clay tiles for a floor. It was comprised of three-sided shapes which fitted together in various cunning patterns, including one which looked like the six-sided shape of the beehive. It was made from six shapes itself, with the sharp pointed ends all together in the middle. She had coloured each shape in either red or orange and it made a pleasing design. Avenda glared at me when she returned and thrust the scrolls into my hands.

'No more scrolls today, I am too busy,' she said and turned abruptly back to her drawings. At least I had managed to get two scrolls I wanted, but I was nonetheless irked by her attitude towards me. I turned on my heel and swept back to my scribeboard wordlessly.

When I put the scrolls down, I looked back to her scribeboard, but she was already engrossed in her work, so I unrolled the first scroll and tried to emulate her.

The first scroll told me much of what I wanted to know about how the orchards and hives in Kashiq were used. Those who grew the fruit trees in the orchards knew that they needed the bees to have good harvest of sweet fruit, and the bees had an abundance of flowers to visit when the fruit trees were in bloom, so the growers planted several types of different trees which all flowered at slightly different times, and then also planted the orchard with low scrubby bushes of sage and thyme which did not need much water to grow. This made the bees happy to stay in their own orchard and to make honey. However, it appeared that the hives were not hung from the trees as they were in Oramia, because if they had been, it might have interfered with the harvesting of the oranges and apricots and so on. Instead, they rested on the ground and were made of clay rather than being carved out of old tree trunks. There was plenty of clay around Kashiq and not so many trees which could be cut down, so it made sense.

The scroll was rather vague about many of the details of the hives and was clearly scribed for someone who knew little about bees, as it concentrated more on the trees than on the hives. It did confirm to me, however, that there were six orchards which surrounded Arbhoun and that they had been there for many ages, since before the age of Rao.

The other scroll was a short piece but was more interesting to me since it described an aspect of the hives which I had not seen so detailed before; that they were capped at both ends by a flat disc and, rather fancifully, one end was designated the working door and the other was called the picture door. The owner of the orchard or the beekeeper only accessed the hive through the working door, which could be moved away to remove the honeycomb frames which were made of wood and fixed to a frame which could be easily pulled out. The working door was constructed from a wooden lattice. The picture door, on the other hand, was made of glazed clay, and decorated with patterns or sometimes the name of the beekeeper's family. The scholar who had scribed the scroll had drawn some pictures of designs they had seen on these picture doors and they included regular patterns such as those which interested Avenda and pictures of people, animals, and plants.

We had not visited any of the orchards around Arbhoun. It was not the season for harvesting fruit which was the usual time when the inhabitants of Arbhoun went to the orchards, to trade for the fresh delicious fruits, and we had no need to go there. However, now that I felt I had established where the pieces of the Orange of Kashiq might have been hidden, I needed to go to them, if only to be able to see for myself. I resolved to suggest this to Achillea and Tarik, and to Ravin. It would be a pleasant way to spend the next Day of Light.

# CHAPTER 15

I
t was Aureus – or rather, the Day of Light, as it was better known in Kashiq. I had come to appreciate this tradition of having one special day in the week which could be assigned to the Goddess or whoever your guiding god was. In truth, this was a question which perturbed me, for it had been easier to simply assign everything to the Goddess than to try to work out where my highest loyalty should lie.

In the end, I was guided by what was normal in Kashiq and considered myself under the guidance of Rao, like Ravin. Perhaps there was an element too of me wanting to be in the same place as him, and to be heading towards the same goals. But there was also a part of me which reserved itself for Ashkana and of course for Asmara the Goddess. Tarik and Achillea did not seem to hold the same sort of allegiances that I had; Achillea was drawn toward Soren, the Goddess of healing and love. It was Soren who guided those who made and administered physics and healing tonics such as we made. She also guided all those who healed in other, less obvious ways – for instance, those who in Oramia would be called Songmakers were, in Kashiq, under Soren because they healed hearts, as Ravin described it. Tarik placed himself under Maliq, the one who guided craftspeople. Tarik was very gifted with making Physics, but it was a mechanical job to him, one which he had learned for its usefulness when he was an OutRider. But when he crafted things, especially anything using metals, his eyes would come alight much as Ravin's did when he talked about drawing

171

out the plans for making some device or other. He spent a lot of time with the metalworkers near the market on the northern side of Arbhoun and was beginning to trade for small items made of scraps of metal he had traded other things for.

We had arranged to meet Ravin at the Place of Prayer close to the orchard on the southern side of Arbhoun. It was the closest of the Places of Prayer to an orchard and so it would not be difficult for us to enter the orchard with our midday meal and sit on a cloth under the orange trees and take a look at the beehives there. I had shown Achillea and Tarik what I had found out, and they thought that I might be right about the pieces of the Orange being hidden in an orchard and being protected by the bees, although whether they might still be there after all this time was unknown. All we could do was visit and see if it might be possible. I told Ravin too, but he seemed somewhat less convinced that the pieces would still be there, although happy to accompany us. I still had not told him anything of the reason why we were searching for the Orange, or indeed that we actually were searching for the Orange, allowing him to think, instead, that it was a whim of mine to have studied it and that I had been partly inspired by him, and wanting to find the Orange for him. I worried that he would try to stop us if he found out, and I also worried about all the things I would inevitably have to talk to him about if I began to explain the whole story. It was not that I did not want to tell him, more that I did not want anything to spoil the heady way in which I now felt about him. If we found any evidence that there were or could have been the six pieces of the Orange concealed there, I resolved to tell him the whole story.

The Place of Prayer was not very full. People came and went as they chose, and many chose to go early in the morning, or in the evening rather than close to midday as we had done. There was a sort of market underneath the main Place of Prayer. Those at the market traded small items for adorning the walls and tables of the gods and goddesses. These were then left as offerings, and then sorted and traded further by those who looked after the Places of Prayer, those under Asmara. They also sat at the market stalls and received the trades which people made for the small squares of embroidered cloths, the little oil lamps, the wooden boxes with scribed prayers inside, the lengths of bright flowers strung together, and the tiny clay figures tied with coloured threads which represented prayers. I had no inclination to trade for any of these things. Perhaps the ways of the Temple were too engrained in me, but the coloured cloths and scented oils we had used to glorify the Goddess seemed more meaningful to me. Besides, these items were simply tokens of what trades you had given for them, and what you traded for them denoted the amount of time they were left out for the gods or goddesses before they were collected up and returned to the trading areas. Achillea, on the other hand, was much enamoured of these tokens, and would always trade a small salve of ointment or scented oil for something, often for a clay figure and some threads which she would tie around it as prayers to Soren. She seemed to feel comforted by this and happily spent time at the place of Soren saying her prayers as she tied the threads. Tarik, I suspected, merely sat quietly at the place of Maliq, thinking through his plans and ideas for his crafting, and perhaps this was the same as prayer for it brought his mind closer to Maliq's.

Ravin and I walked up the single spiral staircase to the Place of Prayer behind Achillea and Tarik. There was a similar staircase which led down and meant there was no waiting for others to go in the opposite direction. The

Place of Prayer had six sides, and each side was dedicated to one of the Gods or Goddesses. The staircase emerged in the centre of the room and we headed towards the place of Rao and sat down on the low woven cushions near the offerings. The place of Rao had, like all the places of the gods and goddesses, a special focus. For those of Ashkana, there was a small statue of the Goddess, for Asmara a large earthenware pot with a tree and flowers planted in it. For Rao, there was, scribed on the whitened wall, a long prayer of gratitude and supplication, asking him for insight in our reading and our scribing and thanking him for the lives of those who in the past scribed their thoughts that they might live forever. It had become a habit for me, as it was for many of Rao, to read without speaking but merely moving one's lips the whole prayer. Today I was indeed grateful for the thoughts of those in the past, especially Finzari, and so I paid closer attention to my reading of the prayer than I usually did.

As we rose to leave, I glanced around me to see if Achillea and Tarik were still busy or if they had already left. Tarik had indeed gone; we would no doubt find him sitting under a date palm outside, whittling a small piece of wood as he waited. Achillea was standing in the place of Soren which reminded me a little of the Temple since it was decorated with coloured hangings and there was a small incense burner which wafted scents throughout the Place of Prayer. As I spotted her, she had been quietly conversing with another woman, but then just as I was about to wave over to her, she began to sing quietly. I had always loved to listen to Achillea sing. There was a purity and a clarity in her voice which somehow seeped through me and, just like the Empath Erayo, it seemed that Achillea's singing could take away your ills. I was too far away to hear the words clearly, and she was only singing softly, but I knew her voice. I stayed Ravin with a hand to his arm and he too stopped and listened as my friend sang. As the song ended, I realised that many other people had also stopped to listen. When she had finished, the woman she was with looked up and smiled in contentment and calm. We moved to go down the staircase and waited for Achillea at the bottom, where Tarik was indeed waiting and carving a small piece of wood into an ornate handle.

'Sorry if you have been waiting for me,' apologised Achillea, her face beaming and her wide eyes gazing blissfully past us.

'What has happened?' asked Tarik, who could see immediately that Achillea was full of joy and anticipation.

'The most wonderful thing! There was a woman there who had come to pray to Soren for healing of her mind's sadness. The only thing which had helped her in the past was to listen to the Song of Soren, for it filled her with light and hope. She asked if there was any there who could sing it for her, and there was nobody except me and I did not know all the words, although I have been trying to learn them, but she told me the words and I sang them for her, and she was blessed with peace afterwards.' Achillea's face shone and Tarik embraced her, moved by her emotion.

'She told me that my singing voice was so beautiful that I should become one of the Singers of Soren who are called upon to sing for healing! I did not even know there was such a thing. And imagine, here in Kashiq, I can be a Songmaker, whereas I could not in Oramia. I can sing as well as make salves and ointments and physics! The woman, called Parline, also told me who to go and see about singing in Arbhoun, and she gave me this as a token of her gratitude for my singing!' She opened her

175

hand and we saw in it a beautifully engraved silver disk with a loop at the top so it could be displayed or worn as a pendant. Tarik picked it up and scrutinised it carefully.

'This is a beautiful piece of jewellery. You could trade it for a great deal at the metal markets.' Achillea laughed. 'I will not trade this beautiful thing for it will remind me of a good day! But Parline told me that there are many who willingly trade well to listen to the healing power of Soren's Song!'

'I am proud of you,' said Tarik, embracing her again. 'My little nightingale.'

'I have always liked to listen to you sing, Achillea,' I said, in agreement. 'I remember telling you a long time ago that you should be a Songmaker. Perhaps I can copy some of the songs which are scribed on scrolls in the Tower of the Wise, and you could learn those.'

We walked out of the Place of Prayer and towards the track which led to the main way out of Arbhoun to the south and to the orchard situated on that southern side of the city. We could see the green area ahead of us and it reminded me of Oramia, with all its trees, and especially of the Osho mountains where I had visited the Empath Erayo. All the settlements in Kashiq were based around rivers or springs of water since the rest of the land was parched by the hot sun. Much of the land was an orange sandstone, with some darker stone outcrops and some lighter coloured hills of sand. The orchards which encircled Arbhoun were fed by channels which had been formed by the Kashiqis out of clay, and which were fed in turn by the spring of Arbhoun over on the east of the city. It was a mystery to me how the water bubbled up from deep under the land and came up here in this otherwise arid land. Maybe it somehow sensed a need within the land for water, or maybe it was the doing of the Goddess.

The orchard we arrived at was an apricot orchard, dedicated to Maliq, where those wonderful fruits which Benakiell had introduced me to only a few short months before were grown. The fruit had all been harvested by now, and the trees stood in rows, their trunks dark brown and pitted with age, with no leaves. Benakiell had told me how these fruit trees lost all their leaves as the cold season came, and then, with the Goddess's blessing came back to life again when the sun began to warm. Having heard many of Ravin's stories about the weather during the hottest times of the year, I was grateful that we had arrived in Kashiq when it was cooler. There was an archway through into the orchard, near which sat an old woman on a date palm mat under a ramshackle shelter to protect her from the sun. She wore a pair of blue trousers and a dark green tunic and headdress. She looked up at us as we came close, her already wrinkled skin furrowing with the effort of peering at us. I guessed she was not able to see very well and remembered the days when Maren had been unable to see. I called out a greeting to her, and relieved, she welcomed us, explaining that sometimes the sun got in her eyes and dazzled her. Achillea looked at her compassionately and asked her what she had for trade. The old woman's face brightened at the thought of a prospective trade and she indicated with her hand what she was trading. On the mat were various items relating to bees; there were simple earthenware jars containing honey from the orchard, small, polished honey spoons made of horn, rough lumps of beeswax, and a small heap of leathery, dried apricots.

'Is this your orchard?' asked Ravin. 'It must be a lot of work for one such as you.'

'It used to be mine,' replied the woman, a little sadly. 'But now, my two sons and their families oversee it for the city of Arbhoun. Our families have cared for the orchard for many ages; my father and my father's father before him all cared for the trees. Some of these trees are more than ten ages old, older than me!' She chuckled, evidently enjoying the interaction.

'Talla here looks after bees in our homeland of Oramia,' chirped Achillea, much to my annoyance. I had told Ravin that I worked with honey and beeswax in the making of the salves but had never fully talked to him about being a BeeGuard – if indeed that is what I was. He looked at me a little sharply, but curiously.

'Come and sit,' urged the woman. 'I am Farin. Take some of those dried apricots and eat with me, for there are precious few visitors at this time of year after the harvests, often it is only me and the bees.' We sat ourselves down, close to her mat and took out our food to share with her. The sharing of food was something I had grown to love since I had left the Temple. There, it had been seen simply as a means of fuelling activity, a necessary thing to do in order to work hard, and the food itself was boring and tasteless. Here in Kashiq, and in the Outer of Oramia, the sharing of food one with another was a symbol in itself. There was effort put into the making of the food, which I particularly appreciated, since I was not adept at making food, and there was a kindness and a care that came from people sharing what they had with you. Ravin and I shared our midday meal every day and it was one of the simplest and yet most fulfilling of pleasures. Farin enjoyed the small pieces of date and almond cake which Tarik had produced, and the oranges which Ravin and I carried and urged her dried apricots upon us. They were chewy, unlike the blissful succulence of the fresh one which Benakiell had first given me, but full of the same sweet, sharp taste.

At last, we got up and told Farin that we would like to walk round the orchard. She happily gave us permission to go where we wished, for there was nothing to take from this place.

'Come back after your walk and talk to me about the bees of Oramia,' she urged me. 'And I can tell you about mine.' Tarik looked thoughtfully at her shelter as we rose.

'Can I mend your shelter?' he asked politely. 'I have some skill in dwelling making, and there are holes and patches in your palm leaf roof which I can fix for you.' She gratefully accepted his offer, and he began to work on the shelter while we walked away to look around the orchard.

'So, tell me some more about these bees you look after, Talla,' suggested Ravin. Before I could open my mouth to say anything, and while I was still trying to formulate what to say, Achillea answered him in a burst of words.

'Oh, Talla is an amazing Beeguard! Do you know, she has never been stung by a bee? And yet she has looked after thousands of them. She looked after my mother's bees when she first came to Mellia and somehow she can make the bees produce the best, most valuable honey! And she never uses smoke or kills a single bee! I have seen her covered in bees and yet not even one of them stung her! It is like magic!' Her voice trailed away as she felt me glaring at her. I was angry with her and the spark in my mind's emberjar snapped and crackled into life. I wanted to scold her, but I didn't want Ravin to hear me do that because I was so worried that he would think ill of me. Achillea looked away at the trees and then continued, in a more subdued tone.

'I know that Talla is angry with me now for telling you about her gifts when she has evidently not told you about them herself. I did not mean to upset you, Talla. But I know you think she is wonderful, already, Ravin, and surely this just makes her even more wonderful?'

Ravin threw his head back and laughed aloud. 'I do indeed think she is wonderful, although I am not sure it is even possible for me to think her more wonderful. But I am intrigued, I must admit.' He turned to me and took my hand in his. It always made me feel comforted and protected when he did this. 'In the place where I grew up, down in the south of Kashiq, in Galdin, there were no orchards nor bees, and we rarely saw such things. Honey was something which was a precious trade, and we did not taste it often. When I came to Arbhoun, I saw bees properly for the first time, and of course tasted many more delights containing honey. Bees interest me greatly, for I have seen the way they build their honeycombs in such regular shapes, and it is amazing that they, with their tiny feet and mouths, can make such perfect shapes.'

I was surprised to hear him say this. If I had told him sooner about my love for the bees, we could have shared many more conversations and discussions about them and I could have shared something more of myself with him, but as it was, I had been fearful of showing myself to him. I resolved to try to be more open with him, but also to ask him more about his early life. I had thought he did not want to talk about it, since he did not often bring it up, but perhaps it was because I did not ask him. 'Many an answer waits only for a question' was written as part of the Meditation of Rao written at the Place of Prayer, and now I thought I understood what it meant. I smiled at Achillea to show her that I was no longer angry, and we continued over to the far edge of the orchard where we found the beehives.

The beehives were similar in shape to those we had in Oramia. They were long tubes, much like the hollowed-out logs which we strung up from the trees in Oramia for our bees. There, however, the similarities ended, for these hives were indeed made of clay. They had been made of rolled sheets of clay, a thumb's width thick, which had been rolled to make a hollow tube and then dried in the sun. At one end, there was a wooden disc with a handle, which presumably was the one described in the scroll I had read, which allowed the beekeeper to access the honey and the honeycomb frames from the hive. At the other end there was a glazed clay disc with a hole in the centre, or slightly to one side. Each hive had a disc with a different picture on it; there were leaves and flowers and animals of all sorts, as well as some which showed people doing various daily tasks. The discs were fixed on with clay so they could not be opened. Achillea looked at them all closely, exclaiming over the patterns which she particularly admired. As we looked, we could see that the bees entered the hives through the holes in the discs, almost as if they were doors of their own into their dwelling. Several bees flew in and out as we watched. I sat down and Ravin sat next to me. Achillea wandered off back towards Tarik and Farin. A bee landed next to us on an old branch from one of the apricot trees. We watched it as it crawled up and down the branch and I put my hand out to it. It crept on to my hand and I brought it up close to Ravin so that he could examine it more closely. He peered closely at it, marvelling at its yellow and black patterns and its fuzzy skin, its tiny legs and fragile wings.

'The Goddess excelled herself when she made this creature,' mused Ravin. 'It is cunning in every way; it works hard, it supports its fellow hive-dwellers, it can craft dwellings and protect itself and even make healing honey. Why, you could almost say all six of the Guides must have come together to make this one tiny thing!'

181

One of the things which I had grown to love in Ravin was the way in which he often seemed to say the things I had thought myself, but in such a clear and articulate way that made them instantly more comprehensible. I smiled at him and took in his smile back at me which warmed my mind's emberjar in quite a different way to the quick rush of heat I had felt with Achillea earlier and which had now completely dissipated.

'She was right, wasn't she, your friend Achillea?' Ravin commented. 'The bee does not sting you.'

'It would not sting you either, probably,' I answered carefully. 'Somehow they seem to know that I mean them no harm and so they do not harm me.'

'Do you think they might sting you if you tried to hurt them or to destroy their hive?'

I pondered. 'I cannot imagine doing that.' I confessed finally. 'There would be no reason to do that. Why would I wish to harm something which is not harming me? They allow me to gather their honey and do not complain at me when I do, for they know I will never take it all. I am comfortable with them, for they make few demands of me.'

Ravin smiled. 'Perhaps they think you as sweet as I do!' He placed his finger in the bee's path, trying to entice it onto his finger but the bee turned when it reached his finger and crawled back towards me before finally flying off and in through one of the holes in the beehive covers.

'Do you think the pieces of the Orange of Kashiq were hidden in the orchards? I am sure they were, but I cannot think how to find them, for the orchards are so big and there are five other orchards of the same size around Arbhoun. If there is one in each orchard it will take us years to try and find out. There must be a way to tell.'

'But if that were so, surely they might have been found by now?' said Ravin. 'That must be why they were hidden here so that nobody might ever find them again. The Lord Rao would not put them somewhere where they could be easily found, for he wanted to protect them, but at the same time he could not bear to see them, so he put them in the beehives to keep them safe but hidden.'

Then, I told him a little more of what I had found out from the scrolls of Finzari; the way in which he had left little clues and codes to where the pieces had been hidden. Why he had done it I could not tell; perhaps it was vanity on his part to think that he alone could understand his clues or perhaps it was a way of ensuring that somebody might one day find the pieces of the Orange if they were determined enough.

'Maybe there are more clues in the scrolls of Finzari you have not yet read,' said Ravin. I groaned. Reading all his scrolls would take as long as searching through all the beehives of Arbhoun. Then I remembered the other scrolls Scholar Mazin had recommended to me; The Poems of the Trees was one, but the other one was entitled Tales of the Orchard. That would be a good place to check and see if there might be any more small clues about the Orange of Kashiq. I told Ravin and he agreed with me, amused by my dedication to the task.

'Now, come along,' he teased, pulling me up. 'Why, I am getting quite jealous of all these competitors for your attention! Why, between the bees and the scrolls and Scholar Finzari and the delightful little Scholar Mazin, I begin to wonder if there is any space left in your heart for me, poor Ravin!'

He pulled a sad face and widened his eyes at me in an attempt to make me take pity on him. I laughed and pretended to turn away from him and he pulled me to him, and for a few moments I forgot all about the scrolls, the bees, the scholars, and the Orange of Kashiq.

# CHAPTER 16

Tales of the Orchard? The tedious tales of Finzari? Have you been persuaded into this by Scholar Mazin?' It was Scholar Avenda who looked up at me the following morning, scarcely able to conceal her scorn at my choice. 'Why do you not study and learn from one who can truly inspire you, one of the masters of design or pattern, or one who can describe why and how things work?' I gritted my teeth, once more annoyed by her superior attitude, and waited silently for the scrolls without responding to her question. 'Your eager follower does not follow all of your interests then, Ravin,' she continued, speaking over my head to Ravin, who stood behind me. She smiled widely at him, continuing to ignore me, and flicking one edge of her headdress to the side. 'Perhaps you should share your meal with me one day, and we could discuss some real learning.' Ravin reached his arm forward and ran his finger down to the base of my spine reassuringly.

'I think I am busy,' he replied airily. 'I have other more important things to discuss.' Scholar Avenda's face fell at his rebuttal and she handed me the scrolls I had requested: Tales of the Orchard and Poems of the Trees, as recommended by Scholar Mazin. Having felt distaste for Mazin and his gushing devotion to Finzari, I now felt that he was positively benign compared to Avenda who, it seemed, was more interested in Ravin than I had realised. It made me feel warm inside that he preferred me, the drab from the Temple to Avenda, the brilliant scholar who shared many of his own interests and was Kashiqi born.

I decided to start with Tales of the Orchard, since it directly related to the orchards where I was now sure we needed to look for the pieces of the Orange. It was a scroll with carved wooden spools, one at each end, around which one could roll the parchment. This one was not made of plant parchment which, while readily available in Kashiq, did tend to crack if it was rolled but rather of parchment and wound smoothly around the spools. Unfortunately, the last reader of the scroll had left it wound to the end rather than to the beginning of the stories, so I had to roll it back again so that I could start at the beginning. The scroll had been ornately illustrated, in the recognisable style of Finzari, his trees' branches extending into the parts where he had scribed the stories. I noted that each story had its own rather wordy title and each one ended with a picture. The stories were not long, and you could position the scroll on the winding spools so that you could see the whole thing in one go. I began to read.

The tales were rather obvious little stories with short lessons in them about the importance of things like trust or freedom or loss. Scholar Finzari had set all the tales in an orchard and most featured either the trees or the bees which lived there. Having read them, I was, truthfully, none the wiser. The stories reminded me of the tales we had been told by the Priestesses when we were in our First Age of childhood to illustrate some tenet or other of the Temple, or some aphorism of Ashkana, and from which we were meant to take instruction. But I was convinced that there was more to this than lay on the surface, and I began to look for points of similarity between the stories, aside from them all being set in an orchard. Below the title of each was a dedication, written in smaller script, almost appearing as an afterthought. Each story was dedicated to one of the six gods and goddesses of Kashiq. Each of the six orchards of Arbhoun came under the guidance of one of them. The one we had visited the day before, on Aureus, was dedicated to Maliq, I recalled. I was convinced now that each tale related to one of each of the orchards which enclosed Arbhoun like a green blanket, softening the harshness of the dry orange sand which lay beyond it.

I talked about it with Ravin later when we went to walk in the gardens and eat our food.

'The pieces of the Orange of Kashiq must have been hidden in the orchards,' I said, frustrated by my inability to see the clues clearly. 'But how can we ever find them, even if they are still there? With nothing clear to find, it is as if Finzari is playing games again with us, raiding our hopes and then dashing them again.'

Ravin frowned. 'Did you not say that the reason you thought the pieces of the Orange might be hidden in the orchards was because Finzari had pointed you in the direction of the bees? Could he have hidden the pieces in the beehives? You are a BeeGuard, so you will know better than I if something made of honeygold could be hidden in such a place for all these long years and never be found? Surely those who tend the bees and take the honey would have found them by now?'

'You must be right!' I looked at Ravin with respect, agreeing with his conclusion. 'Let me think how it could be hidden there without being found.' My hives in Oramia were old tree trunks, hollowed out and roughly shaped, with wooden access panels at either end for retrieving the honey. I felt sure that if a metallic piece of anything had been placed in them, then I would have found it by now, since both panels could be used to enter the hive. Here in Kashiq, however, only the back panel was made of wood and could be removed to access the honeycombs. The front panel was only really for the bees, with its circular entrance hole and its glazed pottery picture disc which was stuck on to the rolled cylinder clay which made up the body of the beehive. Perhaps the pieces of the Orange could be attached to this plate, for, unless the hive were broken, there would be no need to go into the hive that way, and it could not be removed in any case as it was stuck on. The only way into the hive would be through the wooden entrance at the back. I explained my thinking to Ravin.

'But there are hundreds of beehives in each orchard! We can't smash all the hives to try to find only six small pieces of honeygold!'

I cast my mind back over the scroll I had just been looking at. Six stories, six titles, six dedications. What had I missed? Of course, the clue was there. After each story, there was an illustration of a scene from the story. Each of them was drawn in a circular, embellished frame. What if these pictures were pictures of the beehive covers? What if these were the clues Finzari had left for us, with or without the knowledge of his master, Lord Rao? Suddenly I was eager to get back to the scroll to see if my idea could be right. Until I saw the pictures, I would not know for sure. Eagerly I explained my idea to Ravin, and we hurried through our meal, not lingering in our usual fashion to kiss or caress or be close to one another. And yet in that shared goal and interest there was true closeness for we moved and thought with a single aim.

I turned the scroll spindles slowly, stopping at the end of each little story to examine the picture Finzari had drawn at the end. I noticed a feature which I had not previously seen; on each picture there was a small inner circle, incorporated into the design, and I pointed it out silently to Ravin. He recognised, as did I, that this small inner circle was the entrance for the bees on the decorated disc at the front of the beehive. But how could we be sure that we found the exact same picture and thus the same beehive? If only we could somehow take the scroll away with us, but that was impossible. All the scrolls were noted out and in by the Scholar every day and I could not even flatter Mazin and persuade him to let me keep the scroll, for it was Avenda who was the day's Scholar and she already disliked me. In any case, we could not find all the beehives in one night; it might take several days to find the right beehive and after that we faced the difficulty of trying to get into them without being spotted. Ravin was much quicker and more adept with his pen than I was and was accustomed to copying diagrams from scrolls, and by dint of some quiet whispering while Avenda was talking to another student, we agreed that he would copy the six pictures off the scroll.

Scholar Avenda prowled the room from time to time. Much as I disliked Scholar Mazin's florid and oily attention, at least he was quite lazy and rarely hoisted himself off his cushioned perch. Avenda seemed to work in periods of fierce concentration on her own work when she would ignore the students, even those who required a new scroll authorising, or she would restlessly wander round the room. I assume that in some way it aided her concentration, but it detracted from mine, especially now that I knew she had her eye on Ravin. When I saw her approaching us, I coughed abruptly to let Ravin know she was coming, and he smoothly covered over his copy of Finzari's pictures with a long scroll relating to the extraction of honeygold and began making cursory notes on it.

'An interesting topic of study,' purred Avenda over his shoulder, leaning in closely to read the small script. The flames in my mind spat and crackled. I turned the scroll spindle round to the next story, carefully hiding the picture at the bottom, and began to read the story, trying to appear interested in my work.

'I can't believe you can find anything interesting in that tedious nonsense,' remarked Avenda dismissively. 'Still, I suppose you probably don't have a particularly good education in comparison to Ravin and I.' She tossed her head up and one stray glossy curl escaped from under her headdress. It bobbed up and down appealingly, and I noticed she wore tiny golden hoops in her ears as decoration. The inside of my mouth was quite sore with all the biting I was doing to stop myself from retorting as I wished. I put on my Temple masked face, the one which I had developed years ago when I was just a Temple Drab and the Priestesses were upbraiding me for my poor attitude or slovenly work. I cast my eyes down modestly so she could not see my defiance and arranged my lips in a calm line.

'Indeed not, Scholar,' I responded. 'I have much to learn and am grateful for the chance to study the scrolls of one of Kashiq's best loved scribes, Scholar Finzari. His stories are very illuminating.' Behind her, Ravin winked at me and pulled a very droll face, which made me want to burst out laughing. He seemed to know just how to reassure me that it was me who he cared for, and to show me that he had no interest in Avenda, no matter how great an interest she had in him. She turned away from me dismissively and went to peer over Ravin's shoulder, leaning in close to him and pretending to examine the honeygold document.

'Do you have an interest in the honeygold process?' she asked, evincing deep interest. 'Why, that is one of my own interests! When I am not studying pattern making and construction, I study the honeygold. I have in mind an idea to use them both so that you could make entirely regular shapes out of honeygold. They would be excellent for trading. Let me show you a more detailed scroll.' She placed her hand on Ravin's arm and led him off triumphantly towards her station at the end of the room. He looked back at me helplessly as he went. Furiously, I turned back to the scroll of Finzari and began to read the fable written there, which was entitled 'How The Apricot Blossom Learnt That Love Needs Freedom.'

'Lo, there grew in that verdant orchard many apricot trees, and every year they would blossom, filling the air with their soft sweet scent, enticing the bees to come and collect their golden honeydust. There grew on the very tip of a branch of the apricot tree at the furthest edge of the garden a beautiful blossom.

'She was perfectly formed, with five pure white, gently rounded petals surrounding her tiny stalks of honeydust. Many bees did not fly as far as this tree, and she watched sadly as they flew past to visit the more popular blossoms. Then, a handsome young bee alighted gently on a nearby twig and waved his shining wings at her before crawling over and gently making his way to her centre, humming reassurances and compliments. He spoke to her of her beauty, and told her that he loved her, that she was perfect, and she told him the same thing. But when the honeydust coated his fuzzy legs, he prepared to fly away again. The blossom was so angry that he had stayed for so short a time, that she summoned all her strength and closed the petals over the top of him, so he was trapped inside her.

'The bee buzzed around angrily inside the blossom, trying to escape, and eventually, as he paused to gather up his strength, he asked the blossom why she had done that. She replied to him that she did not want him to leave her, that she would miss him too much when he left and that it made her feel abandoned by him. The bee spoke again.

'But blossom, I need to be free. If you keep me imprisoned here inside you, I will die here. I need to be free to go back to the beehive and to take back the honeydust to make more honey. I need to drink the honey to give me strength, and I must visit more flowers, that I might bring back to you their support, so that you can make yourself into the perfect golden apricot I know you are destined to be.'

'The blossom thought over what he had said and asked him if he truly would come back to her, to which he replied that love would always return if freedom was given, but that being trapped was the surest way to end love. She saw that he was right and unfurled her petals once more. The bee thanked her and flew off into the deep blue sky. The blossom waited all that day for the bee to return, turning her face with the sun, but he did not return that day. Sadly, she closed her petals and slept. The next morning, as she unfolded her petals, she saw the bee returning, covered in golden powder which he shook off as he landed, and greeted her lovingly. He told her that while he was away, he had collected and kept the best honeydust for her, and that day he lingered with her, both of them happy.

And the golden dust of their love, born out of freedom freely given, grew into the sweetest apricot there ever was, and from the seed of that fruit grew many more golden sweet apricots and the descendants of the bee visited them always.'

I had become engrossed in the story, for once. I understood the flower's inclination to close tightly around the object of her affections, just as I wanted to do with Ravin. But equally, I understood the bee's need to travel, to learn and to be nourished and I could see that by allowing the bee to be free, the blossom learnt that that gesture only made him love her more. I examined the picture which Finzari had drawn to illustrate this particular fable, and I knew I would not forget what this one looked like, for it was, at first glance, quite simple to look at. If you had not read the story that accompanied it, you might just think it was a picture of a simple flower. If you had read the story, you might wonder where the bee was who played such a pivotal role. The picture was of a white apricot flower with five rounded petals around a centre which had yellow stalks around it. This was where the entrance hole had been placed, and the clever thing was that it would illustrate the story perfectly since the real bees who used the hive would be forever landing on the beautiful flower and having the freedom to leave again and to return.

It felt very satisfying to have completely understood all that Scholar Finzari had tried to convey, and I held him in more respect than I had previously. I turned to tell Ravin of my findings, but he was still talking to Avenda. I wandered over to his scribeboard and eased his copy of the pictures out for behind the other parchment. I saw that he had copied down all the pictures except for the one which I had just read, so I set to work on making a fair copy of it myself. Luckily because it was so simple and so memorable, it was not so difficult to do. The shape of the apricot blossom was very pleasing too, and I thought back to my pounced patterns that I made for Gladia when I first left the Temple. This simple flower would be a good pattern to pounce since it was made of five interlocking circles and a robe or netela sprinkled in these blossoms would be quite lovely. Perhaps one could even find some golden or orange fabric, the colour of apricots, on which to sew the pattern. I wondered if Gladia might stitch it for me when we returned, and I felt suddenly sad and longed for her reassuring company. So much of Kashiq was interesting and beautiful and different to Oramia, but it did not feel like home. Oramia felt like an old friend, familiar and comfortable, like Gladia herself. I suddenly wanted to go home, to Mellia, not even to Gabez which had become my home over the past seven years. To listen to Gladia scrapping with Jember, to hear Benakiell's gentle tales of his travels, to talk with Maren about the bees and to laugh with Achillea over a shared joke. I sighed.

'You look a little downhearted,' came a voice in my ear. 'Did you miss me? Trying to get away from Avenda is like trying to escape from that creeping plant which winds itself around a tree!' Ravin pretended to brush off the clinging tendrils of a plant, and I smiled at him, grateful for his warmth. We returned our scrolls and took our own parchments and left the Tower of the Wise and I told him what I had read in Finzari's fable, and what the last plate looked like.

As we walked down the by now familiar streets towards my dwelling, I told Ravin of my longing to be back at home in Mellia. I asked him if he felt the same way about his own village which lay a long way south of Arbhoun, many days travel away. He had not told me very much about this village, nor about his family or even about his friends from there. I wondered if he ever returned there. A shadow soaked its way across his face.

'I never want to return to Galdin,' he said bitterly. 'I have no longing to go back there. It is not now what it once was, and without the people you love, it is just another place. For, as you have said yourself, it is when you think of the people whom you love that you miss the place where they are to be found. Your village may not be the most beautiful village or the one with the best crops or the most famous scholars, but it contains all that is important to you.'

I put my arm around his shoulders to comfort him. I wanted to ask him more about what had happened, but I did not want to make him sad. After a while, he continued to speak.

'I have no family there, nor anywhere else, in truth. My father died before I can remember him. He was of Yael and his job was in defending Kashiq and, I guess, in bringing death to those who questioned authority. My mother was of Yael too, but she worked with the dying. She was the one who the people in the village turned to when their loved ones neared the end. She brought them comfort and acceptance and she prepared them for burial. My childhood was all about death, in the end.'

We were passing a small shelter where an old man sat, with a pile of small flatbreads and a pot of spicy vegetables. The aroma curled itself around us temptingly. Ravin stopped. He looked in his carrybag for some small object to trade but had only his parchments and his pens. It was hard to find small items to trade for these equally small items. I looked in my carrybag too. I only had a small pot of salve which I used on my lips in the dry heat of Arbhoun. I had found some dry seed pods under a tree close to where we lived and had filled several with a plain salve so that I could carry it where I went. The pod itself was like a tiny gourd, hard skinned and round. I asked the old man if he would trade some of his food for the salve. He looked at me suspiciously.

'What would an old man like me want with a salve? I am not unwell!'

'Try it, Father,' I urged. 'Your lips are hot and dry, sitting there in the sun, and your hands are cracked from your labours. Try a little. If you do not like it, then I will take it back.'

Dubiously he poked his finger into the salve. Privately, I resolved to throw the tiny pot of salve away if he did not want it, for his fingers were ingrained with grime. He spread the salve on his lips which were indeed cracked and peeling, rubbing it into every crevice. He smiled at me, and his face lit up with happiness.

'Why, it is like magic,' he said happily. 'I can open my mouth without it cracking and hurting. Thank you, dear girl.' He swiftly stashed the salve away under his things, as if in fear that I might want it back and gave us each two small flatbreads joined together by the spicy vegetable filling. We walked over to the wall and leaned against it while we ate.

'I needed that,' said Ravin, sounding satisfied by his meal. 'Food can bring us warmth and joy when we feel sad. Do you think that too?'

I pondered. After the dreary and functional food in the Temple, I had revelled in the interesting new flavours I had encountered, first on the Outer in Oramia and then here in Kashiq. I was much tempted by honey and sweet things, but in truth I think that was just a childish greed. Perhaps I did take comfort from eating in the way that Ravin described. I asked him to tell me more about his family.

'My mother died soon after I entered the Third Age of childhood. My older brother was already a man by then.' Ravin had not mentioned his brother before. 'My mother died of some fever or ague. She spent her life with the dead and the dying and I think it was inevitable that she would one day die of an illness she had taken from one of those who died. My brother was terribly angry but became even angrier when I told him I would not follow the path of Yael as he had done, and my parents had done before me. He told me I dishonoured the memory of our parents and that I dishonoured him by turning away from my destiny. He prepared to join the Defenders of Yael and took with him everything of value that belonged to our parents. I wanted to build things, to make new things, not to be with the dead and the dying, or to be the agent of death. He told me to leave Galdin and never to return or he would kill me himself for the fall in honour of our family. I left the same night.' He paused, reflecting, and again the shadows crept across his face.

'Imagine, there I was, a youngster of only fifteen with a bundle of clothes and some food and water walking out into the world, a world which honestly I knew little of. Unless you have done that, you cannot know what it is like.'

I did know what it was like, although I was older than he when I left the Temple for the strange new world of the Outer. Perhaps this sort of kinship was, unbeknownst to us, one of the reasons that Ravin and I were drawn to one another. I wanted to tell Ravin of my past, but I was still wary of talking to anyone about it. Probably here in Kashiq it would not be as difficult as in Oramia where nobody ever left the Temple. But, in any case, Ravin was telling me his story and I did not want to turn the conversation around so that it was about me. He continued, taking another bite of his food.

'I walked from village to village, telling all who asked that my family were dead and that I could work for food and shelter. I changed my family name to that of my mother's brother. Eventually I came to the village of Ebdil where I met my teacher. He needed help at his dwelling since he had injured his back and could not walk properly or carry anything. And so he taught me to scribe and to read and I fetched and carried for him. I cooked for him and cleaned for him and in return he gave me his scholarly wisdom. He taught me to draw and to make diagrams, to measure with measuresticks and to calculate the passing of the days from the sun and the moon. It was for both of us the ideal life.' Ravin's face brightened as he remembered those happy days spent doing the things he was passionate about, recalling the attention and devotion of one who taught him and showed him the path to his own talents.

'I stayed with him, Hurkim was his name, for the next ten years. He was like a father to me and I was like a son to him. When he died, he left a scroll giving me ownership of his dwelling and all his belongings, his scrolls and parchments, his pens and his furniture. Though I would give it all up for him to still be alive. I am not sad now,' he said, turning to me and cupping my face with his hand. 'He was often in pain from his old injury and he was relieved by death. My mother told me that death is not always to be feared as much of the unknown is feared. Sometimes it heralds peace and the completion of a life well loved. What comes before life here is unknown, but it comes into being when a child is born, through Asmara's creation. Likewise, what comes after life is not known to us, but is taken in by Yael. Perhaps what comes after death is just another kind of life. We do not know. Hurkim died in his sleep so perhaps he carries on dreaming in some other way.'

I looked again at my beloved Ravin. All these new revelations about his life only made me love him more. I had never yet borne the loss of someone close to me like he had, and like Achillea had. Achillea had seen both her mother and her lover Ashtun die, one from the ague and one through murder. The pain of that still stayed with her. I knew, of course, of Priestesses who had died in the Temple, but we were not close to them and, in any case, it was always presented to us as if it were a blessing; that the Goddess had called them to her because they were good and were obedient to her. There was no weeping at the Temple when death came, just acceptance. Life continued at the Temple regardless of who was there. The systems which had been put into place worked regardless of who administered them, as long as they did not deviate from the rules.

'After some time, I decided to make my way here to Arbhoun. Hurkim always spoke to me of the wonders of the Tower of the Wise where he had attended when he was a young man. He told me that if I truly wanted to be a scholar, to alter the world with my learning, I needed to go there and see it for myself, and to learn all that I could. And so, I did. The one I live with now, he was someone Hurkim knew when he was a scholar here, and when I came here, I sought him out and told him of what befell Hurkim. He too was becoming old and I am happy to fulfil the same for him as I did for Hurkim. I have been studying at the Tower of the Wise now for two years and I thought my life was full and complete until I met you, my lovely Talla. And now I know it really is complete.' He stood up and folded me into his arms and we stood entwined. My head rested on his chest and I heard his heart beating through his robe.

# CHAPTER 17

A small puff of wind stirred the dust around my feet as we walked back towards the first orchard we had visited. It was late evening and we had come prepared to sleep outside for that night. Achillea had pouted and protested that she wanted to go back to the dwelling to sleep, but when Tarik suggested to her that she could stay at home while we went to the orchard to search for the right beehive, she could not bear to be left out, and accompanied us. I could hear her humming faintly as we walked along. She sang more and more these days since she had been accorded such praise by Parline. She had been to see those who had been recommended to her by Parline, and they too had praised the purity of her song and given her tokens of esteem. Achillea loved these small items, not just because they were beautiful and valuable and she had always loved jewellery and ornament of all kinds, but also because they were symbols to her of how much people valued her singing.

'Do you not think it is a strange thing that I had to travel to another land before I could do the thing I have always wanted to do? In Oramia I had no chance to be a Songmaker, but here in Kashiq, where they live differently, my songs have a more important place,' she commented to me one day as she showed me a small carved box she had been given. In Oramia, we were perhaps more concentrated on the physical. We liked to trade a physical item for another one and a song was so ephemeral that unless you were an official Songmaker, it was difficult to subsist. Likewise, when it came to healing. In Oramia we were gifted at healing physical ills, agues and fevers and wounds. We could make tonics and salves for coughs and old bones and dry lips and earaches, but we did little for the pains of the heart and the soul. Here in Kashiq, where Soren was the Goddess of healing, healing was as important for both mind and body, and music and singing were healing actions.

Tarik had packed some of his metal tools in case we needed them to take off the covers of the beehives. Being Tarik, and always well prepared, he had also brought with him a ball of smooth clay for making repairs. Tarik was such a practical man, always thinking ahead and making plans, and having an idea of how to solve a problem practically. He and Achillea seemed to suit one another perfectly; she was much given to flights of fancy and dreams of all kinds of impractical things, and he was rooted in reality, in dealing with things he could see and do and change. I wondered if Ravin and I were well suited in the same kind of way. Perhaps people who were truly in love with each other were like two sides of the same thing, the inside and the outside of a bowl, for instance; one could not exist without the other. Ravin was good humoured again, lightened in spirit by having told me about his past. I had decided to tell him about my own past, but there had not yet been a time when we could sit together without being interrupted, and strange as it may seem, given that Achillea and Tarik knew most things about me, and had only ever been supportive of me, I wanted for it to just be the two of us when I told him. I was fearful perhaps of his reaction to what I said.

I was a little unsure about the darkness myself, especially in relation to the bees. Bees were so busy working during the daylight hours that they needed to sleep in the darkest hours, to rest before the labours of the next day. I did often take the honey in the early hours of the evening when the bees seemed drowsier so perhaps it would be easier still to disturb them at night but when I thought of myself and how disrupted I felt when my own sleep was disturbed, I wondered if they might try to sting us all, fearing us to be intruders. We had decided to find the right beehive while it was still light and then return to it under the cover of darkness. It was unlikely that anyone would notice or even care that we were in the orchard at night, for what could we hope to steal in the dark? In any case, the fruit was not yet on the trees and the bees were well known for being able to sting any who sought to steal their honey. It felt like a good plan.

Back at the orchard, we were welcomed again by the old lady, Farin, who sat at her shelter with her items for trade, and whose face brightened when she saw us arrive. It did not seem that she had many visitors, or perhaps those who came to the orchard were not interested enough to talk with her. In any case we had come prepared and had brought small items with us to trade for her offerings, including the same kind of lip salve I had traded with the old man. She insisted on making us a drink which was, unfortunately, in my view, not the strong coffee of Oramia, but rather a pale green tea brewed from faintly spicy leaves and sweetened with honey. Ravin enjoyed it very much; it was the normal sort of drink for families in Kashiq, he told me, and it was only really in Arbhoun that people drank Oramian coffee. It was a good thing that we had brought plenty with us. We had agreed before we left that Achillea would occupy Farin and talk to her or perhaps even sing to her and practice her melodies while the rest of us searched the beehives to find one which featured one of the pictures which Ravin had copied out from the scroll. This was the orchard of Maliq, the God who guided those who craft, so

I thought that perhaps the picture might relate to crafting in some way. I had not properly read all the stories which accompanied the pictures except for the one about freedom and I wished now that I had paid more attention to the words, for they might have given us more clues. As I now felt that I had some understanding of the way in which Scholar Finzari's mind worked, I was sure that he would have placed clues in the stories about which orchard they could be found in. However, there were only six pictures to look for, and the designs for all of them seemed quite simple. I was sure we would be able to find the right one.

Arriving at the stacked beehives under the trees, I was impressed again at the ingenuity of their construction. I wondered how they made the clay cylinders dry in such perfect shapes. I thought that perhaps they built them around some kind of inner mould which they could remove once the clay had hardened. Benakiell would be interested in these clay structures, I was sure. I remembered that he had told me about the beehives when I saw him last in Mellia, but I wasn't sure how close he had got to them. The beehives lay stacked up one on top of the other, facing out into the orchard so as to give the bees encouragement to fly towards the blossom of the trees or the flowers which grew in the ground around the trees after the tree blossom had faded. There was nobody here again, but Ravin had assured us that it was lucky that we had arrived at this time of year when there were neither flowers nor fruit on the trees, for the orchards were favourite places for the Arbhoun is at these times and were frequently full, with tradespeople trading goods all around them. We began to examine the pictures on the beehives. There was no one type of picture, but many different styles and colours. I had hoped that the one we were seeking would stand out, and perhaps it had when it was first made, but many others had been added since. Tarik had suggested that it might be found closer to the bottom of the rows of beehives, and this seemed reasonable to me until Ravin pointed out that the length of the row of beehives could have been expanded several times over the ages too. Ravin held the plant parchment with his copies of the pictures on and Tarik and I would occasionally go back to him to re-examine it before dismissing another picture which we had briefly thought likely.

'I think I have it,' said Tarik in a low voice, finally, beckoning Ravin and I to a beehive which was indeed close to the bottom of the beehives. It was ordinary looking; the colours did not stand out and nor did the picture at first. But as we looked at the copied pictures, we recognised that this was indeed one of the beehives which we looked for. The picture was of a honeycomb, its familiar six-sided shapes drawn closely connected. Once again, it had been cleverly thought out, for one of the honeycomb shapes was the entrance to the hive, and instead of being round, had been carefully cut to be six sided so that it fitted in with the picture. To one side of the honeycomb was a bee, and the whole thing had been glazed in colours of sludgy orange and yellow. As we examined it, a bee crawled in through the hole and we turned to one another, smiling in satisfaction. Now we just had to wait for the sun to set. Before we did that, Ravin counted out its place in the row, from west to east and then from top to bottom, so that we could find it again in the dark. Achillea had brought with her a small oil lamp, and an emberjar to afford us a little light.

'Well, my dear,' Farin was saying as we arrived back. 'There is no doubt you have a beautiful voice. I am quite sure that Soren is blessed to have you under her guidance. You will have made all the apricots sweeter!

But now I must go as it will be dark soon and I like to get back to my dwelling before night falls. And you must get back to your dwellings too.'

'Let me help you with your things,' offered Achillea, having seen Tarik's slight nod to indicate to her that we had found the beehive. She and I helped Farin to bundle up her dried apricots and clay pots of honey, while Ravin and Tarik took some embers from her fire for Achillea's emberjar, and then placed the firecover over it. In Arbhoun, they used these firecovers a lot. They were made of the same orange clay as the beehives and were like an upside-down bowl, with a handle on the top which could be placed over the embers of a fire. They stopped any sparks from the fire from escaping and eventually the fire would die for lack of air. Farin left, bustling off, and encouraging us to go home soon so that we did not have to go back in the dark. We assured her we were just about to leave and then waited for the dusk to continue its swift cloaking of the land.

Once all was still, and the sun had sunk beneath the horizon, we made our way back to the rows of beehives. Achillea lit the cotton wick of the small oil lamp from the embers in the emberjar and the small flame flickered in front of the beehives. The bees, like we people, went to sleep in the hours of darkness. They had no light unlike us, and as Achillea put the lamp down on the ground a few bees emerged, confused by the light, and crawled aimlessly about on the decorated covers of their beehives before retreating again. Ravin found the right beehive and indicated it to us. We all agreed that it definitely showed one of the pictures which he had copied, and Tarik took out his tools. Because of the way the beehives were stacked, we could not simply remove the beehive, but instead had to try to take the front plate off it where it lay, surrounded by other beehives. Tarik ran his fingers around the under rim of the hive, trying to work out the best way of taking the front off.

He took one of his sharper metal bladed tools and put it close to the edge of the plate and then took a small hammer and gave it a sharp blow. The blade slipped under the front plate quite easily, but he could not simply lever it off as the plate was too heavy for the blade, so he had to make the same movement in several other places. Each time he did, there was an increased angry hum from the bees inside. I knew how sensitive they were to being bumped. My own bees did not appreciate it when I lowered their wooden hives down from the tree and accidentally banged them. I think they felt the jolts through their wings or their feet, for simple movement of the hive had no effect on them so long as it was smooth.

Eventually, with one final cracking noise, Tarik managed to lever off the front plate. The noise of the bees rose and Ravin and Tarik retreated with the cover at first, but the bees began to follow them, and I called them back. I needed to calm the bees down, to show them that I meant them no harm before they decided to sting. One or two beestings could be easily dealt with but if the whole hive went on the attack, it could be fatal. I called to the men softly, telling them to bring back the cover to the beehive. Gingerly they walked over carrying it, one on each side, accompanied by a cloud of bees. They both looked nervous but as they brought the cover closer to the hive, some of the bees flew back towards their honeycombs inside. I took out one of the clay pots of Farin's honey which had been drawn from these very hives and coated my finger in it and then ran my finger around the rim of the beehive, drawing even more of the bees back to the hive until only a few were still flying around near to the cover.

Achillea edged closer to the hive, trying to peer inside, to find out if one of the pieces of the Orange of Kashiq was inside it. Tarik and Ravin leaned the cover up against the other beehives, and I slowly began to slide out the first couple of honeycomb frames. They had been made of simple wooden pieces and were much like my own honeycomb frames. I could see nothing in the hive, though, and nor could Achillea. Disappointed. I turned round to the men. All our work had come to nothing, for although we had followed the clues correctly, there was nothing in this hive, no part of an orange made of honeygold. Perhaps there had been other before us who had followed the same clues and found the pieces. Perhaps they had been found by somebody who did not even know what they were and had already been melted down and remade into jewellery. My shoulders felt heavy.

As I turned, one of the last few bees still flying around flew towards Ravin and landed on his face. Just as he reached up to brush it away, it stung him, and he yelped and made a sudden movement. As his foot twisted round, it caught the edge of the front plate of the beehive which was propped up near him and flicked it outwards. It rolled and then landed heavily, flat on the hard ground and there was a loud crunching noise. I did not know where to put my attention; on Ravin who was still grunting with pain, for the bee had stung him right underneath his eye or on the presumably shattered cover of the beehive. It would be evident that something had happened to the beehive in the morning, and Farin would no doubt recall that we had been there and tell her son the beekeeper. I tried to do both and said, 'Are you going to be alright?' to Ravin at the same time as I moved towards the cover.

The cover was not broken. It lay smooth and glazed on the ground, the flickering light of the oil lamp dancing on its surface, illuminating the painted honeycomb pattern. The bee which had stung Ravin had crawled on to it and, as all bees must, lay dying on the cover. It had sacrificed its life in the protection of its hive and in leaving its sting in Ravin's face, had condemned itself to death. Its legs twitched briefly before it was still. I lifted up the cover. What had caused that loud cracking noise if it were not the breaking beehive cover? I turned it over onto its back and there, baked into a now cracked and crumbling clay dome lay a small, dull silverish item; one of the pieces of the Orange of Kashiq. It had been moulded onto the beehive cover with some extra clay. You would not have noticed the bulge if you had just seen it and would have thought that it was just a distortion in the clay. Only somebody who knew it was there would be able to find it. The segment was still stuck on to the cover with clay, and Tarik used his sharp bladed chisel to patiently chip away at the dry orange clay which surrounded it.

Picking it up once it was free of the clay, Tarik lay it in the palm of his hand. It was the same size as a real orange segment, and shaped like one too, in a part crescent shape. I peered at it in the flickering lamplight. It seemed too dull for honeygold, but I realised that it had been coated in beeswax to protect it from the clay, presumably. I longed to look at it more closely, but we needed to replace the beehive cover as quickly as we could, and I still needed to tend to Ravin's sting which we had all forgotten about in the relief of discovering the first piece of the Orange. He rubbed it now, and I quickly reached for his hand to stay his movement. It was important not to push the sting further into his flesh. It was already swelling up around his eye and I needed to get it out. I gently scraped my fingernail across his cheek until I felt a tiny obstruction, like a slender splinter. Having found the end of it, I put a little more force on it with my nail and scraped it out. It fell into the darkness.

'I am not sure about being associated with one who counts such soldiers amongst her friends,' joked Ravin, wincing. He smiled at my anxious face. 'Look, you cause me pain and still I love you! Surely there can be no greater proof!' I relaxed a little, recognising his familiar teasing note, and reached into my carrybag for one of the small pots of salve. I mixed it with a little of the honey we had traded for with Farin earlier. I had long believed, for no real reason, that the honey from the same hive as a bee came from might soothe a sting more. I gently rubbed the mixture into his skin. There was little more we could do but wait for the passage of time to ease the swelling.

Achillea had placed the oil lamp down on the ground and was helping Tarik to roll a long rope of clay from that we had brought with us. I thanked the Goddess for Tarik's forethought. I had no interest or experience in clay, but Achillea, having been raised in a small village like Mellia, where many of the simple everyday things were made by the villagers rather than traded for, was adept at using it although she showed little interest in furthering her skill. When I first met Achillea, she had seemed to me to be very lazy, always being indulged by others and doing little work herself. Since I had got to know her better in the ensuing years, I realised that she was very able in many areas of her life, it was more that she was, in general, content as she was. She did not want or need to learn more to be happy. And now that she could sing and be praised for her singing which was the thing she loved to do, she was even happier. I, on the other hand, wondered whether I would ever be content. There was so much to learn in this life of mine, and every new thing I encountered drove me to find out more. I wondered if it would ever be possible to know everything.

Once the rope of clay was long enough, Tarik heaved up the beehive cover and lay it across his knees, upside down so that Achillea could mould the rope along the outer edge and it could be replaced on the hive. She squashed the clay down and then Tarik asked Ravin to help him to replace the cover on the beehive. It was quite heavy and wider than Tarik's chest, so it was much easier to put into place with two people. Once it was matched up to the edges of the beehive, they held it there for some time until they were sure it would not fall off and then we waited a while. The bees had by now ceased flying around at all and all was quiet in the orchard of Maliq. We made our way out of the orchard to the path back into Arbhoun, having blown out the lamp. It was so late when we got back that, after Tarik had carefully placed the honeygold segment into a box, I suggested to him that he should stay the rest of the night at our dwelling. Achillea looked at me wide eyed. I realised what she must be thinking and hastily reassured her that it was only so that Ravin did not lose sleep. Dubiously, she and Tarik retired to their room in the dwelling, and I showed Ravin my own room, sparsely furnished with a sleeping mat and just my few simple possessions.

It was quite cold at night here in Arbhoun, even though it was hot in the daytime when the sun was shining. I wondered if the moon sent the cold to the earth in the same way that the sun sent the warmth. I took off my netela and headband, without thinking and allowed my hair to be free of its covering. Ravin sat next to me and removed his own headdress, folding it up to make a slight cushion for his head. He stretched out and lay down on the mat and patted the space next to him. I lay down beside him tentatively and he put his arm around

209

me, drawing my head up onto his chest. I pulled the tightly woven blanket up and thus we lay, together and warm. Ravin stroked my hair gently. We kissed. Ravin pulled me close to him and I felt my own longing for him reflected in him. He sighed after some time and muttered that we should try to sleep since that was what we were supposed to be doing. Despite my longing for Ravin, however, I slept almost straight away. I had never had any trouble in sleeping. At the Temple all was quiet at night-time and we were trained to sleep in the hours of darkness. It was unusual for me to dream, or indeed to wake up during the night. However, that night, I did wake up and found that I was resting my head on Ravin's chest. I made to move but he held me there and whispered to me that it made him very happy to see me sleeping thus, and so I slept again and did not wake up until the bright slanted rays of sun began to stretch their way through the dwelling.

# CHAPTER 18

Ravin had already risen and left the room when I woke up in bright slanted rays of sunshine. It was rare for me to wake late and I rushed to tidy my clothes and to comb my hair before making my way outside to where the others were all sitting chatting to one another. I could smell the aroma of freshly brewed Oramian coffee, and I sighed in pleasure as I sat down.

'We were waiting for you to arrive so that we could look together at the piece of the Orange that we found yesterday,' remarked Achillea, handing me a clay beaker of black, steaming coffee.

Tarik went to get the box he had placed the piece in and Achillea went to fetch some flatbreads. I crept my hand into Ravin's and he squeezed my fingers. I looked at his face, and the swelling from the sting had died down overnight so that now there was only a small red spot like any other insect bite. He saw me looking at it and chuckled.

'I see you have worked your magic on me. Not only can you manage the bees, but you can sweeten the sharpness of their sting too. You must be the honey in my life, Talla, golden and sweet.' When Ravin paid me compliments, it always made me feel warm, like being pleasantly wrapped in a warm blanket on a cool day. I asked how he had slept.

'I slept fitfully, in truth,' he admitted. 'At first, the sting bothered me, itching and throbbing as it did, but then I found I did not want to go to sleep for fear I might disturb your peaceful sleeping where you were. In any case, I felt comforted and contented to watch you sleeping and to know you were at peace. You know, it is said that nobody can sleep in their enemy's arms, however delightful that enemy might appear to be; that something within our spirit prevents us from feeling truly at peace with one who wishes us harm. And so, it made me feel good that you trusted me and did not see me as your enemy.'

'Does that mean you see me as yours then?' I asked, worried that he might not now regard me as I regarded him.

'Of course not. I was just so full of happiness that I could not sleep. It's quite different. In any case,' he paused and closed one eye at me, 'I found it difficult to sleep while I could see you and feel you near me and yet be unable to be properly alone with you...' He turned as Tarik and Achillea came back, as eager as I was to see this first piece of the Orange of Kashiq.

Tarik took it out of its box and lay it gently on a piece of cloth he had brought out with him. The dull opacity of the piece meant that it looked quite insignificant. I reached over to pick it up. The beeswax that had been applied to it was thick and creamy yellow in colour. I scraped at it with my fingernail and small shavings came off. You could see that the metal was embossed with a design and that it would take many hours of painstaking labour to scrape off every bit of beeswax from amongst the engraving. I put it back, a little frustrated. Tarik smiled a little smugly.

'Don't worry, Talla. We do not have to scrape away every part of the beeswax. There is a much easier way.' He took the segment and held it gently between two carved sticks bound by a strip of leather into a pincer shape. Then he held it over the fire. As the heat of the fire rose, the beeswax began to soften and then to melt off the honeygold. The wax became more liquid and fell in fat drops onto the fire, sizzling and letting off the slight, sweet scent of honey. As the wax fell off, it left behind a bright and shiny piece of honeygold, so shiny that you might have thought it had just been polished. The beeswax had prevented it from tarnishing at all since it had been kept out of the air and so what we now saw was exactly as it had last been seen, perhaps by Lord Rao himself.

Tarik laid the segment gently on the cloth to cool down, and we praised him for his cleverness in so quickly removing the wax. He smiled, modestly this time.

'While I have been learning about the metalworking here in Kashiq, I have also been observing the casting of shapes out of metal which they do using wax and clay. It was that which made me think of this idea.' Ravin looked interested and explained that he had also been looking at the description of this while he had been studying at the Tower of the Wise. Achillea drew our attention back to the segment which lay glinting on the cloth.

'Is it cool yet? I really want to look at it more closely!' She peered down at it and reached a tentative finger towards it to test how hot it was before gingerly picking it up and showing it to me.

The whole of the surface was richly chased in interwoven strands which looked much like the web of fibres over a real orange segment. There was a tiny clasp on the inner edge of the segment and when Achillea pushed it with her fingernail, the segment opened up like a tiny box. Inside was written a word, which Achillea asked me to read. The word was Joy.

'Why is that written there, do you think, Talla?' asked Achillea. I thought back to the stories that Scholar Finzari had written and to what we had read and been told about the Orange of Kashiq. These were the descriptions of the qualities which Lord Rao had identified as the qualities of his love for Ashkana. The six Tales of the Orchard illustrated these qualities of love, and each of the segments of the Orange had been concealed in a different orchard, each orchard being under the guidance of one of the six gods and goddesses of Kashiq. We had been at the orchard dedicated to Maliq, the one who guided crafters, and the quality which Rao, or possibly Finzari, had associated with Maliq was joy. I explained my thinking to Achillea, who nodded thoughtfully and asked me what the story was that went with this word. I thought back to the scrolls I had read, wishing that I had my own copy of The Tales of the Orchard. Having initially been rather scornful of their seemingly sentimental nature, I was beginning to understand how cleverly they had been put together and interwoven. The picture on the cover of the beehive was of a honeycomb, and I recalled that this story had been about the joy the bees felt in building up the honeycomb together; how each one relied on the work of others and how all took joy from their craftsmanship, from the creation of something which was not only beautiful but useful too. I told it to Achillea as far as I could remember it, and she nodded, satisfied.

Tarik took the piece off Achillea's hand and examined it more closely, holding it up to the sun. He was not as interested in the tiny opening clasp which opened the segment as in another tiny ring at the top of the piece, which he examined thoughtfully, holding it up to the light.

'This bit here has been damaged,' he said, regretfully. 'You can see that it would have had a thin wire attached to it here which must have been snapped when Ashkana broke up the Orange.' Ravin leaned over to look at it with him.

214

'This must have been how the Orange of Kashiq was held together to make it look like a real orange,' he murmured. 'I have looked at the drawings made by Finzari and others, but they are not clear in how it worked to open. I do know that there was a central inner stem attached to a leaf shape at the top, so maybe the segments were attached to that central stem by these small wires you talk about.'

Tarik reached for his carrysack, which was never far from him, and, after scrabbling amongst its contents, drew out some fine thread, much like the thread that Gladia used when she was embroidering the netelas and robes she traded. Ravin watched as he tied the thread to the metal stub at the top of the segment and then as he once more rifled through his bag before drawing out a piece of wire. There were men in the metalworking district who made these wires by grasping a piece of honeygold or silver held fast in a clamp with a pair of pincers and pulling it back a length. This whole process was repeated several times as the wireworkers moved on their tracks back and forth, clamping and re-clamping, drawing and redrawing the metal until it became finer and finer. The thinner it got, the more delicate the pincers were that drew it out. This fine wire was rolled around clay cylinders. Those who made jewellery often traded for the wire which they could use to make chains and fine decoration on their pieces, and by the armourers who used the wires to link beaten plates together. For Tarik, these wireworkers were a source of endless interest and he sometimes sat in the evening at the dwelling, fiddling with a small length of wire, softening it over the embers of the fire and then drawing it out, trying to achieve the same evenness of size and shape that these Kashiqi craftsmen managed. Occasionally he would twist the wire into a fanciful shape for Achillea who was always impressed with them and stored them away in her wooden box where she kept her few adornments.

Tarik pushed the wire down into the earth and then tied the thread to the top of it so that the segment lay as if from an opened orange. Ravin's eyes lit up and it was as if he was seeing something which he had seen before. Reaching forward, he murmured an instruction to Tarik, who frowned but then moved the loop of thread so that it lay at the bottom of the wire rather than at the top.

'What are you doing?' asked Achillea, curiously.

'Look, my love,' answered Tarik, joyfully. 'We know how the orange was put together and how it was opened and shut!' And, sure enough, as Ravin demonstrated to us, he drew the looped thread up the central wire and it pulled up the segment of honeygold orange until it stood upright, close to the wire. I recalled seeing some of Ravin's sketches from what he had read about the Orange of Kashiq and the threads or strips around a central column and I understood now what they had been showing. I tried to picture in my head what it might look like if there were five other segments spaced around that same central column and realised that this could indeed be the way in which the Orange of Kashiq had been cunningly made to open and close, just like a real orange, and for it also to show the Lady Ashkana the individual segments, and allow her to read the words which Lord Rao had had engraved inside each segment, those six aspects of love which he had chosen. I leaned closer, eager to take part in this discovery.

'Would the threads holding them up be made of wires too, or do you think they were silk, threaded through these loops?' I asked Ravin.

'It seemed clear in the scrolls I read that the Orange of Kashiq was made entirely of honeygold, he replied. 'But it cannot have just been fine wire for it would have been bent and creased and soon broken with the strain of being raised and lowered many times.'

'Perhaps a fine chain?' suggested Tarik, rubbing his beard with the side of his thumb thoughtfully.

'But then the chains would be seen at the top of the orange when it was closed, wouldn't it?' asked Ravin, equally puzzled by this new obstacle. He pulled the embroidery thread up and down the wire watching the segment rise and fall.

'What we need is to find out more about the leaf and the stem you have seen the drawings of, Ravin,' said Tarik. 'If we could only know what it might look like, we would know how the Orange worked and we might be able to put it all together again.'

Achillea clapped her hands. 'And then we could go back to Oramia and you could give it to Ambar and there would be enduring love forever again!' Too late, she realised what she had done, and covered her mouth with her hands as if to stop the words from leaving, when they had already flown out, like some tiny swarm of bees straight towards Ravin, stinging him with the pain of betrayal as he realised we had not been honest with him about our reasons for finding the Orange of Kashiq.

# CHAPTER 19

The silence spread between us like a creeping puddle of dark water. Achillea looked from me to Tarik to Ravin and back again as if trying to read some ancient scroll. I do not know what she read in all our faces, only that I was full of rage. The emberjar of my mind was full of fire, and, with nowhere to go, it turned inwards on itself, angry and all consuming.

How could Achillea have been so stupid? I asked myself, trying to stop saying it out loud to her. She had risked not only our mission to find the Orange of Kashiq, but, it seemed to me, almost everything else too. Our happy sojourn in Arbhoun would come to an end and we would have to flee back to Oramia. When we got back there, Ambar in his own anger would doubtless make our lives miserable to pay us back for our failure. More than that, I would lose my learning at the Tower of the Wise; I would never find all the pieces of the Orange nor solve for myself my many unanswered questions. But more than all of this, and more precious to me than any of it was Ravin.

I had seen that wounded look that in his eyes as he looked at me. He looked so hurt to discover that there had been so much more behind our quest to find the honeygold orange pieces; that I had intentionally hidden it from him which was as close to lying to him as you could get. I could not now do what I had planned to do; to tell him everything about my life from the time in the Temple through to the search for the Queen and then to our current task. He would not believe me now if I told him I had wanted to tell him everything and had only been waiting for the right moment. I realised that there was a never a right moment for it; that whenever I had told him there would have been questions with difficult answers. And I also realised that it was my own fear for myself that had prevented me from being entirely honest with Ravin; that I was worried that I might lose him and now that seemed inevitable.

'I did not mean to say that...' stuttered Achillea finally, the anxiety making her voice taut and scratched. 'It was me being silly, as I always am. I did not even think before I spoke, and now I have ruined everything!' Her voice broke and she began to weep, pulling her netela over her face. Tarik looked at me and in his eyes I saw that he was concerned for Achillea and for her pain first and that it would lay on me to try to explain to Ravin, even though I felt this most unjust, for we had all three agreed not to tell Ravin everything at the beginning. Tarik got up and went over to Achillea. Gently he persuaded her to stand up and then guided her inside the dwelling, still weeping. I am ashamed to say that I was so angry with her then that I failed to understand how pained she must have felt.

Ravin glared at me. The anger was sliding off him like the sand falls from a sand dune, a perpetual seething movement. From a distance you could not have seen it, for he was not shouting or even talking; there was just an invisible humming wall of distrust between us which had never been there before.

'When were you planning to tell me of this secret plan of yours?' he asked eventually, a formal coldness evident in his tone. 'Was I only a game piece to be played with and used for my knowledge of Kashiq and then discarded? Were you ever planning to tell me that you intended to leave me and go back to Oramia to this Ambar man whom you love? I thought I was the one you loved!' He stood up and paced about angrily. 'I told you things I never told anyone before. Now I know why they say you should never love one from another land!' He stopped and turned to the clay wall and then suddenly thrust his fist into it in anger. I had not yet spoken, nor had the chance to, but the crunching sound of his hand hitting the wall with such force made me wince and I rushed over to him, reaching out for his hand to soothe it. He snatched it away from me and instead cradled it to his chest, blood running from it down his tunic, mutely emanating his rage.

'Can I answer your questions?' I asked, finally, in a trembling voice. I felt hot sliding tears making their way down my face and was unable to stop them. He stood, apparently on the verge of flight, seemingly struggling with whether he could bear to stay in my company. We stood like this for what seemed an age, and all the while there was the humming wall of hurt between us which seemed to get larger rather than smaller as time went by. Eventually, Ravin nodded curtly, and he went to sit against the wall, in the shade, still cradling his injured hand. I trailed after him miserably.

I did not know how to start, for every thread I picked up pulled at another one with which it was inextricably knotted and bound. If I started with Ambar then that accorded him importance he did not have; if I started instead with our mission, that too would seem to demonstrate that it was our higher goal. And all these things drew me back to having to talk to Ravin about my own childhood and how it had shaped me into this person I had become. Truth be told, I was more terrified of this part than any other. I had told myself that I had not explained myself to Ravin because I needed to not speak about our mission from Ambar. But more than that, I did not want to show him who I really was even though I felt more complete in his company than at any other time. I already thought he loved me for who I was, and yet I had not shown him who I truly was, so his love for me was really a mirage, something shifting and unattainable. But I had no choice now. When I had had the choice, I had chosen not to make a choice and now there was but a single path; to speak the whole truth and see what might happen.

'Ask me what you will,' I said eventually to Ravin, since he seemed to be waiting for me to speak first. 'I will tell you anything you want to know. I should have told you it all before, but I was afraid.'

Ravin glowered at me. He seemed to struggle with choosing what question to ask, and I saw them laid out in front of him as he wondered, like me, where this path would take us.

'Tell me of this Ambar,' he said, remotely. 'What does he have that I do not, that you are willing to come to another land and search for a long-hidden object just to gain his enduring love?' He spat out these final words that Achillea had said and I realised that she had inadvertently led him to this conclusion by what she had said. It might have been funny had it not been so serious.

'Ambar is the Lord Vizier of Oramia,' I started.

'I see now why he must mean so much to you,' interjected Ravin, bitterly. 'For I am a nobody of Kashiq, and he is a lord of Oramia. He must offer you riches beyond compare from that position. I had not thought you one to be swayed by such things.'

'Ambar means nothing to me!' I burst out, exasperated by his misunderstanding. 'He offers me no riches and instead only begs me to do his work for him! I do not love him, I love you!'

Ravin looked at me closely. 'It is the first time you have ever said that to me,' he mused. 'It seems strange that you should only utter it now, to try to explain yourself, and not when we were happy together. Tell me who and what he is to you and why you do this task for him if you have no care for him, and why Achillea said that the Orange would bring you enduring love, and why you seek to return to Oramia with a treasure of Kashiq!'

I paused to try to get the threads of my thoughts in order. It was so complicated to try to explain the deceptions I had made to Ravin and the omissions I had made, and, to this day, I do not know why I was not honest with him from the start – or rather, I suppose I do. To trust another wholly is to leap blindfolded from a high place and know that they will catch you. I had been compelled to trust Benakiell and later Achillea, Gladia and Ashtun when I first left the Temple and I had found that difficult even when I had no choice. My Temple upbringing meant that my understanding of trust was somewhat different to that held by the people of the Outer, or by the Kashiqi people. For me, trust was what one had in the Goddess that she would provide for you and that what happened in one's life was of her will. When I ceased to trust in the Aphorisms of Ashkana or in the utterances of the Goddess, I found out more and more which destroyed any simple trust I might have had in the Priestesses as guardians of my fate. Perhaps this was the root of my inability to trust others.

'Do not plan your story too much, Talla,' warned Ravin coldly. 'I will know if you are not telling the truth for I have lost my trust in you already and no longer will I blindly believe everything that you tell me.'

Despite my sadness, this made me feel quite angry and I looked up at Ravin, the snap of rage presumably a flash in my eye, because, for an instant, his mouth moved to curve almost as if he found my anger funny, and it was as though we were how we had been for a fleeting moment.

'Just tell me everything,' he said wearily, but in a softer tone. 'I will listen.'

And so I did. It took me hours as I told the story of my life so far to Ravin. I told him of the Temple and of the mystery of who my mother was and how, for a time I had thought I might be Queen. I told him of the bees and the ways in which they guided me and of my bond with them. I told him of what I had found out about Oramia; of the Angels and the OutRiders and the Queen and of how, in company with Ambar and Tarik, we had found the Queen, Lunaria, and taken her to the Court. Of Ashtun's death and of the manner of Jember's conception I also spoke, and Ravin winced as I told him the details of those two terrible incidents. He listened carefully as I spoke of Ambar's mission; of his desire to find the pieces of the Orange of Kashiq and present the Orange to his love, Lunaria, so that she would marry him and have children by him. He stopped me when I spoke of Ambar and began to question me about him; what he looked like, how old he was, was he knowledgeable, how I felt towards him and so on. I tried to answer him honestly, but I did not always use the right words and in telling him that Ambar was tall and muscled and well groomed, I angered him, even though it was only my view of his appearance. He asked me again if I loved Ambar.

I sighed in exasperation. 'I did not even know what love was when I came out of the Temple. I had never seen a man before save for the traders permitted into the Temple. I did not even know that men and women needed each other to make children; I thought they came from the Goddess! Ambar was the first man who had ever talked to me as if he liked me or liked what I looked like, or even looked at me. He was charming and he flattered me, especially when he thought I was the Queen he had been searching for. I did think that I might be special to

223

him then,' I acknowledged. 'I was like a child, learning for the first time about friendship and love.'

Ravin was briefly silent before he asked his next question.

'But why did you all decide to do more tasks for this Ambar when he asked you? Why did you not refuse him and tell him to find some other way, or tell him that a honeygold orange is no way to prove your love to someone?'

Honestly, I did not know the answer to this properly myself, except that we were all caught up in a common memory of how we had worked together previously when we had found Lunaria. Despite the dangers and the hardships and the bitter disappointments, we had enjoyed it for the most part; the different challenges and the new places we travelled to, the things we had learned. When we had moved to live in Gabez, that too had been interesting and challenging in its own way and travelling back and forth to Mellia and Sanguinea was always a joy. But in the past few years, especially as Achillea and Tarik's relationship had deepened, I had begun to feel a little bored, as if my life in Gabez was no different to my previous life in the Temple, with everyday chores and expectations of doing things at certain times and in certain places. Benakiell's stories of the apricot trees and life in Kashiq had fired up my mind, and it had taken little to persuade me. Tarik, too, was accustomed to travelling and had evidently gained much from our trip to Kashiq, as had Achillea. Achillea always wanted to help others to be happy and she had a tender heart which forgave easily and was always optimistic. She wanted Ambar to be happy with someone he loved, and the tale of the Orange of Kashiq was like one of the old story telling songs she liked to sing. I did not want to mention the special plea Ambar had made of me, and the words he had used to

224

persuade me, but I did say that he had asked me to trust in the mission he had given us and that he trusted us too.

Ravin listened to my explanation, again without interruption. His eyes no longer flashed with deep anger when he looked at me, which he only did briefly, but they were deep, dark pools of hurt and the sparkles which had always seemed to glint off them were shadowed. He had winced as I talked about trust, and I realised how it might sound to him who had not been trusted in the same way.

After I had finished talking, Ravin struggled up to his feet, without putting his injured hand on the ground to push himself up. I stood up to help him, but he turned away from me, stumbling slightly.

'Is there anything else you want to ask?' My voice sounded shaky even to me, and I could feel the tears sliding down my cheeks again. He shook his head and looked at me sadly.

'I need to go back to my own dwelling to think on my own about all of this and decide what I must do. I will tell you when I know.' He turned and walked away, his carrysack hanging forlornly off one shoulder. The breeze caught one end of his headdress which fluttered slightly, and then he was gone.

I remained outside for some time until Tarik and Achillea came out to see me. They must have seen Ravin leave. It was clear that Achillea had been crying for her eyes were swollen and red, and I suppose mine must have been too for I was not given to crying. I was still angry with her for blurting out what she did, but truthfully I was angrier with myself for not having had the courage to trust Ravin myself. I could not blame Achillea for something I was just as guilty of. Wordlessly, she opened her arms to me, and I leaned into her and finally gave in to the storm of grief that had filled me and had no way out. Tarik patted me awkwardly on the shoulder and muttered something about going out for a walk. I tried to explain to Achillea how I felt, and she nodded and put her arm around me and comforted me like a mother with a new-born baby, murmuring little soothing words of nonsense to me as I wept for the loss of love.

Eventually, when I had stopped weeping, Achillea told me that she was going to go up to the nearby market to find something to eat for us, and left, with a small pouch of spices to trade for. Our large supply of spices from Ambar was running low now and I thought momentarily of our task. But why should I care about Ambar's love for Lunaria when it had led directly to the loss of Ravin's love for me? What was the point in trying to find the Orange of Kashiq when it was itself a symbol of broken love? I looked around me dully and gazed at the walls of the small courtyard we had been in, where we cooked and ate and sat in the low sun of evening sometimes. There was a palm leaf besom in the corner, so I returned to my past life as a cleaner in the Temple and picked it up and began to mindlessly sweep the courtyard using the seven-step process I had been taught; three strokes across then three strokes up and then a single swirling stroke across the middle. I focused my churning mind on the sweeping and the counting, and when I had finished, I started again.

As I swept close to the clay wall, I spotted a small plant attempting to grow through the hard dirt. It had had to force its way through the obstacles in its path and still it grew. I felt a surge of concern for the plant as it carried on trying to live through difficult times with little sustenance and drew out half a cup of water from the large clay water jar and poured it around the little plant. I then found a sharp stick and broke up the earth around it to make it easier for the water to sink in. It was as I was doing this that Achillea returned from the market, carrying with her some coffee from Oramia and some food in a palm leaf basket. The Kashiqis used palm leaves for many things. There was an abundance of them here and they were constantly growing new leaves and shedding old ones. The leaves were even conveniently already in strips, so all you had to do was weave them together to make a small bag or basket. You could put food in them or other small items, and they were something in between a piece of cloth and a woven basket of reeds such as we had in Oramia.

Achillea shook some of the ground coffee into the pot of water and waited for it to boil as she unwrapped the food. I did not want to eat, shaking my head as she offered it to me, but she forced it upon me, reminding me that I had done the same to her after Ashtun had been killed. I did not think food would ever taste the same if Ravin were gone forever. He and I had always eaten together, and I associated the goodness of food and the way it brought my senses alive with him and how he made me feel. Achillea had cunningly chosen a sweet cake, dripping in honey and nuts and dried apricots for me and when I ate it, it did comfort me and soothe me like a spoonful of honey might soothe a sore throat. We ate the cake silently together, both miserable in our own way, but nevertheless grateful for the comfort we offered each other. She apologised again for having said what she had said and for the way in which Ravin had interpreted it and assured me that she was sure that Ravin was just angry that we had not told him everything and that he would calm down, given time to himself. I was not at all convinced. She had not seen how deeply hurt he had been by my distrust, and she did not know that only a few days ago he had trusted me enough to tell me all about his own difficult upbringing and about his life before he came to Arbhoun and yet, even then, I had not reciprocated that trust.

After some time, and despite the coffee and the cake, and drinking a physic for pain from Achillea's store, my head bulged and throbbed and I went inside to my part of the dwelling and lay on my sleeping mat, gazing up into the darkness of the roof in preference to the light which came through the pierced walls and eventually I slept, dreamless and bereft.

# CHAPTER 20

There was a sweet yet somewhat sharp scent lingering in the darkness when I awoke many hours later. I had slept the whole day and into the night, and before I woke, I had had a dream. The dream was about the small plant I had found the day before, and in the dream Ashkana and Rao were there, arguing over what to do with the plant. Ashkana was in favour of uprooting it, since it did not belong in the courtyard, and had elected to grow in the most unsuitable of places where it would likely never thrive. Rao, on the other hand, wanted to leave it where it was. He argued that it had survived thus far and that perhaps it was happy where it was, fighting for its place as it had done so far. Perhaps, he argued, it would grow into a useful plant which gave fruit or physic or building material, or perhaps it might be beautiful and heal a wounded soul. Ashkana turned to me and asked me what I would do. It seemed this question was enough to stir me from my deep sleep. Or perhaps it was the scent which had pricked my mind.

I stirred, still dreaming, it seemed, for I felt a hand rest lightly on my hair and a soft, hushing noise – or perhaps that was the breeze in the palm trees. Again, I smelled the scent and then I drifted back to sleep until the first weak rays of sun struck me through the holes in the wall of the dwelling.

I sat up, feeling heavy headed and groggy from too much sleep. I learned later that Achillea had given me a physic full of poppy juice the day before, to take away the pain. It had made me sleep for twice as long as I would normally sleep and had taken the pain from my mind while I slept. As I turned to reach for my netela, I recalled the events of the previous day, and was seized with renewed grief. I lifted my netela off the mat where it had dropped when I went to sleep, and underneath it there was an orange. I might have thought it some strange accidental happening if it had not been for the fact that the orange had been very carefully peeled with a knife, so that each segment of the orange had its own separate piece of peel still attached at the bottom. The pieces had been laid so the segments looked like they had just fallen apart, held together only by a small piece of skin at the bottom of the fruit. I only knew one person who might do such a thing, who would know of its significance. Next to the orange lay a small piece of plant parchment, cunningly cut in the shape of an orange, complete with a leaf. On it was scribed 'Will you share this orange with me?' I held the parchment close to me, and gathering up the orange carefully, went outside, hoping that Achillea and Tarik still slept, for the dawn was only just breaking.

'Are you looking for me?' A familiar voice spoke from where he sat by the wall, covered in a blanket against the chill of the night. I walked towards him shakily, happy beyond measure to see him, and hoping that his message meant what I thought.

'Will you share this orange with me?' I asked Ravin in my turn, holding out the peeled and segmented orange he had left at my side. He patted the floor next to him for me to sit down, and I sat next to him, close enough to feel the warmth of his body but not yet touching. He lifted the blanket which he held around him and pulled it around me too, drawing me to him. He reached for a piece of orange and ate it reflectively before gesturing to me to do the same. I ate it slowly. It was sweet but also sharp, perhaps not quite ripe enough, perhaps with not quite enough of the sun's warmth. Ravin smiled ruefully as he saw my mouth twist.

'That is the message, I suppose, that love must be meaningful in its entirety. You cannot only take the sweet and nourishing parts of it, for without them it has no depth. I cannot pretend that I am not hurt that you did not trust me with the story of your life, as I did with mine, but I believe what you have told me now. I was most angry because I was very jealous of this man, Ambar, who holds such sway over you and your actions. How could it be that you were doing something for him in preference to telling me about it? But I was hot-headed and full of passion. I love you, Talla,' he concluded as he turned towards me, his deep dark eyes once more warm and shining. 'I think perhaps I always will. Even if you had told me you loved Ambar, it would not have stopped how I felt. Tarik came to speak with me yesterday after I left.'

I was surprised and it must have shown in my eyes. I had first met Tarik as Ambar's brother in arms years ago in Oramia when they rescued Gladia and me from some OutRiders. He used to be an OutRider himself, and he had all the loyalty and commitment that that entailed, but it was tempered by his equable attitude and his considered approach. At that time, I always thought of him as being slightly boring compared to Ambar. Ambar had charm in abundance and was adept at getting his own way. He was intelligent too, but impulsive, whereas Tarik was more thoughtful and considered. He had been a good friend to me as well as to Achillea and it had given me great pleasure to know that they loved each other but knowing that he had been to see Ravin after yesterday's events was still surprising.

'He told me about this Ambar, man to man,' continued Ravin. 'How he has a single-minded attitude to life, but also how he loves this lady Lunaria above all others and how I need have no concern about whether he loves you or ever did. He told me that Ambar only ever wanted to find and love the Queen, and that this was set in his mind from childhood by the one who guided him as a soldier.'

I felt strangely annoyed by this small anecdote, slighted perhaps, even though I had no interest in Ambar over Ravin. I realised that Ambar and Tarik must have often talked to one another about such things, and that even when they had met us, they could still communicate secretly with one another using the silent language of the OutRiders. It felt a little strange that Ambar and Tarik might have been discussing me and Achillea in front of us without us knowing. However, I was grateful to Tarik, for he had seen that Ravin needed reassurance from one who was not me, and another man who was no threat to him was probably the best person. I nestled closer to Ravin, and offered him the orange again, taking another piece for myself and biting into it dubiously. This time, however, the segment was sweet and pure and washed away the tartness of the previous one.

Ravin asked me more questions about Ambar's search for the Orange of Kashiq and about the reasons it was so important to him, and he asked me many questions about my life in the Temple. He was fascinated by the strangeness of my upbringing compared to his. It was a relief to me to be able to speak openly to Ravin about this and even more of a relief that he had not turned against me when he had discovered the strangeness of my early life.

The sun had risen further by the time Achillea stumbled out of the dwelling, bleary eyed and ready to blow the embers in the emberjar back to life to make a fire for morning coffee and tea. She was surprised to see us there together, huddled in the blanket. In truth, we were no longer cold, but there was something precious about being enclosed together that had made us reluctant to leave it. When Achillea appeared, Ravin sprang up to make the fire and Achillea apologised to him for her choice of words the previous day.

'It is I who should apologise,' answered Ravin ruefully. 'My head was full of words and my heart was full of feelings I could not control.'

'Let me help you with your hand, at least,' offered Achillea. I had forgotten about Ravin's hand and it pained me slightly that Achillea had remembered it first, but I knew she had skill in the salves. She reached out and took hold of his hand. Now that I saw it in the light, I could see that it was swollen and darkened with bruising. It was the hand he used to scribe with, and I did not think he would be able to grasp a pen for some days. Achillea felt it carefully and told Ravin she did not think it was broken. She had a salve that would bring down the swelling and the bruising, one which Tarik had taught her from the times he made physics for the OutRiders. She bustled off to get it and then gave it to me, suggesting that I might like to rub the salve on. Gratefully, I took the ointment and slowly rubbed it into his poor damaged hand, trying to soften my stroke when he winced in pain.

When Tarik and Achillea joined us to make flat breads and brew tea, Ravin said that we needed to talk about the Orange of Kashiq and our quest to return it to Oramia.

'I do not think it is right,' he said finally. 'The Orange was made by Lord Rao, here in Kashiq, for the Lady Ashkana as a symbol of his love. Even when Ashkana fled to Oramia, she sent the pieces back here to Kashiq where they were hidden by Lord Rao. Surely this orange belongs in Kashiq and not in Oramia?'

I had not thought that he might see it in this way. The three of us who had arrived in Arbhoun to search for the

Orange all came from Oramia and we naturally believed that the Orange might belong in Oramia, in the home of the one for whom it was first made. That the people of Kashiq might feel an equal sense of ownership was not something we had considered.

'It seems to me that it belongs to both equally,' said Tarik, mildly. 'It was, after all, a symbol of the love between two people, which should be equally shared. And so, it should be equally shared between the two lands.'

'But how can it be?' asked Achillea plaintively. 'We cannot only take back half of the orange, the scroll was clear about that, and Silene the DreamReader was definite about the whole orange being needed before Lunaria could marry Ambar and have children with him. If we only take back three pieces, then she will point to it as a failure and use it to say that Lunaria's marriage to Ambar will be a failure too!'

'We only have one part so far,' I pointed out. 'We still need to find all the parts before we can discuss where the orange really belongs.'

'I think we should decide now,' said Ravin stubbornly. 'I may not wish to help you take this treasure out of Kashiq, even though I understand why you want to.'

Our discussion swung back and forth over what our first steps should be. I was relieved that Ravin had no intention of alerting any of the authorities or indeed the Defenders of Yael about our search, but irritated that he had not already decided to agree with us. What we needed was a solution to please all parties whereby everyone could get what they wanted but that seemed impossible. What a shame that the Orange of Kashiq was an ornament of honeygold and not a real orange, for if it were, we could have simply picked another one off a tree and none would be any the wiser, nor indeed know which one was the original orange. A tiny spark of an idea shone in my mind's emberjar. What if we could make an identical honeygold orange?

I turned to Ravin and Tarik and asked them how the metal piece of the Orange could have been made, for it had not been hammered into place as much of the wirework decoration was, but rather looked like it had been poured into that shape, with smooth curves and precise decoration.

Tarik looked at me, curious at my question, but nevertheless explained to me, with frequent interjections from Ravin, how these types of items were made. The item itself was first carved out of beeswax using hot wires and knives. It was carved to be precisely as the item would appear once made of metal, with the addition of a small wax pipe in some inconspicuous place. Then a fine clay would be painted over the wax and dried and painted over again. A further, thicker layer of clay would be added and then another one after that, making sure the wax pipe was kept intact. When it was all dry, it would be gently heated with the entrance of the wax pipe over a fire, and all the beeswax would run down out of the clay, leaving a hard clay mould inside. This would then be carefully turned over and filled, through the wax pipe with molten silver or honeygold. Once this was cooled and hard, the clay mould could be broken off and the metal piece would be made. I pondered.

'Could you make a wax mould the same way? Could you press something made of metal into clay to make a mould and then fill that mould with wax to make a wax model of something, so you can then make a copy of something made of metal?' I asked. Tarik frowned but agreed that it was indeed a possible way of doing things but added that if you already had the metal item, you would not need it twice. Ravin swung round, his face brightening.

'No, that's not what she means! Talla is most ingenious!' Ravin quickly explained to a puzzled looking Achillea. 'If I am right, then Talla may have worked out an answer to the problem of the Orange with two hearts! If we find all the pieces of the Orange, then we can use them to make new moulds, and then somehow we could get some honeygold and melt it and then make copies of all the pieces, then you could take one set to Oramia and one set could stay here in Kashiq!' The words tumbled over themselves as he spoke. I nodded my head to show that this was indeed what I had meant. Achillea clapped her hands delightedly.

'Talla always comes up with good ideas!' I looked down modestly, and slightly uncomfortably. I was not at ease with being the centre of attention and I was still not accustomed to being praised, even though Achillea was one of those sunny people who could praise a person happily for the tiniest thing. At the same time, it did make me feel warm inside that Ravin who, not so very long ago, had been so angry with me, seemed to have left all of that behind him. Tarik looked excited. His interest in metal working was such that anything involving it had become like a shining lantern to a night moth. He nodded thoughtfully.

'I have been talking with some of the men who work in the metalworking and the wirepulling about where they get the silver and the honeygold from. A lot of the time, they melt down the silver and reuse it, but it is said that the honeygold cannot be remelted in the same way – that although you can melt it down very easily, the more times you do that, the duller it becomes until it loses all its lustre. For the shiniest honeygold, you need to use honeygold which has never seen the light of day. They dig it out of the ground in a place called Shiljam two days walk from here in Arbhoun. I might be able to go with them on their next trip if I ask them?' He looked at Achillea questioningly, as if waiting for her comment, or as if she might forbid him from going on this trip, but she smiled at him indulgently and told him that it was a good idea.

Ravin looked hopefully at me, but Tarik stopped the thought of them both going by pointing out that we still had five segments of the Orange to find in the other orchards around Arbhoun, and that Achillea and I could hardly do it on our own when the front plates of the beehives were so heavy. And so we agreed that we three would continue to search for the other segments of the Orange while Tarik went to find honeygold to use to make the copies.

# THE BLOSSOM

## CHAPTER 21

Before Tarik left in search of the honeygold rocks of Shiljam, we agreed that Ravin and I would do some reading at the Tower of the Wise to see if there was any more we could learn about how to make the wax impressions and how the molten honeygold could be poured safely into the clay mould around the wax. I also wanted to reread the Tales of the Orchard by Finzari. We had the copies of the pictures on the beehive covers already, but I wanted to try to remember all the stories that went with them too. Ravin wanted to re-examine the scrolls relating to the mechanism of the Orange, to try to understand how all the parts might come together. He and Tarik had discussed carving a central leaf and stem themselves to take the place of the missing one, of which there seemed little mention save that it remained in Oramia at the time of Ashkana.

As we walked along to the Tower of the Wise from the corner where we had met in the morning, Ravin told me he had thought of an unexpected source of information about honeygold – Scholar Avenda. I was displeased at the thought that he would be spending time with her since she was so obviously interested in him and hated the thought of them being in close proximity to one

238

another. I held his hand tightly. The corner of his mouth twitched.

'I may of course have to make admiring remarks to her to flatter her into sharing her information with me,' he remarked airily. I gritted my teeth, determined to be reasonable, but nevertheless feeling my jealousy of her taking over. Ravin laughed. 'You are feeling a little of how I feel when you speak about Ambar,' he said. I glanced at him, at once concerned that he had brought up Ambar's name again. I hated him even talking about Avenda even though he had assured me that he only loved me. I had assured him the same thing regarding Ambar, but this elusive quality of love called trust continued to be a struggle for me. I trusted Ravin but not Avenda. I had to believe that he would not be swayed by her wiles, and perhaps it was more about myself than him, for I did not believe myself to be much in comparison to her. The women in Kashiq had little of the modesty I was used to seeing in Oramia. Although they wore the headdress, they used it for much more than we used the netela. We decorated the netela with colour and embroidery, but it was still mainly a functional item; a cloth to protect from heat and cold and to conceal ourselves from strangers. Here in Kashiq the headdress fulfilled those functions, but it was also much more than that. Ravin had explained to me that the headdress and its band declared your place in your family and your birth position. Achillea and I had previously spent a long time trying to understand the various patterns on the headdresses but Ravin had explained them to us clearly.

The colours of the headdress were determined by the colours of the days on which family members were born, and the decoration denoted their position in the family. He explained it to us, using his own headdress as an example.

'The main colour of our headdress square is determined by the colour of the day we are born. So, mine is orange because I was born on the day of Aureus. The headband carries on it three pieces of information that you can read: for a man like me, the main band colour is the colour of the day my mother was born, and the decoration is sewn in the colour of the day my father was born. My mother was born on Viridis and my father on the day of Flammeus, so I have a green headband with red embroidery. If I had been a woman, it would be reversed, and I would have had a red headband with green embroidery. The shape of the pattern shows your position in the family; the first born has a circle, the second a line, the third a three-sided shape and the fourth a square and so on. I have a triangle which means I was the third born in the family. I had a sister born first who died of ague when she was only an infant, and an older brother.'

Since he had told us this, Achillea and I had amused ourselves in reading the headbands of the people we had seen around, and in trying to work out what our own might be. Mine, of course was complicated by not knowing anything other than the day of my birth. I had no idea of the days on which my parents were born nor of how many siblings I might have had, and Tarik was in the same position. Achillea on the other hand, was able to work out her own; a blue headdress for Azureus with a yellow headband for her father and purple circles to show her mother and that she was the first (and only one) born.

I had noticed that the women of Kashiq also added other accents of decoration to their headdresses; some stitched shining silver discs on the embroidered shapes or added small metal shapes to the strings with which the band was fixed. Sometimes they pushed the headdress back from their faces until they were placed at the back of the head and the hair was then free of the cloth, and others covered up their hair, but used powdered charcoal as ink around their eyes, and darkberry salve to darken their lips. Avenda was one who evidently paid great attention to how she was seen, for her face was often altered in this way. I tried to push the thought of her away and concentrate on what my own plans were for the day.

While Ravin was finding out about the honeygold process and was also hoping to look more closely at the drawings of how the Orange opened and shut, I was going to re-read the Tales of the Orchard and try to scribe brief notes on the content of each story for the remaining segments of the Orange. It was no surprise to me that it was Scholar Avenda who was working at the Scholars' scribeboard that morning. I had noticed that Scholar Mazin preferred the afternoon; perhaps he liked to sleep in the morning or perhaps he knew that there was less to do in the afternoon. Ravin stood behind me, and Avenda, as usual, hurried through my requests, curling her lip scornfully when I requested the Tales of the Orchard again.

'What may I find for you this morning, Ravin?' she asked brightly before her tone changed to one of concern when she spotted his bound hand. 'Oh dear, have you been injured? Do you need any help in carrying your scrolls? I see your little Oramian friend has already got the scrolls for her study of the tedious tales of Finzari, so perhaps I can do that for you?'

I gritted my teeth, willing myself not to turn around to look at them.

'How kind,' murmured Ravin. 'In truth, I would like to ask you some questions since you are such a well-known expert on honeygold and the honeygold process. I have become interested in it, perhaps through your example. I would like to make some scribings about it, but as you

241

see, I have hurt my hand and cannot scribe today...' His voice trailed off sorrowfully. Avenda's voice became lighter and brighter in response.

'If you want, I would be happy to help you by scribing down some pieces of knowledge for you, Ravin. Your friend will be busy scribing away on her own business and so I am happy to offer myself.' She paused briefly as I seethed quietly to myself. 'And, of course, my scribing to you for your service today. If you have any questions about the honeygold, you can ask me; I am engaged on writing a long scroll on this very subject!' Ravin thanked her warmly and she took the scrolls to his scribeboard for him and then stood closely to him as she helped to unroll the scroll.

I found it very difficult to focus my mind on the Tales of the Orchard and my efforts to commit them to memory. I tried to scribe only the key points from each of the six tales; a description of the picture, a key quality of love which the tale was illustrating, and a short summary of each tale. I spent a lot of time looking at the scroll and barely reading it because I was trying to listen to Avenda and her descriptions of honeygold and how it was used. She did a lot of leaning over of Ravin and touching his arm when she wanted his attention. Occasionally when she was looking the other way or called away to her scribeboard by another seeker of wisdom, Ravin would roll his eyes at me and pull comical faces so that I knew her blandishments were having little effect on him. But still my mind's emberjar rumbled and my thoughts chased themselves in circles.

Eventually, an unlikely saviour appeared in the form of Scholar Mazin. He arrived with much huffing of breath and called Avenda over so that she might tell him what she was doing scribing for another instead of sitting at the Scholar's scribeboard. She explained, and Scholar

Mazin waddled over to stand between me and Ravin. He cast an eye on Avenda's scribings for Ravin and told her that she had done quite enough and then turned his attention to me and my notes on the Tales of the Orchard. He scanned through them quickly, his bright black eyes taking in all the details. He may have had a somewhat comical appearance, but it was clear that he knew the writings of Finzari very well. In a couple of places, he told me that I should emphasise this rather than that, or that it was important to also consider the order of the tales in the scroll as that might tell us something of the thoughts of the scholar. I thanked him for his help, and he bowed with a flourish before making his way back to the Scholar's Scribeboard where he promptly sent Avenda off on some errands for him. I smiled a little.

Ravin and I seized the opportunity while Avenda was busy to go out into the gardens around the Tower of the Wise and eat our meal together, as was our custom. Ravin told me some of what he had learned from Avenda that morning. Some of it we already knew from what Tarik had discovered from the men he had worked with in the metalworking district; that the honeygold was held within rocks found somewhat north and east of Arbhoun, and that although it was not especially rare, the process of removing the honeygold from the rocks was a complicated one, and one which was only known to those who handled the rocks. She confirmed that it was the first use of the molten honeygold which produced the brightest, shiniest honeygold and that if it was subsequently melted down again to be reformed, as all metal eventually was, it would be less shiny each time it was melted again. The most useful thing which Avenda had told him and scribed for him was the process by which the honeygold was moulded into items. This involved carving the item out of beeswax as Ravin had told us, including a long thin pipe of wax which was attached to the item in some unobtrusive place and was later used to pour the molten honeygold into the cast. The clay used over the top of the wax model was made of very finely ground clay, ground in a pestle and mortar so that every tiny detail carved into the wax would be faithfully reproduced in the honeygold mould of it. This was especially useful as it allowed us to plan how to trade for beeswax and the fine clay used by the potters in Kashiq so that we could make the models of the segments. Somehow, it never occurred to us that we might not find the segments of the Orange, or that we might not be able to make them again out of wax moulds. Perhaps it was just that we had the confidence of youth in these things.

Avenda had shown Ravin some diagrams of examples of making metal objects and how the process worked and, together with what Tarik had already found out, these would help us to recreate the Orange segments.

As we sat and talked, I knew that things were different in the closeness between Ravin and I. We had been through a difficult time of learning that trust was important to us both, and although it had been very painful, we had both emerged stronger and perhaps more reassured by the renewed trust between us. I told Ravin about the story from the Tales of the Orchard which had told of trust. It was around the orchard of Asmara, the Goddess of creation and life, she who brought this world into being, the Goddess we had worshipped in the temple, and for whom I had real affinity. It was no surprise to me that Finzari had chosen the orchard of Asmara in which to hide the segment of the Orange relating to trust, for we trusted in the Goddess every day, and she trusted us to take care of her creation. The tale itself was about a bee and the Guardian of the Orchard, a woman named Gulrant. One day a new worker had been in the orchard and a bee had been flying near him on the way to a flower with another bee. His companion bee had stopped and landed on the man's sleeve and the man had slapped at the bee, who was afraid, and stung him and then died. The bee that was left was now fearful of the people in the orchard. Gulrant the Guardian had seen this worker's reaction and had punished him for his hasty reaction, counselling him to take time before reacting so aggressively to one who meant him no harm. She went to sit by the beehive and began to sing to bring the bees out. Soon, all the bees except that one fearful bee were out of the hive. Gently, Gulrant opened the hive and placed her hand inside the hive. The bee did not trust her and turned, as if to sting her, but she did not react to his fear and left her hand there, gently humming songs of sweet flowers and the warm rays of the sun. The bee became calmer and finally he trusted her, for he saw how patient she was with his fear which was the seed of mistrust, and he crawled onto her hand. Calmly she drew out her hand from the hive and brought the bee out into the sunshine and the warm scent of nectar and he flew off. But he always remembered her and often came to ride on her shoulder as she wandered the orchard, and he never worried that she might slap at him.

We talked about fear being the seed of mistrust and about how we had both been driven by fear of the other leaving us into not fully trusting the other. We agreed that we would both try harder to trust and to be patient as we waited for that trust. And then, although we had only been at the Tower of the Wise for half the day, we left through one of the garden gates and wandered back to the dwelling where Tarik was preparing to leave to travel to the honeygold mines of Shiljam. He would meet with a group of perhaps eight men who would travel there over the next few days to find honeygold rocks. He would take with him some of the physic and burn salve that the men might need, as well as food and a water pot. He was excited to set off on this new adventure, but he had asked me to take care of Achillea, and I could see that he would rather have her with him where he knew she would be safe. I assured him that we would look after her for him. Achillea, too, did not want to think of being without him now that the time was near. He had been with us almost all the time since Ashtun had died all those years ago, and although Achillea had a bright and sunny disposition, she could not bear to think of losing another whom she loved. Tarik assured her it was safe and that it was a normal journey made by the metalworkers several times a year. It was hard physical work, but Tarik was a man who always worked hard and had been raised to be fit and strong when he was an OutRider.

When we got back, Tarik was pulling tight the strings on his carry pack. It was a heavy bag, but it would be even heavier when he returned with the honeygold rocks, and he remarked ruefully that he wished that there were horses to ride in Kashiq. I recalled the days that I had spent on horseback in the days following our first meeting with Tarik, and how quickly they covered the ground and how much they could carry. Here in Kashiq, it was much like in Oramia, for only the Defenders of Yael were permitted to ride on horses. This meant that only the determined and well prepared could travel throughout the land, for in many places there were many miles between settlements with no rivers or trees under which to shelter. I could see why those who ruled did not want ordinary people to have the very things which entitled them to their power, but it irked me, nonetheless.

'I shall aim to return on the day of Viridis, a week tomorrow,' Tarik confirmed to Achillea. 'It may be one day more or less, but I will return to you, my little songbird.' He gazed fondly at her face, normally so bright and cheerful, now solemn and anxious. 'You have plenty to do yourself, along with Talla and Ravin, for by the time I return with the honeygold, you will need to have found all the other segments if we are to succeed in this task. You will barely notice I am gone!' Achillea sniffed and smiled a little tremulously at him, not trusting herself to speak in case her voice failed her. They embraced and then we too bade our farewells and watched as he strode down the dusty orange street. He looked back once and raised his hand in salute and then was gone.

Ravin left us shortly after that too, for he had tasks he needed to do for Shafir, the man whose dwelling he shared. He had to trade wood for him to carve more boxes out of, and fill the big clay water jars, clear out the dwelling and sharpen Shafir's woodcarving tools for him. I had not yet met Shafir, although Ravin told me that he had talked to Shafir about me. It was important that Ravin should do the tasks for Shafir and he was happy to do them as it reminded him of his friendship with Hurkim when he was younger.

# CHAPTER 22

We found the next segment of the Orange of
Kashiq very easily. It lay in the Orchard of Rao
on the eastern edge of Arbhoun. It was a large,
sprawling orchard, with only a few dwellings on the edge
of it, which came close to the path which left Arbhoun
and went towards a place called Kafindim. That lay many
days travel away and Ravin had told us that it lay right at
the edge of the land, by the side of a vast body of water
that one could see no end to. I could not even imagine
such a thing, having lived in Oramia where there were
only rivers and small frequent streams and no large areas
of water. In Arbhoun there were the six areas where the
waters deep under the land came to the surface and
whose water was used by the Arbhoun is for their use and
for watering their fields and orchards. These were large,
deep pools of water which never seemed to go down, no
matter how much water was used from them. It was said
that they had been made by Asmara, the creator of all
things in the days when the world began.

We had decided to follow the same plan for each of the
orchards as we had in the first one. Since it was not the
time of year when the fruit trees were either in blossom
or in fruit, there would be less people visiting anyway,
and there might well be some sort of guardian of the
orchard sitting with a small array of goods and honey to
trade, like Farin, who we could talk to while also finding
the right beehive using the drawings which Ravin had
made from the Tales of the Orchard scroll. We needed to
amass some beeswax while Tarik was away so that we

could use it to make the moulds of the segments when he returned, so we went well prepared, with salves and physics and Tarik's wooden latches to trade. We went as the sun began to slip down in the sky.

The Orchard of Rao was watched over by a young man, plainly bored, who sat flicking small pebbles at a target roughly made of palm leaves. He had little to trade for it was late in the day and this route was well used by travellers who would stop and trade for extra food and drink as they left the city. He did, however, have two big chunks of beeswax. Ravin stayed to talk to him, showing him one of Tarik's ingenious latches which could safely lock a door to a dwelling while Achillea and I found the beehive cover we needed. It was the simple depiction of the apricot blossom for the story which I had first properly read. The beehive was on the edge of the row of hives, which made it easy to open up later, once it was dark and the young man had gone home, happily clutching his new latch. I wondered at the Kashiqi Orchard guardians who left their orchards and their beehives unguarded overnight, but, as Ravin pointed out, the bees were the best protectors and would sting to protect their hives and their honey and the fruit trees where they worked. It was only because I was a BeeGuard that we could find the segments with so little resistance.

The segment was placed just like the first one, encased first in beeswax and then in clay and placed on the inside of the front entrance to the beehive. As soon as we had replaced the cover on the beehive, we made our way back to the dwelling. While Tarik was away, Ravin had agreed that he would stay at our dwelling at night in case we needed protecting. Achillea and I were pleased to have him there, and it made Tarik feel happier to know that someone was with us. I would have preferred that Ravin would have slept with me in my part of the dwelling but

Tarik and Ravin between them had agreed that I would sleep with Achillea in her sleeping area, and Ravin would sleep in mine. This seemed to have two different effects on Achillea and I; Achillea slept very soundly, comforted by my presence. I, on the other hand, found that she slept perhaps too soundly, and made small purring noises while she slept which made me less rested than usual. I pondered whether this might be the same if Ravin were sharing my room but thought it unlikely. The more time we spent close to each other, the harder it got to stay apart. Since Tarik was not there, Achillea was never occupied by anyone else and every time that Ravin and I tried to spend some time alone together, she would interrupt us. We had more chances to kiss one another at the Tower of the Wise than in our dwelling.

The next segment came from the Orchard of Soren. Achillea was excited to visit this orchard. Ever since her voice had been recognised by Parline as a gift from the goddess Soren, Achillea had become more and more attached to the guidance of Soren and to finding out about her. On the walk there, she asked Ravin what he knew about the goddess Soren, and he told her as we walked along the path to the orchard on the north east side of Kashiq, close to the fields where food was grown.

'It was told that Soren was the sweetest and kindest of all the goddesses, that she had nothing in her heart but a wish for all to be made whole and to be healed. She knew that there were many people who were hurt, or who felt that something was not balanced in their lives and in all things she strove only to make things better. She learned the arts of using the plants to make physics and elixirs to heal the ailments of the body, but also that there were ragged places in the soul which needed to be healed, some with music and song like yours, Achillea.' Achillea preened herself at this mention and then pressed Ravin for more.

'It is said that Soren, for all her desire to heal, was often the cause of disagreement between the gods. There are stories in the Book of Kashiq of her unwillingness to compromise with others. Only Asmara had the power over her to tell her when to stop.'

'But why would they want her to stop healing people?' asked Achillea, reasonably. 'Surely it is a good thing to be healed and made better? Surely we all feel happier and more purposeful when we are healed?'

'And that was the cause of the disagreements,' replied Ravin, smiling slightly. 'The Gods disagreed about whether it was good for us to always be happy. It is often in the darkest times that we most appreciate the brightness. One who is in the darkest of nights will surely gain more from the light of an oil lamp than one who lives in a constantly bright daylight – for what need would he have of an oil lamp?'

I thought about this. Now that Ravin had put it this way, I could see how it might be impossible for us to fully appreciate the brightness of our joyful times if we did not also have times which were not joyful. But how could we long for dark times? I was grateful that I was not one of the six gods and goddesses of Kashiq and did not have to make choices and decisions about subjects such as this. I was happy to look after my bees – although I recognised that they too had two sides to them – one which made sweet healing honey and one where they would sting and fight to the death.

Ravin continued. 'There was the story told of one who became blind. She was injured by accident, and she used to work making jewellery, so she could no longer work. When she could see, she was always too busy to listen to others, and too busy to try to understand the pain of others. Soren wished to heal her, especially since this woman made supplications to her to return her. But Asmara counselled her to stay her healing, and to wait. The woman began to listen more to those around her. In the absence of her sight, she began to grow in other ways. Because she listened to those around her, they became her friends, and one of them was guided by Soren herself. She encouraged the blind woman to sing her thoughts. Emboldened by her lack of sight, which stopped her from being worried by the expressions of those who listened to her, the woman began to sing. She became more and more well-known for the beautiful quality of her voice and in her turn brought healing to others through her song. And so, Soren learned that healing could take place in many ways. Often, she had to be held back from healing one who was close to death and could only provide peace to them as Yael took his turn to bring them home. It was hard for her to do this, but as she grew older, she understood that healing took many guises.'

The idea of the gods and goddesses having discussions about who should have the right to decide on how a prayer was answered both amused and perplexed me. Achillea, on the other hand, had no trouble at all in accepting it and her simple acceptance of this story and of the characters of those deities reminded me of how I used to accept all that I was told about the Goddess in the Temple. Even though Ravin now knew about my earlier life in the Temple in Oramia, I was still uncomfortable talking about it to my friends. For some unknown reason, I always felt like I was being pitied when I talked about it, but perhaps it was just that I pitied myself.

The Orchard of Soren was a peaceful place. It appeared to have been imbued with a calming healing ambience by the Goddess Soren herself. I asked Ravin if the people of Arbhoun tended toward visiting the orchard whose name was the same as their chosen guide in life. He acknowledged that yes, perhaps that was the case. There was no special ordnance that dictated it but maybe the Arbhounis, like people everywhere, felt more at home in groups of their own kind of people. Those who followed the guidance of Soren had much in common with one another, after all. Achillea was certainly enjoying the visit, and once we had established where the beehives might be, Ravin and I wandered over to them to identify where the beehive we sought was. Achillea lingered, talking to the little group of women who gathered by the guardian's little stand where, in addition to some dried apricots there were all manner of small pots of salve and healing elixirs, as well as some small scenes of trees and flowers painted on plant parchment. I had not seen these sorts of things in the food markets in the middle of Arbhoun. Ravin explained that there were those who thought that looking at something beautiful like a flower could be as soothing and healing to the mind as a song or a salve. I liked them and lingered a little myself before we walked over to the beehives, which were right at the northern edge of the orchard, close to the orange, sandy hills which stretched out to the north of Arbhoun. The beehive cover which illustrated this fable had been beautifully decorated with a mass of simple honeycomb shapes dripping honey in different tones of orange and yellow into different jars and pots. The story compared the sweetness of forgiveness in love to the sweetness of honey.

Ravin and I were becoming rather impatient with waiting for Achillea by the time she finally arrived, full of the names and stories of the women she had been talking to. They formed a small singing group who sang at important times such as the birth of a longed-for child or the death of a beloved parent or partner. They had invited her to join them on the next day of Aureus at the Place of Prayer near the Orchard. She was distracted the whole time we were trying to retrieve the segment, and I had to speak to her sharply when she paused as she was fitting the fixing coil of clay back to the beehive, since Ravin and I were holding up the heavy beehive cover to replace it. It felt as if we would drop it if we held it a moment longer, and I rather selfishly wished that Tarik were here to hold up the cover with Ravin, and to keep Achillea's attention more firmly fixed on the task. I was happy that she was refreshed and renewed by her dedication to Soren. If only she had the same dedication to our quest to find the Orange of Kashiq.

As we made our way back with the third segment carefully knotted into a piece of cloth and tightly tied into Ravin's carrysack, it seemed that everything was progressing well here in Arbhoun. I could only hope that things were progressing as well for Tarik in the honeygold mines, north of that orchard where we had just been. We now had the segments of the orange which represented forgiveness, joy, and freedom; three of the qualities of love which Rao had wanted to share with Ashkana. It seemed from what we had read that Ashkana had been unable to extend her forgiveness to Lord Rao for whatever it was that he had done to her. I thought about how easy it might have been for Ravin not to forgive me for betraying his trust, and how grateful I was that he had indeed shared the sweet honey of forgiveness with me.

The ease with which we found the segment was not, however a sign of how easy it was afterwards. As Ravin held the beeswax encased segment over the fire to melt the coating, part of it fell into the fire along with the beeswax. He quickly pulled the main part away from the fire, but it was clear that the little lid for the segment had broken off from the main part of it. Perhaps Ashkana had wrenched it too hard from the stem when she broke the orange, or perhaps it had been broken as Rao hid it. The section fell deep into the heart of the fire, sizzling as it dropped. Quickly I seized the pot of water which stood waiting to be put on the fire to boil for coffee and tipped it over the fire, quenching most of it. Ravin looked around him and found a long stick which he used to carefully spread out the embers. Achillea hastily crammed some of the still glowing embers into the emberjar which stood by the fire so that we could restart the fire later. All that lay in front of us was a scattered stream of black and grey lumps. There seemed to be no sign of the missing section.

'Where is it?' I asked Ravin. 'There is no honeygold here at all, only soot and ashes. Has it burnt to nothing? What will we do without all the pieces?'

'It will be here,' he replied, calmly, but his eyes showed his concern. 'The metal might have been blackened in the fire.'

'But what if it has melted?' asked Achillea. 'You said, and so did Ravin, that honeygold is easily melted. What if it is just a melted lump? How will we ever make the lid to fit the segment perfectly? All the segments are different from each other and fit together a bit differently.' This was true. Each individual segment we had found so far fastened slightly differently. The way that they were finished affected the way in which they fitted together. I began to feel worried again.

Ravin looked dubiously at the huge, wet, and sooty pile. It was full of misshapen black lumps and would take some time before we could find out if the piece were still intact or if it had been melted. He divided it up into three parts. We had to go through every piece and squeeze it between our fingers. If it were charcoal, it would crumble to powder, but if it was metal it would resist the pressure. We began the task. It took a long time and soon our hands and clothes were black with powdered charcoal from all the crushed embers. Eventually, my nail felt something slightly different underneath it as I pushed down on yet another lump, this one covered in white ash. I pushed against it further. It felt like beeswax, but that was impossible. We had all seen the beeswax sizzle and drip when held over the fire – that was why we were holding the piece over the fire in the first place. I picked it up and scraped at it dubiously. Perhaps the beeswax had melted and then hardened around some charcoal when I threw the water on the fire. I scratched at it a bit more, and eventually made my way through a very thick layer of beeswax, much thicker than it had originally been, to a shiny piece of honeygold. I showed it to Achillea and Ravin. Ravin took it from me and held it to the light wonderingly.

'How can this be? There was not this depth of beeswax around the segment when we first held it in the flames!'

Achillea peered at it and then exclaimed triumphantly, 'It must be Talla! It's because she is a Beeguard! Somehow all the wax has flown to the honeygold piece and protected it all from the flames!' It was typical of Achillea that she saw it in this way; she loved a mysterious tale. There again, I could not explain how it had happened, and neither, by the bewildered look on his face, could Ravin. The broken lid of the segment was thickly protected by beeswax which had not melted in the fire as it had done every other time, but which seemed to have formed a barrier between the precious honeygold piece and the heat of the fire. And yet, when Ravin held the lump close to the fire again, the beeswax just melted and dropped off the metal in large viscous lumps. Perplexed, Ravin examined the fragile little piece that had fallen off as if he might be able to divine some understanding from it, but it looked like all the rest. He pondered over it as he worked on making a tiny hinge with wire to join the two pieces back together but professed himself at a loss to explain it. Perhaps it was as Achillea said; perhaps the bees somehow protected me and my quest again. Or perhaps it was the Goddess Soren, in whose orchard we had found the piece, who wanted us to heal it.

Once the repaired segment was cleaned and carefully stored away in the locked wooden box in which they were kept, we settled down finally in front of the newly rebuilt fire. Achillea began to sing softly, a new song which I had not heard before. It was about the bees collecting from the flowers and its cadence rose and fell like the humming of the bees. It was very peaceful until, suddenly, there came a great banging noise on the wooden door of the dwelling where we lived.

Alarmed, we looked at one another. Had somebody seen us at the orchard? Ravin hastily suggested that he should go and open the door, while we wait behind him, since he was a Kashiq himself and knew more about what might be required. We crept behind him to the door, where the person was still banging in a bad-tempered fashion. Ravin withdrew the wooden peg from the hasp to unlock the door.

'Oh, for goodness sake, in the name of the Goddess, who on earth are you?' came a very familiar and completely unexpected voice. 'I was told that there are definitely two women of Oramia dwelling here and you are not either of them! Where are Talla and Achillea?'

Ravin opened his mouth to speak, but Achillea and I rushed forward to greet our visitor, amazed to see her. Gladia had arrived in Kashiq.

# CHAPTER 23

A re you going to invite me in, or not?' asked Gladia as we surged towards her, both of us asking questions over the top of each other. There was the familiar note of acerbity in her voice, but also a weariness. I took her bundles from her and thrust them into Ravin's arms, telling him to go and put them somewhere and to put the coffee back on again, for I knew Gladia would want sustenance. He went, completely bewildered by the turn of events and not comprehending that this could be the Gladia who I had told him about when I had explained all that had gone before.

When I turned back to Gladia and Achillea, they were embracing one another silently. I hoped that this meant that they were forgiving, finally, of one another's shortcomings. Then Gladia turned and, rather uncharacteristically, embraced me too, pressing me against her warm soft self. Now that I had learned the sweet benefit of an embrace, I was not as awkward as I had been before and embraced her in my turn.

'There is much we need to discuss,' said Gladia finally. 'But I want to sit down somewhere, and perhaps eat something, for I have been wandering around this place for hours now and it has been a long and weary journey from Mellia.' She looked around the dwelling critically and sniffed at the plain fabric which hung between the sections. My mind was darting from topic to topic like a bee presented with too many flowers full of honey dust. What would Gladia think of Ravin? What about her opinion on Achillea and Tarik? Where would she stay? What would she say when she realised that Benakiell was not with us? And most importantly, why was she here? This last question suddenly alarmed me. Had she travelled so far to bring us bad news of one of our friends, or of our land?

Achillea led the way outside to the small courtyard where we had our fire and where we usually sat in the evening, murmured about getting some coffee hot, and then, as we got to the courtyard, about fetching some cake and hurried back into the dwelling to get some. I sighed. Achillea was inclined to do this. In circumstances she found difficult to explain, she took herself away for a little while allowing somebody else (in this case, me) to do the explaining. I led Gladia to the mat at the side, and she lowered herself gratefully down on to it with much groaning and puffing. Before she or I could further speak, Ravin came towards her and made the Kashiq greeting of holding his hand to his heart and then to his head, and sat down himself, across the fire from her, taking the coffee pot from the fire and pouring a steaming cup full in a clay beaker for Gladia. She accepted it and just as she was about to open her mouth, Ravin spoke.

'Are you really that brave and well-loved woman, Gladia, of whom I have heard so much? I am enchanted to be in your presence.'

Gladia blinked and examined Ravin with greater interest.

'I am certainly Gladia,' she responded finally. 'I am not sure who can have been telling you these tales, though. It does not sound like Talla, though it could be Achillea I suppose. Where is Tarik anyway?' She turned to me and demanded, 'And who is this man who I do not know, who knows all about me and yet I know naught of him? I cannot speak with you about certain things with him there listening; I cannot trust a person I have never met. Is he some kind of servant?'

The corners of Ravin's mouth twitched and I could see his mischievous eyes twinkling in the firelight as he waited for me to answer. I struggled to form the words on my tongue. I had tried not to think of telling Gladia of Ravin, preferring to think of her as many, many miles away, in a different land and away from being able to interfere in my life in the same way that she had appeared to interfere with Achillea and Tarik's lives once they had become a couple. Gladia looked at me questioningly. Ravin took pity on me and, presumably because he did not know of Gladia's doughty reputation, spoke to her simply and plainly, with an expectation that she would accept what he said and be happy for me.

'I am Ravin, a scholar of Arbhoun. I am the man who loves Talla, whom you love too, and she loves me in return. We have no secrets from one another, and all I wish is to make Talla happy. I am happy to meet you, for you have come on a long and arduous journey to reach us here. I salute your determination.' He inclined his head towards her. Achillea paused in the doorway where she stood, clutching a fig and orange cake, waiting to hear Gladia's response to this.

'Is that so?' she responded, finally, seemingly lost for words. 'Well, we shall see about that, for I am not ready to take your word for all that, but will ask those I actually know, Talla and Achillea, if the words you speak are true.' She turned to me and poked me hard at the top of my arm. 'So, is this true, what this foreigner says to me, that rather than finding a good man of Oramia, you have taken up with one from another land? Just like your friend over there, Achillea?'

'Tarik is not from another land!' burst out Achillea, defensively. 'He is a man of Oramia, and a good man at that. We are happier than ever with each other!' She ended defiantly, daring Gladia to continue their battle, but Gladia was silent, drinking her coffee mildly, as if waiting for the end of one of Jember's childish outbursts.

'What are you carrying, Achillea?' asked Gladia eventually and Achillea brought the cake over to her, knowing that Gladia, who had a penchant for sweet and tasty food, would want to try the cake. She explained what it was politely to Gladia and then gave her some to try. Gladia ate the cake reflectively, chewing it thoroughly and smacking her lips at the end of it. 'Very nice, Achillea, you must teach me how to make it while I am staying here.'

We looked at each other dubiously. Where would she sleep? Our current arrangements were for me to sleep with Achillea and for Ravin to sleep in my area. We could not put Gladia in with Ravin, so she would have to sleep in Achillea's room, and I would have to share with Ravin. I was very pleased to realise this, for I would not only be escaping Achillea's gentle purring snores but also those of Gladia who I knew, from experience, would often snore much more loudly, although I realised it could be difficult to explain to Gladia. She had only just heard of my relationship with Ravin and may not be ready to consider that we might sleep in the same room.

'You have not told me where Tarik is yet,' commented Gladia after a few minutes. 'Will he be back soon, for the message I bring you from a particularly important person...' emphasizing the last three words, '...is sent only to you three and to nobody else.' She looked pointedly at Ravin. It was difficult to know where to start in the long story, or who should explain what to whom. Should we first hear Gladia's message or should we tell her our own story which included details of a quest which she did not even know about, or should we wait for Tarik to reappear, which might be almost a week away?

Ravin took the lead once more by asking, in a conversational tone, 'Does the message come from Ambar, perchance?'

Gladia gaped at him. I admired his cleverness in this question, for in it he had reassured Gladia that he did indeed know a great deal of what had happened before, at least, although she could not know what task we were now embarked upon for Ambar. Ravin had also shown that he had worked out, from what he had been told of our life in Oramia, that Gladia would be unlikely to travel so far were it not for some urgent reason, and the only urgency he could see was the task of retrieving the Orange of Kashiq.

'Why don't you tell us about the message,' I suggested to Gladia. 'We all trust Ravin, for he is our great friend and while Tarik is away on another task, he is guarding and protecting us.'

'Is he indeed?' said Gladia truculently. 'Well, I only have your word for it, but I suppose that will have to do, since I was persuaded to bring this message with the utmost urgency to you all.' She smiled rather smugly. 'I drove a hard bargain with the High Lord Ambar to come here to you. He seems to have an abundance of riches these days. I shall be able to trade for many silks and cloths to take back with me with these spices and jewels he gave me to do this job.' She chuckled. 'I took him back down a peg or two, I can tell you!'

Achillea giggled and as the two of them laughed, I joined in and soon Ravin did too. 'Tell us your story, Gladia,' he urged. 'For a good story will always be told by a good storyteller like you!'

Gladia preened slightly at Ravin's compliment, and I smiled. I could imagine that Gladia's tale might be as embellished and embroidered as her stitched netelas, but I too was eager to hear it, so we settled down to listen to why she had come all this way, and what Ambar's message could be.

'I was pretty shocked, I can tell you, when Jember came running up to me and told me there was a strange man who had arrived in Mellia and was asking for me, and that there were OutRiders in a little group by the river down the hill! At first, I thought it was one of his silly tricks; he is forever playing tricks on me by hiding or calling out or telling me stories! Anyway, I got up and went out to see who it could be. If it hadn't been for him mentioning the OutRiders, I'd have thought it was Simun, the one who brings the cotton to Mellia for the weavers, but it wasn't. He was sitting underneath that big Paradox tree beside the village and when I got near him, he stood up and came towards and greeted me warmly. You could have knocked me over with a single breath! Just the same as he always was, I might say. Full of warm words which you're never quite sure about. Not like Tarik, he was always the one I could trust.'

Achillea and I exchanged meaningful looks. It did seem as though Gladia had changed her opinion of their relationship, having had some time after my departure and that of Benakiell to ponder on what she really thought. I wondered if she had been to visit the Empath Erayo again because she often returned calmer and less combative after these visits.

'He assumed that one of you might have told me where you were going or what you were doing, but apparently not.' Gladia poked me again, jabbing her finger into precisely the same place as last time. I winced. 'That Benakiell will get the sharp side of my tongue when I see him. You can tell me where he is later. Ambar told me he had to get a particularly important message to you and asked me if I could take it to you. Well, since I didn't even know where you were, it would have been foolish of me to agree immediately, so I waited for him to tell me more.' Gladia chuckled, and Achillea and I did too, knowing how intransigent she could be when she wished. I could imagine Ambar wriggling under her scrutiny.

'He told me a long story about loving Lunaria and wanting to marry her but not being able to because he needed to get some old treasure in the shape of an orange, and he had sent you all here to find it for him. How on earth did he get you to fall for doing all his work for him again? There again, I suppose I have done the same thing! We must all have some sort of longing for adventure. Though, in my case, it had a lot to do with the amount of goods he was willing to give me if I accepted. He did say I was his only hope, and that he had always thought of me as the reliable one in the group.'

I rolled my eyes at Ravin. Ambar was always a master of flattery, with his compliments and his warm eyes and his honeyed voice. He had such a capacity to make you believe what he was saying. We were still waiting for Gladia to tell us what the message was, but I suspected we would be waiting for some time yet.

'Once we had agreed terms, I packed up my best stitching along with the other things, and of course the message and told Bellis and Maren that I was going to Gabez to see you two and Tarik. I couldn't think of a better excuse than to say I wanted to ask your forgiveness and to reconcile with you. It was the only reason I could see that they would accept, which they did. And now, I suppose, I will actually have to do that since I have told everyone that's what I was going to do.'

She shuffled uncomfortably. Gladia was not always particularly good at admitting when she was wrong, like many of us, but she did usually do so, and I respected her for it. She had given me good advice over the years, and had been kind to me, and forgiving of my many outbursts when we had first met. I was grateful that she could go to all this effort to try to make amends with Achillea and Tarik. Achillea, being the person she was, immediately forgave Gladia her previous actions, and assured her that all would be well with Tarik too when he returned. I marvelled at Achillea's ability to do this; to sunnily move on in life, leaving much of the difficulty behind, even when she had already endured the deaths of dear ones and was living in a different land.

Achillea patted Gladia's hand. 'Tell us some more of your story, Gladia!'

'Ambar said it was very urgent to get this message to you in Arbhoun, and that I should make haste. Though I suppose what he means by make haste and what I mean are quite different. Since he has a horse and is fit and slender. I shudder to think of having to ride on a horse again though. I still remember how sore I was after we had ridden on those horses. Anyway, I joined a group of people who were walking along the road to Gabez and they let me walk with them, so I wasn't alone. When we got there, I made my way to your dwelling, just in case you had returned or had never gone in the first place. For all I knew, Ambar might have been making the whole thing up. There was a woman there, Kazima, who told me that you had gone away on a trip to Kashiq and she was looking after the garden.'

Gladia frowned critically. 'Looked to me like she was just letting it run to weeds. I noticed she started tidying it up as I left, so hopefully that sent her into action! Ambar had already told me that I had to get the message to you safely, but also that I would have to cross the bridge in Gabez over to Pirhan and to pay the soldiers the tax for bringing in items to trade. Ambar gave me some bundles of cinnamon to use for the tax. How did you get on with the tax? Can't imagine Benakiell paying taxes every time he comes to Kashiq. He's never mentioned them.' I thought back to our journey on the boat across the river at night, north of Pirhan, Benakiell's way of avoiding paying the taxes and pondered on how we might leave Kashiq without Benakiell's boat. If we went through Pirhan to Gabez we would have our carrysacks searched and the Orange would be found. Before Achillea or I had time to respond to her, however, Gladia had moved on to the next part of her story, clearly relishing being in the limelight.

'I hid the message in my clothes, in a small pocket I sewed under my tunic, here. There are not many soldiers who would be searching an old lady like me in that place, let me tell you! It is only a small message anyway, so I was fairly sure I would be safe. Once I got to Pirhan, I stopped there for a day, and did some trading for food and water gourds, and tried to find another group of people to travel with, but the people here are a bit odd, aren't they? No offence to you, young man,' she added hastily in Ravin's direction. 'I suppose I was dressed differently to most of them, and they have that complicated way of speaking where they add all kinds of words on that you don't need.' Ravin's mouth twitched. I had told him of Gladia's plain speaking before, and now he was witnessing it in action. Gladia had never been fearful of saying what she thought, and rarely hid her words to make them more palatable. She continued hastily before anyone could interrupt her story.

'The first day I just walked on my own. I came to a place called Rishkar, but even though I really wanted to go there and see whether I could make good trades in their market, I remembered what Ambar had said about not drawing attention to myself and steering clear of bigger places until I got to Arbhoun and found you, so I camped at a place a little way out of Rishkar, where there were some other women who were travelling to Arbhoun. After I had shown them some of my embroideries, they got friendlier, and told me that I could do good trades for them in Arbhoun. They really liked a new one I have been working on with Bellis, which has little yellow flowers on it. I walked the rest of the way here with them, and I started asking around if anyone had seen you or knew where you lived and eventually I found someone who told me where to find you.' Achillea and I exchanged glances. Gladia had been awfully close to discovering where Benakiell actually was, and, if she had ignored Ambar's advice, would have had an unwelcome surprise, and found out about Shira.

In the silence which followed after Gladia's story, which had, in the end not contained any flowery embellishments, we all pondered the events and what might happen in the future. Gladia now looked tired. It had been a long hard walk, not least for one of her age and her weight and it was clear that it had taken more from her than she cared to admit. There was one thing, however, that we needed to find out from her before we could let her sleep, and that was what Ambar's message was.

'What was the message from Ambar?' I asked, hoping that it was a clear one. Neither Ambar nor Gladia could scribe or read and so, if there was a written message, it would have relied on Ambar finding a trustworthy scribe to scribe it for him. There was danger in that, but I could not think what could have provoked this message. A message so urgent that he had seen fit to seek out and send her many miles into another land to have it delivered safely.

Gladia blinked wearily, and then a slight smile played on her lips.

'Always Talla, getting to the heart of the matter,' she murmured and patted my hand affectionately. I was more accustomed to her poking my arm and was warmed by her words though others might not have been. She reached to her robe and then paused.

'You, young man, will have to leave the courtyard while I retrieve this message. I sewed it into the folds of my robe, and I will need the help of these two to retrieve it from where it is hidden!' Ravin rose and bowed. He said he would go and organise the sleeping areas while Achillea and I retrieved the message. When he had left, Gladia whispered, 'Are you sure you can trust him? I do not want to get the message unless you are sure.' We reassured her that Ravin was part of our group now and that he was just as trustworthy as Tarik or Benakiell, and she showed us where a small patch had been sewn into her robe, in an area which was much folded and full of fabric due to Gladia's love of a loose robe which she found more comfortable. The patch was around the shape of my outstretched hand, and rather than the folded piece of parchment I had expected, there was a knobbly shape beneath the cloth. Achillea picked at the stitches with her nails and then her teeth, for Gladia had sewn the pocket strongly, twice over. Eventually she had one side unpicked and reached her fingers inside it to draw out the strange object inside it.

'Ambar insisted you would know what it was, and why it was important, said Gladia. 'He said to tell you that he found it hidden in a chest in the Queen's Court.' She looked at us expectantly. 'So, what is it? Is it really important, or has Ambar persuaded me to do something I shouldn't have bothered with?'

Achillea held up the object, smiling. I reached over and touched it. It had a thin engraved central stalk, and a sliding ring with six tiny loops attached to it, each of which bore the remnants of a broken wire. At the top was a beautiful, shiny, honeygold leaf, which resembled a real orange leaf in every way, down to the thin network of lines which traced its surface. It was the central mechanism of the Orange of Kashiq which we had been searching for and which Ravin had been trying to work out how to replicate ever since we had found that only the segments had been returned to Kashiq. Now, all we would have to do would be to establish how the segments were joined to the leaf stem and we would be able to reconstruct the complete Orange of Kashiq.

# CHAPTER 24

The leaf and stem piece which Ambar had found fascinated Ravin. It was late at night by the time we had managed to sort out a sleeping mat and a blanket for Gladia and encouraged her to go to sleep. Since we only had the light of the fire and the small oil lamps to look at the stem, we decided that we too should rest, and look at it again in the morning.

We had to continue with our task of regaining the other three orange segments before Tarik returned, but now that we had the stem and leaf, we could also make another one of the stems using the same method as we had planned for the segments. Ravin examined the stem carefully. It had a sliding ring around it which could be moved from one position to another. The ring had six smaller rings attached to it and presumably this was the mechanism by which the orange could be opened and closed to allow for the segments to be examined. Ravin thought that they were probably attached with very fine wire threads, and that if the ring was pushed down, it would cause the orange to open, and if it were moved up towards the leaf, it would close the segments up so that the whole thing looked just like an orange made of honeygold from the outside. From what he had read in the scrolls, the intent was for only Rao and Ashkana to share the orange, that it was a cunning hidden trick solely for them, a shared secret. The underside of the leaf had a small clip on it which would allow it to be latched into place, on one of the segments. It must be on one of the ones we had not yet found since we looked at the others and saw no signs of it.

When Gladia woke up, we showed her the segments of the Orange that we had already found. She showed some interest in it but expressed her surprise that such an ornament could be of such importance to Ambar and Lunaria.

'Why on earth does it matter whether you have a beautiful trinket like this if you really love each other?' she frowned. 'It is a lovely thing, beautifully made, but it is still just a thing. Do you think Ambar really loves Lunaria? Or that she really loves him?' She turned her gaze on me, questioningly.

'Why do you think it would make a difference for Lunaria to have this Orange, which, from what you have told me, was made by Rao for Ashkana and which she then sent back to him when they didn't love each other anymore? I mean, isn't it more of a sign of broken love than whole love now?'

When Gladia put it in this way, it was hard to disagree with her. Why did Lunaria want this Orange so much? Had she just been swept along by the supposed dream reading of Silene? Had she stopped to think that Ambar might actually try to get her the Orange, or was she sure that he would never be able to find it and thus she might never feel obliged to marry him or bear children? Or was it more to do with the fact that it had been made for Ashkana, she who began the Temples all those ages ago? Did the proof that Ashkana had felt love allow Lunaria to feel love for Ambar? The difficulty was that Lunaria was always so opaque. In the Temple she was well mannered and obedient to the wishes of the Priestesses and the Goddess and seemed to be confident in her own abilities and position in the world. When she had found out about her unexpected role as the new Queen, she had accepted the role with equanimity and serenity. But I did not know very much about her aside from what I had learned in the Temple and in the few days before she arrived at the Queen's Court. She was attractive, there was no doubt about that, with her clear skin and her long dark hair, and her wide eyes. But did Ambar love her, and did she love him? I was doubtful, especially when I thought of my own love for Ravin. I could not picture them sharing tender moments together or making one another laugh. But the Orange had belonged to Ashkana, she who was honoured and elevated in every Temple in Oramia, and perhaps it was this, more than its symbolic meaning which attracted Lunaria.

Ravin told Gladia the full story of Ashkana and Rao, insofar as we knew it, for all we had to go on were the scribings of long dead scholars, and the fragments of scrolls we had read. When Ashkana went to Oramia after her love for Rao was broken, she had started the Temples dedicated to Asmara, the Goddess, and all the other gods and goddesses who were venerated here in Kashiq were blown away like fine grains of sand in the desert wind. Gladia listened to the story and sighed at the end of it.

'I don't know, sometimes I think we would be better off without this kind of love, which makes us do things we later regret. But what would I know? I have never even been married, nor known the joy of raising my own child.' Her eyes took on that faraway look which I had first seen when we went to visit the Empath Erayo. I had taken on her feelings after that time, briefly, and had known that she had those longings for Benakiell, although she kept them well hidden, playing the role of a concerned friend who had known his dead wife, Velosia. I felt angry suddenly with Benakiell, who was at this very time enjoying a life of pleasure with Shira, in a land far from Mellia and who did not see the one who loved him who lived in his home village. Achillea patted Gladia kindly on the shoulder and asked her all about Jember and Bellis and how they all were, since she had not seen them for so long. Brightening, Gladia began a long story, punctuated with chuckles and tuts about how big Jember was growing and how he had been learning to look after Maren's garden, and how to collect sticks for the fire, and collect paradox fruit from the tree.

We were planning on going to the Orchard of Ashkana later that day to retrieve the fourth segment, but I wasn't sure what to do about Gladia. She would probably want to come with us, but she was not always the most unobtrusive person and might draw attention to us more. In the event, we did not even need to discuss it, for Gladia, as usual, made her own choices.

'I will stay here tonight,' she announced firmly. 'I have done far too much walking and carrying in recent days to want to go out again already on some quest to an orchard. I will be resting here and sorting out my stitchings so that I can do some trading tomorrow. I need to organise the things I have brought with me and decide which of Ambar's goods can be traded first, and which I might consider keeping for myself if my own trades do well here.'

'Will you show me some of your stitching?' asked Ravin. 'Talla has always admired your abilities to stitch.' Gladia snorted at this idea but was nevertheless flattered and pulled out some of her latest embroidered cloths to show to Ravin. He was genuinely interested in the craftsmanship behind the stitching and I could tell that he was thinking about some kind of application her stitching might have for a future project, He was much taken by a stitch she had used to outline a red flower on one piece, where she had looped the thread and stitched it so that it looked like a chain. He asked her to show him how it was done and watched carefully as she flicked the needle in and out on a scrap of cloth. Then he asked if he could try to do the same stitch himself. Gladia gaped at him.

'Men don't stitch! It is a job for women, at least where I come from!'

Achillea explained to her that here in Kashiq, jobs were not divided by whether they could be done by men or women, but by which of the gods and goddesses were the guides for that work. Gladia raised her eyebrows and muttered, but handed over the needle and thread to Ravin, who made a good try of stitching. It was certainly better than my own woeful attempts to stitch. Lunaria was the most talented sewer I had seen, and her work, when she had lived in the Temple, had been exquisitely fine. I wondered if she still stitched, now she was Queen of Oramia.

'So, who would be my guide here in Kashiq then,' asked Gladia. 'I suppose I had better know these things so that I can chat to people in the market as if I know what I am talking about!'

'It would be Maliq,' replied Achillea, smiling slightly. 'The same one who guides Tarik.'

Gladia raised her eyebrows again and said, 'I wonder if he too will want to learn to stitch from me when he returns.'

Achillea giggled at the thought of Tarik wielding a needle and thread, but I did not think it was too difficult to imagine him using such a thing if it were to be part of his metal working. His work was becoming much finer and it was clear that he was learning a lot from the metalworkers of Arbhoun. I wondered idly if Achillea and Tarik would ever return to Oramia, for this land of Kashiq seemed to suit them both so well. It pleased me too, but I had only been here for a few weeks and there were parts of Oramia that I missed. I missed my bees most of all, for there were not many opportunities here to keep your own bees, as all the hives were stationed in the orchards. The bees seemed perfectly happy in their clay tube hives, but I still thought my own bees must be happier in the hollowed-out log hives, hoisted high into the trees with less interference from people. And I missed the trees. There were trees here; orange and apricot trees and date palms and other similar sorts of trees but there were none of the huge, grand Paradox trees which we saw in Oramia, which offered big patches of cool dense shade. Having Gladia here made me nostalgic for my homeland.

Acquiring the fourth segment from the Orchard of Ashkana proved to be the easiest one of them all. I had the fanciful thought that Ashkana was watching over us, and that, because I knew all the aphorisms of Ashkana, and indeed repeated one of them to myself throughout the task, she blessed us with good luck in our quest. Perhaps also she wanted us to find the Orange segments and put together the Orange of Kashiq again. Perhaps she missed the love of Rao still, so many Ages later.

There was nobody guarding the orchard or sitting trading small items as there had been in the others. This orchard was to the northwest of Arbhoun, beyond the path which came in from Pirhan in the west and alongside another path which led further to the north, following the line of mountain gorges from which the river which flowed into Arbhoun arose. There were fields of crops here too, and all those who were guided by Ashkana in the area were out in the fields, working hard on tending to them, weeding and trimming and shading small seedlings. Ashkana would be proud, I thought. It made sense that they would be in the fields rather than in the orchards, for it was not the time of year when the orchards needed tending, and they moved to where the work was. 'Only in your work will you succeed in finding contentment' was one of the Aphorisms of Ashkana, and knowing what I now knew, it was impossible for me not to feel some of the hurt that might have existed before she uttered those words. Loving Rao had not brought her contentment, in the end and she preferred to rely on working rather than on other people to uphold her.

We wandered around freely, and once the workers in the fields had reluctantly packed away their gardening tools, we swiftly found the correct beehive and removed the segment as we had done before. The story which Finzari wrote to accompany this clue related to the quality of mutual respect between the inhabitants of the orchard; the bee needed to respect the apricot tree, for it gave freely of its flowers, and the tree needed to respect the bee for it carried the honeydust from flower to flower and without the bee, no fruits could be made, nor new trees grown from their hard stones. They needed each other, and respected that each had gifts which the other did not, and that together they could achieve great things. I liked this story, although I felt that perhaps this respect had ebbed away between Ashkana and Rao until they could no longer see where the strengths of the other lay and that they lost respect for one another as independent people. I thought of how the couples of people that I knew complemented each other: that Achillea's sunny, singing personality contrasted with Tarik's quieter, more reserved nature, but that his calm strength provided a sanctuary for Achillea's fears and weaknesses.

It also made me pause to consider Benakiell. If I thought of Benakiell with Shira, the woman we had met some time before in Rishkar, I could see that she was an attractive woman, that she was accomplished in her chosen occupation and that she was kind and sociable and clearly cared for Benakiell. I could see too that

Benakiell liked to both be needed and to not be needed by Shira. He was a man who liked to have time to himself; he was not afraid of action, but he also liked to think about how things worked whether they were building tools or the way in which the OutRiders acquired the Angels. His wife had died so long ago; I had never met her, and he did not speak much about her, so I did not know whether she was closer in nature to Shira or to Gladia. For me, it was difficult not to think that Benakiell and Gladia should be a partnership; there was an ease which came from having known each other for many years, but maybe that was an obstacle as well as an advantage, and after all Benakiell had never said anything to indicate that he loved Gladia except as an old friend.

I asked Achillea what we should do about talking to Gladia about Benakiell and where he was. She looked at me a little blankly, and I remembered that although I always thought of Gladia and Benakiell together because of their long history and of course Achillea had known them longer than any of us, it was only I who really knew the depth of Gladia's feelings for Benakiell and even then she did not know I knew. I had felt her feelings run through me when I had seen the Empath years before, and I knew from the feelings which coursed through me that Gladia had loved Benakiell deeply for many years and longed for him to feel the same way about her. At least, that was how she had felt then, I reminded myself. Perhaps many things had changed in Gladia's heart in the ensuing seven years, just as they had in my own.

'Benakiell is with Shira,' Achillea reminded me. 'We talked about this when we first met her in Rishkar. We love Gladia and we love Benakiell, and we want them both to be happy. It is not for us to decide how that might be, just because it makes sense to us. Look at me and

277

Tarik or you and Ravin! If someone had told me when I was with Ashtun that one day I might end up with one who used to be an OutRider, I would have laughed. And if, before this trip, another had told you, Talla, that you might find love in a strange land with a man you had only known for a few weeks, you too would have found it unbelievable, and yet here we are. Love is not something that we choose, but rather a grace from the Goddess herself.'

'I am still concerned about Gladia,' I confessed. I knew that Achillea was right, but I could not shake my feeling that Gladia would be hurt by Benakiell's new relationship. 'I am worried that she will be upset when she finds out.'

'Maybe we should just leave it alone,' counselled Achillea. 'Benakiell knows that we know about Shira, so he will understand that he will have to tell Gladia about her at some point. Or maybe we do not need to worry so much. Maybe Benakiell will tire of Shira and wish to return to Mellia and Gladia's bossy ways!' She laughed at the thought, and I smiled with her, but I was still uneasy and unable to apply the rules which I could apply to myself to others. But we agreed we would not say anything to Gladia about Shira, and would merely tell her, if she asked, that Benakiell was in another town, doing some trading while we worked in Arbhoun.

# CHAPTER 25

Ravin was intrigued by Gladia's stitching, and she had given him some threads and one of her needles. He learned how to sharpen the needle against a rough stone so that it would go through the cloth easily. He had brought Gladia a small wooden box carved by Shafir. The box was just big enough to keep Gladia's needles in and she was delighted with it, declaring it much better than the old piece of cloth she had previously used to keep her needles safe. Ravin did not use the needle and thread to sew on cloth however, but by wrapping the thread in a loop and then pulling the needle and thread through it, he was able to make something which resembled a tiny chain.

There were those who made chains in the metalworking district, but they made each link individually and it was a long and time-consuming business. Most of them were made of big, heavy links and were used on buildings like the doors of the Council of Guidance where, it was rumoured, great treasures of gold and honeygold and silver were kept. The Council of Guidance seemed to be the equivalent of the Queen's Court here in Kashiq. There was, however, no queen or other single leader. Rather, the land was ruled by the Council of Guidance itself, which was a committee of thirty-six people, six in each of the groups guided by the gods and goddesses, each with their own leader. These six prime leaders made the decisions about how Kashiq was governed. Ravin had told us that each member served for six years and they took it in turns to represent those they guided as the prime leader. It all seemed very orderly and organised, but I thought that the system in Oramia probably appeared that way to outsiders too. Even the people of the Outer in Oramia did not understand how their land was governed. It did not surprise me that great wealth was held behind those doors. If the Kashiqis had had the Orange of Kashiq, that would be where it would be found. I suspected the Court of the Queen had large stores of wealth too, as did the OutForts, and possibly also the Temples. Sometimes I thought it would have been interesting to have become a Priestess if only to find out the answers to these questions.

There were some jewellers in the metalworkers' quarters, accustomed to working with fine metal wires, who painstakingly made much tinier individual chains into bracelets and necklaces. Unsurprisingly, these were costly trades. Ravin's version with the thread was not a true chain, but it was strong and flexible, and it would serve his purpose well if he could make some lengths of it in fine wire, to use for the mechanism which lifted and lowered the segments of the Orange from the central stem.

Gladia herself was much refreshed by her long sleep and was itching to go to one of the markets in Arbhoun with her stitching. She had brought some netelas, and although they did not wear them here, preferring the colourful headdresses, I thought that perhaps there would be those who might like them for decorating their homes, or to make tunics for small children. Gladia bridled a little when I suggested this to her, but I reminded her that it was the trades in Kashiq that she was interested in, and she grumbled her way to her bundle to withdraw a small pile of treasured netelas which she did not want to be traded in this way, and then she and Achillea departed for the market, quite as if they had never had a long argument spanning months.

Ravin and I were going to meet them later, at the end of the day, at the market in the northern quarter of Arbhoun, close to the orchard of Asmara, and we would go on from the market to get the fifth segment of the orange. I was not sure that Gladia would not draw more attention to us, but there was also the chance that she might be able to draw attention away from us by engaging guardians in conversation, for example. In any case, Gladia was the one who had brought us the honeygold stem from Ambar, and she wanted to join us and take part in the rest of the task.

They were sitting on the edge of a low mud wall when we arrived at the market, which was set out on the customary layout of differently coloured squares which was used throughout Kashiq. It made the market much more orderly, but there was something lost, perhaps in the careful divisions made between the traders. Very few traders traded for more than one type of item on a given day, so those of Maliq might trade their carved boxes and jewellery, but not items they had received in return for those things until another day, and one guided by Ashkana might come to market with a pile of lemons and a pile of tomatoes, but not any of the clay pots they had traded their food for until another day. In Oramia, trading was much more mixed and perhaps more efficient too, for one could easily acquire in one day whatever one needed. In Arbhoun, it was more set out and one had to plan more carefully.

'Did you trade well?' asked Ravin as we approached them.

'Yes,' replied Gladia rather smugly. 'It would seem that there are many in Kashiq who want to trade for my cloths sewn with flower patterns. I have traded almost all of what I brought with me already, and I have had people ask me if I can make them more. Luckily, I have managed to trade for some brand-new needles to keep in that box you gave me, and some more cloth, even some exceptionally fine silk which you cannot get in Oramia. In fact, I don't know if I can even take it back to Oramia; they might take it off me at Pirhan. I also had to try a cake with apricots and almonds and got some more to take with us to this orchard we are going to. We might get hungry!' She looked wistful. 'I wish I could take some back for Jember and for Bellis and Maren. They would love them!'

Achillea and Gladia continued to tell us about their trading as we walked to the entrance of the orchard. The Orchard of Asmara was well known in Arbhoun for it was the site of the Mother Spring. It was called this because, Ravin explained, it never ran dry, just like a mother's love for her children, and the Goddess Asmara's love for her people. I rolled my eyes in irritation. How could someone like me, who never knew their mother, understand the depth of that feeling? Who was to say that my mother's love for me had not run dry shortly after my birth and that was why I had ended up at the Temple?

There were six springs in Arbhoun, each one roughly serving one of the orchards that grew there. The springs bubbled up from under the orange sandstone and sand and fed small lakes of water from which people took water for washing and growing crops, and for building and crafting. Water for drinking was taken from several wells which had been dug close to the springs, so that the drinking water was kept pure and unsullied by its other uses. In Oramia, we had very few lakes, although Benakiell had told us that there were lakes north of Sanguinea and Aderan. Oramia had rivers and streams, though, which ran from the tops of the mountains, and which the settlements were based around. It did not take too long before you came across a small stream or river in Oramia, and although they went down very low in the hottest weather, they never seemed to fully dry up. Gladia was impressed by the Mother Spring and gazed at it, enjoying the colour of it which lay somewhere between the colours of Viridis and Azureus. I wondered idly how the priestesses of the Temple might argue over which of the days these springs might belong to, and how what might seem to be the green of Viridis to one might yet appear to be the blue of Azureus to another.

There were a lot more people in this orchard than there had been in any of the others and I began to worry about whether they would leave as it began to fall dark. The other orchards had been a little way distant from the springs but here in the Orchard of Asmara, the orchard almost surrounded the spring and people were continually using the spring to gather water. Gladia gave her cloth bundles to Ravin, who took them good-naturedly as she strode off towards a knot of women who were sitting with their wares, close to the spring, but who seemed to be doing more chatting than trading. We looked around for the beehives of the orchard but could see none. We walked along the river which fed into the Mother Spring from the mountains further north and peered through the rows of apricot trees which were interspersed with nut trees but could see no sign of the beehives. Until now, we had had no difficulty in finding the pieces of the Orange which we sought, but I became worried that we could not easily see the wall of piled up clay beehives as we had done in other orchards.

'What if they don't have beehives here?' I said, fretting. 'Maybe they have moved them somewhere else and maybe the bees from the orchard of Ashkana come to this orchard too? What will we do if we can't find it, and we still have another one to find?' Ravin looked at me.

'I am sure we will find it,' he replied. 'And even if we do not, we may be able to make a copy of one of the other ones, now we know what to do.' I had not thought of this, but Ravin with his mind which delighted in understanding how things worked and how their patterns coalesced, had seen that the segments we had recovered so far were very similar except for the words which were engraved within. Feeling a little relieved, I took his hand and we walked back through the trees to find Gladia waiting for us.

'It may not be as easy as we hoped,' warned Achillea. 'We do not know where the beehives might be for this orchard and we have looked through almost the whole orchard.' Gladia looked at her impassively.

'Hmm,' she said, a little mysteriously. 'Well, show me around any way. Why don't we go and look at that strange piece of old building over there?' She gestured towards the edge of the orchard where there lay the remnants of some old city wall. Ravin had told us that in ages gone by the city of Arbhoun had been surrounded by walls to defend itself from invaders, but that the wall had been knocked down as the city grew and now there were only a few places where one could still see the old pieces, jutting out from the sand.

'We are supposed to be looking for the beehives,' I reminded Gladia, irritated by her demand to go and see an old piece of wall.

'Well, we can,' she retorted, poking my arm. 'Just let's go and look at that first and then you can take us wherever you like.' I subsided. I knew that sometimes it was not worth going into battle with Gladia over small things. We walked towards the old wall, some of which was still standing. There were trees growing close to it, whose branches hung over it.

'Let's just look what it's like behind, too, shall we?' said Gladia in a bright tone. I was beginning to feel suspicious that she was up to something. We followed behind her as she led us on around the wall. There, away from the crowds of people in Asmara's orchard were the rows of beehives.

'Oh, how interesting,' said Gladia. 'I wonder what these things are...'

'They are the beehives we are looking for,' started Achillea and then, looking at Gladia's face, and realising that Gladia had known all along she laughed ruefully. Gladia's eyes twinkled.

'I did fool you, didn't I? It's amazing what you can find out if you bother to talk to those who sit and trade all day. All I had to do was ask them innocently what this place was – and they could see I was not from Kashiq because, unlike you, I am still wearing my Oramian robe – and they told me all about it. Where the best place was to draw water, where the best place was to trade, where to go if you wanted to find a place to camp for the night. They told me not to camp behind the wall because that was where the beehives were! Your faces are a picture! I only wish that Benakiell had been here and then I could have fooled him too. I'd have loved to see him as surprised as you three!'

'You are very observant,' commented Ravin, impressed. 'Without you, we would have never known where to look.'

Gladia's face shone. I noticed how happy it made her when she was praised and resolved to try to be better at complimenting her. It was easy to forget to say good things to her when she was being irritating and even easier to forget the many ways in which she had helped me over the years with no expectation of thanks.

After dusk, we made our way to the beehive with the cover on it which showed the picture for the story about trust which Ravin and I had discussed before. Gladia sat, leaning against the wall, watching out for any curious people, but although there were still people down by the Mother Spring, they were intent on their tasks, and because the small oil lamp we had brought was behind the wall. It attracted no attention and we soon retrieved the segment.

Gladia was fascinated when we showed her the piece encased in beeswax later and told her about how we could make two Oranges.

'There should have been two in the first place really,' she remarked. 'One for Ashkana and one for Rao.'

'It was never intended that it should be broken at all', Ravin reminded her. 'It was always Rao's intention that he and the Lady Ashkana would remain together always, and that the Orange would symbolise that.'

'So, if you make two,' asked Gladia, 'will you give the original Orange to Ambar for Oramia and Ashkana for whom it was intended, or will you give the original Orange to Kashiq for Rao who made it and hid it?'

This was indeed a quandary. We had previously agreed between us that we would make a copy of the Orange of Kashiq and that we would take one to Oramia and one would stay here in Kashiq, but not which land would get the copy, and which would get the original Orange.

Ravin smiled. 'I think that the fairest thing to do would be to mix the two, don't you? For love is not an object like an orange to be given by one person to another in its entirety. Love is more like a lake of water which flows between two shores, like the Mother Spring. It is ever the same and yet ever changing. And the two different sides of the land are joined by something which is not land and yet which connects them. Something which is the same and yet different for both. Talla's love for me is different from my love for her, and yet it is of the same water. The refreshment and replenishment which I gain from her love is different from that which she gains from mine and yet it is still replenishment. The pieces of the Oranges should be mixed so that we do not know which is old and which is new, only that they are symbols of the same thing between two different people and from two different times.'

Gladia nodded thoughtfully, a faraway look in her eyes. I wondered if she was thinking about Benakiell. Perhaps it was because of his scholarly upbringing and the number of scrolls that he had read, but Ravin always seemed to be able to express clearly in words the things that the rest of us struggled to say. I leaned my head against his shoulder, tired from the day's activities but content. Gladia rose to go inside and sleep after a little while, yawning loudly and groaning as she heaved herself up. Achillea followed shortly after her, advising Ravin and I to make sure that we got a good amount of rest ourselves, and reminding us to save some of the members in the emberjar. When they had gone, I leaned my head back on Ravin's shoulder. He tipped my face towards his and nudged my netela so that it dropped to my shoulder and ran his fingers along my hair lightly. It heightened my senses and made me shiver slightly.

'Are you cold?' murmured Ravin, his lips brushing my ear. 'I can think of a way in which I could warm you up...' His voice trailed off suggestively as he sought my mouth with his. I responded to him, pressing up against him. It was becoming difficult for us to stay apart, and now that Achillea would be sleeping with Gladia, it was even more difficult. But there were only a couple of curtains between us and them, and my cheeks burned to think of Achillea or, even worse, Gladia hearing us. We made our way to sleep, fitfully, in my room, both of us longing to be even closer.

# CHAPTER 26

I t's not fine enough.' Ravin was exasperated. We were trying to make a clay fine enough to reproduce exactly the details on the segments of the Orange, but the grains in the clay were too large. We were waiting for Tarik to return to Arbhoun, having acquired all the six segments of the Orange of Kashiq. The sixth one from the Orchard of Yael had been as simple as the others. My mind toyed with the idea that the Goddess was guiding our actions and protecting us from harm. But perhaps it was something about the Orange itself; nobody was expecting to find the pieces of the Orange because nobody knew they were there, aside from Finzari and, of course, us. So, there was no real reason for anyone to be suspicious of us as we wandered around in the orchards of Arbhoun. Kashiqi people did spend time in gardens and in areas where there were trees. Much of the land was a dry sparse orange sand, except where the rivers flowed in gorges down the steep, stony mountains, and the places where water flowed and plants grew were welcome respite from it.

The Orchard of Yael was only unusual in one regard; it was near the place where the dead were returned to the Goddess. At least, that is what we called it in Oramia. In the Temple, there was no ceremony or fuss when one of the old priestesses died. We knew that it meant the Goddess had called her home to herself, to the place where she had first begun. Here in Kashiq, they believed that death came under the guidance of Yael. That Yael was the one who ushered people out of the world in the same way that Asmara ushered people into the world at their birth. Ravin had told me about his parents and their different roles serving under Yael; his father was a soldier, one of the Defenders of Yael who were sanctioned to kill, and his mother cared for the dying and the dead. There were also those who dealt with the burial of the dead. The burial ground for the dead of Arbhoun lay next to the orchard of Yael. In Oramia we did not mark the place of burial, except, perhaps with a boulder to prevent others from burying there. In Kashiq, the site of burial was marked with a small clay dome. Some had names scribed on the domes, or pictures of flowers and trees or patterns. The body was buried there for an Age; that is seven years. After that, the dome was broken, and the place used for another, for, by then, the hot sand and the herbs of death buried with them had taken away all the flesh and only bones remained. I learned a great deal from Ravin as he described these things to us, for of course he had much knowledge of these things from his parents. Achillea shuddered, perhaps thinking of her mother and of Ashtun who were, by now, only bones in the earth too.

As we looked out at the small domes which lay on the sand, marking the dead, however, I thought how peaceful it seemed there, quiet and away from the bustle of the city. The Orchard of Yael was a mixture of orange trees and lemon trees and the scent in the flowering time must have been heavy and intoxicating. I thought it would be no bad thing to be buried here for a time, with only the sand and the scent of the orange flowers and the murmuring of the bees, who had given up the sixth segment of the Orange with barely a hum of interest.

'I wish I had been the one to bury Ashtun,' said Achillea suddenly, breaking the silence. 'At the time, I could not bear to think of it, to think of him being dead and no longer there for me. But perhaps it would have given me peace. It would have been nice to know where he was buried, for at least the people of Kashiq can have a place to grieve for seven years. What happens at the end of the Age, Ravin, when the dome is broken?'

'We celebrate their life, if we wish. By then it is time to give them up, for Yael has taken them home to the Goddess and she has made their spirits live again. Not all in the same person, but you could see it as though the Goddess were making a cake. She would add some nuts from different trees, and some honey from many bees to make that cake. Just so does she make the soul of another one born. You have doubtless met people who have reminded you of those you have lost, like Ashtun.'

Achillea pondered on what he said. Gladia too, looked reflective. Although I had seen many Priestesses called to the Goddess, I had never thought about what happened after they died, just accepting their fate as we were taught to do in the Temple. Ashtun was the only person I had known somewhat better who had died, and we had had an uneasy relationship much of the time, both of us united only by our regard for Achillea.

'You know, Jember has that headstrong way that Ashtun used to have of making his mind up and never wavering from it,' said Gladia thoughtfully. 'Perhaps he has a little part of Ashtun's soul within him.'

Achillea brightened. 'I must watch him closely when I next come to Mellia!' Gladia smiled and I saw that she realised that Achillea planned to return to Mellia, at least at some point. It was a sign to Gladia that Achillea really had forgiven her intolerance over Tarik. Whether he would feel the same way was not certain, but he loved Achillea so much that he would undoubtedly be guided by her.

Ravin, too, looked reflective. 'I often see small elements of my mother in people that I meet. Perhaps in the way they shake their head, or in the way they admonish their children. Even, sometimes, just in the way a person might look at me from behind half closed eyes or adjust their headdress. Of course, her grave marker will be long since gone, and I never saw it anyway because I left so quickly. But when I see those little gestures or flashes of her soul in others, I am content, now. For I know she lives on in other ways and in other lives.' Ravin had never spoken to the others about his earlier life and I was surprised by his openness.

And now, the next day, back in our dwelling, which lay north of the orchard, we were trying to make a fine enough clay to take a perfect impression of the segment so we could cast it again in beeswax to mould the new segments with the honeygold which Tarik was going to bring back. Achillea had traded for some fine clay in a pot but it still seemed too coarse.

'Can you mix it with something finer?' asked Gladia. 'Like flour or sand?' Ravin looked interested momentarily but then recognised that the grains in each of those were no smaller than those in the clay. I tried to think of something which made a fine powder and suddenly remembered the way in which I used to pounce patterns on cloth, and the ground charcoal I used to make the pattern.

'What about charcoal?' I suggested. 'We use it to make a fine powder in some salves and physics, and in ink We could mix the charcoal with clay!' Achillea went to get some charcoal from the fireplace outside, and I found two smooth stones to act as a pestle and mortar. Having ground down the charcoal into a fine black dust, we mixed it with the clay so that it formed a speckled substance which was indeed much finer than before.

Ravin pressed one of the segments into it, first on one side and then on the other. As he took it off, a wide grin spread across his face.

'It's perfect! We can take impressions of both sides of the segment and then fill them with beeswax. Then we can seal the two halves together and do it the other way round, with a thin wax pipe to pour the honeygold down.'

'Would that be the honeygold which I have here?' asked a tired voice from the doorway. It was Tarik, returned from his trip. Achillea gasped and leapt up, running towards Tarik to embrace him.

'You will not be so eager to embrace me when you smell me,' he said ruefully. 'I have not bathed for more than five days and it has been hot and sweaty work.' He looked around him. Gladia was sitting on a mat, placidly winding her embroidery threads, looking for all the world as if she had always been there. He looked at Achillea, uncomprehending.

'Greetings, Tarik,' said Gladia, cheerfully. 'I will get up and greet you better when you have bathed and changed your clothes. I know they say that love is blind, but I never heard that it could not smell either! Achillea, get him some water and put some cedar wood in it else we shall smell him all night!'

Achillea giggled and pushed the bemused Tarik indoors, explaining Gladia's presence and telling him of all we had done while he had been gone without him uttering another word. We all laughed, and Ravin, having carefully pressed the orange segment into the clay poured a little melted beeswax over the top of it. He had heated the beeswax in a small clay pot over the fire and intended to build up the wax impression in layers once the first layer had set, to ensure a crisp outline. After all, we still had to make the clay shell for the wax model before we could fill it with honeygold.

# CHAPTER 27

It was late when Tarik finally reappeared, cleaner and more fragrant than he had been on his arrival. Achillea had made him wash his clothes while he washed himself, and he laid them out on the wall to dry. The evenings were not as cool anymore, and every day it was a little warmer. Soon the blossom in the orchards would be out and the bees would recommence their busy work. He sat, content, next to Achillea, who had provided him with some of the nut and honey cake which Gladia eyed enviously. It was clear that Achillea had spoken to him about Gladia's surprising reappearance, and her even more surprising apology for the way in which she had treated Achillea and Tarik. Granted, Gladia had not yet admitted she was wrong, but no one of us expected her to; that was not Gladia's way. Tarik began, then, to tell us of his travels.

'It took us all of a day of hard walking to get to Shiljam where the mines are. It took us a little longer to get back, for the honeygold stones are heavy and we could not walk as fast. I wish I had had a horse such as I used to have when I was an OutRider. I could have got there and back much more quickly. There were plenty of horses there though. The Defenders keep a close watch on the caves and take a big share of what is mined. For every stone you take for yourself, you must give two to them. They load them onto the horses, and they are brought back here; they say to the Council of Guidance.

'It was really fascinating to see where and how the honeygold is mined,' continued Tarik, who, once he had everyone listening to him, was fond of detailing things with great precision. I was not myself, interested in every tiny detail about the mines, but I knew that there would be no hurrying Tarik, so, like the others, I settled down to hear it.

'Shiljam is a strange place, with outcrops of oddly shaped rocks. Some are like pillars and some like trees or dwellings. The honeygold mines are found beneath these rocks. Somehow, many ages ago, it seems that the honeygold was made and pushed the rocks upwards from the earth. There are paths which lead into the mines. The paths are big enough for a single man and a flat basket to go down and to pass one another, but no more. The mines have been dug out over years and years, and now go deep underground. There are other things in the mines too, silver and iron and coloured crystals for jewellery. There are orange carnelians, which at first I thought were just dull orange stones, but the men showed me how they look when they are polished, and they are beautiful.'

Tarik got up and went over to his carrysacks which he had piled up on the floor by the wall and reached into one of them. He withdrew a small piece of cloth tied at the top with a knot, carefully untied it and took out a smooth stone, highly polished, like a shiny orange berry. It was translucent and almost seemed to glow in the firelight. He gave it to Achillea and told her that he would make it in a necklace for her, to remember these times. I was a little envious. The stone was so smooth and pure, it reminded me of a drop of dark honey, a sweet and unctuous thing. I wondered if it would be easy to find another such stone to trade for in the markets of Arbhoun. Tarik began to speak again, and I hoped that he would soon tell us about the honeygold that he had found, and how we might use it, rather than telling us so much extra detail from the beginning.

Ravin, on the other hand, was fascinated by Tarik's tale and leaned forward, concentrating on every one of those details which I so wanted to ignore. I looked at him as he listened to Tarik. The light and the shadows of the fire moved across his face like a gentle breeze, illuminating different parts of him. His face was so dear and so familiar to me now, and yet each time I looked at him carefully, I seemed to see something new, whether it was in the line of his eyebrows or in the expression of his mouth. I was paying more attention to Ravin than to Tarik now, so I reluctantly drew my gaze away from him and concentrated on what Tarik was saying.

'The walls in the caves where the honeygold is found are very bumpy, and the strangest type of rock I have ever seen. The men who work there use a tool they have made especially for this job. It is of iron, and has a sharp blade at the end, but it is also curved, and you use it much like a wood carver might, using a hammer to guide it around the lumps in the wall. Each of those lumps is a honeygold stone.'

'How do we get the honeygold out of the stone?' asked Achillea. 'I hope it is not too difficult to do.'

Tarik smiled. 'It is the most amazing thing that I have seen, and something which I did not know until I went to the mines. The lumps of rock are shaped a little like an egg, and quite smooth on the outside. In the cave where they are found, it is dark and cool compared to the heat of the midday, though warm compared to the cool of the night. If you were to take a honeygold stone in that heat and break it open you would find that the honeygold was hard set in the middle of it, bound to the sandstone around it in tendrils so fine it would take you many months to chisel them all out.' Once again he reached into the carrysack and drew out an egg-like stone which fitted comfortably into the palm of his hand. We were all fascinated by now, even Gladia. who put down her sewing threads and looked at it carefully as we passed it around. When it lay in my hand, I could feel how heavy it was, even though it looked like a piece of light sandstone. It was faintly warm to the touch, almost as if it were alive, like an egg from beneath a chicken.

Achillea's face fell at the thought of how long it might take us to chisel out the honeygold we needed to make the new pieces of the Orange. We knew that by now Ambar would be getting impatient and we had, after all, told him that we would get back to him by the month of Aureus.

Tarik patted her hand kindly. 'Ah, do not worry Achillea, and put back your lovely smile! For the thing that is amazing is that when you heat up the honeygold stones on a fire, for only a short time, the honeygold inside melts. Then all you have to do is make a small hole in the stone with that tool I told you about and there you have it; you can pour the honeygold out of the rock as easily as you can pour water from a clay jar.'

We all stared at him. This felt like something from one of Finzari's fanciful stories, the invention of somebody's imagination. This meant we could continue with our plan of casting new segments and we could do it all here, at our dwelling, where nobody could become curious about what we were doing or why. I was fascinated and looked forward to being able to see this phenomenon that Tarik had described. It was getting late, however, and Tarik had been walking all day with a heavy load. It seemed that we were all ready to sleep until we realised that our sleeping arrangements would have to be changed again.

With only two rooms, we soon realised that the only course of events possible would be for we three women to share one of the rooms and for Tarik and Ravin to share the other. Achillea's face fell when she realised that she would not be getting the much longed for private reunion with Tarik after all, at least not for a few days. She went to change over the mats and blankets in the rooms again as Tarik rose wearily to move the bags of stones. Ravin motioned him to sit back down again and began to move the bags to a more sensible place, somewhat hidden from a casual glance by some palm fronds. Gladia shuffled uncomfortably, realising that no matter what Achillea might have said in explanation for Gladia's past actions, Tarik would be a harder person to make things right with. He had been hurt by what she had said to him and by her insinuation that he would never be good enough for Achillea, and that he was no better than the OutRiders who had so hurt Bellis. Tarik did not mean to make it easy for her, and sat quietly, waiting for her to speak first.

'I hope that you will come to Mellia after we have finished with this Orange thing you have all got yourselves involved with,' she began, before realising that she still sounded truculent. 'What I mean to say is that I would welcome you back in Mellia when you return to Oramia. Achillea would like to visit her home village, I am sure, and you have friends in the village who would like to see you again; Maren and Bellis and Jember of course and Benakiell – though you have seen him more recently than me.' Gladia paused. She found it so hard to acknowledge when she had said or done the wrong thing. Normally she tried to bluster past it, or to ignore it in the hope that it would go away.

'And what about you, Gladia? Would you be one of those who would be happy to see me again?' asked Tarik quietly, looking straight at her. 'You told me that I was not fit to love Achillea, that I should remain some sort of outcast for the rest of my life, belonging neither to Oramia nor to the OutFort, and never becoming worthy enough for Achillea. But I intend to spend the rest of life with her, and we pray that in time the Goddess may bless us with our own children.'

Ravin glanced at me at this point. My eyes widened. Although I thought that Tarik and Achillea would always be together, I had never heard Tarik state it in such unequivocal terms. I tried to imagine Achillea with a child and somehow, I found it hard. Perhaps it was because to me, Achillea had always been the same person. Ever since I had turned up in Mellia a lost and outcast Drab from the Temple, she had warmly welcomed me as her friend and yet I never thought of us growing older and doing all the things which people did as they grew older.

Tarik continued. 'Achillea and I will not be parting from one another. And although it would sadden us both greatly, we would not want any child of ours to feel unwelcomed, as they would be if you cannot accept or support us being together.' He sighed, and for a moment looked older and wearier than I had seen him before. Others would have left this conversation for another day, but Tarik liked to finish things off properly. Gladia frowned, struggling to balance her desire not to be wrong with her desire to be part of Achillea's future life and the possibility of children who were so attractive to Gladia, all the more so since Jember's birth and her involvement in his life.

Eventually, she spoke. 'I was wrong,' she said firmly. 'I wronged you and Achillea, and I am sorry. I was worried about Achillea because I love her, but I see how much you love her and how much she loves you. Who am I to stand in your way? I know you work hard, and you are kind to Achillea, and you will look after her.' She looked down, embarrassed. 'Maybe I was jealous of you both. You live the sort of life with each other that I used to dream about when I was young, and now I never will.'

Tarik smiled warmly at her, and I felt a rush of gratitude for his kind nature. 'There is no need to stop dreaming now, Gladia,' he replied. 'We never know when the Goddess will see fit to grant our dreams and hopes. When I was an OutRider, I often dreamed of what it might be like to be someone different, but I believed it was my destiny to always be that soldier. Now I see my destiny differently. For me and for Ambar and for Talla, our lives have diverged from the paths we had been told were our fate. You may yet find a life which brings you even greater happiness. Now, tell me some more about that young rascal Jember. What has he been up to now?'

Gladia settled down, relieved, and began to tell him of Jember's exploits. At first, he was attentive and then slowly his eyes began to drop, and his head hung forward. Gladia huffed as she got up from her place on the floor and called for Achillea.

'He's gone to sleep in the middle of me talking!' she exclaimed. 'Some thanks that is!' But we could all hear the chuckle in her voice as she made her way to the sleeping room.

# CHAPTER 28

Tarik positioned a ring of firestones around the fire to hold two or three of the honeygold stone eggs upright as they were heated up slightly. It only required a little heat to melt the honeygold within, and if it had been later in the year when the hot sun beat down more ferociously, we might not have had to heat them at all. The cave in which they were found stayed at the same temperature all year round and the stones were always solid when they were found, but Tarik had told us that many metalworkers went to get their honeygold from the Shiljam mines at the hottest time of the year for it meant they did not have to heat the stone eggs up, but just left them in the sun all day and then cast with them in the evening. I wondered who the first person had been to discover that there was a much easier way to extract the honeygold than to painstakingly chip it out. Probably it had been some chance discovery where one of the stones had been left in the sun and then a miner began to chip at it. I imagined his surprise as the liquid honeygold flowed out of the stone.

Ravin had, by now, made wax and clay copies of all the segment parts of the Orange of Kashiq, and had then added on to each piece a thin strip of beeswax. Each segment was cast in two parts: the main piece and then the little hinged lid. Now we were trying to reconstruct it, I could see how fiddly it was and I was already impatient with it, but Ravin and Tarik both enjoyed this detail. Achillea and I had been out to the bigger market area in the north east of Arbhoun where there were several traders of honey and beeswax. They had come to know us, for we used the beeswax to make our salves, and it was no surprise to them that we might want to trade for more. Gladia had given us some of the spices which Ambar had given to her. She had been rather reluctant to do so, but Achillea promised that we might find her some fine silks to sew and a cake or two in addition to the beeswax, and she was mollified by this, and was now sitting with her sewing laid down at her side, having finished off the date and honey concoction which Achillea had found for her. It was a long time since Achillea and I had been able to sit still like this, with nothing urgent to do, and we too had enjoyed a small piece of the date and honey cake. I looked across to Gladia.

She sat with her round face tilted towards the sun and her eyes closed. She was wearing a purple netela today, embroidered with tiny white flowers and green leaves. It was slipping off her head as she leaned it against the wall and I could see her hair, cut short and sprinkled here and there with the grey hairs of wisdom. As youngsters in the temple the Priestesses had told us that the Goddess left them there as a sign to others of the wisdom of the elders. I was not convinced that all the older people I knew were any wiser than me at the time, but I knew they must at least have more experience than a younger person. Gladia's cheeks had had beeswax and lavender salve liberally applied to them and they shone. The tired droop to her face and her shoulders which we had seen when she first arrived had gone and the weight of the disagreement with Tarik and Achillea had been lifted, and she looked peaceful and relaxed. Her eyes fluttered open and caught me looking at her.

'Don't you have anything else to do, Talla?' she asked crisply, shaking herself awake and heaving herself up, a little embarrassed at being caught napping. 'I must go inside and see if I can find that ball of tangled threads for you to unpick since you have the luxury of being able to sit idle!' She bustled off into the dwelling and Achillea and I laughed together. The men were preoccupied with the casting and I got up and wandered over to watch them work.

The wax segment pieces had been encased in the fine clay we had made, and Tarik held each small clay lump over the fire with a pair of metal tongs which he had traded for with one of the miners in return for some honeygold stones. Once he was sure the wax had melted, he turned it over and the hot beeswax trickled out through the fine pipe onto the fire where it spat and smoked and filled the air with the unmistakeable scent of honey. I wished I were back in Gabez with my bees. Each day here in Arbhoun had been filled with new discoveries and new knowledge but I was ready to be back home and sitting quietly in the garden thinking about what I had learned. In the Temple, Ashkana's words had exhorted us to be always working and busy and I had only recently recognised that thinking over new knowledge and skills was indeed working. In fact, my mind often worked more vigorously when I was sitting surrounded only by the plants and the murmuring bees.

Once the wax had completely dripped out, it was time to pour in the honeygold. Before placing the stones on the fire, Tarik had used a small iron spike and a hammer stone to bang a hole into the stone. It went down into the rock about half a finger's length. Then using the tongs, he lifted the honeygold stone off the fire and very slowly tipped it over the tiny hole in the clay mould which was being steadily held by Ravin. I was fascinated by the molten honeygold. I had once had a bee made of honeygold and it had been exceptionally beautiful. I wondered now if it had been cast in this way, perhaps even here in Arbhoun. That bee necklace turned out to be the property of the Queen, and although Ambar had first given it to me, I had returned it to Lunaria when she became Queen. The honeygold dripped viscously, like honey, oozing into the mould slowly. The whole process advanced slowly, but once the top of the pipe of honeygold was visible, Tarik would replace the honeygold stone on the fire and Ravin would place the cast piece to one side and pick up the next.

Gladia had not re-emerged and I suspected that she had taken the opportunity for a rest inside where she would not be so keenly observed. Achillea was once more scrubbing Tarik's clothes which were still stained with the vivid orange dust of the Shiljam mines. She thumped them vigorously against the flat washing rock in the courtyard, muttering and throwing in scented herbs.

'Is Tarik here?' came an exhausted but somewhat familiar voice. It was a woman's voice, but I could not place it. I went to the arched doorway of the courtyard, looking behind me at the men who quickly threw a cover over the cast pieces and took the honeygold stone off the fire and propped it up against the wall. It would have to be reheated later. Reassured, I pulled up the peg from the lock and opened the gate. Outside was the bent and twisted figure of a man and the woman who had asked for Tarik. I looked more closely at the man. His face was contorted in pain. His beard was straggly, and his clothes were covered in dust. His foot was bound with strips of cloth, apparently hastily torn from some clothing and this bandaging was stained with blood and infection. But the eyes were the same eyes that had first greeted me when I left the temple. It was Benakiell and Shira.

Shira slumped with relief, and I saw that she had been supporting Benakiell, along with a rough stick which he was holding in his other hand. She was dusty and exhausted.

'Can we come in?' she asked tiredly. 'As you can see, Benakiell is gravely injured and we have need of Tarik's physics and your salves.' Benakiell murmured tiredly. I could not catch his words, but they sounded rambling and incoherent. I called Tarik and Ravin to come over and they carefully supported Benakiell over to the wall which lay in shade and helped him down on to the mat, where he lay, silent and trembling. Achillea went to Shira, who was standing limply and encouraged her to sit down too and gave her a beaker of coffee. It was only lukewarm because the men had been using the fire, but she sipped it gratefully, nevertheless. I looked at Achillea meaningfully. What were we going to do about Gladia? Not only was Benakiell here, but so too was Shira and she had brought to us a gravely injured Benakiell. She looked anxiously towards the door, but it was still quiet, and I felt sure now that Gladia must be sleeping in our room.

Tarik asked Shira what had happened to Benakiell and how they had arrived in Arbhoun. She explained that she and Benakiell had decided to set out several days ago from Rishkar to come and find us as Benakiell had promised. Benakiell had brought with him some of his reeds to trim and shape and trade in Arbhoun, and Shira had brought with her some of her cakes. They had stopped to rest just over halfway to Arbhoun and while they sat in the shade, Benakiell had decided to work on the reeds so that he had some more ready to trade. He was trimming one braced against his leg when the sharpened reed slipped and went right through his foot. When Benakiell tried to pull out the reed, it seemed to get stuck, perhaps behind a bone, and splintered off. Being Benakiell, he then tried to get out the remaining reed fragments with his knife. He did remove some, but the foot was very painful to walk on. It was closer to walk to Arbhoun than to walk back to Rishkar, so they began to walk on, slowly.

'Did nobody help you?' asked Achillea, horrified. Shira said that some had but they had barely met anyone anyway. One traveller had offered the cloth with which his foot was bound, and another had given them extra water. One had given the walking stick which Benakiell had used. But mostly, they had been on their own and their progress had been very slow. This morning when they had woken up, Benakiell had been feverish and was not making sense, and the foot had become hard and red. It had taken all of Shira's strength to get him to us.

Tarik had washed his hands free of the clay dust from the casting. Gently he unwrapped the cloth from Benakiell's foot, wetting it where it had stuck to the wound beneath to peel it away. He asked Achillea to get poppy juice to feed to Benakiell for his pain, and she went to sit by his head, dripping the sleeping potion in, a few drops at a time. I fetched some white honey from our dwindling store and put it on to a flatbread for Shira, who ate it lifelessly, sitting next to Benakiell, her eyes sharp with worry. Once the cloth had been removed, Tarik looked more closely at the wound in Benakiell's foot. There was the sweet, cloying smell of infected decay. His foot was very swollen, and the edges of the wound were rimmed with crusts of pus. Achillea winced.

'I need to pierce the swelling,' muttered Tarik, a worried tone in his voice. He laid his hand on Benakiell's leg and then on his forehead. Benakiell groaned. 'We need a needle.'

Achillea opened her mouth, no doubt about to say that she would fetch one from Gladia and then shut it again. We looked at each other. Ravin stepped in and told Tarik that he had one, that he had been using it in his trials to make tiny chains. He took it from where it was laying, along with his other scrolls and small tools and held it in the fire briefly to burn off any dirt. Tarik took it and plunged it deep into Benakiell's wound. There was a creeping smell of decay as the pus oozed out, slowly but seemingly never ending. Benakiell stirred and moaned with some relief as the pressure eased. Tarik still looked concerned. The wound was ragged round the edges where Benakiell had tried to take out the splinters of reed buried deep in the flesh of his foot. Tarik said he would need to clean out the wound more, and maybe even cut it open more so that he could take out all the pieces of reed that were embedded in Benakiell's foot.

'What is all this noise about?' came Gladia's slightly grumpy voice from the doorway. 'A woman can't even rest for a few moments without being dist...' She broke off, looking down at the prone figure on the mat next to Tarik. 'But that looks like Benakiell!' Her eyes washed with brief relief at seeing him again. 'What has happened to him? Oh, poor Benakiell!' Before anyone could answer any of her queries she bustled over to the mat where Benakiell lay and had sat down next to him and taken his hand before she had even realised that there was another woman there, sitting on the other side of Benakiell, also holding his hand. 'But who is this?' she asked, gesturing towards Shira in that offhand way she had. 'Has she brought him in? Thank you very much for bringing him to us, his loved ones. It was kind of you to help a stranger like that.'

Shira drew herself up and glared at Gladia.

'I don't know who you are, although I know Tarik and Talla and Achillea. I do not know him,' she waved over at Ravin and then continued, her voice raising and quivering slightly as she spoke. 'But I can assure you that I am one of Benakiell's loved ones! I am Shira, of Rishkar and Benakiell lives with me when he is not travelling or in Oramia. He is as my husband, and beloved to me.' Her voice quavered and finally she broke down and wept. We all seemed unable to move, like silent sandstone pillars in the desert. What could we do but watch as the winds of change blew the sand from one sand dune to another?

Gladia was silent. She who almost always had a retort, or a sharp, pithy response had nothing to say. Her face sagged. Her shoulders slumped. Her deft, capable fingers twitched the edge of her netela, compulsively rubbing it back and forth as if to try to remove the joyous embroidery which edged it. Achillea widened her eyes at me, not comprehending the situation which unfolded in front of us and surprised at Gladia's uncharacteristic silence.

Gladia turned from the doorway. As she turned and pulled her netela up and over her head I saw the glistening track of a tear drop making its way down her face, that same face which had looked so contented and happy earlier in the day. I had never seen Gladia cry, even when she had been tortured by the OutRiders. I got to my feet.

'Shall I come with you?' asked Ravin, seeing that I intended to go to Gladia, but I shook my head. This would be between me and Gladia, and no other.

'I will be back later,' I said. 'Achillea, the rest of the honey is inside if you need it for Benakiell's wounds.' Shira was still miserably snuffling and stroking Benakiell's hair. This situation was worse than Gladia's tangled embroidery threads, for it seemed unlikely that we would be able to resolve it to the satisfaction of all. I imagined how it might feel if I learned there was another, like Avenda who loved Ravin. But I knew that Ravin loved me and we did not know Benakiell's true feelings on these tangled relationships of his. I went into the

308

dwelling and was just in time to see the door being shut. Gladia had left. I opened the door hastily and could see her walking down the street to the east, stumbling a little. I followed her for some time as she plodded aimlessly about. Eventually she got to the Orchard of Rao and then looked around her vaguely, completely lost. I caught up with her and took her arm.

'Come, Gladia,' I urged her gently. 'Let us sit over there in the shade of the date trees.' She walked with me, silent and we sat, Gladia leaning up against the date palm and me, cross-legged by her side. She could not speak. She kept trying to form words but could not find a way to say what she was thinking or feeling. She did not know that I knew how she felt for Benakiell, but now she needed to. If I had learned from my argument with Ravin, it was that there were times when it was important to be honest, especially with those you loved. I did love Gladia. I loved Benakiell too. They were the closest thing I had had to parents and no matter how aggravating they both could be, I knew that I could depend on them, and now it was time for Gladia to be able to depend on me.

'I know.' I said to Gladia, simply. 'I know how you feel about Benakiell.'

She raised her eyes to me blearily. 'What on earth do you mean? Of course, I am worried about Benakiell. I have known him for years and it was a shock to see him injured like that. I just need a few minutes to get used to it and then I will be back to help. Don't worry about me!' This time her attempts to bluster her way through this were not going to work.

'No, Gladia.' I was firm. I also hoped that I was right, else I would look very foolish. 'You love Benakiell.'

She tried to evade me again. 'Well, of course, he is an old friend, like I said.'

'You love him, like I love Ravin,' I said gently. 'I felt it from your heart after we went to the Empath Erayo. You have loved him like that for years. You have waited and hoped for years for him to feel the same for you. And now you have met Shira who tells you that she is the one whom Benakiell has chosen to spend his time with, the one whom he loves. I do not know what Benakiell and Shira feel. I only know what you feel, and I know that now you feel hurt, pain and grief.'

Gladia's eyes filled with tears and she obstinately turned her head away from me, unwilling for me to see how distraught she was. She was so accustomed to hiding her love for Benakiell that she could not cope with the thought that another person might know.

'How did a Drab from the Temple come to know so much about love anyway,' she muttered. 'Maybe you got some strange mixed message from Erayo which meant nothing.'

I put my arms around her and pulled her close to me, sensing that words would not convey what I needed her to know. She rested her head on my shoulder. I could smell the lavender from her face salve and the smoke in her netela and the sweat. Her soft, plump body leaned into mine and she wept, great racking sobs and groans of pain. I sat with her, as she had sat with me all those years ago when I had sobbed. Before I came into the Outer, I had been trained not to display or indeed have feelings except those of devotion to the Goddess. We did not cry after the Second Age of Childhood, and rarely cried after the First Age except when in physical pain. We were often quoted Ashkana's words 'Tears will not water a garden.' And 'Tears will not scrub the Temple'. Knowing what I knew now, I wondered how many times Ashkana had wept for Rao before her heart was hardened and she rejected the whole concept of love forever. Achillea had told me, from her conversations with Parline and others under the guidance of Soren, that it was Soren who sent tears because they were healing to a person. Tears allowed a person's feelings to spill out and to ease and that, while tears could be linked to physical pain, they were most closely linked to love or to the loss of love, which is what grief is. I still did not cry very often, at least not in comparison to Achillea who often wept tears of happiness and sadness over the smallest things, but I had learned to allow them when they came, and to have no shame.

Eventually, Gladia drew away and sniffed, wiping her face on the already sodden netela which hung loosely on her shoulders. She looked at me blearily.

'I don't know what to do. Benakiell has always been my friend, from when Velosia first brought him back to Mellia. She was my best friend, you know, she had been from childhood. She was the only one apart from my parents who saw my baby girl, the one they left at the Temple. We had a bond, she and I because neither of us was ever blessed by the Goddess with children after that. But Benakiell loved her and she loved him and then when she died he was in such pain. He was so kind to me and stayed friends with me, and I tried to do for him what Velosia might have done. Somehow it changed into love from me, but he never seemed interested in me in that way. I kept it well hidden, or so I thought. I went to Erayo once or twice a year and it would soothe me and take the feelings away for a little while. It didn't matter when he did not want any other woman either, for I thought he was still grieving for Velosia, and understood it. But now,' she broke into fresh sobs, 'He loves another! I was there all that time and he could have had me any time he wanted, but he loves that woman Shira, who doesn't even come from Oramia either! And she is beautiful and loves him too! And he must have never even mentioned me by name to her when they spoke together.' She sniffed noisily and then turned to me angrily. 'And why didn't you tell me? I have been here for days now and you have said nothing to me, even though she said she knew you! Why would you let me shame myself like this?'

I shifted uneasily. 'We did not want to hurt you, Gladia. We wanted to tell you, but it was hard to do. And remember what a big surprise it was to us that you had even arrived? We did not think we would see you until we returned to Oramia and then we would have told you, honestly.'

'Who else knows of my feelings?' demanded Gladia suddenly. I assured her that I had told nobody, not even Ravin. I also told her that both Achillea and Tarik had agreed she might be upset by it but only because Benakiell was such an old friend and that she might be disconcerted by the commencement of a new relationship. She made me promise not to tell anyone else ever, and reluctantly I promised her. I could not see how she would be able to avoid it coming out though.

'I will manage,' said Gladia stoically. 'I must. I will just have to tell myself I have never loved him in that way. I will return to your dwelling in some time when I am better composed. I need an excuse.' The date tree we were sitting by had shed some of its fruit, and we began to collect it. Once we had some, we walked to the spring near the orchard and Gladia washed her netela at the washing slab. She was better being busy, and I mused on whether this was how Ashkana had developed her ideas about work as a replacement for love. Perhaps she too had found solace in working hard. Gladia lay the netela in the sun to dry and then we walked back, the dates wrapped in Gladia's netela. I was not sure what she planned to do, but I was willing to be led by her since she had now calmed herself. I knew there would be more heartache for her but that she was coping as well as she could with this blow, and I needed to support her and look after her, just as she had supported and looked after me.

When we returned, Achillea met us at the door.

'Where did you go to so quickly, Gladia? Shira is worried that she has upset you. She was tired and distraught about Benakiell, that is all.'

Gladia waved an arm airily, and I marvelled at her acting skill. 'Oh, of course, I quite understand. I just thought it better to leave Tarik in peace to work on Benakiell; I know how skilled he is with the physic. There were a lot of people there. I thought I'd go and get some dates to feed our guests and then Talla found me, so I got her to show me where I could wash my netela which was covered in this dust which lies everywhere. I'm sure you will agree it looks much better.' She babbled on and Achillea looked at me curiously. I shrugged my shoulders and tried to look as bemused as her. We walked into the courtyard of the dwelling. There was no sign of Benakiell and Shira who were both resting inside, and Ravin was working on the honeygold moulds.

I was, by now, concerned not only for Gladia and Benakiell and their very different problems, but also for us and the completion of our task. When we had left Benakiell at Shira's dwelling, he had told her nothing of the effect of the scroll he had brought back to show me nor of our quest, and I was uneasy with yet another person knowing what we were doing. But how could we carry on with the casting while they were both here, and more to the point, how would we all fit into the small confines of this dwelling which only slept four comfortably? I discussed this with Ravin and Tarik in a low voice while Achillea sat with Gladia, talking of this and that. Whichever way we tried to place people, there was a problem of some sort. I began to wish that Benakiell and Shira had never arrived. I then felt instantly ashamed.

The place where our dwelling was, in the south eastern section of Arbhoun was full of dwellings. Some of them were traveller homes like the one that we were in, reserved for those who would only stay a few weeks or months and then leave again. They were administered by the markets, which were in turn administered by the Council of Guidance, and received trades from those who stayed in them, a sort of tax on what they were selling. Some who came to Arbhoun brought with them fabric tents and sticks, and made their own dwellings outside the city limits, and others stayed with friends. Ravin offered to go and look if there were any other dwellings nearby where Benakiell and Shira could stay while Benakiell's leg healed. It was not a busy time of year in Arbhoun yet, for the orchards were not yet in fruit. When they were, it would be extremely hard to find a dwelling. Ravin left, with a pouch of sandalwood that we had brought from Ambar and returned soon after, victorious, and with half of the sandalwood still in his possession.

'I knew one of Shafir's friends lives near here. He has a traveller dwelling next to his own. It is only small but big enough for two and with a small courtyard. He was happy to let me have it for a good trade because Shafir has spoken well of me to him.' Ravin smiled, happy to have helped to solve a problem. I could see that he was longing to get back to the making of the two Oranges. Tarik wanted to complete the casting, which might take the rest of the day, but was also concerned for Benakiell's foot. Tarik had twin interests; the physic and the metalwork, and although recently the metalwork had been his focus, now that there was a crisis, his knowledge of physic was once more becoming important. He was most accomplished in the treatment of wounds and certain types of fevers and agues, all the types of things which the OutRiders might see most often; falls from horses, injuries from weapons and so on. This injury of Benakiell's allowed him to use some of that knowledge.

By now, Gladia was sitting and sewing, looking for all the world as if she were content, not as if her heart was grieving for her lost and unfulfilled love. Marvelling at her strength of character, I went across to her and told her that Ravin had found a place for Benakiell and Shira to stay and cautioned her against talking about the Orange of Kashiq in front of Shira. She snorted and observed that she knew how to hold her tongue even if other people didn't. I looked at what she was stitching. It was a small tunic, with stitching round the neck and cuffs in a pattern of orange and purple triangles. Gladia's plump fingers guided the sharp needle in and out of the yellow fabric, as regular as breathing and I could see that she found the sewing as soothing as I found working with the bees.

'Who is this for?' I asked.

Gladia smiled a little wistfully. 'It's for Jember. He is growing up so fast, that boy! I wish he could just have stayed little forever! But he will love the bright colours on this tunic, and more to the point, Bellis and I will be able to spot him easily when he is trying to hide away from his chores!'

I laughed, amused at the idea of Gladia outwitting the little rascal Jember. I thought of how she had given up her own baby and how she had longed for a family of her own since then. It did not seem fair that she had sacrificed so much. I thought too of how easily she had taken to the maternal role to Bellis and Jember and how it seemed unlikely that such a thing would ever happen to me. I had, after all, gone through childhood with no parents and having been told that I would never have children of my own. I had no yearning for a child, though, for there were too many other things to learn and do for myself without being responsible for someone else's learning and doing.

Some time later, Shira emerged from the dwelling. Tarik had put them into the men's room so that we could get anything we wanted from our room. Most of what Ravin and Tarik needed was outside by now, hidden under mats and fabric.

'Benakiell is asking to see you, Tarik,' she said, quietly. 'I think the fever is starting to ease for he knows we are in Arbhoun now I have told him, and that he is injured. He asks to speak to you alone,' she added, glancing at Gladia suspiciously. Gladia continued to sew methodically, but I could see her fingers tightening around the small needle and an increased ferocity in the stabbing of the needle.

'Talla, can I have some of your white honey?' asked Tarik. 'I have seen it used before, for infected wounds such as Benakiell's. I need the swelling and infection to come down before I try to get the rest of that reed out of the wound.' I rose and went into the dwelling to fetch one of the last few small gourds of my white honey from Gabez. I had grown flowers and herbs with healing qualities in my garden in the hope that the bees might pass some of it on in their honey. I was a little regretful that it would not be eaten and would instead be used to cover the wound, but I hoped it would ease Benakiell's pain. However much I disapproved of his avoidance of talking to Gladia about Shira, I hated the idea of him being in pain and unable to think properly, and wanted to see the old Benakiell reappear, with his gruff ways and his occasionally twinkling eyes, his disregard for authority and his steadfast loyalty to his friends. Surely there would be a way for him and Gladia to still be friends with one another?

Meanwhile Tarik had taken some cloth strips and soaked them in a physic of goldenrod and yarrow. He took them and the honey and went inside to Benakiell. Ravin smiled at Shira in a friendly way, and I was grateful for him being there with his open attitude and his kind heart. He did not carry with him any of the old memories the rest of us had and did not even know Benakiell although I had told him about him so his welcoming attitude to Shira was natural and unforced.

'My name is Ravin,' he introduced himself with the Kashiqi hand to heart greeting. Shira looked relieved to find a fellow Kashiqi in this dwelling of Oramians and returned the gesture, smiling. She looked a little less drawn, and more rested, though a little stiff, which was understandable since she had been supporting Benakiell on their journey to Arbhoun. Nevertheless, it was clear that she had paid some attention to her appearance before she emerged; her hair was combed and shiny and she was wearing clean clothes and wearing an orange blossom scented oil. She carried with her a woven pouch of the sort used here in Kashiq to carry food.

'I greet you,' she replied and then turned to the rest of us. 'It is amazing how much some few hours of sleep can do for how one feels.' She turned to Gladia. 'I am sorry for being so quick to anger earlier. I did not know who you were, then, and I was tired and worried for my Benakiell.' I winced inside at her possessive words and what effect they might have on Gladia, who paused slightly before answering Shira.

'Worry will do that to a person,' she answered, looking up from her sewing. 'I did not know who you were either.' Ravin stepped in again.

317

'Would you like some Kashiqi tea?' he asked Shira and then turned to me, grinning, and put his arm around me. 'Talla and her Oramian friends love to drink coffee all the time, but it can be a little strong and bitter for me. I can make us some mint and honey tea if you prefer.' Shira smiled and accepted his offer. While he busied himself with the leaves for the tea, Achillea poured the rest of the coffee which had been left in the pot into cups for us. Shira reached into the woven pouch and brought out some carefully wrapped, dense date cake. I remembered her profession and my mouth watered in anticipation.

'I brought some cake with me to trade and to share,' said Shira, opening it up. 'This one has dates and powdered almonds, dried apricots, honey and orange blossom oil in it.' She broke the cake into pieces, carefully counting a piece for everyone and offered us a piece. When the cake arrived at Gladia, she put her sewing down and took a piece, thanking Shira. It was delicious. It felt to me like a kind of alchemy, that a person could put ingredients together like this and create such a taste. I loved the different foods I had tried here in Kashiq but knew that I would be unlikely to ever be able to reproduce them. I could cook simple foods to keep myself alive, but everyone was a better cook than me. The dried apricots were like small golden jewels in the dark, rich cake, and the orange blossom oil had been dripped on the top of the cake adding another level of taste to it. I glanced at Gladia and could see that she was savouring this treat too, regardless of who had made it, and silently applauded Shira for her gesture. I wondered if she had spoken to a more lucid Benakiell about Gladia yet, and whether he knew that Gladia was here.

# CHAPTER 29

avin had been working on the tiny chains he had made with the fine wire for the segments of the Orange. He and Tarik had by now made copies of all the parts of the Orange, and the new pieces of the second Orange had been hinged together to make the small compartments for Rao's words of love. We kept them separate from each other for now, the original from the copy, but in truth it was difficult to tell the difference. The thin metal pipes left on the recast pieces were fragile enough to be cut off, and the pins for the hinges had been made with thin pieces of honeygold wire. The stem piece which Gladia had brought from Ambar formed the central section which held all the segments together. It was six sided when you looked carefully at it, and each tiny flat side had a notch running down the middle of it where the segment rested when it was closed. There was a small flat disc at the bottom of the stem which the segments rested on and a six-sided ring which could be pushed up and down the stem.

I loved to watch Ravin working. He often worked with a piece of plant parchment next to him and a charcoal stick, and scribed measurements and sketches of what he was doing. The scholars of Kashiq, of whom he was undoubtedly one, at least in my eyes, took the skills of reading and scribing very much for granted and used them in all parts of their lives. Even those who were not of Rao often learned to scribe and read after a fashion, and it was a real disadvantage for those who did not know how to do it. In Oramia it was rare to meet one who could

319

scribe and read who was not of the Temple or the Queen's Court, and in Oramia my skills were extremely useful and sought after. But those skills were inextricably linked to the seats of power and subjugation of the people of the Outer, and so naturally caused suspicion. I did not use my scribing or reading in my day-to-day life in Gabez, although I practiced whenever I could. I liked to see how naturally it occurred here in Kashiq and it was just one more thing which enhanced my feelings for Ravin. His fingers were long and elegant and equally at home holding a pen or manipulating a tiny chain or being trailed suggestively down my back as they were now.

Achillea and Gladia were out together. Their reconciliation had seemingly driven them closer together and Achillea wanted Gladia to hear her sing for Parline and the other women she had met. They had asked me to go too, but I was happier to remain at the dwelling with Ravin. We had barely spent any time alone together of late and this was our opportunity. Tarik had gone over to Benakiell and Shira's dwelling to change Benakiell's dressings and to try to remove the final parts of the splintered reed, so we knew we had some time to ourselves.

Ravin slid his hand underneath my tunic and smoothed his hand up my back, drawing me firmly closer to him, and bending his head to kiss my neck just behind my ear. The touch of his hand on the skin of my back was simultaneously comforting and exciting. It felt as I had felt when the channel of empathy had first opened in me when I wore the bee necklace, like something alive which danced between us. I slid my hand underneath his tunic, and he wriggled us closer together. We stood like this for some time, warm and melting together, before Ravin led me into the dwelling.

It was not something I had known anything about, this secret dance between lovers. In the Temple there was no mention of it save the fact that babies were born to women of the Outer, and what I learned afterwards about the ways in which the OutRiders used the Angels had made me confused and angry. But this was none of that. It was at first shy and then bold, selfish and selfless, as important to please as to be pleased, a union of body, mind and heart and a way of expressing that which we could not put into words, both a yearning and a fulfilling.

When we returned to the courtyard, some time later, I realised that, at any time, the others might return. I had not been aware of the passage of time while Ravin and I had been together. I hastily began to clean the coffee pot out, using the ground pieces of coffee to scrub it clean. Sure enough, not too long afterwards, Tarik arrived back, with an unexpected visitor; Benakiell. Tarik had fashioned a crutch with a leather cushion fixed to the top so that Benakiell could rest it under his shoulder in comfort. His foot was well wrapped and padded with new strips of cloth and he was clean and rested, though clearly still weak and in some pain when his foot brushed the floor.

'Greetings Talla,' he said, with the ghost of a smile. 'It is good to see you again, although Tarik here tells me you have already seen me when I arrived, with Shira. Is anyone else here?' He looked around him, his eyes lingering briefly on Ravin. I shook my head, relieved that Gladia was not here.

'I thought it a good idea to talk to Benakiell on his own,' said Tarik. 'Now that he is lucid and can understand what we tell him, for things have progressed in these weeks of being at Rishkar.' Benakiell looked somewhat abashed. It was clear that his initial interest in the quest for the Orange of Kashiq had been diluted by his interest in Shira. Having made this introduction, Tarik wandered over to Ravin and started looking at the mechanism again and left it to me to try to explain to Benakiell what we had achieved so far. It was only at this point that I realised how much we had done and how much had changed in these weeks at Arbhoun. I had to explain some things twice over to Benakiell, but by the end he had grasped that we were very close to completing our task and that we would need to get the orange back into Oramia to give it to Ambar. He asked to see the pieces of the Orange and I called to Ravin to bring them over to show him, which he did. While Benakiell examined the pieces, Ravin stood behind me and ran his finger down my arm playfully.

Benakiell looked up from the Orange sternly. 'And who are you, young man, that you take such liberties with Talla and that you have earned such trust from my friends?' He was gruff but stern, and Ravin moved his finger hastily from my arm. I had forgotten that Benakiell did not know Ravin, for it felt by now that I had known him forever. I stuttered to explain until I saw Benakiell's eyes twinkling at me from beneath his hooded eyebrows and I knew he was teasing me, and that either Tarik or Shira had told him about the relationship between me and Ravin. He turned to Ravin again.

'In the absence of another, I stand in the stead of Talla's father. If you should hurt her, not only will I come after you, but so will Talla and she is much more frightening than me!' Benakiell chuckled. I was touched by his words, put simply but reaffirming his place in my life. Ravin looked relieved at the laughter, but assured Benakiell that he only wanted for me what would make me happy. I wanted to talk to Benakiell about Gladia and the pain he had caused her, but I could not. Gladia had asked me not to speak of it, and even if nobody else had been there, it was not for me to tell it. So instead, I asked him about Shira, and if she knew about our task here in Kashiq.

Benakiell confirmed that he had not told her about it specifically but had only told her that we were here to find out more about a story that I had read on the scrap of scroll that he had brought back from her dwelling months ago from the Tower of the Wise. He had not found the other part of the parchment and asked us not to tell her anything more.

'I do not want Shira to worry herself about any dangers we might face. It has been hard enough for her to have to drag me along the path to get here to Arbhoun.' It seemed only protective, but I wondered if Benakiell preferred to keep the two parts of his life separate from one another.

'Will you stay in Kashiq with Shira?' asked Ravin innocently. 'For she told us you are as a husband to her. Or perhaps she will return with you to Oramia, to your village with you and with Gladia.'

Benakiell winced and closed his eyes. 'I do not know,' he admitted finally. 'I like Kashiq, but I like Oramia too and Oramia is my home. But Kashiq is Shira's home. Perhaps I will continue to travel between the two. Anyway, what do you plan to do? For you are of Kashiq and Talla is of Oramia, and soon she will be going back to Oramia. What will you do, for you are the same as me?'

I closed my eyes. This thought had been hanging in my mind like a fine spidersilk. Almost invisible and yet a barrier. I did not know how we could make it work except perhaps by my frequently crossing the bridge at Gabez to Pirhan and by him living nearer to Pirhan. Ravin, however, seemed to have no concern about it at all.

'I will go where Talla goes,' he said simply. 'Perhaps we will travel between the two lands, sometimes in one and sometimes in the other. I shall be content if I am in the same place as her, wherever it may be. I shall certainly return with her to Oramia with the Orange for I have a curiosity about her homeland.'

Benakiell looked at him carefully. 'You will have to learn to dress as we do in Oramia,' he said. 'There are many less Kashiqis in Oramia than there are Oramians in Kashiq. Perhaps we are more suspicious people. You wouldn't be wanting to get the likes of Ambar worked up about your motivation for being in Oramia.'

Ravin smiled. 'I am sure I will manage. Tarik has already promised that I can use some of his clothes, and I am sure that Gladia will trade one of her fine tunics for a needle box full of needles.'

'Will I indeed?' came Gladia's voice as she bustled through the dwelling. She had heard only the end of Ravin's sentence and was taken aback when she got to the door and found Benakiell sitting there by the wall. He looked up and smiled at her.

'Greetings old friend,' he said, talking into his beard somewhat. 'I never thought to see you here in Kashiq.'

Gladia raised her eyebrows. The smile she had put on her face hastily did not reach her eyes.

'No,' she said finally. 'I don't think you ever did think I would come to Kashiq, did you? You have quite a different life over here, to that which you have in Mellia.'

Benakiell looked down, embarrassed at her implication and well aware that he had been caught out in his subterfuge. Perhaps also, though, there was a spark of relief glowing in his mind. A glad feeling that now he did not have to separate out his life so much, and that perhaps things would be easier from now on. Looking at Gladia's set mouth, I was not sure.

'I should have told you,' he said. 'But I was concerned about how you would feel.' I wondered if Benakiell was aware of Gladia's love for him when he said this, but he went on to say, 'You were Velosia's oldest friend and I was worried you might be angry with me on her behalf, that I had found another to love after her death.'

Gladia turned to the fire and pushed another stick into it roughly. A cloud of ash and spark flew up, and she dabbed at her face with her netela, as if to remove the ash from her eye. I knew better. She coughed too, as if she had inhaled the smoke. This all gave her some time to calm herself before she responded.

'I can't pretend I am finding it easy,' she said finally. 'It will take me a while to understand it well enough for it to be normal. But Velosia would have wanted you to be happy, and so, if you are happy, then that is important. But remember, there are people who care about you at home in Mellia too. Jember misses you when you are not there, and he looks up to you like a father. In fact, he asked me to tell you to come home soon and to bring him some more oranges and apricots!' With that, she bustled off, back into the dwelling.

'When will you be ready to return to Oramia?' Benakiell asked Tarik. Tarik frowned.

'What day is it now?'

'Viridis,' said Ravin, who seemed to recall the days despite not having any colours or scents to remind him.

'We should aim to leave on Lilavis,' said Tarik. 'We need to get back to Ambar by the beginning of the month of Aureus, at the latest, which is only two weeks away now. Much as we may be enjoying this stay in Arbhoun, the most difficult part of this is going to be getting the Orange back to Ambar in Oramia. I am not sure your foot will be ready to walk on by then,' he said to Benakiell, frowning. 'You and Shira may have to stay here; we might be able to get you back to Rishkar, but you will not make the long trip back to Mellia yet.'

Benakiell looked slightly relieved, I thought. Although he was never afraid to confront wrongdoing or to protect his friends with no thought of his own safety, he did not like to be involved in argument and discussion, and the prospect of staying out of Gladia's way would no doubt be appealing. Gladia too might benefit from some more time to try to guard herself against more pain before he returned, knowing what she knew now.

'How will we get back though?' I asked. 'For Benakiell's boat could only carry four of us, and there are five of us now. Gladia came through Pirhan to get here but if we go through Pirhan they will find the pieces of the Orange when they survey our goods for taxes.' There was a good chance that we could still get the Orange of Kashiq over the bridge and past the guards on each side; the Defenders of Yael in Pirhan and then the OutRiders in Gabez, but if even one of the segments were found and confiscated as a simple piece of honeygold for taxes, all our work would come to nothing.

'You will have to split up,' said Benakiell, stretching his foot out in front of him. 'Tarik, you will have to take the boat back over the river and take the Orange back with you that way.'

'He can't go alone,' said Ravin. 'I will go with him. We will take the Orange and some of the goods and get you and Shira back to Rishkar. If you struggle to walk, you will need two strong men to hold you up anyway. Shira cannot do it on her own again. Talla and Achillea will have to go back to Oramia with Gladia over the bridge at Pirhan.'

I knew that what he said made sense, but I was nonetheless annoyed with Ravin for deciding things for me. I had hoped to spend the trip back with him, telling him about Oramia and describing the land more and the names of the trees and flowers. I must have looked disappointed, because Ravin smiled at me and assured me that it would soon be over and we could then spend more time together, and I could show him my land as he had shown me his.

Benakiell got up after this to return to the dwelling that he and Shira shared to rest, and, I suspect, to escape from Gladia, who was bad-temperedly tidying up and sweeping with a palm leaf besom. Achillea had left again shortly after she and Gladia arrived back. She was going to sing for one of Parline's friends, who had recently given birth to a much longed for child. Achillea had composed a song especially for the child and her parents, which told of the journeys of birds and the growth of trees, of how the baby was nurtured in a nest in the tree and of the care she would receive from her parents and the tree. It was a good song and Achillea's beautiful voice sang the refrains so sweetly, and it had such a soothing rhythm that I felt sure that the parents would soon be singing it to their baby themselves as they tried to get it to sleep. I wondered how she would feel to go back to Oramia where she was not a SongMaker and would no longer be able to do the thing which she most enjoyed.

Ravin had returned to the Orange along with Tarik and together they were hooking up the tiny, knotted links of wire which Ravin had made with the needle to the little links at the top of each segment, and then attaching the other end of the chain to the sliding ring which moved up and down the stem piece of the Orange. At first the sliding ring got stuck a lot, but once the stem had been waxed with beeswax, it slid smoothly up and down. Eventually, the last segment was attached to the stem and Ravin called me over, along with Gladia to see how it worked.

Ravin asked us both to close our eyes. Gladia grumbled, but in a good-tempered way, and I think she was as excited as I was to see this ancient artefact restored to its original state. I felt the weight of the honeygold orange being placed gently on the palm of my outstretched hand and opened my eyes. It was the size and shape of a normal orange, and there was a stem with a leaf on it which emerged from the top. The outside was engraved and chased to resemble a real orange and it shone in the late afternoon sun.

'Now we must open the orange,' announced Ravin, his eyes sparkling with excitement. Tarik smiled too and I could sense their feeling of achievement at having completed rebuilding this special ornament made so many years ago. I lifted it up and peered at it closely. In a normal orange there was always a tiny disc, a sort of scar which showed where it had been taken from the branch, and there was here too, but it was made by the sliding ring which went up and down the inner stem.

'Show us then,' urged Gladia impatiently. She had no interest in trying to work things out as I did.

Ravin slid the leaf on the stem round. It was on its own sliding ring which locked into the other ring and unclipped the tops of the segments from the small disc. Slowly, Ravin pushed the central ring down the six-sided stem and as he did so, the tiny chains which he had made unfolded and the six segments of the Orange of Kashiq opened out and lay splayed out, joined only by the flat disc at the bottom. Each one could be gently unclipped from its place and the lid opened to read the six words of love which Rao had chosen for Ashkana. I read them out to Gladia.

'Trust, Joy, Respect, Freedom, Forgiveness, Loss.'

Gladia ran her fingers over the tiny words inside each of the segments thoughtfully and repeated them after me as if to memorise them. Then Ravin replaced them in the lower disc and slid the ring back up the stem. As it moved up the stem, it drew up the segments with the tiny chains until they were standing up again and ready to be locked in place with the leaf. It was a wondrous thing. Hundreds of ages before this time, Lord Rao had thought his love for Ashkana so important that he had this thing cunningly crafted for her. For some unknown reason, their love had been broken and Ashkana had, in her turn, broken the Orange and returned it to Rao. And now, we had rebuilt this symbol of love so that another man, Ambar could give it to another woman, Lunaria as a sign of his own love for her. In my heart, I did not believe that Ambar felt the same love for Lunaria that I felt for Ravin or indeed that Lord Rao had felt for Ashkana. I wondered whether Lunaria would, now that the Orange of Kashiq was made whole again and in her possession, placidly accept it as a sign from the Goddess that she should proceed down this path of marriage to Ambar and having heirs to her throne. She had been a Priestess of the Temple and had a strong faith in its teachings. Once she had realised she was indeed the Queen, she had accepted it and moved into that role. If the Goddess had apparently ordained that she should have the whole Orange before she was married and had heirs, then that was probably what she would do.

Gladia seemed to read my mind. 'And Queen Lunaria can now love Ambar, can she? This piece of carved metal tells her that she can? It wasn't even made for her! Why does she believe these things so firmly? If it were true that it had that power, well then we would all be finding love...' She broke off and her eyes looked away over the wall of the courtyard. Here she was, in Kashiq, alone amidst three couples who did indeed love one another. I hastened to fill the silence she left.

'Well, it was really just a ruse, wasn't it, made up by Lunaria's DreamReader, Silene. She never thought that

THE ORANGE OF KASHIQ

Ambar would be able to find the Orange of Kashiq and give it to Lunaria, and she was hoping that that would give her more influence over the Queen.'

Gladia snorted scornfully. 'Hmmm, well it's not as if Lord High Ambar has done very much, is it? All he did was get somebody else to do his dirty work as usual! If it had been left up to him, it would never have been done!'

Tarik carefully put the Orange of Kashiq away, wrapped in a piece of cloth, in a box. There were still the other pieces for the second Orange which we had cast. Once the pieces were polished, it had been impossible to tell the difference between them. Ravin and Tarik had just chosen six for one Orange and six for the other. It seemed entirely right that the two should be so interlinked and blended. In the same way, the love between two people was interwoven until it was hard to tell where one person's love melted into the other's. We had agreed that we would not make the tiny chains for the pieces which we were leaving in Kashiq, for it was known that it had been broken anyway. We would replace the six segments in the beehives in which we had found them, but not in the protective domes of clay that had originally been moulded onto the covers, because that would take too long, and in any case it was not necessary. If another person came along and solved the clues in Finzari's manuscripts and scrolls and went to the beehives they would still find the pieces of the Orange. We would encase the honeygold segments in beeswax and then simply drop them through the bees' entrance hole in the front of the beehive since they were small enough to fit through. It seemed a shame to not be able to leave the other Orange fixed together somewhere in Kashiq, but it was just too dangerous. We were, except for Ravin, from Oramia, and questions would undoubtedly be raised about why we had been searching for the Orange of Kashiq in the first place.

# CHAPTER 30

The sun seemed to rise more strongly every day. Kashiq was a hot land, full of sand and dark orange sandstone pillars and gorges. The only places where trees seemed to grow were the places where settlements had grown, where the river springs emerged out of the rock and brought life to the earth. These springs emerged from deep underground and never dried up. I walked with Ravin to the Tower of the Wise, and as we entered the southern gate, we passed through the avenues of orange trees which had been planted there. There was, on the warming breeze, the sweet yet sharp scent of orange blossom on the air, the first I had smelled since we had come to Kashiq, save in the oils and perfumes at the market. In amongst the dark glossy green leaves emerged small white flowers just like the ones which Gladia had embroidered on my veil when I was masquerading as Priestess Neroli. A whole age of seven years had turned since then. Ravin picked one from the tree and held it under my nose.

'It is beautiful and smells so good,' I said.

'Neither its scent nor its appearance is as beautiful as you,' said Ravin, stopping me as we walked. 'You are the only woman I have loved, the only one who has loved me as I am, with all my faults. Asmara must have been saving all the best pieces for your soul to be made.'

Ravin had a gift with words. I knew the same feeling but could not articulate it like him. He seemed to know that I loved him however, and that was enough. We kissed beneath the orange trees. He placed a blossom in my hair, under my netela and I playfully planted one in his beard. We laughed and then continued to the Tower of the Wise.

It would be our last visit to the Tower. It might be my last visit forever, although I had every intention of returning here in the future. There was so much more that I wanted to read and to find out about the worlds of Oramia and Kashiq and other lands about which I knew nothing but their name or some long distant legend of their people. Ravin was accustomed to being able to read scrolls and scribe notes, to copying ideas and scribbling down designs. Oramia would be a quite different place for him, and I knew that he would not be able to manage for long without his scrolls and scribings. He had arranged for another scholar to assist Hurkim for the next four months, after which he would return, either to remove all his belongings and move on or to go back to his normal life. It was hard for him to do this, not knowing when he would be back and yet unable to tell Hurkim more. At the same time, I was looking forward to returning to the land of my birth, to seeing trees again, however scrubby they might be. To the earth which grew plants and grasses and flowers and to the solid stone mountains that rose from the plains, and to my small dwelling in Gabez where bees gathered honeydust. My mind drifted as we walked, and we arrived at the Scholar's scribeboard at the entrance before I was aware of it.

Scholar Mazin was perched on his cushion next to his scribeboard. He preferred to sit there when he read scrolls, and only stood up to scribe names or make his own notes. His eyes brightened as he saw us.

'Ah, the young Oramian with such an interest in Finzari's scribings!' he exclaimed. 'I had thought you might have left since I have not seen you here in some days. Nor your companion either,' he added hastily, glancing briefly at Ravin and then returning his gaze to me. 'Which of the Finzari scrolls would you like to see today? I have copied almost all of them myself so that I can read them when I am at home. Perhaps you might like to do the same? I assure you that the more you read his stories, the more they unfold.' He smiled at me expectantly, and I asked him for the scroll of the Poems of the Trees and then, as an afterthought, I asked him for a scroll about the life of Ashkana.

'There are many of those. What part of her life are you interested in?'

Suddenly I wished I had more time to read. I had spent all this time chasing after the Orange of Kashiq and I could have been understanding how Ashkana had become who she was and learning why the Temples had emerged in Oramia in the way that they had.

'Her later life in Oramia,' I replied.

'Ah yes, indeed,' said Scholar Mazin. 'Of course, we do not have so much material on that; only a few mentions and descriptions. But I can see why you might be interested, since that is where you are from.' He heaved himself up and went to search for the scrolls. Ravin had walked over to the scribeboard where he had been working the last time we were there. He had left a few charcoal sticks and reed pens, and a small pot of ink, as well as some plant parchments and scribbled notes. He had asked for some unrelated scrolls about the rivers of Kashiq and boat designs, so I guessed he was trying to find out more about the river crossing in Benakiell's boat which awaited him in a few days' time. As I waited for Mazin to return, I saw that Ravin was reading some closely scribed parchment and when I got to my scribeboard and stool, I asked him what he was reading.

He handed it over to me wordlessly so that I could read it too. I started to read it, a little puzzled.

'I must tell you now of my great admiration for you. I would call it love. I have observed you for many months now and have waited for you to notice me and to feel the same way for me. But you seem to have lost your mind and are attending only to the pathetic little Oramian who follows you about like a lost child. Surely you would rather be with a real Kashiqi woman who knows what you want and need? The Oramian will bring you nothing but disaster, whereas I can give you fulfilment and an equal mind...' The scroll continued in the same vein for some lines before ending with an invitation to Ravin to meet the scribe on the day of Aureus at the Place of Prayer near the Orchard of Rao. 'Come alone,' was almost unnecessarily added to this and the whole scroll was signed with a flourish. Avenda.

'Do you think I should go?' teased Ravin. 'After all, what can you offer me, you little Oramian?' He laughed. I could not believe that she would scribe all of that on a scroll that anyone here could have read. Did she not care what anyone knew? And how dare she presume that Ravin would prefer her more?

'You know,' murmured Ravin, his lips close to my ear. 'Your eyes are incredibly attractive when they spit with fire like that. Perhaps I will read this scroll to you again when we are alone in the dwelling and then we can explore your feelings more!' He kissed my ear and moved back to his scribeboard. We did both have work to do before we left here for the last time and so we dedicated the next few hours to finding out more.

The scrolls which Mazin had given me were of some interest. They told me stories which Kashiqis who had travelled to Oramia to trade had heard and passed on in ages gone by, but it was unclear how true they were. Once a story had been told many times and through many years, it began to slowly change. The scrolls said that when Ashkana had left Kashiq in anger and distress at the loss of love between her and Rao, she had spent more than a year living on her own in one of the western forest areas of Oramia.

The Goddess Asmara ensured that she came to no harm and provided for her so that she never ran out of food or water, but otherwise left her alone. The Goddess was the creator of Ashkana, but she was not Ashkana and only Ashkana could decide how she wanted to live. After this time alone of reflection, Ashkana realised that the only time when she did not grieve over her lost love was when she was working in the fields and in her dwelling, or when she was speaking with the Goddess Asmara. So she planned to make a place where women like her could go to work and be cared for and communicate with the Goddess. The first temple was thus begun, and it was named The Temple of Prayerfulness. This same Temple still existed now, north of Sennaret. However, instead of this endeavour helping Ashkana to heal, it merely made her more bitter, for there were so many women in those early days who were grieving the loss of love. She became more and more concentrated on their lives being made fuller and fuller of work so that they had no time to feel the pain of love any more. She wrote the Aphorisms of Ashkana when she was in her seventh age. She had never recovered from the loss of Rao and she felt it made her weak. The scribe of one of the scrolls was amazed at how quickly so many Temples had grown up in Oramia some ages later. I wondered when the system of the Angels, which so revolted me, had been decided upon by the Priestesses or the Queen or indeed the OutRiders. Had Ashkana had a hand in this too? Had it really been used in this way for many more years than I had been given to believe?

I thought about Lunaria, the Queen. Did she love Ambar? Or did she just know that, according to the rules, she needed to produce daughters to carry on the line of the throne? I could not imagine her full of passion, and yet it seemed that Ambar loved her. Or did he? Perhaps he just loved the idea of being in power, and of being the consort to the most important woman in Oramia. I shook my head. Here I was, having spent months of my life in a foreign land searching for an ancient symbol of love for him to give to her so that they could feel it for themselves. After this, I swore to myself, I wanted nothing more to do with either of them.

There was one more job to do while we were here. I had decided, together with Ravin, that we would conceal the second stem and leaf we had cast within one of the scrolls of Finzari. Someone would eventually find it and perhaps show it to the Scholars, or take it away themselves, or maybe even solve the puzzle as we had done and find the other pieces in the beehives. There were several copies of Finzari's scrolls in the tower of the Wise, so it was unlikely that anyone would find it until long after we were gone, especially as Finzari appeared to be a rather unpopular Scribe, despite Scholar Mazin's enthusiasm. The scroll I had requested, The Poems of the Trees, was held rolled up in a hard leather case and it was a simple job to drop the small stem and leaf into the case once the scroll had been replaced. I fixed the lid firmly closed, and we gathered up the items from our scribeboards and bundled them up before leaving the scrolls in the baskets by the Scholar's desk to be returned.

We did not tell Scholar Mazin that we would not be back. It might be some days before anyone realised, but the Tower of the Wise was always full of new learners and they would barely notice for long. Except, of course, for Avenda, who would, I thought to myself smugly, be disappointed on the day of Aureus, for by then we would be in Oramia, far away.

# THE FRUIT

## CHAPTER 31

Pirhan was a dusty, busy town. We got there after four days of walking. We had split from the others at the fork in the road to Rishkar where Benakiell and Shira would remain while Benakiell continued to heal. We had walked more slowly than usual because of his foot and although the padded stick helped, his foot was still tender. Tarik had made a padded leather covering for Benakiell's foot to protect the honey-soaked dressings from the sand. Once again, I wished we had the horses we had used in Oramia. I said this to Gladia, and she shuddered.

'I never want to get on another horse as long as I live!' she said. 'All that bumping up and down!' But the horses allowed you so much more freedom to travel for long distances and to carry heavy loads and even to move injured people about. Tarik looked wistful and acknowledged that he missed riding the horses too. Achillea had not enjoyed riding them but admitted that she would have preferred to get back in a faster time instead of walking all day in the increasing heat. She looked pale and admitted that she did not feel very well. Tarik was attentive, giving her Kashiqi tea instead of coffee and adding ground ginger root and honey to it. Gladia cast her a sharp look but said nothing.

339

The men had taken the bulk of what we were bringing back with us from Kashiq. We had traded almost all of what we had taken, both our own things and the valuable items which Ambar had given us, but we returned with different things; dates and oranges, dried apricots, orange blossom oil, carved boxes and the honeygold rocks which were left. Achillea had asked Tarik to take her box of necklaces and ornaments which she had earned through her singing. We tried to carry with us simple things which an Oramian might trade in Pirhan and then go back with and had given the more unusual items to Tarik and Ravin to take back to Oramia on the boat. Gladia had told us how the system worked. The OutRiders would stop those coming over the bridge into Oramia and the Defenders of Yael would stop those entering Pirhan. Occasionally, they might stop those passing back the other way if they were especially suspicious, but since we would not have with us anything like that, we were not worried about them.

Pirhan was full of traders. Even though it was only across the bridge and a few miles from Gabez, I had never been here. Partly it was because of the numbers of OutRiders who waited by the bridge to tax the traders. I had first-hand experience of how cruel and vicious the OutRiders could be, and they still ruled over the people of the Outer with their strength and power. I had hoped that it would stop once Lunaria became Queen and Ambar was in the court, for he had left the OutRiders himself because they did not behave nobly. It was true that I had heard less tales of horror about them since, and there were certainly less stories of them looking for the maids from the Temple. In fact, we did not seem to hear any stories about the Drabs as they called them in the Outer. Perhaps they kept them all. Despite all this, I still felt a rising fear at the thought that the OutRiders might pick us out.

'Don't worry so much,' said Gladia. 'I don't worry like you do, and they hurt me more than they hurt you. I'm sure Achillea here will smile at them and they will just let us past.' She turned to Achillea, who smiled weakly, and trudged on towards the square in Pirhan.

'Is she alright?' hissed Gladia. 'She looks very peaky to me. I've never seen her looking so ill.'

'Maybe she is worried about Tarik,' I said, for I knew I was worrying about Ravin. We would only know that they were safe when they arrived back in Gabez.

'Hmm,' Gladia was unconvinced. 'There is more to it than that, mark my words.'

Once we got to the square, we sat down in the shade to catch our breath. We had been walking since just before the sun rose and we were tired and hungry. Gladia sat fanning herself with her netela and Achillea took some sips of the cold tea Ravin had made for her. I looked in the carrysack and pulled out some cake, which Shira had given us. Gladia's eyes lit up. She might not like Shira, but she certainly liked her cakes. Ordinarily, Achillea did too, but she only nibbled at it listlessly.

'How long since the sign of the Goddess, Achillea?' asked Gladia abruptly. I turned to her surprised that she would ask such a thing out of nowhere. The Goddess sent a sign to all women every few weeks to remind them of how blessed they were as creators and holders of new life, and as a sign of their sacrifice. But it was not something that many discussed unless they were seeking physic to ease the pain. Achillea looked up, as surprised as me.

'I do not know exactly,' she confessed. 'Since we have travelled to Kashiq, I have not been counting the days in the same way as I do in Oramia. Why do you ask?'

Gladia pursed her lips and looked troubled, as if fighting some internal battle, before continuing with her questioning.

'Have you been feeling sick for long?'

'Only a little while,' answered Achillea. 'It gets better after I have got up and when I drink Tarik's ginger tea.'

Gladia sat back, smugly. 'Well, it will be a while before you feel better from that sickness,' she said. 'In fact, I would say, sometime in the month of Lilavis.' I calculated in my mind how far into the future this was, and it was five Oramian months away, thirty-five weeks. How could she possibly divine how long Achillea might feel unwell for? Gladia snorted at the look on my face.

'It might be years since you left the Temple, Talla, but they trained your mind well in there. Never to think of the real meaning of the Goddess's blessing. I suppose it's a good thing that nobody ever did lose the Goddess's blessing while they were in the Temple!'

Achillea was looking at Gladia in a strange mixture of shyness and pride tinged with shock.

'Are you saying that I have truly been blessed by the Goddess?' she asked.

Gladia smiled a wistful smile at her, and her eyes took on that distant film as she thought of events long ago.

'Yes, Achillea. I remember as if it were yesterday how I felt when it happened to me. Except of course I was too young, and my father saw it as a curse not a blessing. I was extremely sick.'

My mind was still trying to put everything together that I had just heard. Even though Achillea and I were such good friends, my natural reserve meant that we did not talk about such intimate things. When I realised finally what Gladia was saying to Achillea, my mouth fell open and I stared at Achillea. Her face, still wan and tired looking, was nevertheless shot through with a shining joy.

'Talla, I am going to have a baby!' she said. 'I thought I had some awful Kashiqi ague and might die like my mother. But now I know what it is, I can cope easily! What do you think Tarik will say? I can't wait to tell him!'

Gladia was silent for a while as Achillea chattered on, suddenly animated by the news that Gladia had imparted. I still felt shocked. Achillea was to be a mother, and Tarik a father. There was no doubt that they would do a fine job of rearing a child, I was sure, but part of me felt a little sad because Achillea would, no doubt, drift away from my friendship. She would talk to others who had had babies like Gladia and Bellis, and I could offer her nothing – I had not even realised what it meant when the Goddess's blessing did not come.

'Soren must have asked the Goddess to give me a real blessing,' said Achillea. 'When I sang the song for the friend of Parline and their baby, it must have touched her heart.' She began to softly hum the song.

'I hope it may bring you joy,' said Gladia finally. 'And that Tarik will look after you both well. Perhaps you will come to Mellia with the baby when it is born. Jember will like that. And I must stitch you some looser robes to wear, since you won't be fitting into such tiny clothes as you do now for long.'

We sat for some time under the trees, silently exploring this news in our own minds. Achillea was happy, I could see that, but I did not think I would feel the same if the Goddess thought to bless me in a similar way. For much of my life, there had only been space for myself and for the Goddess. Later, my friends added to the warmth within, and, recently, Ravin had entered, causing the flames to spark and crackle and fill me with warmth. There did not seem to be space for anyone else.

We crossed the bridge a short time later, joining the line of Oramians and Kashiqis heading towards Pirhan. There was a large group of OutRiders waiting to take their tax from the bundles. Each person would have their goods examined and one in seven items would be taken. Of course, it was the same going the other way, so by the time a person had gone both ways, almost a third of their items would have gone to either the OutRiders or the Defenders. There was no wonder they were so eager to maintain their grip on power when they received all these goods for no effort at all. I was not surprised that Benakiell had found his own way to cross the border and wondered how many more there were who travelled in that way. However many there were though, there were still many more, mostly the women or the older traders, who were accustomed to the taxing and who made allowance for it in their trading.

The OutRiders spoke to one another using their hands silently. They all wore armour, and the horses they rode stood close by in a shelter from the sun. The shields which bore the emblem of the Queen hung from the saddle, but their bows hung on their backs and I knew they all carried throwing knives. We shuffled on, scuffing the dust as we moved until eventually, we arrived. There were several areas smoothed over with clay where one laid out everything in the bundles. They were well practiced at spotting the goods from Kashiq and interested themselves in these most. I unknotted my cloth bundle and let the goods spill from it. The OutRider turned them over with the edge of his foot, which was encased in a sort of leather shoe.

'You don't seem to have done very much trading,' he commented with a sneer on his face. 'Not much point bothering in going over to Pirhan just for this lot.' He picked out his tax of the fruit I had brought back and took two vials of Orange blossom oil and two gourds of orange blossom and apricot honey, then gestured to me to tie them up again and move on. I cast my eyes to the ground, ever grateful for the fact that I could pretend respect while cloaking my disdain. I glanced across at Achillea. The OutRider who was taxing her reached his hand towards her face, forcing her head out of the netela and headdress so that he could see there was nothing concealed there, and that she was not wearing elaborate, golden Kashiqi earrings. She stood mute while he examined her. He exchanged some silent gestures with his comrades who laughed in a crude way. He ran his hands over her body, announcing that he suspected she might have hidden something in her clothing. Achillea stood quietly as he did this, his hands lingering suggestively in certain places.

Gladia stood by my side, watching impassively. We knew from our own experience that the OutRiders could not be persuaded by appeals to their decency. The angry flames in my mind's emberjar flared. I started to move but Gladia laid a firm hand on my arm.

'Now is not the time,' she said. 'We will work from the top. Ambar will pay dearly for his little trinket.' Her lips tightened grimly, and I knew she was thinking of Bellis and the countless other Angels who had had to endure this debasement at the hands of the OutRiders and the system which had been created to feed the desires of the OutRiders for women and the desires of the Temple for their babies and their slave labour on the Temple buildings. She was right too, that we should wait. I had always felt like I had failed Gladia when I did nothing to stop her torture at the hands of the OutRiders, but she had never held it against me; instead, she had supported me against Benakiell and Ashtun and even Achillea and told them that I had no choice. Eventually, the OutRider moved away reluctantly from Achillea and she put her remaining items back together wearily and came to join us. Gladia patted her on the shoulder comfortingly.

'Put them out of your mind. Think instead of Tarik, and what a good man he is, and about your baby sent to you by the Goddess. She knows who to bless.'

# CHAPTER 32

The boat was just where we left it,' said Tarik. 'Benakiell has found a good place to cross the River Gabish, that's for sure. We waited until night to cross, because we had seen some Defenders riding along the river during the day. It is lucky that there is so much of those water reeds they make the plant parchment from. It made it easy to stay out of sight.'

Ravin took up the story. They were relishing telling us about their trip back to Gabez and had just arrived back at our dwelling three days after us.

'I have never been in a boat before, although I have heard tell of them, for there are towns in Kashiq which lay at the water's edge. There are boats there which carry many men, they say. It is a strange and uncomfortable feeling to be unable to use one's legs to move and to nevertheless move. Tarik said the river was higher than it was when you crossed it which must mean there has been rain in the mountains to the north. The current was strong and we both had to paddle with all our might to reach the other side without being blown down the river and into the rocks. Luckily, we made it across, and nothing was lost, although both of us were very wet! We left Benakiell's boat where he had told us to, under the branches and then set off back here. He will come to Oramia through Pirhan when he comes back next time, and then take the boat back.' He looked around him. We were sitting under the Paradox tree, on a woven mat. All around us was the sound of bees as they greedily gathered their honeydust. It was calm and soothing sitting here in the shade, and it felt a relief from the endless sand of Kashiq to be in a land where a large tree like a Paradox tree could grow and give its shade to all who sought it. I noted that Tarik must have lent Ravin one of his robes to wear, and that he had carefully put away his Kashiqi headdress. He was indistinguishable from other Oramian men around him now. His skin was perhaps a little darker, and his beard worn a little longer. It was strange to see him without the headdress. Everyone wore them in Kashiq, whereas here in Oramia it was only the women who wore the netela and of course the Priestesses who were fully veiled. His hair caught the evening sun and glowed with a dark red tone which normally I would not have seen. The only times I had seen him without his headdress were at night when there was little light anyway.

'More importantly than all these heroics of yours, did you manage to get the Orange back safely?' asked Gladia, briskly breaking into the tale.

'Hmm,' said Tarik, a worried look on his face. 'I am not sure about that. Can you remember where we put that Orange, Ravin? Was that what bounced out into the river as we crossed over?'

'Yes, you're right, I watched it rolling down into the depths...'

Achillea pushed Tarik. 'Stop joking about losing it! Wait, you are joking, aren't you?' We all laughed. Tarik liked to make little jokes up for Achillea and she fell for them nearly every time. Tarik explained that he had the Orange tied to him all the way, under his robe. He unwrapped it and we looked at it again. Honeygold was such a strange metal which seemed to have varied tones of warm gold and cool silver in different lights and times, but it appeared to have more of a golden glow now we had returned to Oramia. If the Orange could choose, I pondered, which land would it see as home? Would it be Kashiq where it was made, or would it be Oramia where its owner took it? Was its allegiance to its land or to its owner, to its creator or its receiver?

'Anyway, how are you feeling, my little nightingale?' asked Tarik, looking at Achillea. 'You look a little better, or at least a little happier. I wonder what it could have been to make you feel sick; you are never ill.' Achillea beamed. She had been dancing from one foot to the other since the men had returned, waiting for the moment to tell Tarik her news. She had told Gladia and I not to say anything as she was going to tell Tarik when they were alone, but we should have known that she wouldn't be able to contain herself until then.

'I will be better in a little while,' she said. 'Though it may take four or five months.'

Tarik frowned. 'Who has told you this? I can think of no illness that lasts so long in all my years of caring for the OutRiders.'

Achillea chuckled gleefully. 'Ah yes,' she said, 'but they were all men, were they not? And anyway, I am not ill, I am simply different.'

Tarik looked at her. 'Do you mean that you are...?'

'Having a baby? Yes! Just imagine, Tarik, we are going to be parents! We are going to have the best baby in the world!' Achillea flung her arms around Tarik who looked shocked at the news, and then delighted. Ravin beamed and clapped him on the back.

'Your wish came true already!' He explained that he and Tarik had been talking about what they wanted to do in their lives, and that Tarik had said that he hoped to be a father one day. I wondered what Ravin had said in his turn to Tarik but did not dare to ask.

Gladia sat back and beamed. Her spirits had lifted since we returned to Oramia and it seemed as if the sad weight she had been carrying with her ever since she had learned of Benakiell's relationship with Shira had been eased. Perhaps it was just that she could anticipate seeing Bellis and Jember again, and, of course, Maren, who had by now moved in with them. Gladia had little enough to say about this new relationship except to confirm that Maren and Bellis seemed to love one another and that it would be good for Jember to have another adult there to keep him in check. I felt for Gladia. All around her, people were building intimate relationships with others, and she must have felt quite alone. For all her faults, Gladia was a strong and loving woman who had much to offer. I hoped she would find her own happiness.

Later, after we had eaten, we discussed when to let Ambar know that we had recovered the Orange of Kashiq.

'Don't be in too much of a hurry just yet,' advised Gladia briskly. 'He can wait a day or two. First we need to decide what he will be giving us in return. This journey has come at a cost to all of us, and Ambar will be getting the rewards of it by marrying the Queen when he gives her the Orange. What will we get?'

We fell silent. None of us had entered the quest for any kind of gain, but now that it was completed and we looked back over our endeavours, it did seem that we had been to a lot of effort for Ambar, especially when none of us really seemed to know him anymore. Maybe it was just the pull of historical friendship which made us feel as if we were still fighting for a common cause which had pushed us on.

'Well, if none of you have thought of anything, I have an idea,' said Gladia. I wondered what it was. Gladia always drove a hard but fair bargain when she was trading her sewing in Sanguinea and it would be interesting to see what she thought was a good exchange for the Orange of Kashiq.

Gladia turned to Ravin. 'Tell me – what is the purpose of your Tower of the Wise in Arbhoun, where you and Talla spent all your days?'

'It is so that we can learn more. We can gain knowledge and wisdom from the thoughts of others and in doing so, we can better ourselves so that, in turn, we can offer our own knowledge and wisdom to others.'

Gladia smiled triumphantly. 'You see! Now, I have no interest in scribing and reading like you two do, I don't see the point of it, but you never even mentioned the scribing and the reading. It was all about learning and wisdom and improving yourself. I have had this dream for a long time, ever since we found Bellis. I think that something like your Tower of the Wise could be made for some of the Angels. I could teach them how to live in the Outer. They could learn from me and Bellis and Maren. We could show them how to sew and how to grow their own food and how to trade. And they could learn from each other and from others like Bellis who have been through the same experience as them. I have in mind that Ambar can exchange the Orange for two promises. I will not ask what he cannot deliver, but this, I think, he can. He can give us enough materials to build a large dwelling with space for ten or more people to stay. Benakiell can build it when he comes back to Mellia. It will be a good experience for him,' she added. 'Since he spends less time here in Oramia, he should put some effort in while he is here.'

I smiled to myself. Gladia would make Benakiell work hard, I had no doubt, and it would afford her a degree of satisfaction to see him working hard for her. Gladia continued, buoyed up by our interest in her plan.

'And the other promise must be that he will deliver to me one Angel for each month of the year and for the three weeks of the Goddess. Each year we will have ten new women to care for. At the end of the year that they live with us, they will be able to choose to go wherever they like. Some will stay in Mellia and live there, I am sure. But others might want to go far away on their own and start again by themselves.' She shot me an astute glance. 'It depends on their character, after all. And I will ensure that Ambar sends me at least five who are with child, like Bellis was.' She looked around at us triumphantly. 'What do you think?'

Tarik looked uncomfortable. I know that he struggled with memories of his past as an OutRider. His upbringing was not his fault, any more than mine was my fault. All people were born into their lives and their struggles were their own. There were those among the Priestesses who had always told us that the Goddess sent us trials and difficulties in our lives to test our faith, but this seemed to me unlikely. Trials and difficulties in life came from many directions and we all reacted to them differently. It was, perhaps, more likely that the Goddess sent us the skills and strengths to cope with what was visited upon us, which came to us randomly like the offerings borne by a capricious breeze which picked up this flower but not that and stirred this dust pile but not the other and carried the scents of both decay and fragrance.

'Do you think Ambar will countenance such a plan?' he asked, clearly worried that Gladia was asking too much. 'Are you not fearful that he will just take the Orange away from you by force or attack us all if you suggest this to him? I do not want Achillea, or indeed any of us to be put in any danger.'

Ravin had been listening carefully to Gladia's plan. There was so much for him yet to learn and find out about Oramia and its ways and the history between us all, but he seemed to take it all in, as if he were reading one of those long scrolls which detailed the designs for a complicated machine or concept.

'Perhaps I can help with that too,' he said. 'For here I am, a man of Kashiq. This Ambar is not expecting to see one such as me in any part of this quest. Perhaps if you tell Ambar that I demand it as a representative of Kashiq's Council of Guidance or else the Defenders of Kashiq will come to Oramia in search of the Orange of Kashiq stolen from its lands by those working for him?'

I could see that Ravin relished this idea, since it would put him in power over Ambar. My own fear with Ambar was that he would promise smoothly to deliver what Gladia asked and then just not keep his word. It would be nice to think that we could trust him, but past experience had shown that he followed his own changing loyalties. But perhaps there really was still that part of Ambar which had led him to search for the new Queen in the first place, for his ideals of a more noble and glorious land rather than one based on lies and subterfuge. Tarik nodded thoughtfully.

'I think that is a good idea. Ambar is much swayed by issues of state and he would not want for the Queen to find out that he had done anything that might endanger Oramia. If nothing else, Ambar is a very loyal servant of Oramia.'

'We must all stand together,' said Achillea. 'We must all be absolutely firm, so we are as one voice when we speak with Ambar. If he loves Lunaria as much as he says he does, and surely he must do to go to all the trouble he has gone to in finding this thing for her, what Gladia – and all of us – ask for is a small thing. We are not asking to change everything all at once, just to make a difference to some.' She turned to Gladia. 'When my mother died of the ague, I felt so lost and alone. I have not been through what the Angels endure, but I know what it is to feel powerless and empty. At the time, you helped me, Gladia, you and Benakiell. And you helped Talla too when she left the Temple, and Bellis when she came to us, so sorely injured and distressed. The Goddess herself must be calling you to do this work, for she could not have picked a better person! What do you think Talla?'

They all turned to me, for I was the only one who had not spoken, although I had been thinking about what everyone else had said.

'It was Talla who inspired me,' said Gladia. This surprised me very much. 'Her anger when she found out about the Angels was even fiercer than ours who knew that there were ways in which our land is broken. She came from the Temple and yet she did not defend it. Talla has no blind loyalty, but a mind which unpicks things and tries to make them better, and her anger is just – at least usually.' Her eyes twinkled at me.

I felt flustered by her praise. I spent so much of my life trying to dampen down the flaring rage I felt that I barely thought of it as a quality worthy of praise. I cast my mind back to the time when I had found out from Bellis what the Angels were and how they were used by both the Temple and the OutFort. I thought of Bellis curled up, injured and starving, carrying a child whose father she had never known, for he was one among many, and I knew that Gladia was right. This would be something that might be small in the enormity of a whole land, but it would be enormous in the lives of those who could be saved. I thought fondly of Jember and his mischievous ways, his ready laugh and his cheeky grin and pictured a time in the future when Mellia might have a thriving community of women who were healing from their difficulties with the help of those like Gladia who had strength and love and those like Bellis and Maren who knew their pain.

'What will you say to the people of the Outer?' I asked. 'For we all know that Ambar will not let us have this if it might mean that other people know what the Angels are. How will you explain this new place to them?'

Gladia waved her hand dismissively. 'We will tell them all they are girls who have been unwell and are here to learn sewing skills from me. Everyone knows that I am a good stitcher.' I must have looked dubious. 'Do not worry, Talla. Most people will not even have any interest unless they are trading for something. Mellia is a quiet place, as you know, just a small village, off the main tracks.'

We all agreed that we would stand as one against Ambar to achieve this, and that he would only get the Orange of Kashiq once he had delivered the materials and goods and the first of the Angels to Gladia. He would be desperate to get hold of the Orange of Kashiq, and I did not think it would take him long. His carved box of cinnamon would be left for him in the morning in the place he had told us to leave it. It was common, Tarik told us, for the OutRiders to leave signs and messages like this in secret places and we knew the message would get to him. Although the OutRiders did not read or scribe, they were adept with their own languages, and in some ways it made it more possible for them to transmit their secrets – after all, only the OutRiders knew the silent language, and only the OutRiders knew the meanings of various signs and symbols such as the box we were to leave for Ambar. Then we would travel to Mellia and wait for his response.

# CHAPTER 33

T he leaves in the Paradox tree rustled in the dry wind. The heat was becoming harder and sharper, and we were grateful to be sitting in the shade now, in the late afternoon. Tarik and Ravin were busy cutting the tall reeds used in dwelling making and repairing. They had become good friends, these two, and relished being busy. I had shown Ravin where my dwelling used to be and introduced him to Maren and Bellis, and of course to Jember.

Jember had been excited both to see his uncle Tarik again and to meet Ravin. Whenever there was a spare moment, he would plague Ravin with question after question about life in Kashiq until eventually Ravin would throw his hands up in despair and set him a building puzzle to keep him quiet, or a complicated errand to run. Today, they had taken him with them so that he could gather up the cut reeds and had promised him a story at the end. I had been clearing the gardens of weeds. Achillea declared herself to be feeling unwell, and, rather uncharitably, I mused on how this sickness seemed to emerge at very convenient moments these days. Bellis and Maren had been delighted to hear the news of her blessing and fussed over her endlessly. I observed how both these two had blossomed since they had discovered their love for one another. Bellis was less watchful and more peaceful, and Maren was more confident, carrying herself lightly. Both smiled more. Having done our work, we were all sitting with Achillea when Jember came running up to us. Presumably, the men had finished their work too.

'Aunty Talla!' I looked up, surprised to be the one being called for first. 'There is a travelling trader in the village! He has brought all manner of things in a big red bundle. He told me to go and fetch you. He is trading with some of the people from the village now. He says he knows you and wants to greet you.'

I looked across at Gladia. It was clear to me that it must be Ambar or one of his men, for I did not know one who traded who would know me and ask for me by name. I got to my feet and smoothed down my robe and arranged my netela on my head demurely.

'We will follow along soon,' promised Gladia, with a glint in her eye. I hoped that Tarik and Ravin would also be arriving soon. Jember hopped about, waiting for me.

'I've been an extremely helpful boy today,' he informed me proudly. 'Uncle Tarik says I can nearly do the work of a man already!' He puffed out his chest and strutted next to me. 'Do you think the trader will want to trade for any of our reeds? Maybe Tarik and Ravin will let me have something, like my own reed knife or something, or maybe he has oranges like Benakiell brings back and you brought back, and I wonder when Benakiell will come back again...' He could talk endlessly, and every new thought seemed to set off another. Fortunately, Jember never seemed to need a response.

'Do you have honey to trade?' Ambar's voice was as smooth and charming as it had always been. It took my mind back to the time we had first met in the market in Sanguinea, when he had persuaded me to trade with him for the little bee necklace, which now resided at the Court of the Queen. I looked at him. His light brown eyes were alight with excitement and anticipation. The other villagers had drifted off back to their dwellings, having

357

seen what this trader had to offer, and would soon be back with their trades. Jember poked around the items, trying to find something he wanted and could plead for.

'I have some honey,' I replied mildly. 'I also have oranges from Kashiq if you would like to trade for one.'

'I am sure we can come to an arrangement,' murmured Ambar. 'A lady as lovely as yourself will no doubt drive a hard bargain.'

Jember gave him a hard stare. 'You'd better be careful,' he counselled Ambar 'Uncle Ravin won't like it if you talk to Aunty Talla like that!' Ambar glanced at me sharply. Just as I was about to respond, Tarik and Ravin came around the corner and down the path towards us. They walked with little urgency, talking to each other in low voices, occasionally looking up to the supposed trader.

'Perhaps you could return later, on your own, to finish that trade for honey?' suggested Ambar in a low voice. 'I do not wish to talk of our trade in front of strangers.' Some of the villagers were starting to drift back with items to trade, so I agreed, and told him to call at Gladia's dwelling when he had finished. I could see he was itching to continue the conversation without Jember being there, and to further quiz me about Ravin. I turned away and followed Jember as he skipped up the path toward the two men, chattering away. I could not speak of Ambar in front of the child, so we turned towards the dwellings, catching up on the day's events.

After the sun had set and we had eaten, we sat at the fire, and when Jember, Bellis and Maren had all departed to their dwelling for the night, I told the others of what Ambar had said and that he would be coming soon to settle our bargain. I stood up to walk towards the Paradox tree to look out and see if I could see any sign of him. Ravin came with me and we stood together, looking out at the vast darkness which lay in front of us. He laid his hand on the back of my neck under my netela and drew his fingers down my backbone. I turned to him and he bent his head to mine and kissed me as we stood there, alone in the dark indigo of night. I longed to be able to return to my dwelling in Gabez with him so that we could be alone together again.

A small cough pierced the silence, and we broke apart. It came from behind a tree just a short distance away. As we watched, Ambar slipped out of its shadow and walked towards us. I wondered how long he had been standing there watching us while we thought we were alone and reminded myself of how skilled he was in this art of passing unnoticed. Ravin's hand tightened around my waist and we turned to look at Ambar as he moved into the light.

'I thought we would be alone,' muttered Ambar, looking petulant. 'I need to speak with you privately about our trade.' He looked Ravin up and down dismissively. We turned to walk over to the fire where Gladia, Achillea and Tarik waited. They greeted Ambar and we sat down. Ambar looked pointedly at Ravin and began to converse with Tarik in the silent language of the hands. He could not forget that Tarik had once been an OutRider like him, and indeed his comrade. Perhaps he missed his friendship now that he lived high up in the Court of the Queen. Tarik understood what Ambar wanted to do but refused to communicate back to him in the same language, instead speaking plainly to him.

'You ask me to send away this man whom you do not know, but I will not. His name is Ravin, and he is a part of this quest you have sent us on. He knows everything, in any case, and as you see, he loves Talla and she loves him. We here know the full story of the Orange of Kashiq and can tell you about it, but not if Ravin is sent away. He is a true and trusted friend to us all.' Tarik's voice remained calm, but I could sense the strength and the threat implicit in what he said.

Ambar bristled briefly, but then accepted what Tarik said. He glared at Ravin who returned his look coldly. They reminded me of two roosters, strutting in the dust. There was silence for a few moments and then Ambar spoke again.

'Do you have it? Do you have the Orange of Kashiq? Your message said that you had it. I can't believe you have managed to find it for me. Lunaria will be so surprised that I have managed to find this most precious thing for her. It will prove my love and show that I am the one whom she will marry and whose children she will bear.' His eyes lit up.

'Well,' interjected Gladia, smoothing the skirt of her robe firmly. 'We do have good news for you, but we have had to endure many hardships to acquire this thing for you. Why, Benakiell almost lost his foot because of it. So, we will need to be recompensed well for all our hard work, as I am sure you understand. You have come to Mellia as a trader and now we will trade.'

Ambar looked shocked when Gladia mentioned Benakiell's injury. He had thought well of him and admired his loyalty to his friends and could see he was not here with us now. He asked after him and Gladia told him dramatically that Benakiell had had to stay in Kashiq for a while as his foot had not yet healed. I smiled slightly as I observed her using this to add weight to her bargaining. There was no wonder she always did so well at market in Sanguinea.

But Ambar was an astute trader too and had spent much of the time he had roamed the land in disguise as one.

'I will not begin to trade until I see what I am trading for,' he retorted. 'It may be damaged or perhaps it is not as it was described to the Queen. You may just be trying to get valuable goods from me in return for nothing.'

Gladia snorted. 'You have about as much faith in us as we do in you, Lord High and Mighty. Of course, we have the Orange of Kashiq, and we even have here an expert from Kashiq, Ravin, who can swear that it is as we say. We do not need much of your abundant wealth; that might be a little too easy a trade. Instead, we require from you an oath, and in return we too will promise never to speak of this to the Queen or to her DreamReader. Tarik, would you show the Orange to Ambar, so he can see what he will be getting?' Gladia was enjoying this and I was enjoying watching it.

Tarik went into the dwelling so that Ambar could not see where the Orange was hidden, and came back with it in his hand, covered in a cloth. He stood next to Ravin with it, forcing Ambar to come to them. Tarik took the cloth off and we all gazed at it again. Its honeygold exterior glowed in the firelight, the light polishing the edges of the decoration. Ravin unclipped the leaf and slid the ring down the stem so that the Orange of Kashiq fell apart, its segments held by the tiny chains. He picked up one of the segments and unlatched it, showing the word inside to Ambar who looked at it with little understanding.

'Oh, do you not read?' asked Ravin with a dry little smile, knowing full well that he did not. 'Let me assist you.' He read out the word inside, which was Respect.

'Isn't it beautiful?' asked Achillea from where she was sitting. 'Lunaria will love it and you, Ambar. The story of how it was made is so romantic. Talla and Ravin can tell you the full story and then you can tell it to Lunaria. She will be amazed at what you have found for her!'

Ambar looked greedily at the little ornament, swayed by Achillea's words, and reached towards it. Tarik stepped back from him.

'I only wanted to touch it,' protested Ambar. Tarik shook his head firmly.

'No, brother,' he said. 'You trusted us and made a great deal about the fact that we were the only ones who could be trusted to do this for you. Now you must prove that the trust is real. You cannot have the Orange of Kashiq yet. Only when you show us that you can keep to your side of the trade will we give it to you.'

Ambar's eyes flashed in anger, but he calmed himself and asked what our expectation was. He expected, no doubt, that we might demand tradeable goods in exchange for the Orange. He sat back confidently, waiting to hear what we had to say. We turned to Gladia.

'Lord Ambar,' she began, formally. 'I know how much you love the Queen. Why, I have seen it with my own eyes. I know how important she is to you and how important it is for you to give her this. But I beg you to think of those who may never have the chance of love. You want this thing so that you can marry Lunaria and share the Goddess's blessing of children with her. But here in Oramia there are still those you call the Angels. Even though we do not see the Temple Maids released from the Temples anymore, nor witness their capture here in the Outer, we know it must still happen somehow.' Ambar opened his mouth to speak, no doubt to protest, but Gladia swept on, ignoring him completely.

'We will trade the Orange of Kashiq for the freedom of ten Angels a year, especially those with child. They will never return to the OutFort. They will come to me here in Mellia where you will build me a large dwelling where they can live, and enough materials for them to live and work with. For our part, we will give you the Orange of

Kashiq and we will never speak of our part in finding it to either the Queen or to the Council of Guidance of Kashiq.'

Ambar leaned back, disconcerted by Gladia's request. He turned to look at each of us in turn, trying to see how we felt.

We looked back at him.

'What if I refuse this request?' he said finally. 'I could just take this Orange, and nobody would believe your story.'

Ravin laughed drily again. 'We have protected ourselves from that possibility,' he said, taking the lead. 'I, who am from Kashiq, have scribed two scrolls detailing all that we have done and that we have been asked to do. They are both safe. But should anything happen to any of us, or should Gladia's request not be fulfilled, one scroll will be sent to the Council of Guidance of Kashiq, and they will know that the land of Oramia have sent spies into Kashiq to take away something which was made in Kashiq and returned to Kashiq and belongs to Kashiq. No doubt they will then wish to take it back...The other scroll will be sent to the Court of the Queen of Oramia. She will hear of its contents from her devoted Dreamreader, Silene, first...'

We had discussed using Ravin's position as a man of Kashiq to our favour, but he had come up with this idea on his own. I wondered if he really had written it all down on two scrolls as he had said.

Ambar examined Ravin through slightly narrowed eyes but betrayed no other outward sign of anger aside from a pulse at his temple when he clenched his jaw. He turned deliberately away from him and faced only me, excluding the rest of the group.

'Talla,' he said, looking at me searchingly, so that I felt he was inside my mind. 'I have always felt a connection between us, when we first met in Sanguinea, and later, as we rode back to Besseret with Gladia. I ask you now to help me understand that which you ask of me, and to make up my mind about how much I can trust you.' I was startled because I did not know that he had felt that channel too. It had occurred when I was wearing the little bee necklace. I had first become aware of it when Gladia and I had visited the Empath Erayo and there had been a stream of feelings from her to me. When Ambar and I had been close to one another, physically touching, the channel of empathy would open again, and I would sense what he was feeling. Perhaps Lunaria now wore the necklace and experienced the same feelings. I raised my eyes to Ambar's, looking back at him without fear.

I knew that Ravin had no liking for Ambar, that he was jealous of him and of his former role in my life. Achillea always saw the good in everyone. Gladia respected the power he had and wanted to take advantage of it. Tarik must have felt a little like me; his former close friend and companion who now lived a life far distant from the one which they had shared together. We did not know which Ambar was the real one – and possibly Ambar himself did not either – or which one was trying to seal a trade with us.

'I appeal to your noble aims, Ambar,' I said, finally. 'I remember your anger when you saved Gladia from those OutRiders and again when you saved Bellis. I saw how it flashed in your eyes. If we do indeed share a connection, then I beg you to use it to know how angry I am that the promises you made then about the fate of the Angels have not come to pass.' He opened his mouth as if to interrupt, to explain, to gloss over things. I gave him little chance and continued with my words.

'I know that you view things differently now. Perhaps you see and understand things I cannot about how this land is controlled. But there are things which are never right and never justified. I know that you watch us in secret, and that the task you sent us on was for Lunaria. I know that you love her and want only for her to love and to marry you and to bear your children. I know what it is to love someone now. What Gladia asks is a small step towards a better life for a few women. What does the Goddess Asmara think, I wonder, when she sees what she created now? She, whose only task is creation, cannot step in to heal the wounds her own people have made; they must heal them on their own. Imagine if it were Lunaria, or me or Achillea who were taken to be Angels! Try to imagine how you would feel. And think also of how it will make you feel to know you have saved the lives of ten women every year!' My cheeks were flushed with the anger I felt anew, and my voice had risen in outrage.

Ambar nodded slowly. For all that Ravin disliked him, I knew that deep within him there was a man who had been given the right ideals in his life, at an early age, by his OutCommander, the one who had treated him like a son. But he had become so entangled in his own ambitions that he had lost sight of those noble aims. Loving Lunaria seemed to have made him less noble, not more.

'I will agree to this on two conditions,' he said, finally. 'The scrolls written about this must be burnt in front of me. No more will be spoken of it again. Instead, Talla will scribe a new scroll which will tell of my commitment to this place of learning that Gladia will make, for the next seven years.' He raised his hand as Gladia opened her mouth, ready to protest. 'After seven years are past, I will meet with you again and we will talk of how it works. If it is a success, you will get another seven years. If not, that scroll too will be burned and my part in this will be over.'

We had agreed that Gladia would do the negotiating with Ambar, for the reward that we would get for the

Orange was her idea, and that she would decide when she had a good deal. Ambar did not want these scrolls to exist, that much was clear. He did not read himself and, like many who did not read, saw it as a sort of mystic talent, rather than a skill which could be learned as easily as shooting an arrow. The thought that other people might be able to read about his scheming and plotting, and of him effectively asking people to steal something from another land to gain the favour of the Queen was awful to him. But, if we burned the scrolls, we would have nothing to hold over Ambar to compel him to keep to our arrangement and would instead have to rely on trust. On his past behaviour, that seemed a risky choice.

Gladia leaned back thoughtfully, considering the trade she had been offered. She would not let Ambar direct all the decisions, even if she were fully aware of his power. She tapped her fingers and then set her jaw firmly. 'That will not work for us,' she said crisply, surprising us all with her certain resolve. 'If we burn both those scrolls, you could just deliver one Angel to us and a few materials for building and then never bother again and we would have nothing to make you keep to your side of the bargain.' She fixed Ambar with a sharp look. He opened his mouth to protest against her assessment of his character, but she began to speak again before he could. 'No, you may choose which one of the two scrolls you wish to have burnt. We will abide by that. But the other scroll will remain with us, in a safe, hidden place, far from here. After seven years have passed, we will talk again, as you have suggested yourself. That will at least mean that we will be able to work with many more Angels.'

I looked to the ground, my mouth twitching at Gladia's sharp negotiating skills. Ambar's shoulders slumped slightly, but he maintained a calm exterior apart from the pulsing jaw.

'I see you have lost none of your keen bargaining skills,' he remarked finally. 'Very well. I will have the scroll burnt that would have been sent to the Court of the Queen. I will take the Orange of Kashiq with me now, to maintain its safety. We do not want anything happening to it after all the effort you have exerted to find it.' He continued to try to assert his authority and control over the situation, even though those of us who knew Gladia were well aware that he stood no chance against her.

Gladia snorted disrespectfully at this suggestion. 'You can have the Orange of Kashiq when you deliver the goods and the first of the Angels here to Mellia. I will speak to Maren and Bellis. I won't tell them of the work we did for you in exchange for this, I will just tell them that it was your brilliant idea, much as that might pain me.'

Ambar laughed. It was the first time he had let down his guard since he had been here, and it felt like there was a return to the man we had first known. His eyes crinkled up at the corners and his even white teeth gleamed in the firelight. Tarik chuckled too. He knew how much it must have taken for Gladia not to tell everyone about her part in bringing the freed Angels to Mellia, as we all did, and soon we were all smiling and laughing together, even Ravin, who had moved to sit next to me.

'I will arrange the goods to be brought here this week,' said Ambar, before he left. 'They will be left by the track next to Benakiell's dwelling at night. It will be your job to build the dwelling. I will work out how to acquire the Angels for you.' I could see him thinking through various possibilities relating to the Angels and realised how hard this would be for him to organise.

'The one who will be left for you to care for, will be left outside your door, in the night. You will find her there one morning and you will know. After that, I will come again myself to get the Orange of Kashiq.' His voice trailed off and there was a distant look in his eyes as he thought of what would be to come when he presented Lunaria with the Orange. I wondered how Silene the DreamReader would react to this, for she could not go back on her word since it purported to come from the Goddess herself in a dream. And perhaps it did. For we only had Ambar's word that Silene was cunning and plotting against him. Maybe she really did have a talent given to her by the Goddess and was only trying to protect Lunaria. It was so hard to judge one whom I had not yet met and whom I had only ever heard about from someone who you might consider to be her enemy.

'Imagine,' he said finally. 'Imagine that one day soon I will be married to the Queen of Oramia, and she will have my children. And they in turn will rule our land...' He turned to Tarik, his old comrade.

'Remember all those years ago, when we used to talk about what it might be like to be a father? We could not even imagine how it could happen to us. And now, it will soon be happening to me!'

Tarik smiled at him properly for the first time.

'I'm afraid that if this were a race, I would be the winner,' he said simply. 'Achillea and I will be parents ourselves in four or five months.' He beamed at Achillea and she smiled back a little tiredly.

Ambar looked shocked. Perhaps it had never occurred to him that Tarik might become a father before him.

'May the Goddess bless you both,' he responded finally, smiling warmly, and then he turned to me.

'And what of you, Talla?' he asked. 'Are you just as blessed by the Goddess, for you and Achillea always used to like to do things together!' Beside me, I could feel Ravin bristling at Ambar's question, and replied before he could inflame things further.

'Ah no,' I replied. 'I have many years ahead of me yet. The Goddess will no doubt bless me when she sees that I am ready for such a task. Meanwhile I will help Gladia as much as I can, and Ravin and I will then return to Gabez.'

With that, Ambar rose and collected his bundles and then melted away into the darkness. The OutRiders were masters of the art of moving and communicating silently and it seemed that Ambar was still well versed in this skill. No doubt the building materials and the Angel herself would be left with as little noise.

# CHAPTER 34

'Talla, wake up!' I blinked the sleeping dust away from my eyes. It was still dark inside the dwelling. Ravin stirred in his sleep next to me. I fumbled for my netela and tiptoed to the door, bemused by such an early call from Gladia. Her supposed whispers were not that quiet, and I thought that if she had ever whispered a secret to anyone, she would have ended up letting everyone know.

A thin, pale orange line drew itself across the horizon, a golden edge in a darkened world. Dawn was rapidly approaching, so perhaps it was not as early as I had first thought. Gladia stood impatiently waiting for me. I had guessed that my early wakening meant that Ambar had delivered the first of our Angels to us. In the few days beforehand, we had awoken each morning to find piles of goods stacked neatly outside Benakiell's dwelling. You would not know, unless you knew his dwelling area well, that these were not just piles of Benakiell's building materials, waiting for him to return. This was, in fact, what Gladia had told the other villagers in Mellia. She had come up with a story that involved her embroidered items being traded for precious items in Gabez and that she had thought to build a dwelling to encourage more people to stay in the village. It seemed a shallow story to me, but the whole village respected and trusted Gladia. Besides, there were still only a dozen or so families who lived in Mellia. Her plan was to start off small and build a dwelling big enough for four or five, and then build another next to it. She said she would wait for Benakiell to build it, but that Tarik could make a start, along with Ravin, who always wanted to learn more. They would take themselves off to the cleared land to work on splitting the reeds for the dwellings. In Oramia, dwelling making was man's work and prohibited to women. Ravin, not being of Oramia, had no problem with telling me how the dwelling was made, which Benakiell had always steadfastly refused to do.

'Hurry up,' urged Gladia impatiently. 'She is here.' We walked back to Gladia's dwelling along the dusty path, still dampened by the morning dew. By the side of her clay veranda was a mat. On the mat lay a rounded form, curled up and covered with a rough blanket. She was sound asleep due to the poppyjuice she had undoubtedlybeen given.

'What shall we do next?' asked Gladia. Now that her plan was beginning to unfold, she seemed less sure of herself. The dwelling was only halfway finished, so she would have to stay with Gladia. In any case, she would need the comfort and security of other women around her as she got accustomed to a new life. Even now, seven years afterwards, Bellis still experienced pain in her heart and her mind when she recalled the events of her life as an Angel. I was the lucky one, for I had escaped from the Temple without ever being recaptured and sent by the OutRiders to become an Angel. The Angels who toiled on building the Temples and the OutForts and no doubt the Queen's Court too. The Angels who were used by the OutRider force for their own pleasure and who, when they were inevitably with child, were forced to have their babies taken away from them and returned to the Temples to start the cycle all over again.

We did not know how this woman might react when she woke up in a strange place surrounded by strange people. She might try to run away, or to fight. She stirred, making a small snuffling noise.

'I will sit with her,' I offered. 'You go and make coffee. Achillea can help us later with some physic for her, and Maren can look at her and see when her baby might come.' She had not yet become fully rounded with her unborn child, but I was no expert in this, and Maren was a BirthMother. Her knowledge would be crucial. Bellis too would be an important part of this endeavour, since she was the only one amongst us who knew what this woman had endured, from the fateful Choice ceremony at the Temple to the recapture and life as an Angel to giving birth to a child whose father was unknown and unloved. Gladia bustled off, relieved to be doing something practical. I settled down next to the woman and stroked her hand gently.

I looked out over the land. Gladia's dwelling was on a slight hill, raised somewhat from the other dwellings. The thin orange line of dawn had widened and now filled the sky. The tiny clouds were edged with the same golden colour. The land itself was waking from its rest. The birds began to sing and somewhere in the village a rooster crowed to ensure that all those who slept would wake up. A bee flew by, searching for early flowers. It alighted briefly on the woman's blanket, a small flash of gold against the dull grey. It crawled further up towards her head which was partly covered by an equally grey netela and onto her face. I reached my hand down towards the bee, not wanting it to sting her awake. It crawled up my hand and I lifted my hand up to my face and then gently blew on it, and it flew away, as if satisfied by the encounter. I smiled and looked out again towards the rising sun.

'Who are you?'

Her voice was young and confused. I looked back towards the woman hastily. She must have been woken by the bee. Curiously, its tiny feet had stirred her awake even when nothing else had.

'I am Talla,' I responded calmly. 'You are safe here. What is your name?'

She pushed herself up on her elbow and looked around, dazed.

'I was Rubra, before. But they do not call you by your name anymore.' Her brain struggled to put her entangled thoughts in order, befuddled by the sleeping physic. She sat up, dull and exhausted by a life she could not yet remember.

'You will be well, here.' I reassured her, looking round for Gladia. I did not feel that I could manage as well on my own. 'This is your new home, for you and the baby. Gladia will take care of you here.'

Rubra pushed her grey netela off her head and rubbed her head, looking confused. Luckily, Gladia appeared then, carrying the coffee pot and a basket of flat breads.

'Oh, you are awake now, are you?' she said briskly, but kindly. 'Well, everyone feels better for some good coffee and a flatbread with honey, don't they?' She lowered herself down next to Rubra, puffing. She took a flatbread from the basket and gave it to Rubra and then poured coffee into a beaker she had brought with her. I could not help wondering why she hadn't brought more beakers with her so that I could have one too. Rubra looked from Gladia to me and then back and rubbed her head again.

'It will all make sense soon, don't worry,' said Gladia. Rubra began to nibble at the flatbread, her eyes darting between us as she tried to come to terms with her changed surroundings. If it had just been me, I would have started out talking to Rubra and asking her questions and wanting to find things out from her straight away. But Gladia's calm practicality meant that she started by addressing Rubra's more pressing needs first. Eating and drinking soothed the body and the mind and calmed an anxious heart. Having started out by gobbling the food as if she feared it might be taken away from her, Rubra gradually relaxed and slowed down, finishing her flat bread and her coffee and looking round her speculatively.

'Am I here to do some special kind of building work? The AngelMother said that some are called to more important work by the Goddess. I can work well with a chisel and can carve designs in stone.' She looked eager to please, her head still full of the necessity of pleasing the Goddess and the AngelMother who worked her. It was the cruellest title, this. The AngelMother sounded so good and nurturing and yet it was she who oversaw the Angels for the OutFort. She who chose which ones would be used to labour all day and which ones would be put aside for the OutRiders. She did not behave in any way as a mother might, trying to protect her children from hardship and support them in time of trial. The emberjar of my mind crackled as I thought about this and I resolved to find out more about how this all worked: who were the AngelMothers? Were they Angels who felt a kind of enjoyment in seeing their fellow Temple Maids reduced to this, or did they receive a valuable inducement to do the job? Perhaps they were even Priestesses, specially trained to do this most unpalatable of jobs and justified it by purporting it to come from the Goddess herself.

Gladia patted her hand kindly. I saw Rubra tense up as if she were about to be hit.

'You are not an Angel anymore, Rubra,' she said. 'You are starting a new life here in Mellia. We will help you. Maren will look after you until the baby is born, and

Bellis will teach you how to care for it when it arrives. You can learn a new way of work here; I can teach you stitching if you are good with your hands as you say, or perhaps you will be good at growing things or making physic. We will find out. There will be a lot to accustom yourself to, but it will be a better life.'

Rubra struggled to comprehend what Gladia was telling her, and I was not surprised. I recalled when Bellis first came to Mellia, and how long it took for her to be able to talk to anyone about her life as an Angel. She looked at me for confirmation of what Gladia told her and I nodded my head.

'It is as she says. It is undoubtedly the wish of the Goddess herself,' I said firmly. 'She has blessed you with a child and has chosen you to live here in the Outer.'

Rubra nodded slowly. Her eyes began to droop again, and it was clear that the poppyjuice was still in her. Gladia made her comfortable and she curled up like a small animal and went to sleep.

# THE SEED

## CHAPTER 35

The bees crawled over the outside of the log hive I had brought down from the tree. I was pondering the differences between Oramian and Kashiqi beehives and which ones the bees might prefer. The clay Kashiq hives were easier to care for since they stood on the ground rather than hanging from tree branches as mine did, but I still thought the bees must prefer to live in wooden hives. They did not need to have the honey harvested yet; Maren took good care of them, and they did not need cleaning either, but I still wanted to spend some time with them. Ravin and Tarik were finishing off the dwelling today and then all it would need would be to be waterproofed when Benakiell next returned home. Achillea was with Rubra and Bellis talking about babies to Maren. I could not sustain my interest in that subject for long, and I had left them there together. Rubra still bore an air of bewilderment on her face but was starting to talk to others now. We were all just waiting for Ambar to return to collect the Orange of Kashiq and then we could return to our old lives. Although, of course, our lives would never be what they had been before our trip to Kashiq.

'I used to do this often, you know.' A quiet voice came from behind the Paradox tree. Ambar slipped out and came to sit opposite me on the low grey stone.

'Not here in Mellia,' he continued. 'But in Besseret, with Maren's bees. You thought you were alone, but I was often there, as I have been here for some time, just watching you with the bees. It makes me feel ... peaceful, I suppose.'

He was wearing dull grey and brown clothes which allowed him to blend into the landscape. It reminded me for a moment of the drabcoat which I had worn years ago. That too had the effect of making you anonymous and unnoticed. Especially when the Priestesses were so colourfully dressed. He smiled at my face, which must have shown how annoyed I was that he had been there when I thought I was alone.

'Don't worry. I do not often spy on people anymore. Although the temptation is always there for one as intriguing as you, Talla. I find myself thinking of you often, especially since our meeting before you went to Kashiq. Do you sometimes think of me?'

I was disconcerted by his question. When it was just the two of us, he was humbler, more interesting and seemed less focused on his ambitions. I had sometimes thought of him, of course, although not in the same way that I thought of Ravin. Ravin was the one who was like a constant star in the sky, and Ambar was like a shooting star which lit up the sky and then was gone. I did not answer him and just smiled and asked if he had come for the Orange.

'I think you will agree that I have upheld my side of the trade, and so I am here to receive the Orange of Kashiq – although perhaps we should call it the Orange of Oramia now!' He smiled. 'But do not fear, I have no wish for war with Kashiq, they will not know that we have their Orange. If they ask, we will just say that we have had our craftsmen draw up the plans to have a copy made, or some such story. Don't forget to bring the scroll Ravin scribed so we can burn it.'

I offered to go and fetch the others so that he could hear about how Gladia's plans were developing as I went for the Orange and the scroll. He looked rueful.

'I do not think that any of them welcomes the thought of seeing me, aside from you, Talla. Gladia blames me for the Angels' existence and Achillea has always blamed me for the death of Ashtun and for filling his head with ideas about being an OutRider.'

I had never thought this to be the case. Ashtun was perfectly capable of deciding things for himself and had always been more than eager to learn to ride and shoot and wear armour. His only fault was to defend Achillea. She had certainly never mentioned any such thoughts to me. Ambar continued.

'Benakiell is not here - and in any case, he no doubt feels the same way as Achillea when it comes to Ashtun, who was like a son to him. Tarik, who was once as I imagined a brother might be, has turned his face firmly away from his OutRider brother. He is lucky that he had my protection, for anyone else would have died for attempting to leave.'

Once more, Ambar had surprised me. He seemed to have spent much time dwelling on the events of the past and turning them over and over in his mind. We all did, I suppose. I had not realised that attempting to leave the OutRiders resulted in death. Tarik must have been very sure of himself and of Ambar's reaction when he declared his intention to be a man of the Outer.

'As for Ravin ...' Ambar looked towards the sky briefly. 'Ravin hates me. He may be polite and calm, but inside his hatred for me burns strongly. He hates me almost as much as he loves you, I suspect. He does not want me anywhere near you – and I do not blame him. For he has won a precious prize in you, Talla. When I thought you were the lost Queen of Oramia, my heart was full of joy, but then, when Lunaria was proved to be the Queen, I knew my fate lay with her instead. I have grown to love her in my way. I do not know if she truly loves me, but the Goddess has dictated that she will love me if I give her Ashkana's Orange intact again.'

Ambar seemed in a very reflective mood, sitting here with me in the garden. I did not understand his view of love or his belief in destiny or fate. It seemed convenient that he believed that his destiny was to marry the Queen and have children with her which would incidentally put him into a position of great power. I asked him why he thought it was his fate to love Lunaria.

'I have been told this since I was a small boy by my OutCommander, the one I told you about, the one who was like a father to me. He told me that one day I would meet and marry a queen and be happy. Perhaps you think he was just trying to be kind to a little boy and give him a future to dream of, but to me it has always felt like my destiny. It comes from inside my heart.' He reached for my hand and placed it just inside the open neck of his tunic. His skin was warm and smooth, and I could feel his heart beating under my hand. I pulled it away, disconcerted by his intimacy, and stood up.

'Will you do this for me, Talla? Will you fetch me the Orange of Kashiq without telling anyone until after I have gone? I prefer to leave without ceremony. And I am sure they too would prefer it that way.'

I could see no reason why I should not do as he asked of me, and I nodded, suddenly mute. He stood up.

'I will wait for you here, by the tree.'

379

I walked slowly up the path and when I turned to look back, he had already disappeared back into the shadows. Back at the dwelling, I took the Orange of Kashiq from its box and took one last look at it. Ravin had made many careful drawings and diagrams of how it was made and how it worked, but none of them conveyed the warmth of it. It seemed almost alive, glowing in the sun. I traced my fingers over the surface of it, and the six segments which contained Rao's words of love for Ashkana. Knowing its history, it seemed to me an uneasy choice of a love token. I also took an old scroll which Ravin had made for us to burn as part of our bargain with Ambar.

Returning to the garden, I was suddenly eager to hand it over and be done with it, for Ambar to go and for us all to move on. I sat down on the flat rock and waited for Ambar to reappear, which he did a few moments later.

'Do you have it?' he asked eagerly. I placed it in his outstretched hands gently. He unwrapped the cloth and looked at it, his eyes lighting up and then wrapped it back up again, almost tenderly, and placed it in a leather bag he carried on his back.

'And the scroll which tells of how the orange was obtained?' I handed him the scroll, knowing that he could not read what was written there. Ravin had never written that scroll, but it had proved a useful bargaining piece for Gladia's suggestion. He gave it a cursory glance, trusting me to have given him the scroll he had asked for. This small subterfuge made me feel uneasy, but I reasoned there was no harm in it.

'Do you have an emberjar?' he asked, and I gestured towards the clay emberjar which was resting on the rock in case I needed to light a fire. He quickly built up a small pile of leaves and dry twigs and pushed one of the embers on to it. He bent down and pursed his lips to blow the flame up from the ember. When it was bright and the leaves and twigs had caught fire, he placed the plant parchment scroll on top and watched it until it had burned to powdery white ash.

'I will bid you farewell, now, Talla. I will not forget your kindness.' He turned to leave and then turned back to me and swiftly, before I knew what was happening, he kissed me lingeringly. It was both sweet and sharp, like biting into an orange.

'I have often wondered what it might be like to kiss you,' he said. 'And now I will always know.' And, with that, he was gone, as if he were a trick of the light.

# CHAPTER 36

We returned to Mellia almost two months later.
There had been some surprise when I told the
others that Ambar had been and left with the
Orange of Kashiq without speaking to them. Gladia
muttered about wanting Ambar to see her work so far on
the dwelling for the Angels, but in truth she was probably
more disappointed that she couldn't have tried to get
more out of him than about the loss of his opinion. Tarik
raised his eyebrows and said he was surprised that
Ambar had not wanted to speak to the rest of them.
Despite his reserve and his attitude toward Ambar, I
thought he was hurt by his erstwhile comrade's actions.
Ravin was more concerned with why Ambar had only
sought me out rather than someone else, like Tarik to
make the exchange with. I tried to explain that Ambar
had merely appeared to whoever was on their own that
day, which just happened to be me, but Ravin was
unconvinced and asked me more about what Ambar had
said to me and why I thought he had said it.
Unsurprisingly, I said nothing of most of what Ambar
had spoken to me about, and certainly did not mention
the kiss. Ravin and I had agreed to trust one another's
love, but that did not necessarily mean telling one
another everything. After all, it had been Ambar who had
kissed me, not the other way round, and I could not be
held responsible for his actions.

Tarik and Ravin had finished off the dwelling before
we left. It was a fine place, large enough for three or four

to live in comfortably. Inside it was quite dark, with only the light coming through the upper light spaces and the door. It smelled of the sweetness of dried cut reeds and thatching grass. Gladia had asked Ravin to make some wooden frames, as tall as a person, and had hung old cloths from them to make partitions, so that each person sleeping there had their own space but was nevertheless with other people. Then we had left for Gabez again, promising Gladia that we would return before Achillea had the baby.

Achillea was now well rounded and halfway through her expected time. She no longer felt sick, and her face and her skin shone. She was happy to be back in Mellia, with people who wanted to make a fuss over her. I was still unsure of her new situation. I had rarely even seen a woman who was having a baby before I left the Temple and had not grown up with them around me. In the Temple, the babies were kept in the BabyHouse and unless you worked there, you did not see much of them. Tarik worked hard on things to make and trade in the markets in Gabez and had brought some of his pegged door locks with him to trade in Mellia. He was intent on trading for whatever Achillea thought she needed for the baby, which was not a lot, in truth; some cloths to carry it and wrap it, some salves and tonics and some little carved toys which he spent his evenings making; models of goats and hens, balls and blocks and rings.

Ravin and I lived together in my dwelling in Gabez. He had begun to make pictures on plant parchments to trade. He stuck them on to thin sheets of wood and they became popular; they reminded me of some of the pictures the Priestesses put on the bottoms of scrolls. They were scenes of flowers and trees and little animals, or of mountains and rivers. I marvelled at his skills. When he was not making these, he often scribed. I asked him what he was scribing, and he told me he was making a record of all that had befallen him, and of all that he was learning in Oramia. Sometimes we would gather with Achillea and Tarik in the evening, and he would read to us from his scrolls. It made me ponder on whether I might try to do the same thing one day about my trip to Kashiq. It also made me realise that although Ambar had asked for a scroll to be burnt to take away the proof of how the Orange of Kashiq had been acquired, a new scroll could easily be scribed. In fact, what was scribed need not be the truth either.

Benakiell was also back in Mellia. He had not brought Shira with him and planned to only stay for a few weeks before returning to her in Rishkar. Gladia had set him to work waterproofing the new dwelling and he happily worked on it together with Jember who was delighted to see him back and had begun to swagger round the village doing 'important secret errands' for Benakiell, relating to dwelling making, most of which seemed to involve collecting nuts from the Paradox trees around the village. I suspected the errands were so long and complicated in order to keep Jember otherwise occupied while Benakiell worked.

There was much to do with the Paradox nuts once Jember had collected them. They had to be taken to Mariam, one of the women in the village, who ground them into small pieces and then mixed them with water and slowly heated them several times over so that the Paradox oil could rise to the surface of the pot and be skimmed off and placed in clay jars to be traded. She traded her Paradox oil with Benakiell in exchange for him repairing and waterproofing her dwelling every year. She also traded some of the Paradox oil with those of us who used the oil to mix with beeswax to make creams and ointments. Jember was the ideal errand boy because he liked nothing more than wandering around picking things up. He had a sharp eye and often found the Paradox nuts which had been missed by others. Bellis had given him a square of cloth and he gathered the nuts in that until it was full and then carried it back to Mariam, who might then set him on to cracking the shells with a convenient rock.

Rubra also seemed to be settling in. By now she was close to giving birth. The others in the village had accepted the story they had been told by Gladia and were happy to see another young woman in the village. She lived now in the dwelling along with another Angel who had been delivered in the same way to Gladia's dwelling. This other woman was called Flora. She was much more withdrawn than Rubra, who really seemed to want to work and be part of her new village, and, instead, was listless and silent. Every day, Bellis spent time with Rubra and Flora, talking and listening to their experiences. Nobody else was allowed to attend, so that they could talk openly. There was a lot of work involved in this idea of Gladia's and a good deal of effort was required to try to heal the damage that these women had suffered at the hands of both the Priestesses and the OutRiders. I talked to Gladia about it one evening, and she smiled.

'Why, imagine the work that is involved in rearing a child, Talla. If you asked Bellis, or Achillea when she has had her baby, they would tell you that you put everything into that child. You work hard to protect them and to nurture them and to grow them into good people who work hard. Well, I am working hard on these young women because they are like my children. I will not ever have more children, but each one of these reminds me of the one who was left at the Temple. I will never know her fate, but I can care for these ones and they will be as my children. I will put everything into them and protect them and support and make them good people.' She looked at me and smiled widely.

'It makes me happy to do this, Talla. And it is taking my mind slowly off that other matter.' She looked meaningfully down the path to where Benakiell's dwelling was.

We were back in Mellia for a special reason, however, and not just to see how everyone was. Achillea and Tarik were going to be married here in Mellia. It was a brief, symbolic ceremony, and not all chose to do it. Tarik, however, very much wanted for him and Achillea to be joined formally before the baby was born.

Here in Oramia, it was a simple ceremony often carried out before the birth of the first child. Each person to be married brought with them three strips of cloth of the same length, and in the colour of their day of birth. The cloths were sprinkled with oil from that day's scent. Tarik, of course, did not know the day of his birth, but had elected to use Viridis with its scent of cedarwood and Achillea, of course, had blue cloths for Azureus, and the sharp spice of Rosemary. We gathered around them as they were symbolically joined. They had asked Gladia to say the words for them to follow as they made the steps of binding.

'My parents made me with the Goddess's blessing.'

First Achillea laid down two of her strips and repeated the words, and then Tarik did the same, carefully laying his strips counter to Achillea's and so that they formed a sort of cross shape.

'With the Goddess's blessing, we are bound.'

This time the third strip was woven between the other two, under and over until the final result was a piece of simply woven cloth which was carefully lifted up and then passed around those present who all stitched a few stitches around the outside to hold it all together in one square shape. There were nine of us there to make our stitch, and later, Gladia would stitch it more carefully around the edges to hold it firm. When the baby was born, Achillea might use this cloth for it while it slept or to soothe it. As the cloth travelled round us, it brought with it the sweet mingling of the two perfumes and I thought how comforting it might be for a baby to have that scent around them in the cloth, almost as if their parents were there.

After the weaving of the cloth, the final step of binding was the pot making. Tarik poured water into the orange clay dust which Achillea had gathered on a stone, and together they kneaded it until it was clay, and worked it until they had made a tiny pot.

'Once you are bound, you will always be made of something new. Alone, you are the dust and the water, but together you are the clay that can be moulded, used, and broken. Binding the dust and the water makes something new. Let your binding, in turn, make something new.' Gladia looked around rather self-consciously. It was the first time she had been asked to say the words of binding but Achillea and Tarik just beamed back at her, clearly joyful after her words. The small pot would be kept and drops of both their perfumes would be put in it. No doubt Achillea would keep it safe in her box of treasures.

'Time to celebrate!' said Benakiell, breaking the silence. 'I have brought you some cakes from Shira. Jember, go and fetch that green cloth bundle in my dwelling!' Jember sped off with alacrity. Gladia looked pleased, though whether that was with the completion of the ceremony or the thought of eating the cakes, I could not tell.

Achillea came over to me, still beaming, carrying the pot wrapped in the cloth. She put it down and then flung her arms round me and embraced me.

'It might be you and Ravin next!' she exclaimed. 'Now that Gladia seems to have got over her views on the women of the Outer marrying those who are not of the Outer, you will have her blessing, I am sure, as well as the Goddess's. I wonder if the Goddess is happy that we built the orange again and I wonder if Lunaria is happy now that Ambar has proved his love?' I ignored her remark about me and Ravin. I had already endured a vicious poke to the arm and a similar message from Gladia which I had likewise ignored. Ravin himself was much amused by the suggestions being made to us and pointed out that in Kashiq, a couple must live together for a full year before they were permitted to marry. I was grateful for this. I was certainly not ready to commit myself to a life of motherhood and marriage however much I loved Ravin.

'Do you think the Goddess thinks like a person does?' I asked Achillea.

'Oh yes,' she replied confidently. 'I imagine her as just like one of us, except of course that she lives forever and spends her whole time creating. Like a mother to all of us.' She placed her hand on her belly. 'It does make you feel powerful, knowing you have created even one new person. Imagine how the Goddess must feel.'

I had puzzled over the existence of the Goddess for many years now. What kind of being was she? Each Temple contained a statue of the Goddess, carved from a smooth polished stone which reflected the colour of the hangings which surrounded it. She sat with her knees folded under her, and her hands folded peacefully in her lap. She was rounded and full of life, and around her head was a circle. As children, in the first age of childhood, we were told by the Priestesses that the circle was a sign of the light which shone from the Goddess. In the third age of childhood, we were told that it also stood for the unending nature of creation, that the circle had no end nor yet any beginning. But I had been confused by what I had read and found out in Kashiq. If Ashkana was a human chosen by the Goddess, then how could she too be a Goddess? For Rao was also chosen by the Goddess, as were Soren and Maliq. And both Rao and Ashkana, at least, were real people who had led real lives and had fallen in love and then out of love and had finally died, unlike Asmara, the Goddess, who lived forever. What had happened to them had changed the way the world had developed; if Ashkana had not fled from Rao into Oramia, she might not have started the Temples. Did our remaking of the Orange also affect the Goddess if she existed?

Luckily, at that point, Jember returned before I could tie my thoughts up in any further knots, and we gathered around and ate the cakes which Benakiell had saved for this event. Heavy with dates and nuts and with the distinctive taste of honeyed orange peel running through them, they were delicious. It all felt quite different from when I had been in Mellia all those months ago, when Benakiell had first shown me the parchment, for everyone now seemed to be content.

# CHAPTER 37

L unaria stood at the window, looking out from her room in the Court of the Queen in the dying light of the day. It offered a far-reaching view over the surrounding plains. She could see the vague shapes of larger trees and pockets of forest, small villages, and the larger buildings of the OutForts. Turning to the western sunset, she screwed up her eyes and thought that she could just make out the place where her Temple might be. She dipped her head and recited the Prayer of Thankfulness.

'We thank you, Goddess, for your blessings.
We thank you, Goddess, for the gifts of night and day.
We thank you, Goddess, for the gift of the earth, the water, and the sky.
We thank you, Goddess, for the people to serve you.
We thank you, Goddess, for the work of the Temple.'

The scent of lavender swirled out from the oil burner on the low table. It was Lunaria's day, and she wore a deep purple robe which she had embroidered herself with tiny heads of lavender. She could have had somebody else do the work for her, of course, but there was a comfort in stitching here, by the window, when she was not making decisions on how the OutFort and the Temples should work or rather, agreeing with carrying on with the ways things had always been. That was her job as Queen; to maintain the old ways. There was a tap at the door. It was past the time of working and past the time of eating. She smiled to herself. It would be Ambar.

He had been very attentive recently. He had been her constant companion for seven years, and she trusted him where she trusted no other – apart from Silene, perhaps. Because, after all, the Goddess spoke through Silene. Sometimes, when the Goddess spoke through Silene, it seemed as if it were Silene herself who was speaking, but there were other times when Silene seemed to be taken over by another spirit, possibly the Goddess herself. Lunaria sighed. She had never considered marriage when she was in the Temple. One of the first things she had learned as a Priestess was that Priestesses were chosen by the Goddess to dedicate themselves only to her. That all the Goddess's power that was, in ordinary men and women, used up in caring for other people, could instead be used for the good of the temple and the Goddess herself by the Priestesses.

Being told, when she became Queen, that she would be expected, in time, to marry and give birth to a daughter who would, in turn become Queen had been a terrible shock. She was told by the old Queen's officials that she must have children by the time she reached her Third Age. Ambar had been understanding, had reassured her that it would happen when it was fated to happen, but was equally adamant that he was part of that fate. He came to her every day that he was at the Court, in the evening. He told stories about his day and she talked to him about problems that she had to resolve. She always felt safe with Ambar, the way she had felt when she had first ridden on the horse with him and had had to hold on to him tightly to stop herself from falling off.

Lunaria invited Ambar in, looking forward to hearing about what he had been doing. She did not tend to move from the Queen's Court herself. There was a small Temple in the grounds of the Court which had previously fallen into disuse, the old Queen having no desire for it.

Lunaria, however, had ordered it to be cleaned and restored, and it became her personal Temple. She made sure that beautiful, embroidered hangings were changed each day, and it was always scented with the day's scent. There was no need for Lunaria to travel further, and Silene had warned her of the dangers of travel. Here, on top of the steep hill where the Court was based, she was safe. Ambar, however, had no such strictures. In fact, Silene had said she thought it was good for him to travel around the land, to keep an eye on it for the Queen, even though it meant that she saw him somewhat less and Silene somewhat more.

Ambar came in, with a spring in his step, and greeted her. They sat on the cushions and talked of this and that for a while. Then, he took her hand.

'You know that I love you, my lady Lunaria,' he began. 'But it has been a long time since I first told you this, and you told me then that you loved me too.'

'I do love you, Ambar,' replied Lunaria. 'As far as I am able. But the Goddess, bless her name, has spoken to me in my dreams, which Silene my DreamReader has read for me, as you know. It happened once, to our beloved Ashkana herself, that she loved someone and, because she did not ask the Goddess for her blessing and guidance, that love did not last. Only the Priestesses know of this,' she added hastily, seeing Ambar's surprise at her words.

'Because of that, the Queen is always fated to lose her love and her children, until the symbol of Ashkana's love, the Orange, is found and made whole again. But you know all this already, Ambar How could I marry you, knowing that I would lose both our love and our children if we did not have the Orange? Silene says that this has become more and more important through the ages,' she added.

'So, if I found Ashkana's Orange and it were made whole again, then you would marry me and have our children?' asked Ambar, fidgeting slightly.

'Of course.' Lunaria grasped his hand. 'I have told you this, Ambar. It will happen, I am sure of it. Silene says we must just be patient and wait and hope for the intervention of the Goddess in showing us where this Orange might be.'

'Hmmm,' Ambar murmured noncommittally and then reached into the leather carrysack he always had with him before withdrawing his hand. It contained a knobbly round item wrapped in orange silk.

'Close your eyes, my Queen,' he said, and then placed the item on the palm of her hand, having unwrapped it. He placed his own hand over the top of it and intertwined their fingers, so that they were holding it together and told her to open her eyes.

Slowly she opened her eyes and then looked down on their clasped hands.

'What is it?'

'Look and see.'

Slowly she peeled back his fingers and then looked down at her hand. There it lay, nestled in her hand, like a real orange but made of honeygold.

'Is it really Ashkana's Orange?' Ambar noticed how she had changed its name, without thinking. To her, of course, this was the important thing about it; that it had belonged to Ashkana who was venerated as the one who established the Temples dedicated to the Goddess. He nodded.

'Let me show you.' Ambar turned the leaf and stem to unclip them and then slowly pushed the stem downwards, opening the orange out. The six segments, attached with their tiny, fine chains lay around the stem.

'These are the six words of love.' In turn, he opened the tiny segment boxes and showed her the words. He had memorised the list which Talla had read to him, so that although neither he nor Lunaria could read the words, he still knew what they were, and, if Silene read them, she would read the same words.

'Joy. Respect. Trust. Freedom. Forgiveness. Loss.'

Lunaria repeated them after him wonderingly and traced her thin, agile fingers over the words.

'But how? Where did you find it? Silene told me she thought it was lost forever. But I knew if anyone would find it, it would be you!'

'My Queen, and my love, will you now marry me and declare your love for me? Will our children be the ones who will rule this land after you?' Ambar asked her, eagerly.

'Yes. For the Goddess has ordained that it be so,' she answered formally, her fingers still tracing over the words. 'Imagine Silene's surprise when I tell her!'

'Imagine,' agreed Ambar, smiling slightly sourly. 'But let us not wait. We have waited for too long. Let us go to your Temple now and be married under the sight of the Goddess herself. Then, in the morning, you can tell the Court, and they will no doubt wish to congratulate you and celebrate an end to the curse. Let this be between us and the Goddess who made us all. It will make it more special.'

'I will bring the Orange with us,' said Lunaria. 'We will put it in front of the statue of the Goddess. She will bless it and us at the same time.'

'She will,' agreed Ambar, smiling again. And he and Lunaria went down to her Temple. The Goddess was still decorated with the colours of Lilavis, and the faint scent of lavender hung around the statue. Absently, Lunaria took a wooden spoon of oil from the nearby jar and dripped it on to the feet of the Goddess. She rubbed the oil in and then took Ambar's hands.

'With the blessing of the Goddess, the creator of all things, we dedicate ourselves in marriage to this her land of Oramia. We also dedicate this Orange to her, as a sign that her Queen can now marry and bear children to her glory.' Lunaria spoke the words confidently and together they placed their hands over the Orange of Kashiq and then embraced. Ambar wondered briefly how she had known the words to say. Perhaps she had often thought them in her mind.

'My Queen.' A voice came from the doorway as they stood close to one another, embracing. A tall thin shadow came forward into the light of the oil lamps, and they could see it was Silene. She wore her customary dark gown, her hair covered by an equally dark netela. Her angular features seemed even sharper in the shadows cast by the lamp. Her finely plucked eyebrows were drawn tightly into the crease of a frown.

'Stop, my Queen, you cannot marry without the Orange of Kashiq! The Goddess herself, bless her name, has ordained this in our dreams! Do not let Ambar persuade you into the path of unhappiness. You must wait and see if he is indeed the one.'

Ambar turned to her, triumphantly, the Orange in his hand. 'I am the one, DreamReader Silene. I have brought the Orange of Ashkana back to where it belongs, as the Goddess ordained. And now, as you yourself have said, there is no obstacle to our Queen marrying and so we are already married in the sight of our Goddess. You will, I am sure, be as joyous as your Queen!'

Silene's eyes narrowed, and the smile which she had coaxed onto her face for the benefit of Lunaria did not meet her eyes, which, instead, flashed with fury that she had been outwitted by Ambar. She turned her attention to Lunaria who stood happily smiling next to Ambar.

'You are indeed blessed, my Queen,' she murmured. 'May I see this miraculous thing – and perhaps hear the tale of how Lord Ambar managed to find it...'

Lunaria showed her the Orange, and how it worked. Ambar asked Silene to read the words inside the segments. She did so but paused when she read the word 'Loss' and raised her fine eyebrows at the Queen and Ambar.

'This one worries me,' she said. 'For how can loss be part of love? Think how joyous you now feel. Loss would not bring you that feeling, surely?'

'How can loss not be part of love?' asked Ambar, pleased to have listened carefully to the explanations of Talla and Ravin, Tarik and Achillea. 'For without love we cannot feel deep loss. And sometimes it is only when we lose someone that we really understand how much we love them.' He turned deliberately away from Silene and any further questions and faced Lunaria, saying 'Come, my lady, it is your wedding day; let us go and feast and then we will be together for the rest of time; all else can wait.'

Lunaria smiled and took Ambar's hand and walked with him from the Temple. Silene remained, still in the shadows, and watched them as they went out into the light.

# CHAPTER 38

I looked around me. I had taken the honey and the salves to the market to trade, because Achillea tired easily now. It was a normal day in Gabez. We only needed a few things; soapballs, salt, cooking spices and needles for Ravin who continued to work with the needles and fine wire, making different types of chains and linking threads. They were not to trade, but he and Tarik used them in different devices they were designing. Having acquired those things, I sat down with what was left to see what other interesting trades there might be. One always had to keep in mind the need to keep stocks of things for when you needed them. Those who traded millet flour for the flat breads were always able to trade but finding something they wanted was not as easy. Luckily, we made a honey tonic which soothed their throats and dampened down the coughing which was a result of working with the flour every day and so we were never short of flour.

A woman walked up to the place where I sat. She was tall and thin and wore a dark grey robe with no embroidery, and similar netela, the shade of deep charcoal. I imagined Gladia's face if she had seen such a dull robe and smiled at the thought.

'You seem happy,' said the woman, in a curiously dead voice. Her eyebrows were so fine as to look as if they had been drawn on her face and made her already sharp features look even more severe. Her voice was deep and low and reminded me of the carefully modulated tones of the Priestesses of my childhood. In fact, everything about her reminded me of the Priestesses.

I kept the smile on my face. 'It is a lovely day is it not?' I knew that some customers demanded a little chat first before settling down to the business of trading. It was not something I found easy. Years ago, I had blamed it on my Temple upbringing and their requirement that all talking should only be necessary for work or for prayer. Now, however, I was coming to realise that I was just one of those people who found it harder to talk about trivialities for any length of time, unlike Achillea or Gladia.

'Is it?' Those fine eyebrows raised slightly as the woman looked around her. She reached down and picked up one of the small gourds of honey and examined it. Her long fingers stroked the smooth brown exterior.

'What do you wish to trade?' I did my best to be polite, but I was tiring of the market in any case. Unless this strange woman had something new to offer, I planned to pack the things up into my bundle and return to the dwelling where I could pick some beans and plant some pumpkins in the garden.

'I have little to offer,' she answered. 'Some say I read dreams and tell the future. Perhaps I could do such a thing for you, in exchange for this good honey. As you see, I have not had much to eat.'

I looked down to hide my annoyance. There were those in the Outer who loved to engage with such as these. Achillea herself enjoyed nothing more than a discussion of the meaning of this dream or that, or a telling of her future. I had noted that all the futures being told were joyful and good; there was no wonder that people were willing to make small trades with these people. But she was indeed very thin, and perhaps a small gourd of honey was not so very much to give away. Besides, it might be interesting to see what she forecast for me, since I had never taken part in such things before. The last time I had done anything like this was when I had been to the Empath Erayo all those years ago with Gladia. Gladia still visited her twice a year and tried to persuade me to go too but I did not wish for a repeat of what happened last time.

'Very well, you may have the honey,' I said.

She settled herself down on the ground next to me and closed her eyes. I looked at her carefully while her eyes were shut. You could see under her netela that her hair was cropped close to her head. Some of the Priestesses had done that, especially as they got older. She raised her fingers to her temples and pressed them hard until it must have hurt. I waited, ready to hear tales of my future happiness.

'You have journeyed a long way, but it is short compared to where you must now go. You are loved, but that will change, for love is fickle and cannot be trusted. There is one who seeks you out, but he will bring great danger if you ever see him again.' She paused and opened her eyes briefly to stare at me with eyes as dark as caves. I stared back at her, unnerved by the calm way in which she was telling me this and then she shut them and began speaking in that deep, flat voice again.

'Harm will befall your children and all you know if you do not flee this land. You must protect them from those who seek to destroy you. Remember the Goddess in all you do, for she will see your actions and judge you. Your destiny was written before you were born.'

Her eyelids fluttered. She raised her thin hand to her head and rubbed it. Her eyes once again focused on me but this time they were only normal dark brown eyes.

'I hope your future is a good one, and that all I have said comes true,' she said, in an almost cheery fashion. 'I do not know what I say to people; it just seems to come out while I am in a kind of trance, and they are normally delighted.' She peered at me. 'You do not look as happy as you did before. Was it something I said?'

I smiled back at her tightly. I had no intention of telling her what had been said to me, even supposing that she told the truth and did not know what she spoke of, and every intention of forgetting everything she had just told me, if possible. For now, I just wanted her to go away.

'Thank you very much, sister,' I said, politely. 'Here is your honey; I hope you enjoy it.'

She rose from the ground, holding the gourd of honey, brushing off the orange dust. I rose too, preparing to bundle up my things.

'You are Talla, are you not?' she said as she turned to leave. Startled by this, I asked her how she knew my name.

'Oh, one of those traders over there told me who you were; they said you traded honey,' she answered, waving her arm vaguely. She smiled faintly; her lips set in a thin line.

'And who are you?' I asked as I looked away briefly to the place she pointed to, annoyed that she knew my name and I did not know hers.

But when I looked back, she had gone, like the mist of the night disappears into the warm morning air, leaving only a sour taste in my mouth. It lingered with the woolly pervasiveness of pith and her words ate into my thoughts. Laying in solitude where she had been sitting only minutes before was an orange. I reached down for it, shaking my head at her actions. She had told me she was hungry, and yet she had left me an orange, which must have come from Kashiq, or at least from a Kashiqi trader. Its peel was a dark orange in colour, mottled almost with red. I picked it up with the rest of my things and headed back.

When I got back, I went down to the garden and sat there, unable to rid my mind of what she had said. The emberjar inside my mind kept flaring up as I recalled a different part of what she had foretold for me, as if small dry sticks were being sprinkled on a fire. When Ravin arrived later, I told him what had happened. He frowned.

'It is not like you to be so upset by the ramblings of an old woman who is probably not in her right mind, or more likely trying to get better trade from you before she gives you a better fortune!' He smiled, trying to encourage me to do the same, but I could not shake my unease as we walked back to the dwelling together, he holding my hand, interlacing his fingers with mine.

'My love for you is not fickle, Talla, it will not change, you know that. This silly woman has just thrown things together to make them sound important.' I tried to make myself believe him, but somehow, I believed her flat, dark words more. What she had told me had sounded more like a warning than a foretelling. I showed him the dark orange she had left behind. He looked at it curiously and then began to peel it so that we could eat it. For he and I, sharing an orange had come to be a cherished way in which we affirmed our love and reminded ourselves of it. But when Ravin pulled the segments apart from the peel, and one of them split, it looked disturbingly strange, for it seemed to be bleeding. I drew my hand away from it fearfully. Ravin laughed.

'Don't worry, Talla, it isn't blood, though some say these oranges are grown on blood. That's just a story though. They get like this because they are grown near the high mountains in the north, where the days are warm, and the nights are cold. It is just a different colour but tastes much the same. I wonder how she got it. No doubt she uses them as devices to make her so-called fortunes more startling.' He chuckled again and ate one of the pieces of the blood orange and offered one to me. I took it dubiously, and closed my eyes as I ate it, but Ravin was right; it really did just taste like an orange, albeit a sweeter one. In my heart, I knew that she had left this blood orange as a warning to me too.

When we got back to the dwelling, I took down some plant parchment and a metal nibbed pen I had acquired in Kashiq. I took a small clay pot of dark ink from Ravin's set of coloured inks. Tarik had made him a scribeboard, like the ones we used in the Tower of the Wise, and I stood at it, in the courtyard. I scribed exactly what the woman who purported to read dreams and tell fortunes had said and done, so that I would not forget it, and then rolled up the parchment when the ink was dry and tied it with a thread and put it in the wooden box along with some of Ravin's scrolls.

'There!' I said brightly to Ravin. 'Now it can be forgotten about, for I have scribed it and it will live there instead of in my mind.' He looked at me appraisingly but did not comment further. I asked him not to tell Achillea and Tarik about the woman, explaining that I did not want Achillea upset so close to when she would give birth, and he agreed to tell them nothing of it. My own worries were hard enough to quell without introducing the weight of Achillea and Tarik's worries. After all, Achillea was much given to over dramatic interpretations of dreams and such things, especially now the baby was nearly due.

Later, however, when I was on my own, I took out the scroll, and reread the words. There was one who sought me out, which I was sure must be Ambar, and seeing him again would put me and those I loved into danger. I needed to leave Oramia if I wanted to preserve myself from the danger that Ambar might bring if he sought me out again. I rolled it up. I did not believe in dreams and portents however unsettling they might be. I had dreamed many a dream which made no sense and had never come to pass, after all. But this message seemed to be clear. I could stay in Oramia with those I loved and place them in some sort of unknown danger, or I could leave and protect them. Or I could ignore it.

A bee flew past, heading towards the hive with great determination, its legs heavy with the orangey-yellow honeydust it had gathered. It flew into the safety of the hive, away from the dangers of the world. The bees did not think of the future. They went out to work on the flowers every day and completed their labours. They ate and they rested. Sometimes they fought. New bees were brought forth to continue the work of the hive. But none of them knew what might come tomorrow, and none of them could even imagine what might come tomorrow, let alone worry about it. Their present was their world. And here I was, worrying over some few words which could not possibly be true, for nobody could foresee what had not yet happened.

Smiling to myself at my earlier foolish imaginings, I let go of my thoughts, and having harvested the beans, took them over to Achillea and sat out in the sun with her and listened gratefully to her own foretellings of the future; the things her child would be and achieve and the bright happiness that it would bring to all of us.

# ACKNOWLEDGEMENTS

First of all, I'd like to thank you for reading my book! I hope you enjoyed it. Please do recommend to a friend or lend your book to someone you think will also enjoy the story or consider writing a review.

I'd like to give my heartfelt thanks and gratitude to my Beta readers for their time and energy and for their thoughtful responses to my first drafts. They are a wonderful crowd of people and I am indebted to them.

This book has been inevitably delayed by the Covid pandemic – finding writing time, space and focus has been tricky and all the associated tasks have taken longer too. My thoughts are with those who have struggled through this time and who have been affected by illness and loss. I hope the world of Kashiq will allow you some respite and escape.

The lovely cover art has once more been created by Amy Yeager. You can find her at www.amyyeagerart.com or on Instagram at @amy_art.illustration.

If you have enjoyed reading *The Orange of Kashiq*, you may like to visit my website where you can find extra information on The Emberjar series, including character lists and pronunciation guides as well as further information about the lands of Oramia and Kashiq, and Book 1 of the series, *Flammeus*. You can find the website at www.emberjar.com.

Thanks again to my readers – a writer really is made complete by their readers, and mine are a fabulous bunch of people!

# THE ORANGE OF KASHIQ

Printed in Great Britain
by Amazon